FOR HER BABY

&

THE MIDWIFE'S SON

BY
SUE MacKAY

MILLS &
BOON

DOCTORS TO DADDIES

The biggest role of their lives…

No demands. No commitment. That's how hot-shot doctors Grady O'Neil and Jackson Wilson like to conduct their relationships. Women feature in their lives like the revolving door of the A&E.

But, returning home to the small island of Golden Bay, Grady and Jackson meet two women and their delightful bundles of joy… and everything changes. These two dedicated bachelors suddenly find themselves yearning for the one thing they've never wanted:

fatherhood!

Meet the women and their babies who melt their stubborn hearts in

the **Doctors to Daddies** duet by Sue MacKay

Available June 2014

Read Grady's story in
A FATHER FOR HER BABY

Read Jackson's story in
THE MIDWIFE'S SON

A FATHER
FOR HER BABY

BY
SUE MacKAY

MILLS &
BOON

Published in Great Britain 2014
by Mills & Boon, an imprint of Harlequin (UK) Limited,
Eton House, 18-24 Paradise Road, Richmond, Surrey, TW9 1SR

© 2014 Sue MacKay

ISBN: 978 0 263 90770 4

Dear Reader

Golden Bay is one of New Zealand's gems. There's only one road in, but it's well worth the effort to go there. I've spent a few summer holidays staying at one of the beaches there, enjoying the fishing, swimming and just relaxing. I also have family living there, and attended a wonderful wedding on their lawn which gave me ideas leading to these stories.

Sasha and Grady, Jessica and Jackson—all have family connections and history from when they were teenagers. But people have to leave the bay area if they want to attend university, and not everyone comes back. Of course I had to bring these four back. I hope you enjoy their ensuing relationships and how they find love again.

Cheers!

Sue MacKay

PS I'd love to hear from you at sue.mackay56@yahoo.com or visit me on www.suemackay.co.nz

With a background of working in medical laboratories and a love of the romance genre, it is no surprise that **Sue MacKay** writes Mills & Boon® Medical Romance™ stories. An avid reader all her life, she wrote her first story at age eight—about a prince, of course. She lives with her own hero in the beautiful Marlborough Sounds, at the top of New Zealand's South Island, where she indulges her passions for the outdoors, the sea and cycling.

Recent titles by Sue MacKay:

These books are also available in eBook format from www.millsandboon.co.uk

CHAPTER ONE

As SASHA WILSON reached the first sharp hairpin bend on her descent from the top of Takaka Hill into Golden Bay she eased off the accelerator, moving even slower than her previous snail's pace.

A shudder rolled through her chilled body, nothing to do with her friend's entreaties for her to move back to the city where her biggest mistake ever lived but all about the treacherous road conditions. While there was frost on her heart, it was the black ice at every corner and coating most of the road that required her undivided attention right now. As it had done for the more than five hours she'd been driving home from Christchurch. Where her headlights swept the grass and tree-covered banks, blinding-white frozen water glittered back at her.

'Winter sucks,' she growled, and swiped the back of her glove-covered hand across the condensation on the windscreen. 'If only it wasn't so important to be back for work in the morning, I could've waited until the weather cleared.' Then her voice softened and her hand briefly touched the bump over her stomach. 'At least you're tucked up nice and warm in there, Flipper. And safe from that selfish man who accidentally fathered you. The man who wanted me to terminate you.'

Gasp. 'Wash my mouth out.' Flipper wouldn't pick up on her thoughts, would she? Because no matter her own opinion of the man who would remain nameless, she wasn't ever going to visit that on her daughter.

Gripping the steering-wheel, she continued her diatribe. 'It's like someone threw a switch on my life. Winter's always been about chasing the best snow and hurtling down ski slopes, and going to those amazing après-ski parties to rub shoulders with some of the best skiers in the world.'

Not any more. Her skis were in a cupboard at the back of her parents' shed. Her fancy outfits were folded away in cases filling the wardrobes in the tiny cottage she now lived in on the edge of the family orchard.

'We don't even like the cold, do we, Flipper?'

The baby kicked none too gently.

'You're quite the swimmer, aren't you?' Sasha smiled as she sucked in a breath. 'The inside of my tummy must be bruised purple from your feet.' Pregnancy was amazing. Every day seemed different. She already loved her little girl. Completely and utterly. Fiercely. She'd protect her with her life.

On the radio a song finished and the announcer piped up in his false cheery voice, 'Coming up to eleven-thirty on the clock, folks. I hope each and every one of you is tucked up warm and safe by now.'

'I wish. Big time.' Sasha flicked a glove-covered finger in the direction of her radio. 'You obviously haven't listened to your station's weather forecast, buster. It's been blowing a blizzard up and down New Zealand for most of the day and some of us are struggling to get home in the resulting chaos.'

Successfully negotiating a tight bend, she let relief

spread through her. 'One down.' The relief evaporated instantly. 'Plenty more to go.' If only she was pulling up outside her house now. She was so over this trip.

A new, cheerful song filled the interior of the car as Sasha leaned forward to peer through the windscreen. 'It's hideous out there, Flipper.' Not even the possums were out partaking in their nightly forage for dinner. She shivered and hunched her neck down into the warmth of her leather jacket.

Her mouth stretched wide as she yawned. She was tired beyond tired. The long drive down to Christchurch on Thursday, the pre-wedding celebrations, in which, as bridesmaid, she had an active role, and then the wedding yesterday—she'd been on the go non-stop for three days. And then today's endless drive from hell. If only keeping her job wasn't so important that she had to get home. But it funded her decision to return to the one place on earth where she felt safe, where there were people she could trust, where her family lived. Where Mum needed her.

Golden Bay with its small township of Takaka had become her bolt-hole, the place where she could lick her wounds and harden her heart, the district she wanted to settle down in and raise her daughter. Earlier she'd briefly considered calling one of the doctors she worked for and explaining that she'd be a day late getting back, but they'd been adamant she had to prove her reliability if she wanted to get a permanent position at the medical centre. No days off for anything except illness, she had been told on more than one occasion. Her reputation from her long past high-school days just wouldn't go away. Small communities had a lot to answer for. But that was why she was here, that sense of a blanket being wrapped around her and keeping her safe and warm had also drawn her in.

Another yawn lifted her shoulders, filled her lungs. Rubbing her eyes, she spoke loudly in an attempt to banish the loneliness suddenly enveloping her. 'Hey, Flipper, ready to tuck up under our quilt? I know I am.' She really was nuts, talking to the baby like this. But it made a change from yakking to herself all the time. And it was good to talk to her baby even before she was born, right? Who cared? She'd do it anyway. There'd be people who said it was the right thing to do, and others who'd say she was bonkers.

'Unfortunately the cottage will be cold enough to freeze the boll—' *Oops, mind your language in front of the baby.* 'It'd be great if your grandma has gone down to light the fire for us. But somehow I doubt it. She doesn't trust the safest of fireboxes.' Mum had always been overly cautious. Mum. Sasha's mouth drooped into the antithesis of a smile while her eyes misted.

'What has Mum ever done to deserve the disease slowly wrecking her life, taking over her body?' she asked around the lump clogging her throat. Her beautiful mother, who'd always been there for her and her brother, refusing to accept the disease taking hold in her body would never let go.

Sniff, sniff. Life could be so damned unfair. Sasha's hands tightened on the steering-wheel as she leaned forward, all the better to see, but it didn't make the slightest difference. This final stretch of road seemed interminable.

'What the heck?' Red lights blinked from the edge of the road ahead, right on the bend of the next hairpin.

Random. Definitely out of place. Suddenly her heart beat a rapid rhythm.

'I don't like the look of this.' Her bed beckoned even harder. Swallowing a yawn and resisting the urge to slam on the brakes, she gently slowed to a stop right beside the rear end of an upside-down truck poking up from the bank it'd gone over. 'Bad parking.' But hardly surprising, given the hazardous road conditions. And why she hadn't relaxed at all despite getting close to home.

Sasha carefully turned her vehicle so the headlights shone onto the wrecked truck, with its black tyres pointing up into the night. Downright eerie. A shiver ran down her vertebrae. For a brief moment she wanted to drive on home to that cold bed and not face what might be waiting in that buckled cab. Not because of her need to be home safe but because all the years working in emergency departments hadn't dulled the fear she might fail someone who desperately needed her help. Neither did her nursing experience make seeing people suffering any easier to deal with. She felt for them, had cried tears for them.

'Get on with it,' she said. 'You can do the emotional stuff later when everyone in that vehicle's safe.' Because the truck hadn't driven itself off the road, and the glowing headlights suggested it hadn't happened long ago.

None of that stopped her muttering, 'Please, please, be empty.' Her churning stomach mocked her. 'Okay, then be safe, not seriously injured.'

Tugging her woollen hat down around her ears and pulling at the zipper on her jacket to try and close the gap caused by her baby bulge, she hauled in a lungful of warm air before elbowing the door open and gingerly stepping down onto the frozen road. Instantly her feet skidded sideways and she grabbed for the door, hung on as she righted herself. This wouldn't be a picnic, and these days, with Flipper on board, she had to be extra, extra careful.

Her cheeks instantly tightened from the cold, while her unease increased. Initially the night seemed silent but now the cracking sounds of hardening ice became apparent. Or was that the truck shifting?

'Nice one, Sasha. Scare yourself, why don't you? Move your butt and stop overthinking the situation.'

Collecting her medical kit and the heavy-duty torch she always carried, she gingerly crunched over to the edge of the bank, and gasped. In the half-light the Golden Bay Freight Lines logo on the side of the truck was distorted but readable. Sam and Lucy Donovan's truck.

'Sam, is that you? It's Sasha.'

'Help me.'

'Sam, are you on your own?' Please, she muttered. Talk about needing a lot of favours in one night.

'No, the missus is with me. She's hurt bad, Sasha.'

Damn, damn, triple damn. The Donovans were the greatest neighbours her parents had ever had, always there for them, there for her too nowadays whenever she needed help with Mum's orchard. Which she didn't. Not because she was stubborn or anything. Of course not.

Sam hadn't finished with the bad news. 'I can't move my legs.'

'I hear you.' First she needed to get more help. Fast. Her heart sank. What were the chances there'd be cell-phone coverage? But she couldn't do this on her own. 'Has anyone driven past since you went off the road?'

'Not that I heard.' Sam's voice cracked. 'Hurry, Sasha. Lucy's bleeding from the head.'

Things were looking up. Not. Her heart squeezed for

the middle-aged couple stuck in that cab. 'Sam, you'll have to hang in there while I get the rescue crews on the way out.' She swallowed her growing worry. Like worrying helped anybody. Thinking logically was the only way to go.

Tugging her phone free of a pocket, she touched icons. No coverage. Sasha glared upward at the stars blinking out of the now-clear sky. 'Thanks very much. Can't someone up there make it a little bit easier to save my friends?'

Crunch, crack. She jerked. Had the truck moved? 'Sam?'

'Sounds like another car coming.'

Yellow light slashed across the white landscape, swept over her. Relief poured through her tense muscles. She glanced upwards again. 'Okay, I take it back. Looks like there was already a plan in action.'

A car pulled up beside her. The driver's window opened a crack. 'What's going on? You need a hand, lady?' a voice she didn't know asked.

I'm not standing out here for the hell of it. The air in front of her face turned misty as she sighed. *Give the guy a break. At least he stopped.* 'A truck's gone over the bank with two people inside. We need emergency services urgently.' The risk of hypothermia was enough to want to rush everything, to drag Sam and Lucy out regardless of injuries. Which was so not how to go about rescuing them. 'I'm not getting reception. Can you call it in from further down the hill? Or stop at the first house you see? Tell them Sasha Wilson is here.'

'On my way.' The car was already moving away, thankfully cautiously.

But as she watched the lights fade in the distance that

loneliness grabbed at her again. Until help arrived, Sam and Lucy's fate depended on her.

'Your problem is? You're a nurse. Not a bad one either. Get on with doing something practical. Sam will be getting desperate.'

With all the ice about the place she wasn't in for an easy time getting down to the truck, something that never normally fazed her. But with Flipper to consider there'd be no leaping over the embankment like a sure-footed goat. 'Hey, I can do careful,' she whispered. 'This is one time where I have to go slow and steady.' Now, there was a first. Her lips pressed hard together, the skin of her cheeks tight.

Maybe if she'd gone slow and steady with that grease-ball back in Christchurch she'd still be up to leaping over edges without a care in the world. Might not have a baby under her belt. 'Sorry, Flipper. I'm not trying to wish you away, sweetheart.'

Wrong time to be thinking about this, with the Donovans waiting for her. Taking a steadying breath, she let her medical pack slide down the bank. Then, with her torch gripped tight in one hand, she sat down on her bottom and shuffled and slipped down, too.

'Hey, there.' She mustered a cheery tone as she reached the driver's door.

Sam blinked in the light from her torch. 'Am I glad to see you.'

'How secure do you think the truck is?'

'I haven't felt it move at all. From the sound when we hit I think we're jammed against rocks.'

Some good news. At least they weren't about to plummet down to where the road twisted across the hillside directly beneath.

'Sasha, I'm real worried about Lucy.'

The fear in Sam's voice had her squatting down by the shattered window to shine the torch inside. Blood had splattered over most of the interior. Lucy hung upside down, half in, half out of her seat belt, a huge gash across the side of her head.

'She hasn't said a word the whole time.' Sam's voice trembled. 'What if—?' he choked.

'Hold that thought, Sam.' Darn, but she hated it when friends were hurting. Placing her free hand on Sam's shoulder, she tried for a reassuring squeeze. 'I'll check Lucy over. But what about you? Where are you hurting?' At least he was upright, though what injuries he'd sustained when the truck had rolled didn't bear thinking about.

'To hell with me. Look after Lucy, will you?'

'Okay. But keep talking to me.' The way his voice faded in and out didn't bode well. 'Tell me where you hurt. Did you bang your head?' He had to have, surely? 'Are you bleeding anywhere? Stuff like that.' Talking might keep him focused and make the minutes tick by a little faster than if he just sat watching and worrying over his wife. Really? That was the theory but theory often sucked. 'Shine my torch so I can see what I'm doing.'

Hand over hand she grabbed at the edge of the truck's grille and made her way to the other side. Not easy clambering over frozen rocks with a bump the size of a basketball under her jacket. Flipper must've got the seriousness of the situation because she'd gone nice and quiet with those feet. Automatically rubbing her tummy, Sasha muttered, 'Thanks, sweetheart. Mummy owes you.'

Reaching through where the window used to be, she

felt carefully for Lucy's throat and the carotid. 'There you go. Lucy's got a pulse. She's alive, Sam.'

One big sniff. 'Thank you, lass. Can you get her down from that seat belt? I don't like her hanging like that. Can't be doing her any good.'

'We're going to have to wait for the rescue guys. I could do more damage than good if I cut her free.' Tilting her wrist to see her watch, Sasha counted Lucy's pulse. Slightly low but not too bad, considering. 'You haven't told me about your injuries yet, Sam.'

Carefully feeling Lucy's head, neck, and arms for injuries, she tried to work out how long would it take for the rescue crowd to get here. How long since that car had driven away? Had the driver got that this was an emergency? Swallow hard. Toughen up. It would be at least forty-five minutes before anyone showed up. Make that an hour by the time everyone'd been phoned. Then there were the road conditions to contend with.

Focusing on diverting Sam's attention—and hers— she said, 'You and Lucy were coming home late.'

'Been to tea with the kids in Nelson.' He went quiet.

A glance showed his eyes droop shut. 'Sam.'

He blinked. 'Roads are real bad.'

'Very dicey.' It wasn't the first time she'd driven this road in the aftermath of a winter storm, and it probably wouldn't be the last. Unless she changed her mind about staying in Golden Bay like Tina wanted. Now her friend was a happily married woman she seemed to think she had the right to fix Sasha's life. Worse, the guy Tina had thought would solve all her present problems had been nice—in a wet blanket kind of way. Tina was probably making up for the fact she'd introduced the greaseball to her in the first place.

'Sorry, Tina, but which bit of no more men for me didn't you get?'

'Who's Tina? Is someone else here?'

'Talking to myself. A bad habit I really should get over.'

Taking a thick cotton pad from her kit, Sasha taped it over Lucy's head wound. Hopefully that would slow the blood loss. She kept prattling on about anything and everything in an attempt to keep Sam with her. Having him slip into unconsciousness would make it harder for the rescue crew to remove him.

Glancing at her watch, she stifled a groan of despair. Twelve-twenty. The rescue crews couldn't be too far away now. Could they? What if the road was worse between here and Takaka? Don't even go there. She knew those men, had gone to school with some of them, now worked with others. They would come through. It might take some effort and time but they'd be here as soon as it was humanly possible.

'S-Sasha, h-how's Lucy?' Sam's teeth clacked together as shivers rattled him.

Sasha winced. A couple of thermal blankets would be very welcome right about now for her patients. Her own toes were numb, her fingers much the same since she'd removed her gloves to attend to Lucy, and she wasn't stuck, unable to move. At least Flipper would be warm. She answered, 'Breathing normally and the bleeding's stopped.'

After what felt like a lifetime flashing lights cut through the dark night. Relief slipped under her skin. 'The ambulance's here. Now we'll see some action.'

The first voice she heard was Mike's, one of the GPs

she worked for at the Golden Bay Medical and Wellbeing Centre. 'You down there, Sasha?'

She stood upright, grabbing the doorframe for balance. 'Yep, and I've got Lucy and Sam with me.'

Before she'd finished telling him, Mike had joined her. Rebecca, one of the ambulance volunteers, was right behind him.

Mike asked, 'What've we got?'

'Sam's legs are caught under the steering-wheel. Lucy's entangled upside down in her seat belt.' Sasha quickly filled them in on the scant medical details. Above them a tow truck pulled up, quickly followed by another heavy four-wheel-drive vehicle. Then the fire truck laden with men equipped with cutting gear and rescue equipment arrived. 'I love it when the cavalry turns up.'

Mike grinned. 'Guess it does feel like that. You want to wait in the warmth of the ambulance? Thaw out a bit before we send one of these two up to you?'

For once she didn't mind being set aside so others could get on with the job. She wasn't in a position to take the weight of either Lucy or Sam as they were freed and lifted onto stretchers. The strain might affect her baby in some way and that was not going to happen. 'On my way.' Though it wouldn't be as easy going up the bank as it had been coming down.

Mike read her mind. 'There's a rope to haul yourself back up to the top, as you're more of a small whale than a goat these days.'

She swiped at his arm before taking the end of rope he held out to her. 'Thanks, Doc.'

'Is that Sam's truck? Is he hurt badly? Anyone with

him?' The questions were fired at her before she'd even got her feet back on the road.

Doing her slip-slide ballet manoeuvre and with a lot of men reaching for her, she managed to stand upright and steady. 'Lucy's unconscious and Sam's fading in and out.' Sasha glanced around at the mostly familiar faces, relief that they were here warming her chilled blood.

Then she froze. Like the air in her lungs had turned to ice crystals. The heat left her veins. Her eyes felt as though they were popping out of their sockets. *Tell me I'm hallucinating.* Her head spun, making her dizzy. Her mouth tasted odd as her tongue did a lap. *Can't be him.* Her numb fingers hurt as she gripped someone's arm to stay upright. *Not now. Not here.*

But, of course, she wasn't imaging anything. That would've meant something going in her favour for a change. Grady O'Neil was for real. Eleven years older and more world-weary but definitely Grady. No mistaking that angular jaw, those full lips that were nearly always smiling—except not right at this moment—and… Her shoulders rose, dropped back in place. He hadn't been smiling the last time she'd seen him either. When he'd told her he didn't love her any more he'd had the decency to keep at bay that wicked smile that made her knees melt. The first man to hurt her. But he didn't have that on his own any more. There'd been others. She so didn't do well with picking men.

The urge to run overwhelmed her. Her left foot came off the ground as she began turning in the direction of her vehicle. *Sliding on the ice and falling down hard on your butt would be such a good look. And could harm Flipper.* Deal with this. Now. Breathe in, one, two, three. Breathe out. 'Grady.' She dipped her head. 'It's been a while.'

A while? How's that for a joke? Why wasn't he laughing? A while. Far too long. Huh? No. She meant not nearly long enough. Didn't she? Oh, yeah, definitely not long enough. Yet here he stood, a few feet from her, as big and strong and virile as ever. And that was with layers of thick warm clothes covering that body she apparently still remembered too well.

You shouldn't be remembering a thing about that amazing year. You're long over him and the hurt he caused. True? Absolutely.

She fought the need to revisit Grady and everything he'd meant to her, instead aimed for calm and friendly, as though his unexpected appearance didn't matter at all. 'What are you doing here?' Big fail. Her voice rose as though a hand gripped her throat. Memories from those wonderful carefree days she'd stashed away in a mental box some place in the back of her head were sneaking out and waving like flags in a breeze, threatening to swamp her.

Swallowing hard, she focused on now, not the past. Why had Grady turned up? Golden Bay was her territory. Not his. He'd only come for summer holidays and that had been years ago. He'd be visiting. But who? Not her, for sure. Her tummy sucked in on itself, setting Flipper off on a lap of her swimming pool, nudging Sasha every few seconds, underlining how unimportant Grady was in the scheme of things.

Sasha dug deeper than she'd ever done before for every bit of willpower she could muster to hold off rubbing her extended belly. She would not draw those all-seeing blue eyes to her pregnant state. That was hers alone to cope with. She certainly didn't need Grady asking about her baby.

His smile seemed genuine, though wary. Which it damn well ought to be. 'Hi, Sash. This is a surprise. I didn't expect to run into you while I was here.'

Sash. That certainly set free a load of hot memories. Her nipples tightened, her thighs clenched. Grady still drawled her name out like he was tasting it, enjoying it.

He couldn't be. He'd lost any right to those sensations the day he'd told her he didn't love her enough to spend the rest of his life with her. Yet he was checking her out. Her pulse sped up as that steady gaze trawled over her, starting with her face and tracking slowly down her chin, her throat, over the swell of her breasts under the thickness of her jacket, on down to Flipper. As his gaze dropped further the breath she'd been hanging onto trickled over her lips. He hadn't noticed the six-month bulge. Guess the thick jersey and heavy jacket she wore made her look larger than normal anyway.

Now his gaze had reached her legs—forever legs, he used to call them. Another memory leaped out of the box. Grady's strong hands gently rubbing sunscreen from her toes to the tops of her thighs. Slam. The lid shut firmly.

Then Grady stepped right up to her and enveloped her in those strong arms she would not remember. Her head bumped against the chest she'd never found the likeness of again. And out of nowhere came the need to lay her cheek against him and tuck her hands around his waist. Even to tug that shirt free and slide her hands over his skin.

No, Sasha, you can't. Are you that stupid you've forgotten his parting words? That memory never went into the box. That one you kept out in the open as a warning never to make the same mistake.

Except she had got it wrong again. Had learned nothing in the years since Grady. She jerked backwards. Too quickly for him to let go of her, so that her baby bump shoved forward, right into his solar plexus.

His head snapped up, those startled eyes registering shock. He pulled away from her fast, as though he'd walked into an electric fence. In the shadows and flashing lights from the emergency vehicles she saw a multitude of questions spinning her way. He pushed his hands deep into his jacket pockets, forced his chest out and splayed his legs slightly. Such a Grady stance. The don't-mess-with-me posture even while his face showed how much he wanted to ask her about that bump.

Tough. Her baby had nothing to do with him. He'd want to know who the father was, no doubt wondering if it was someone he knew from way back when they had been part of a whole crowd of teens at the beach. He could guess all night long, he'd never get it right.

He looked away, looked back at her. Tugged one hand free and rammed his fingers through his thick hair. Stumped.

She blinked as her throat clamped shut on the delayed shock charging up her body, opening that box of memories again, wider than ever. *I remember you very well, Grady O'Neil. Too well. I remember—too many things I'd prefer not to.* The air trickled out of her lungs. Those memories were capable of melting all the black ice on the Takaka Hill road.

Why had she never considered this moment might happen? Because Takaka had been their playground only when they'd been teenagers knocking around together. Knocking around? That was one way of describing what had gone on between them. They'd been inseparable. Totally in love with the intensity of teenagers overdosed on hormones. She'd stupidly thought they'd be together for ever.

So wrong about Grady. So wrong about the grease-ball she'd walked away from four months ago. She really needed a 'how to' book on establishing perfectly balanced relationships with the opposite sex.

She closed her eyes. Opened them. Nothing had changed. Grady still stood in front of her, questions blinking out, begging for answers. No way, sunshine. Not telling you. Swallowing the lump in her throat, she croaked, 'I didn't realise you knew Mike.'

'I met him two days ago when I dropped by the medical centre. He and Roz invited me to have dinner with them tonight, which is where I was when this call came in.'

Jonty called from the open back doors of the ambulance, 'How do we get these stretchers out of here?'

Saved by the fireman. Sasha hurried to clamber inside the wide vehicle and unlock the stretchers from the wheels they wouldn't be using tonight.

'Ta.' Jonty grinned. Then pulled a grim face. 'We're bringing Lucy up first so you and Grady can do what you have to with her in the warmth of the ambulance.'

I have to work with Grady? Her skin broke out in goose-bumps, even as she gathered her strength around her like a mantle. 'Sure.' She pressed her lips together and started getting out equipment they'd need. She'd work with the devil if it meant helping Sam and Lucy.

The devil might be easier to get on with.

Blinking back a sudden rush of tears, she tried to concentrate on the job. Damn her tear ducts. They'd taken on a life of their own since she'd become pregnant.

The ambulance rocked as Grady clambered up the

step. Did he have to suck up all the air? Surreptitiously she studied him, saw the pinching at the corners of his delectable mouth. Absurdly she wanted to reach out and touch him, run her finger over those lips and say, Hello, how've you been? *Great idea, Sasha. Not.*

'Sash, can you move back a bit so I can get inside?' His vivid cerulean eyes locked onto her and the bottom fell out of her stomach. That memory box lifted its lid again as she looked deeper into those eyes that used to twinkle at her while sending her hormones into a dance, eyes that had undressed her, grown slumberous with desire. Eyes that had turned the colour of thunderclouds as he'd told her they were over. Eyes that now held nothing but a simple request.

So he was playing the friends card. She'd do that too. Cool, casual. Aloof even, but friendly.

Flipper chose that moment to kick hard, making her gasp. Sinking down onto the stretcher frame, she rubbed her side. Felt another nudge from her girl. This baby had an attitude problem. Reminding her mum exactly what her new life was all about—her daughter.

CHAPTER TWO

'Sasha Wilson, I've never forgotten you.'

He sucked cold air through clenched teeth. Unfortunately his mind remained fixed on Sasha.

'Not for lack of trying, believe me. You've hung around in my skull, annoying the hell out of me, reminding me continually of what I destroyed. My one chance of extreme happiness blown out of the water because I couldn't figure a way to make the future work well for both of us at the same time as looking after Mum and my sisters.'

What had he done to deserve this turn of events? Opening up old wounds had never been on his agenda. Especially Sasha's hurts. Coming to Takaka had been such a foolish idea, but he'd thought spending four weeks here would be safe. That he'd visit, get his house sorted and on the market then leave, without Sasha factoring into his plans—because she wouldn't be here.

When Mike had mentioned her name earlier he'd struggled to absorb the shock and warmth that had hit him. But it seemed no preparation could lessen the slam-dunk feeling he'd got when he'd actually seen her. His ability to think straight had vamoosed. He'd been sorely tempted to hold her, kiss her, devour her. The struggle to keep himself together while he'd given her that friendly hug had caused knots in his shoulders and neck muscles.

And then her pregnant belly. That had really put him in his place. He didn't belong here. Certainly not with Sasha. But, then, that was why he'd come, to get shot of his house and move on with his life. Once and for all.

Sash hadn't lived here for years, or so he'd been told. If anyone had told him she was working at the local medical centre, however temporarily, he'd have said they needed to see a shrink. Golden Bay was far too small for a personality the size of hers. Always had been. *They'd* never planned on living here any time in their future. The future he'd deliberately destroyed to set her free.

He didn't want to think about that baby she carried. But how could he not? His heart slammed his ribs. A little bit of him had died right then. Sasha was pregnant. With another man's baby. Yeah, well, the point being? Pregnancy usually involved a man and he hadn't been around for a very long time. Bile soured the back of his throat. She'd got on with her life like he'd told her to, proving how final his words had been.

He'd spoken them but had he understood the true depth of what he'd told her? Hurting her had been unavoidable if he was to make her get on with her life, unhindered by his problems with his family that had suddenly tied him to Nelson and stopped him going away to med school. He'd spent hours trying to come up with a way to break off with her without causing her distress and pain, hoping to leave the door open for later. Of course there'd been no answer other than to say it straight out. Go, get on with your life, leave me to mine. It had hurt him as much as her, but she hadn't seen that.

Now Sasha had a family of her own. Without him. His loss. His big loss.

Was that what had brought her back here? Family? The baby's maternal grandparents lived here. The slower-paced, outdoors-orientated lifestyle was perfect for a young child. Sasha had lots of friends here who were probably starting families round about now. Who had she settled down with? Someone local that he knew? Or an outsider who'd fallen under Sasha's spell? Like he had the very first time he'd set eyes on her as she'd rowed her dinghy into the beach and tossed the anchor at his feet. He'd been young and horny and in lust. Which had quickly turned to young and horny and in love.

Where was her man anyway? Grady scowled. *He* wouldn't have let her out alone at this hour, driving in these horrendous conditions. Yeah, but this was Sash. The woman who never listened to anyone's advice. The girl with enough confidence for a whole team of down-hill skiers. That had been one of her attractions. That and her smarts, and her enthusiasm for just about every-thing—except spiders and mashed spuds.

Never in a month of dry Sundays had he expected to feel so disorientated when he saw her. He'd honestly be-lieved he'd be cool, calm and casual. He'd had an hour to prepare. He'd been sitting at the same table as Mike, listening as the guy had rung around the emergency volunteers, getting them on the road to help Sasha with a road accident.

The only word that had registered in his brain had been 'Sasha'. Immediately excitement had rolled through him. He was going to see her. For eleven years he'd stayed away, wondering how she fared, if she'd forgiven him, and could they be friends again—and now all he could think was what he'd missed out on. His gut roiled. Sasha, his one true love. Out of reach for ever. And no one to blame except himself.

How could I have been so stupid to think I'd get over her if I tried really hard? Talk about impossible.

Pain bounded around his chest. His head spun so fast it hurt. His gut had crunched down hard, feeling like it held a solid ball of concrete. So much he wanted to know, yet he couldn't ask her a thing.

'Ask what?' came the sharp tone of the woman he wanted to pretend wasn't within touching distance.

Inside the ambulance he ducked to avoid smashing his head on the overhead cupboards. 'Nothing,' he muttered, because he truly couldn't think what to say. Most things that came to mind would be incendiary. Certainly not conducive to good working relations.

A cupboard door slid shut with a bang. 'What area of medicine did you specialise in?'

So she knew he'd finally trained as a doctor. She must've thought of him occasionally, then. Was that good? Or bad? He told her, 'I chose general practice. I like the community aspect best.'

'I get that.' Sasha surprised him with a smile. A very brief flicker but he'd take it. It melted some of the forced wariness that had settled on his heart the moment he'd seen her head popping up from behind that bank where the truck had crashed. The chill had been about him, not her. A hopeless attempt to shut down any leftover feelings he had for this beautiful, feisty woman.

She'd been a girl-slash-woman when he'd fallen in love with her. Seventeen going on thirty. Unafraid of anything, whether it had been taking her dad's plane up for a spin, galloping her horse at breakneck speed along the beach, or diving for scallops out in the bay. She had always got her own way by sheer willpower. People had either gone with her or stepped aside to watch with envy her latest escapade. Watching her now, she seemed very much in control.

Voices reached them, and then thankfully men appeared at the entrance to the interior of the ambulance. Jonty was telling them, 'Go easy with that stretcher, guys. Lucy doesn't need any more knocks.'

Sasha took the top end and guided the stretcher onto its frame, before deftly clicking all the locks in place. Lucy wasn't going anywhere she shouldn't.

Grady moved closer, looking their patient over, fighting to ignore Sasha's presence as her arm rubbed against his when they both leaned over the stretcher. Heat spilled through him. Heat that woke up parts of his body best left asleep right now. Heat he did not need around Sash. *Focus on Lucy.* Head wound, right arm at an odd angle, suggesting a fracture, laboured breathing. Sliding a hand under Lucy's torn blouse, he carefully felt her ribs. No problems there. One point in her favour.

'The GCS was nine when I first checked Lucy and it hasn't changed,' Sasha informed him. 'She came round twice very briefly earlier and asked about Sam, before losing consciousness again.'

The Glasgow Coma Index. Borderline severe. Not a good sign. Grady's fingers worked along Lucy's hairline then over her head. 'I'm guessing she hit the dashboard when the truck flipped.'

'The wound above her temple was still bleeding moderately when I reached her.'

He gently lifted the padding at one corner. 'It's stopped now.'

'One thing to be thankful for.' Sasha's tone was perfectly reasonable, normal. Totally unaffected by his presence.

Guess she'd long got over him. Which, considering her pregnancy, should be mighty obvious even to his sluggish brain. He must've done a good job of telling her to get on with her life without him in it because the results were very clear. Sash was going to become a mother in a few months' time. She hadn't done that on her own.

The green-eyed monster lifted its head, roared inside his skull. Who was the lucky bastard? Did he treat her well? Did she love him? Completely and utterly? Passionately? Of course she did. That was the only way Sash did anything. Grady wiped his hands down his jeans, removing a sudden coating of sweat. 'We need to splint Lucy's arm.'

He'd spoken more brusquely than he'd intended and received a perfectly arched eyebrow kind of glare for his trouble. 'Sure.'

It was as easy as that for Sash. Except her fingers had a slight tremble as she handed him the splint. Interesting. And confusing. Talk about mixed messages. Not only were those fingers trembling, they were covered in rings. Was one of them a wedding ring? The silver one on her wedding ring finger had a tiny butterfly etched into the metal. Not a likely wedding ring, even for Sasha.

They worked quickly and efficiently, routine emergency care that neither of them had any difficulty with. Grady asked in as nonchalant a voice as he could manage, 'Where have you been working? Before Takaka?' Sasha had been planning on starting her training only weeks after the last time they'd been together. They'd finished high school and had been enjoying their last summer holidays before hitting the adult world.

'In the emergency department at Christchurch Hospital for a year.' She gently lowered Lucy's arm by her side. 'Now I'm the community nurse around here while the centre's usual nurse is on maternity leave.'

'Must be something in the water,' Grady muttered.

'Here I'd been thinking it was all to do with loving relationships.' Suddenly her tone could have slayed rampaging bulls.

A quick glance showed the anger spitting out at him from those beautiful emerald eyes. Anger and something else he couldn't make out. Hurt? Disappointment? It had come and gone so fast he didn't have time to work out exactly what that emotion had been.

'Sash, I'm sorry. I didn't mean to sound flippant.' Once he'd have been able to say anything to her and get away with it. That had been before bust-up day. Eleven birthdays and Christmases ago. A doctor's degree ago. Two broken relationships ago. Relationships he hadn't cared enough about to make work.

'My name is Sasha.' Words as cold as that ice outside fell into the silence.

Not to me you're not. His heart cracked wide open at her rebuff. He hadn't set out to be overly friendly by using his pet name for her. But he'd *always* called her Sash. He hadn't learned not to. All these years he'd thought about Sash, not Sasha. That was everyone else's name for her. She used to protest at anyone calling her Sash—except him. Seemed he'd been relegated to the slush heap. His shrug was deliberate and heavy. 'Sasha.'

The door opened and cold air hit them as Mike and

the guys hoisted the second stretcher on board with Mr Donovon strapped down tight.

Their patient roused himself enough to croak out, 'How's Lucy?'

'She's stable, Sam.' Sasha held the older guy's hand for a moment, spoke in a very caring way, nothing like she'd talked to him. 'I'm glad you're out of that truck.'

'You and me both, lass.'

Mike nudged his way between Grady and Sasha. 'Let's take a look at you, Sam, before we get on our way.'

'Are you driving over to Nelson?' Sasha's eyes widened. 'I've just come over the hill and it's not good. Took me a lot longer than normal.'

'No choice. The rescue helicopter flew to Wellington on an emergency run four hours ago and has been grounded after a wind gust flicked it sideways, causing damage to a rotor,' Mike explained. 'Jonty has offered to drive while Rebecca and I keep an eye on these two.'

Rebecca poked her head through from the front, where she'd been having no luck in her attempts to raise the Nelson ED on the radio. 'I don't have a lot of confidence driving on ice, whereas Jonty's had plenty of practice.'

'You want me to come along?' Grady asked Mike. 'I'm happy to help.' Though it was getting crowded in here.

Mike shook his head as he cut down through the centre of Sam's trouser leg. 'No point in all of us missing out on a night's sleep. Rebecca and I can handle this. Grady, you hitch a ride back with Sasha. She lives on her parents' property, close by your house.' Mike really didn't have a clue about anything.

He saw Sash stiffen for a brief moment. Then she

returned to helping Mike, for all the world completely unperturbed by the other doctor's suggestion. Mike's idea made perfect sense. She lived very close to his house. He used to be able to get to Sasha's in under a minute on his motorbike if the road was clear. Bloody lucky he'd never come off on that tight corner by the Wilsons' gate. 'Okay with you, Sasha?' he drawled.

Why did his mind play these games to annoy her when really all he wanted was a bit of peace for the rest of his stay here? He must quit giving the woman a hard time. She hadn't asked for him to barge back into her life. 'I can go back with the fire truck if you'd prefer.'

Her mouth tightened, her eyes darkened, and she tugged those small shoulders back hard, automatically pushing that baby bump further out between them. She wouldn't back down from what she'd been asked to do. But she glared at him as she said, 'Might as well come with me. I warn you I'm not in a hurry. Too much ice to drive like I'm handling a racing car.'

Now, that was something new. Sash had always driven like she had to win. 'Works for me.'

'Let's go.' Sasha was blunt. 'I'm more than ready to be home tucked up in bed for what's left of the night.'

Air whooshed out of his lungs. Sash and bed. The memories he'd been trying to deny for the last thirty minutes reared up bright and dazzling. Sash—gregarious, generous, sexy, funny. A full-on, crazy, risk-taking kind of girl. An exciting, adventurous lover whose kisses had always left him breathless. And wanting more of her. What he wouldn't do for one of those now.

Huh? Man, he had a problem, and he was about to hitch a ride with her. He watched her carefully lower to the ground, holding onto the safety rail in case her feet went from under her. So unlike the Sash he knew. But he wanted, needed, to get to know this version.

Mike tapped him on the shoulder. 'Sorry about dragging you up here, but that's Golden Bay for us medicos. The isolation means no one can ever totally relax.'

'No problem,' he answered mechanically, his eyes still fixed on Sash as she moved away awkwardly, taking each step extra-carefully. Her back ramrod straight, her head high. He knew her chin would be jutting forward, her mouth tight.

Exactly like that last time he'd seen her. On the sand at Pohara Beach below Dad's house, now his house. She'd turned to walk away from him, the summer wind flattening her burnished gold curls and sandblasting her arms. Her long legs, forever legs, showcased by barely-there shorts, had eaten up the ground as she'd put distance between them.

Those green eyes, big in her fine-featured face, had been fixed on something in the distance at the far end of the beach. Only minutes before they'd been filled with love for him. Love that had rapidly turned to disbelief, and pain, as he'd spewed out his sorry attempt to make her go away so she could have the future she'd already mapped out long before they'd got together. The only kind of future that would suit Sasha. Certainly nothing like the one he'd suddenly faced, brought about by Dad's death.

If he had a dollar for every time he'd wished his words back over the intervening years he could have retired already. But there'd be no undoing what his mouth had spilled that day. His deliberate attempt to send her on her way had been highly successful. Though he'd been thankful it was done, there'd been a part of him that had wished she'd fought him, made him accept there was no letting go of what bound them together, that theirs was a love that would see them through anything and everything.

Now he had to sit in a vehicle with her for as long as it took to get home. He would not spend the trip remembering her fingers playing over his skin in moments of wild passion. He would not recall how she'd call on her cell phone in the middle of the night and talk dirty till he lost control. Or how she'd climb on the back of his motorbike, slide her arms around his waist and hang on, laughing at the wind in her face. Not. Not. Not.

His heart squeezed painfully. He'd missed Sash so much that even if he could, he didn't want to go away again without talking to her. Could they bury the elephant between them? These weeks might be his only opportunity. He could put the time to good use and put the real Sasha up against the one in his memory. That might prove interesting. Maybe the biggest disappointment of his life. But then he might finally be able to move on.

'You going or what?' Mike asked.

Grady shook his head, concentrated on the here and now. 'On my way.'

He hadn't even got the car door shut before Sash turned the key in the ignition. She mightn't intend driving fast but she wasn't wasting time hanging around. Glancing his way, she kept her face inscrutable. 'Ready?'

'Yes.' Shrugging back into the corner, he couldn't stop his gaze wandering over her. His breathing stuttered. She'd grown even more beautiful than he remembered her to be. Her pearly whites were now straight and orderly. The braces she'd hated wearing had done a fantastic job, though he missed the gap between the two front teeth. That had been kind of cute. Sasha's curls had grown into a long, burnished gold ponytail held firmly in place with a purple clip thing. She still stared directly at everything, everyone. Including him.

And there—in those eyes—he finally recognised something from way back. Those eyes held the same all-seeing, missing-nothing gleam, and they were focused entirely on him. Looking for what?

Then she blinked, turned her head and began backing the vehicle onto the road, before concentrating on taking them down the hill. Her hands were firm on the steering-wheel, her body tilted forward as she peered out the windscreen. She was in control. Nothing new there. But she wasn't fighting the situation, instead using the gears to go with the conditions outside.

Grady relaxed further back into his seat, clicked his seat belt in place. The vehicle was in capable hands. Unless fate had some ugly plans for them he'd soon be back at his house, warm and comfortable again. And hopefully getting some sleep. Something he seriously doubted was likely to happen.

The only sound was the purr of the engine and the intermittent flick, flick of the wipers. Sasha had never liked silence. But she wasn't doing anything about filling this one. Grady's mouth twitched.

Ironic but he wanted to hear noise, her voice, words, anything but this quietness that smothered him.

Her gloved right hand lifted from the steering-wheel and did the gentlest of sweeps across her belly.

His gut squeezed tight. He wanted to place his hand on top of hers, to feel whatever she felt. To be a part of this scene, not an observer. Her gesture had been instinctive, a mother-to-baby touch. Sash was obviously comfortable with being an expectant mum. It suited her.

From what he could see in the dull light from the instrument panel her face had softened, the glint in her eyes quietened, and that chin didn't point forward. Yes, she was at ease with her situation, if not with him.

The tightening in his gut increased. He wanted to ask about the father of her baby, why she was living back here, how long before she left again, if she was happy. Instead, he looked out the windscreen and went for, 'How are your parents? Your dad still flying?'

At first it seemed she had no intention of answering. But just when he was about to try again she answered. 'Dad's set to retire at the end of the year. He's getting tired of long-haul flights, finds each one a little harder to recover from than the last. But he doesn't want to go back on the domestic route. Says that's for the up-and-coming pilots to sharpen their teeth on.'

'I've never understood how pilots manage all those hours in the air, their bodies not really coping with all the time-zone changes. It can't be good in the long run.' Yet he remembered Ian Wilson always having abundant energy. Working their avocado and citrus orchards when he was at home, going fishing, flying his plane, taking his family away for hiking weekends. He'd never stopped. His daughter had the same genes.

'You haven't seen Dad for a while. He's looking older. And he doesn't move as fast any more.' Sadness laced her statement. 'He's only sixty-three, for goodness' sake. He shouldn't be slowing down.'

'Are you worried about it? Enough to suggest he see a doctor?'

'No, it's life catching up, I think.' She changed gear

to reduce speed for a sharp bend. 'Jackson's working in Hong Kong so they catch up whenever Dad flies that way.'

So Dr Jackson Wilson, Sasha's older brother, now lived halfway round the world. No surprise. The guy had been in a hurry to leave the bay the moment he'd finished high school. Guess he hadn't stopped when he'd reached Auckland either. 'What does your mother think about Ian retiring?'

'She's the reason he's not stopping as soon as he'd like. I think she's afraid he'll take over her orchard and leave her with little to do.'

'Hardly surprising. It's been her baby for years.'

Again Sash went all quiet on him. This time the silence hung heavily between them as she concentrated on negotiating the final hairpin bend, her eyes focused straight ahead, her lips pressed hard together. He sensed the tension in her thighs, arms and the rest of her compact body. Because of the road conditions? Or the fact he'd used the baby word?

He broke the silence. 'When I went for a walk yesterday I noticed the orchard's been expanded. There's a lot of work there for anyone to cope with.' If Ian was sixty-three then his wife had to be a similar age. Time to relax a bit, surely?

It took a few minutes but finally she answered so quietly he had to strain to hear her. 'Mum tries, and I help when I can.'

'Is that wise in your condition? Orchard work's quite heavy.' Seemed his runaway tongue had no problem with talking. Then his head jerked forward as the car skated to an abrupt halt.

'By the time you've walked home you might've

learned to keep your unwanted opinions to yourself.'
Sasha stared out the windscreen, not even dignifying
him with a glare.

'I'm sorry. Again.' He waited. He had no intention of
getting out into the night and waiting for the unlikely
event of another vehicle coming along.

*Might try and learn to keep your trap shut while
you're waiting. Because up until now it's done nothing
but get you further than ever offside with Sasha. If that
was possible.*

Something akin to fear slithered under his skin. What
if he never got to laugh with Sasha again? Never saw
her eyes light up into that brilliant summer green that
hit him right in the heart? Could he still go and knock
on her door and say hi?

She wouldn't need that from him. Those bases would
be covered with the father of her baby. Nausea rolled up
Grady's throat. He hadn't been able to do any of those
things for years. Long, lonely years when he'd looked
for her in every woman he dated.

Suddenly he really, truly, understood how coming
back to Golden Bay had little to do with working on his
house. He could've paid a carpenter to do that. No, this
mad idea had been all about Sasha and their past.

But it had to be friendship he was looking for.

Nope. Not at all. But it was all he'd get.

But first he needed a ride home.

He did the one thing he was very good at, had been
doing for years. He waited.

CHAPTER THREE

Sasha snapped the shower off after a quick soap and sluice job and snatched at her towel. She'd slept in. She'd be late for work. The one thing she'd do anything to avoid. And on a Monday morning it'd be bedlam at the medical centre. Hopefully, Mike and Roz would give her some slack because she'd been helping Sam and Lucy. There'd be no problem with Rory. He was more laid back than his medical partners.

Why hadn't she heard her alarm? Hard to believe she'd fallen asleep the moment her head had touched the pillow, that there hadn't been hours of tossing and turning while Grady ran amok in her skull.

But the moment her eyes had popped open this morning he'd been there. That wary, lopsided smile clawing at her heartstrings. His gravelly voice thrilling her deep, deep inside, stirring hormones into a dance. The lid had lifted off that memory box again.

'Grady O'Neil, I've missed you so much.' Nothing or nobody in the intervening years had filled the hole he'd torn out of her heart. Out of her soul. There'd been men, for sure, but none had touched her as deeply as Grady. Not even greaseball had hurt her as badly. Could be she was getting used to being tossed aside by the men she'd cared about. Thank goodness. She wouldn't have survived a repeat of the kind of devastation Grady had caused, leaving her hollowed out.

Kick, kick.

Until the advent of her baby. Flipper would go a long way to making her feel complete again. Flipper would soak up all the love she had to give. 'My baby girl.'

Swiping the condensation off the mirror, Sasha studied her belly. So round, smooth, life-giving. Her fingers splayed across the taut skin and she turned sideways for a different view. 'Oh, wow.' Tears misted her eyes, clogged her throat. 'You're beautiful already.'

She never tired of this view. Pregnancy had turned out to be amazing. Hard to believe that a wee baby girl was growing in there, getting ready for the big, wide world. What colour were her eyes? Her hair? 'My baby. My love.' Sniff. 'I promise you, Flipper, I'm going to be the best darned mother you'd ever wish for.' Sniff. 'I love you so much already.' Would love cover all her failings? Help her make wise decisions regarding just about everything? Would her love make up for the lack of a father?

Tossing the towel in the general direction of the drying rail, Sasha fumbled for a tissue and blew hard.

No, Grady, the job's not up for grabs. As much as my baby needs a dad, I'm not letting you in. It's bad enough you shoved my love back in my face, and on a bad day I might even take another chance on you, admit extenuating circumstances, but what if you left again? That could hurt Flipper, which is non-negotiable. So, byebye, Grady.

But, for the record, her real father's out of the picture, too. He made it clearer than a fine winter's day that he wants absolutely nothing to do with this child. As far as I'm concerned, he's had his chance.

Kick.

'Hey, baby girl. You should be sleeping in after your late night.' Dropping the soggy tissue in the waste basket, Sasha picked up her knickers and stepped into them. Reached for her bra, which got tighter by the day. 'You know we're running late, Flipper? The centre will be buzzing with people who've knocked themselves about over the weekend, playing rugby or netball, plus the usual line-up of colds and flu.' The zip on her pregnancy trousers caught. 'Flipper, you're putting on weight.'

As she shoved her arms into her blouse there was a loud pounding on her front door. 'Who the heck?' Just what she needed, a visitor when she should already be on the road. Then she relaxed. It'd be Jessica. There'd been a message on the answering-machine when she'd got in to call her friend urgently, no matter what the time of day or night. Fairly certain Jessica would be phoning to warn her about Grady's reappearance, she'd opted to wait until she saw her at work rather than talk for what had been left of the night about how to deal with him.

Heading for the front of her cottage, she left buttoning her blouse and tugged on a woollen cardigan. She swung the door wide, shivering in the cold blast that immediately whacked her. 'Hey, you can save your breath. I already...' Her voice petered out as her eyes encountered the one person she'd never expected to see at this moment.

'You already what?' Grady asked in such a normal tone, like he always dropped by her place, that the temperature of her blood went from normal to boiling in a flash.

Remain calm. Breathe deep. 'What are you doing here?'

Grady's eyes widened but otherwise he remained unperturbed. 'I need a ride to the medical centre. My car's at Mike's.' His hand slid through that wonderful, nearly shoulder-length black hair that she refused to remember running her fingers through. 'I presume you're heading that way shortly.'

The heat in her veins evaporated immediately. A ride to the centre? In her car? He was doing something so mundane as asking a neighbour for a lift and yet she wanted to yell no at him. Yearned to close her door in his beautiful face and lean back on it, while pretending that the guy on the other side meant no more to her than yesterday's lunch. So much for not letting Grady get to her.

Be calm, act rationally. Do the right, the sensible thing. 'No problem. Give me a minute. I'll grab my jacket and bag.' She didn't try to sound chirpy. Too tired for that. And wired. Grady mightn't have kept her awake last night but she hadn't forgotten for an instant that she'd seen him, that he was back, that she'd *missed him* more than she'd ever guessed. That her body went a little crazy whenever he was near. Shouldn't pregnancy dull the sex buzz?

A buzz he didn't seem to be feeling as he said, 'Thanks. I'm covering for Mike this morning while he catches up on much-needed sleep. They didn't get back from Nelson until about five.'

The vague hope that she could drive fast, dump Grady at Mike's and get on with her day vanished. They'd be in the same building most of the morning until she headed off on her rounds. She'd be unable to avoid him. Even if she didn't see him she'd hear his deep voice when he talked with patients as he led them to his consulting room or when he took a coffee break in the kitchen. So? What happened to doing friendly? Grady seemed to be managing that. Surely she could? Or didn't he feel anything about the past? Had he got over it so well that he really thought friendship was possible?

Get real. Grady told you he didn't love you any more. What was there to get over?

Spinning on her heel, she left him on the doorstep and headed for the kitchen to collect her gear and something to have for breakfast once she got to work.

'Sash,' he called after her.

Spinning back, she glared at him, holding in the pain that using the diminutive form of her name caused. Today she would not lower herself to plead that he refrain from using it. Instead, she slapped a hand on her hip and, barely resisting tapping her foot, waited.

'Sorry. Sasha.' His chest lifted, fell back into place under that navy jersey that fitted him like a second skin, accentuating all the details of his chest she'd prefer to forget. The tip of his tongue appeared at the corner of his mouth. 'You might want to take a few more minutes and finish getting dressed.'

What? She glanced downwards. Great. Her blouse was only half-buttoned, exposing her new, getting-bigger-by-the-day cleavage. Her feet were bare. Heck, she hadn't put any make-up on yet or done her hair. 'Make that ten minutes.'

Grady watched as Sash did that spin-on-her-heel thing again. Her back was straighter than straight, her long, mussed hair bouncing as she charged away. And his belly squeezed hard on the boiled egg he'd eaten half an hour ago. Did those golden locks still feel like silk? Did she still enjoy having them hand-combed by someone else?

The wind roared across the lawn, pelted his back with cold and knocked the door against the wall. He stepped inside and closed winter out. Now what? Did he wander through the house like he was welcome? Or wait here just inside the door like a nervous kid outside the head-master's office? Like he'd ever done that.

He strode towards the door opposite where Sash had disappeared, hopeful of finding the kitchen. What if her partner was there? Then he'd front up, introduce himself and explain why he was here. He would not say he'd de-liberately come by to meet him, to find out who he was and see if they already knew each other.

That baby bump was still there, hadn't disappeared overnight. Hadn't been a figment of his overactive imag-ination. Breakfast rolled over. Regurgitated egg tasted disgusting. Hadn't tasted that flash first time round, come to think of it. He'd eaten on autopilot, knowing he'd regret it later if he didn't have breakfast but not overly interested in what he ate. His head space had been filled with images from last night of Sash. Angry, cautious, smiling—not at him—shocked, and very, very protective of her unborn child.

The cupboard that was obviously the kitchen was empty. No partner here. Grady didn't know whether to feel relieved or disappointed. The moment of reckoning had only been delayed.

'Right, let's go.' Sasha's hand appeared in the pe-riphery of his vision as she snatched up keys lying on the bench.

'Sasha.' Grady knew he should stop right there but the words kept on coming. 'Do you live here alone?'

'Yes,' she called over her shoulder, as she strode away to the front door. Her hand on the door handle tightened then she whipped around to face him, her annoyed-looking eyes locking with his. 'Yes,' she repeated more emphatically. And then she waited, apparently understanding what he wanted to know and not making it easy for him.

'The baby's father doesn't live with you?' *What part of living alone didn't you get?*

'Definitely not,' she snapped, then blinked and turned away, tugging the door open, but not before he saw anger flicker across her face, widening her eyes.

Not sure how he should be feeling right now, he followed her outside. If there wasn't a father in the picture then maybe he could spend some time getting alongside her and see where that led. Probably fooling himself, setting himself up for heartbreak.

What about that baby? Do you want to be a part of its life? Because if you're wanting Sash back then she comes with extras.

Something to think about. Though his need to get alongside Sash might override any concerns about the child. At the moment, anyway.

Watching her closely as those keys she'd snatched up flew from one ring-laden hand to the other and back while she waited for him to come outside, he had to resist the urge to wrap her up in a big hug. Nothing sexual. A completely caring and friendly embrace. A hug to take away some of that despair she was valiantly trying to hide behind anger.

The front door closed with a bang. Then the locks on

that canary-yellow car popped. Sash's feet slapped hard on the pavement as she closed the gap to her vehicle then swung back to face him. She'd applied make-up in those few minutes she'd left him standing around, yet her face appeared ghostly pale. But her spine had clicked dead straight again.

'I am going to be a solo mother.' Fierce words spoken in her don't-screw-with-me attitude. So Sash. Watch out anyone who gave her a hard time over that. And there'd be plenty. Small communities might turn out to support anyone who needed them but there was always the gossip doing the rounds, too. Which was why her brother had left so long ago.

'I'm sorry to hear that.' And he was. He mightn't like another man in her life but he was big enough to acknowledge single parenthood would be no easy feat and he really didn't want Sasha having to face it alone.

'Don't be. It's for the best.' She slid into the car and shoved the key into the ignition. 'Coming?'

Why did I just tell Grady that? It's absolutely none of his business. At the gate Sasha lifted her foot off the brake too quickly and the vehicle jerked forward. *It's not a secret. Probably best to put it out there so he's not badgering me with more questions.*

When she'd spilled the truth there'd been something in Grady's eyes that had curled her toes with warmth, as though he was on her side. Which had to be the dumbest thought she'd had in a long time. Why would he be? And why had the idea of Grady being there for her in any way, shape or form made her feel a smidgeon better than she had five minutes ago?

She *was* doing this alone. Jessica, as friend and midwife, would see her through the pregnancy and birth, but the hard yards were all down to her. Her parents would always stand by her, but in the end the baby was her responsibility. *Hope I know what I'm doing, Flipper.* Her hand dropped to her extended belly and did a quick lap over the bump.

Unable to stop herself, she glanced sideways, met Grady's steady gaze, saw wonder all mixed up with yearning gleaming out at her. Oh—my—goodness. A sensation in her chest of something like a mouse on a treadmill brought tears bursting into her eyes. Her neck clicked as she flicked her head forward, taking her eyes away from that unrealistic sight.

If only that picture was for real, like they were a happy couple expecting their first child. It should be true, would've been if he hadn't dumped her. Grady would make an awesome dad. But not for her little girl. Flipper was not going to grow up believing Grady would always be there for her only to discover he left when she wasn't looking.

Back up. Grady had put his mother and sisters before her, before them. His family had desperately needed his undivided attention and support at the time. He'd also put training to become a doctor on hold. It hadn't only been about not wanting her. With Mum's illness beginning to make an impact on her family's lives she was beginning to understand what he'd been facing. But he should've talked to her, told her everything. Shared his problems.

Toot, toot. A car pulled up beside her vehicle, stopping in the middle of the road. Sasha looked out. Mum's head was poking out of the driver's window, surprise widening her eyes as she peered past her. Oh, great. Now for the forty questions.

Best cut her off at the pass. 'Hey, Mum, how's things? I'll have to find someone else to take the lemons over the hill tonight. Lucy and Sam had an accident last night and are in hospital so I'm not sure what's happening with their freight run.' *Shut up. You're babbling.* Anyway, Mum hadn't heard a word, she was too busy sussing out the man sitting beside her.

'Grady, it's good to see you. I heard you were at the house, and hoped to catch up with you in the next day or two to ask you over for a meal. Ian will be back to-night. Sasha's joining us for dinner tomorrow so how about you come along?' Now who was babbling? At least Mum hadn't said it would be just like old times. Yet. 'It would be—'

Sasha held her breath.

Mum continued, 'Lovely to catch up with what you've been up to since we last saw you.'

Thanks for the loyalty, Mum. Where was the 'Who the heck do you think you are, coming back here when Sasha's finally moved back home?'

Grady leaned forward, shot a quick look at Sasha that told her exactly what he was going to say. 'Hello, Virginia. I'd love to catch up with you and Ian. I'll bring a bottle of wine.'

'Lovely.' Mum beamed. Mothers had no right to invite ex-boyfriends to dinner. They should know better. But, then, Mum hadn't really seen the devastation Grady's defection had wrought on her, hadn't known that she'd gone from wild to wilder for twelve months. Hadn't known how many pieces her heart had broken into and how, when it had come to putting it back together, it had been like a jigsaw with bits missing.

Sasha swallowed her annoyance. 'Mum, did you hear

me? Lucy and Sam crashed their truck last night. They're in hospital.'

Finally Mum's attention flipped to her. 'What? That's terrible. How badly hurt are they? I'll go over and see to the chooks and dogs.'

'Leave it, Mum. I'll see to that after work.'

She got a glare for an answer.

'Mr and Mrs Donovan will be in hospital for a few days,' Grady informed them. 'Mike says their injuries are not serious.'

Repeating herself, Sasha said, 'I'll ring the other carriers and see if we can get the citrus cases picked up from your shed. Otherwise I'll load them after work and take them into the depot.' The fruit needed to be at the market early tomorrow morning. 'But right now I'm late for work. See you later.'

Putting the vehicle in gear, she slowly drove away. Mum looked more tired than usual this morning. Thank goodness Dad was nearly home. He'd be able to do some of those jobs Mum insisted she was still capable of doing. Like driving into the township for supplies. Like loading heavy cases onto the ute and delivering them to the depot. Which was definitely *her* job whenever Mum would listen.

She hated this illness; hated the thought Mum would slowly lose the ability to do all the things she loved doing. Mothers weren't meant to get ill. They were meant to be there for ever. *Well, I'm going to be here for ever, watching, helping, looking after her. Doing everything possible to make life easier for her.*

She'd ring Mum later and see if she needed anything picked up. Grady was in for a shock tomorrow night. By the end of the day her mother didn't always have the strength for cooking so they could very well get heat and eat on a foil plate. Nothing like the wonderful home-cooked meals Mum used to be famous for in Takaka.

Deep in thought, she hadn't noticed the silence in the cab until Grady broke it with, 'You're annoyed I accepted your mother's invitation.'

Was she? Probably. Seemed he was getting into her space too much, too quickly. 'A little. But I'll get over it.' Please.

'I can beg off if you want me to.'

'Leave it, Grady. Mum would be disappointed. Just…' How did she explain without explaining?

'Sasha? Is everything okay? You and the baby are doing fine, aren't you?' Talk about a left-field question. How did he go from discussing her mother to asking about her baby? His concern could be her undoing. If she let it.

Her lips pressed together and her eyes blurred as hurt for Mum gripped her. Blinking furiously, she focused on the road in front, thankful for the lack of traffic at this time of year. Shaking her head from side to side, she managed, 'Everything's hunky-dory. But it can be a little out of whack at times so be prepared for anything tomorrow.'

And that was all he was getting. The ache in the back of her throat grew but at least her vision cleared. She could feel Grady watching her closely. There'd be questions in those beautiful eyes that always saw too much. She would not look at him. There was plenty of time later if she wanted to talk to him about the disease devastating her family. And whether she did or didn't depended on lots of things, but mainly on how well they got along over the next few days.

Grady had skin thicker than the steers she could see in the paddock alongside the road. 'What's this about you loading the boxes of lemons? You can't do that in your condition.'

Condition? Like I'm sick or something. 'Trust me. I won't do anything that could hurt my baby.'

'I believe you, but do you recognise when you're doing too much? I remember those boxes. They weren't light. You should leave the job to someone else.'

Like who? 'When did you turn so bossy?'

'I had two teenage sisters to deal with. They never made anything easy for me. I probably didn't make it easy for them either, trying to fill Dad's shoes and be the man about the place. I wasn't ready for that job.'

'It must've been hell for you all.' She relaxed, tossed him a smile. 'But go, them. Where are they these days?'

'They're both in London with Ma and her husband. Collete's a lawyer and Eve's a gym instructor.'

'Your mother remarried?'

'Yes, two years after Dad died.' His tone quietened, deepened.

'That didn't make you happy?'

'I'm fine with it. Carrington's a good man and Ma's blissfully happy. She's not the kind of woman who can live on her own for long. She doesn't cope well with finances and making sure the insurance or rates are paid.' His turn to stare out the window at the passing paddocks. 'That took me a while to realise and when I did she'd made some bad calls with money. She wouldn't let me take total control so we agreed to sell the trucking business and invest the money to give her a monthly payment. It worked, sort of. Then along came Carrington and he took care of them all.'

'Leaving you free to get on with your medical training.'

'I took the remaining six months of that year off, went north to pick fruit, tried my hand on a commercial fishing trawler, pulled beers in a pub. Generally let loose for a while, knowing that once I started at med school there'd be no let-up for a long time.'

'Makes sense.' While Grady was okay with talking about himself she'd absorb every detail going. It was getting harder by the minute to keep him at arm's length. She craved information about him, what he'd done, where he'd lived, who he loved.

Who Grady loved? Did he have a partner? Was she in Auckland, working while he dealt with this pesky little issue of a house out in the back of nowhere? Her heart rate picked up speed. What did any of that matter? She wasn't getting back with the guy and she'd be the last person to wish him anything but happiness.

With relief she pulled into the car park at the back of the medical centre. At least there'd be more air in the centre, fresh air that didn't hold that spicy scent that was Grady, and she wouldn't starve for oxygen because he'd sucked it all up.

'There you go. Delivered safe and sound.' Wasn't that what Jessica would say when she put Flipper in her arms? Giving Grady a ride had seemed almost as traumatic, though not as painful.

'So uneventful I thought I was dreaming.' A hint of laughter in his voice had her head spinning round. He added, 'I don't remember a single time you ever drove or flew me anywhere that was downright steady and safe.'

Yeah, she'd been a little on the wild side then, had got worse after their bust-up. 'That was before Flipper.'

Long, long before. Recently life had become so sedate she bored herself.

'Flipper?' His mouth twitched into a heart-wrenching smile.

'Baby. Commonly known as Flipper for her swimming antics that feel like what I've seen the dolphins doing out in the bay, rising and falling through the water.'

'Her? So you're having a girl.' His smile died, his gaze turned wistful. 'A little Sasha.'

Why wistful? This was her, the woman he'd professed not to love, at least not enough to hang around with for the rest of his life. 'Yep, a little me. Guess I'm in for payback time for all the worry I put my parents through. Dad keeps warning me I'll have heart failure every time she moves, wondering what antics she'll get up to and if she'll be safe.'

'Ian encouraged you to do those things. It was your mother who had the heart failure.' Thank goodness the laughter had returned to his voice. She didn't like Grady being sad. It didn't fit her memories, the ones that had escaped the box overnight.

He'd always been full of fun and laughter, teasing, happy. Ping. Another memory. The day his father had dropped dead on the golf course. Grady had never been Grady afterwards. The shock had knocked him and his mother and two much younger sisters to their knees. Mr O'Neil's passing had been completely unexpected. He hadn't had a sick day in all his adult life. Never been to a doctor. Hadn't swallowed pills for anything. A big, solid man, who'd adored his family, worked hard and given generously. Died at forty-four of a massive coronary while swinging an iron at a golf ball.

When Sasha had heard the appalling news she'd gone

home and hugged her dad hard and long. It had been impossible to imagine what losing a parent would be like, but she'd known how much she'd loved Mum and Dad and had never stopped telling and showing them ever since.

That day had been the beginning of the changes that had overtaken her and Grady's lives. What if she'd been too impatient with him? Selfish in her own wants, not hearing beyond what he'd actually said? She'd moved on, trained as a nurse, done pretty much anything and everything she'd wanted, and now was preparing for a new challenge—becoming a mum. But what if she'd failed Grady? Was that why men left her? Because she didn't stack up when the chips were down?

The sound of a car door slamming broke into her reverie and reminded her she was already late. At least Mike wasn't here to give her a hard time about that, and Roz might just be more relaxed and prepared to give her a chance after last night's events. 'Better get cracking. Monday mornings are hectic, without fail.'

She didn't wait for Grady but headed straight inside, anxious to put some space between them. Until last night she hadn't considered if bringing up Flipper alone was wrong. Sure, all kids needed two parents, and that was on a good day, but those who only got one seemed to do okay. Until Grady's reappearance she hadn't worried too much about that.

CHAPTER FOUR

'HEY, YOU DIDN'T call me.' Jessica looked up from her desk in the nurses' office as Sasha slipped inside and opened her locker.

'Get growled at for waking you at two in the morning? I don't live that dangerously. Any more,' she added under her breath.

Jessica fixed her with a compassionate look. 'Sasha, I want to warn you…' She hesitated.

Sasha dived straight in. 'Grady's back.'

'You know? Who told you? No one at the medical centre knows about your past with him.'

Sasha's lips flattened. 'I had the privilege of giving him a ride home in the early hours. I came across the Donovans caught inside their truck after sliding off the road last night and when the rescue crews turned up, guess who lined up with them?' Shrugging out of her jacket, she went for broke. 'I've also brought him into work as he's covering for Mike this morning.'

'You okay with this?' Jessica's chair scraped the floor as she pushed it back to stand.

'Do I have a choice?' The hand hanging up the jacket shook hard. No, she wasn't okay. About Grady's reappearance in her home town. About him coming to dinner at her parents' home, like old times. About him working at her workplace. About anything.

Jess's arms surrounded her, pulled her in for a hug. 'Want to take a sickie?' she whispered.

'A four-week one? Yep, I do.' Which only showed how rattled Grady made her feel because she never, ever ducked for cover when the going got tough. Hadn't had it this tough for a while, though.

Stepping away, Jessica gave her a twisted smile. 'Which doctor will you ask to sign the leave form? Roz or Rory? Or Grady?'

'Now, there's a thought.' Retrieving her yoghurt and fruit to put in the fridge, she asked, 'Want a coffee before mayhem arrives?'

'Too late. It's already here. You've got a stack of patient files higher than my dirty dishes at home.'

'Then I'm never going to get done today.'

'Let's go grab that coffee anyway.' Jessica led the way to the kitchen. 'Bet you haven't eaten this morning.'

'You know me too well.'

'Eat that yoghurt and banana before you start work.'

'Why is it that because I'm pregnant everyone thinks they can tell me what to do? You're not the first today.'

'Let me guess. Grady been giving you orders, too?' Jess actually smiled around her question.

Traitor. 'Don't act like that's a good thing,' Sasha said as she tugged the foil off the yoghurt pot. Because it was out of order. He had no place in her life. And her friend's role was to support her, no matter what.

Jessica's smile widened. 'Mrs Collins is waiting for you to take her stitches out. Brought us a chocolate cake for morning tea as well. Which is good because that's not enough breakfast for you and your baby.'

'Chocolate cake?' The thought of it made her gag. And she wasn't insulting Mrs Collins's cooking. Those chocolate cakes she made were the best on the planet. If only her stomach wasn't in a riot of nerves. 'Flipper might like some.'

Jess threaded her arm through Sasha's. 'How is my favourite baby?'

'Bet you say that to all your mothers.'

'Of course I do.'

'Cheers.' One of the best things to come out of returning home to have her baby was discovering that Jessica had also returned to Golden Bay only weeks earlier and would be her midwife. She couldn't think of anyone better to be there when she delivered. They were forging a strong friendship. Jess had been in Jackson's year at school so they hadn't known each other well. Jess's family life had been hectic and chaotic back then.

Inside the kitchen Sasha stopped, suddenly overwhelmed by everything. She studied her hands as she asked quietly, 'Jessica, I am going to manage, aren't I?' She swallowed a huge lump that had risen to block her throat. 'I know nothing about bringing up a child. Apart from my nursing training I haven't had anything to do with babies. What if I make a right royal mess of things? Get the award for worst mother of the year? Flipper will grow up hating me.' She blinked as moisture threatened to spill down her cheeks.

'You? Worst mother? Not possible. You haven't got a hopeless cell in your body.'

'Every cell feels more than hopeless at the moment.' This debilitating sensation hadn't happened before. Until this morning she'd been quietly confident she'd get parenting mostly right, and if she got stuck she had her own great parents to turn to. Even with the problems they were facing at the moment, they couldn't wait to be grandparents. Staring at her shaking hands, she almost cried. 'What's come over me?'

Jessica hugged her. 'You're hormonal. It's quite normal in your condition. I was a blithering idiot at six months.'

'Hormonal? That covers a multitude of things.' And ignored what might be the real reason for her distress. That man she'd brought to work with her. Hugging Jessica back, she stepped away, headed for the kettle, plastering a false smile on her dial and bracing herself for the day.

'Did you bring photos of the wedding with you?' Jess asked.

Duh, of course. 'The camera's in my bag.'

'I'll grab it. Can't wait to see Tina in all her finery.'

'She looked gorgeous,' Sasha said, the moment Jessica stepped back into the kitchen. 'Stunning, as did Paolo. And when they said their vows I cried.' Just like she was doing now. Fat, silent tears rolled down her cheeks. 'They are so happy, so in love, it's like magic.' Her heart swelled with emotion. 'It was the most beautiful wedding I've ever been to. They walked under an arch of skis and the theme of the reception was all about skiing.'

'I should learn to ski and go to Italy, find myself a gorgeous Italian man like Tina did.'

'Didn't work for me.' Sasha smiled genuinely at last.

Jess held the camera in one hand, deftly clicking through the photos, and wrapped her free arm around Sasha's shoulders. 'Hey, the bridesmaid looked gorgeous, too. That shade of emerald really suits her.'

'I tried to hide the bump as much as possible but it wasn't easy.' Sasha hiccupped and dashed at her cheeks with the back of her hand. 'Tina kept telling me to stop worrying but most of her wedding photos are going to have my pregnant belly as the centre of attention.'

Jess squeezed her shoulder. 'If Tina hadn't wanted Flipper in her photos she'd have taken you up on your suggestion she find another bridesmaid. She's a true friend.'

More tears fell. 'I'm a right mess this morning,' she muttered as she sniffed hard.

'Babymones.' Jess grinned around her made-up word for pregnancy hormones. Then the grin slipped as she leaned close. 'And a little bit of disturbance in the two-metre package that just walked past the door.'

'I wish…' Sasha hauled in a deep breath. 'You know, I haven't a clue what I wish when it comes to Grady. I seem to be having some positive thoughts, memories…' Again her voice trailed off and she shrugged.

'You've got Flipper to think about. Leave Grady to his own resources. And if it gets too bad you come see me. Okay?'

'Okay.' She was so lucky with her friends. They really cared about her. As she did them. Tina had insisted she be bridesmaid, saying after all the things they'd done together during the two years they'd nursed in Dubai the small matter of a baby wasn't going to stop her having Sasha beside her as she said her marriage vows.

And now Jessica and her little boy, Nicholas, had become an integral part of her life. She really had nothing to complain about, and everything she could wish for.

Except a father for her baby.

* * *

Grady tapped his fingers on the top of Mike's desk. George Browning had gone, happy with a prescription for his cholesterol and something to clear his chest infection.

He should be heading out to the waiting room to collect the next patient but he needed a moment. He'd overheard Sasha talking to Jess in the kitchen, heard the raw uncertainty in her voice. So unlike the Sash he remembered. From the highest hair on her head to the ends of her toes she'd always emanated confidence. Always. Too much sometimes, but that was better than not enough.

Admittedly, being responsible for a tiny baby had to be different. Scary. Daunting. Especially doing it on her own. His fingers shoved through his hair. Sasha was having a baby. It still rocked him to think about it. And he'd thought about it for what had been left of the night after she'd dropped him off at his house. Sasha Wilson. Once the love of his life. *You are still capable of rattling me, turning my heart upside down, making me want you and to be a part of your life.*

Grady visualised Sasha holding her baby, crooning sweet nothings, placing delicate kisses on her forehead. She'd throw herself full on into motherhood, as she'd always done with anything. That baby she carried didn't know yet how lucky she was to have Sasha for a mum. If he ever had kids, their mother would have to be just like her.

Just like her? Or her?

His hand clenched, banged down on the desk. His mouth dried. Yeah, sure, Sasha having his kids? After the way he'd treated her?

'Knock, knock. Are you all right?' Roz appeared in his line of vision, a worried look on her face.

Forcing a smile, he leaned back in the chair. 'Absolutely.'

'I just wanted to say thanks for stepping in for Mike. He's been putting in some long hours lately and getting quite exhausted. Last night didn't help.' Roz parked her backside on the corner of the desk.

'You're welcome. I didn't feel very excited about painting this morning anyway.' He'd taken one look at the boring off-white colour and banged the lid back on the tin. That house needed vibrant colours to bring it alive again. It needed people. Laughter echoing in the rooms. Music playing in the background. Which was why he was selling it, remember?

'Where have you gone?' Roz knocked on the desktop.

'Sorry. I'm happy to help you and Mike out further if either of you need a break.'

Roz grinned like she'd got something she wanted. 'We'll take you up on that.' Her finger scratched at the desktop. 'Having you here won't be a problem for Sasha? I didn't realise until Mike said something about it this morning that you two had history.'

'No.' He hoped not. 'It's very old history. We met when I used to come over here for summer holidays but until last night I hadn't seen her since the year she left school and Golden Bay. My family never came back here after that summer either.' Too many memories of Dad for all of them to cope with. And, for him, memories of Sash.

Roz stood and smoothed down her skirt. 'Can I ask you something? Just in case she annoys you or does something irritating? Can you go easy on her? There are a lot of things going on in her life at the moment and she's very fragile.'

'Sure.' Sash fragile? She'd always been strong. He stared at Roz, hoping for an explanation, but the woman was heading for the door.

One of us doesn't know Sash very well. Was that Roz? Or was it him? Did this explain the need to hug and protect Sasha he'd felt last night? And again this morning when he'd knocked on her door and found her in a dishevelled state? It was a gut-level feeling that gripped him whenever she came close. A feeling he'd never had for her before.

Earlier, when he'd heard Sash ask Jessica about her coping skills, he'd wanted to rush in and yell, 'Yes, of course you'll do a fantastic job.' He'd wanted to hug her tight to keep those fears at bay. As if she'd listen to him. But she'd sounded so frightened. Alone, even, despite the midwife being there for her. He'd be the last person Sasha would want overhearing that short conversation, let alone offering comfort.

Anyway, what did he know about raising a child? Grady could hear the distain colouring her voice now. She'd really get stuck into him. And he'd had enough of that from her last night. Even if he had deserved it.

'Got a moment, Grady?' Sasha appeared in the doorway.

This office was busier than a bus station. 'Got a problem?' he asked.

Her green gaze cruised over him while her mouth lifted and dropped as though she hadn't made up her mind how to treat him.

'Go for friendly.' He smiled broadly, practising what he preached.

She blinked, squinted at him. Her shoulders rose and fell quickly. 'Is there any other way?' But her return smile was kind of sad.

'You wanted me?' Or a doctor?

'Can you take a look at Mrs Collins for me? She came in to have stitches removed from a gash in her left calf muscle. Apparently she had an accident while chopping wood last week. The wound is inflamed and oozing. She needs a new prescription for antibiotics.'

So Sasha wanted a doctor, not him. Get used to it. She was setting the tone for the rest of his time here.

Didn't mean he had to take any notice, did it?

The stars were beginning to show by the time Sasha turned into the orchard's drive and headed for the packing shed. She ached with exhaustion. It had been a long, hard day following a long, hard night. Her last patient, nearly an hour away out past Collingwood, had been in need of some TLC more than anything medical. She'd changed a dressing and drunk milky tea and eaten week-old lemon cake.

Ruth Cornwell lived in the falling-down house she'd been born in seventy-nine years ago, and no one would be getting her out of there unless it was in a box. Ruth's words, which Sasha had heard on numerous occasions, today being no exception. A tough old lady, she was now very lonely after falling out with most of her neighbours over the years. But suggest she move into a rest home? You'd better be able to run fast.

'Okay, Flipper, let's get those lemons loaded. Then we can take them to the carrier's yard before heading home for a hot shower and dinner.'

Dinner. Her shoulders slumped. She hadn't been to

the supermarket, and her cupboard was bare. A yawn dragged her mouth wide. If it weren't for Flipper she'd head home, eat the last yoghurt and fall into bed. But she shouldn't be doing that. Bad mummy practice.

Just inside the shed door she patted the wall, found the light switches and filled the space with light. And gaped. Where were all those cartons Mum had presumably packed over the weekend? They should be stacked by the bench for Sam Donovan to pick up. Mum had better not have taken them to the yard. She'd been warned time after time by Mike and her and Dad: do not lift those full boxes. 'Mum, I love you to bits, but you are so in trouble right now.'

The gravel on the driveway crunched and headlights swung across the yard. Mum's ute turned into the carport at the side of the shed.

'Right, Mum, we're about to have a talk.' Switching on the outside lights, Sasha stomped outside and followed the side of the shed to the carport. But even as her mouth opened she was hauling on the brakes to halt her words.

Grady was locking the ute's door. He had a laden grocery bag swinging from one hand. He'd also changed in to butt-hugging jeans and a thick, woollen outdoors shirt with a roll-collar jersey underneath. Drop-dead gorgeous. Except Sasha felt she might be the one to drop dead with the need unfurling deep inside her. Her swallow was audible in the quiet night.

'Hey, Sasha. I heard you were going to be late back so I dropped those cases off at the depot. Hope that's okay?'

As he approached, the need to lean into him and let him take over for an hour or two nearly floored her. Click, click, her back straightened with difficulty. 'Sure. Thank you.' Try again, Sasha. That was feeble. 'I mean it, Grady. I am grateful. I hadn't been looking forward to loading up and going back into town.'

'I'm not surprised. Whenever I've seen you today you've looked shattered. Not enough sleep last night, huh?'

'That and a big weekend.' Maybe that yoghurt would have to do tonight. Unless she raided Mum's pantry before going home.

'You still like pasta?' Grady seemed to be holding his breath as he waited for her answer.

'I love it. Especially spaghetti carbonara.' That yoghurt seemed very unappetising now.

His hand delved into the bag, brought out a package. 'With bacon?'

Her mouth watered as she nodded.

'And cream?'

'If you're teasing me, Grady O'Neil, you'd better start running for the hills.' What was he up to? They'd managed to keep their distance all morning at the medical centre, acting polite and friendly in an aloof kind of way.

'I'm scrounging a ride home. Again. I'll cook you dinner.'

She swallowed, blinked back the tears threatening to spill over. 'Your house is five hundred metres from here. Oh…' She lightly slapped her forehead. 'It's dark and cold. Of course. Hop in and I'll run you home before the bogeyman comes up from the beach.'

Grady's laugh filled the chilly night air and lifted her heavy heart. For the first time all day she didn't feel held down with fear and need and the sense that time was running out. She also didn't feel that she should be avoiding Grady. Why she felt any of those things she had no idea. It was as though something was lurking on the periphery of her mind, worrying at her like a dog with its bone. But right now, here in her parents' yard, in the dark of nightfall and the cold of midwinter, she felt warm and safe. Felt she could cope with everything again. Why? She had no idea and wouldn't even try to find out.

Nothing to do with Grady, then? She certainly hoped not. Because even if she fell head over heels in love with him, what were the chances they could make it work? She carried another man's baby.

Backing the four-wheel drive round to face down the drive, she asked her passenger, 'Are you really putting your house on the market?'

Grady stretched his legs as far as they'd go under the console—not far at all. 'You've avoided the dinner question.'

And he'd avoided the house question. 'I should be making you dinner as a thank-you for taking those cases to the yard. But I'm guessing sharing a pot of yoghurt and a banana wouldn't cut it for you.' She eased on down to the road.

'We didn't used to thank each other for every little thing we did for the other.'

'We knew where we stood with each other back then.' Why had she said that? Brought the elephant into the car? 'Forget I said that.'

'I will, on one condition. That you tell me whenever there's a stack of boxes to be loaded onto the ute for delivery. They weigh a lot for someone who's carrying a baby.' Grady's tone was still light and friendly but steel backed it.

'Dad's home tonight. He'll be doing the orchard jobs until his next trip.' Don't ask why Mum can't do it. I'm not ready to talk about that yet.

Thankfully he changed tack. Read her mind? Nah, it was a minefield in there and he looked relatively unscathed. 'Do you usually eat yoghurt every meal? I saw you scoffing some before you started work. I'd have thought you'd be into the fresh vegetables and salads, all the healthy stuff.'

'Anyone point out that it's winter and salad ingredients are hard to come by? When I do find them they're tasteless.'

'So carbonara it is.' So sure of himself. So—so friendly and ordinary. Ordinary in a 'we used to be lovers and now don't know what we are' sort of way.

'How can I turn down such an eloquent invitation?' Passing her cottage, she continued towards Pohara Beach and Grady's place, every metre of the way wondering if she'd just made a monumental blunder.

You're only going to eat a meal with the man. Not jump his bones.

Her vehicle jerked to the right. Grady reached over to grip the steering-wheel and straighten their direction. 'Sash?' There he went, one little word all full of heat, care and—sex.

Panic flared hard and fast. Her lungs worked overtime. 'I think I'll give the pasta a miss.' Coward. A total fraidy-cat.

'Your call.'

No pressure, then. Cool. He'd probably already decided he'd made a mistake by inviting her to share his meal. He had more sense than her at the moment. But she had babymones brain, remember? That was the best excuse for just about every darned mistake she made. Excuse? She needed an excuse to get out of spending an hour in Grady's house with him? Wouldn't it be better

that she went and showed how little his return affected
her? Show that the past was well and truly the past, that
she didn't care enough to get all in a twitter whenever
he was near?

Then Grady added, 'What does Flipper think about
yoghurt for dinner when she could be having carbonara?'

Big pressure. 'Low blow, O'Neil.' But the panic had
receded, replaced with soft warmth.

'Yep.'

Did he have to sound so smug? That alone should
have her kicking him out of the vehicle and heading for
home. She turned into his drive and stopped, looked
around at the familiar and yet different yard. The lid
snapped off the memory box. She shoved it back down
tight. 'Looks like whoever lived here last didn't know
much about lawnmowers.'

'Or hammering boards back on the fence. Or unblock-
ing drains. Or cleaning the oven.'

'Got your work cut out, then.' Curiosity rose above
the need to drop Grady and go. 'Is there a lot of damage
around the place?'

Grady pushed his door wide. 'Mostly superficial but
time-consuming. The family who rented it for ten years
only came for holidays. Guess they didn't want to waste
time doing any work around the place.' When he stood
up she could no longer see his head or half his chest.
Though those well-defined thighs were filling her vision
and tickling up her senses a treat, sending her stomach
into another riot—this time with desire. Then she heard
him ask very casually, 'Come inside and I'll show you
what I've got planned for the place.'

'As long as you remember my name is Sasha.'

CHAPTER FIVE

GRADY INTERNALISED HIS GRIN. Sash was rattled. That had to be good. If she didn't care two dots about him and them then she wouldn't give a rat's backside what he called her. But he'd hold back on overusing the Sash word, would endeavour to call her by her full name most of the time. Because first of all he needed to know her situation.

If she was head over heels in love with that baby's father then he would be out of the bay and on his way back to Auckland quicker than it took for the paint to dry on these walls. He might want her back in his arms but he'd never break up her relationship for his own needs. But if those often sad eyes were anything to go by, he doubted Sasha was in love. Unless it was unrequited love. His heart turned over for her. For him.

She'd followed him inside and now stood in the open-plan living/dining/kitchen space, looking around as if searching for something.

He went for casual. 'I'll put a pot of water on to boil for the spaghetti before anything else.'

She didn't comment, merely walked across to the long wooden table and ran her hand over the now badly worn finish. If he'd been staying he'd have sanded it back to the wood and revarnished it. Sasha's look was wistful, snagging him in places he didn't want to be snagged. He could see the memories in her eyes, and felt his throat clogging as images he'd refused to think about over the last few days came roaring to the fore. Dad was in most of them.

'He loved it here, didn't he?' She knew he'd get who she was talking about.

'His favourite place to be. For weeks before Christmas he'd be packing his gear in readiness for coming over the hill. Then he'd have to unpack because he'd need something. For Dad summer *was* Takaka. *Was* this house. *Was* the beach at the end of the lawn. His boat, the fishing, scalloping, barbecues.'

And I'm selling it.

I shouldn't have invited Sash in. I've mostly managed to avoid this since I arrived.

Yet two minutes inside and Sash went for the jugular without even trying. This house was full of wonderful memories of his family that even after all this time he struggled with looking through. Like photos in an album, those memories now flipped over before his eyes. Dad grinning as he held up a nine-kilo snapper. Dad smirking as he tipped his scallop haul out on the lawn. Dad cuddling his daughters in their wet swimsuits. Sash in her bright yellow bikini helping Dad shuck those scallops. Sash backing the big boat into the water.

'The water's boiling.' Sash leaned her butt against the table and crossed her ankles.

Concentrate. He blinked, swallowed, turned away from the understanding and sympathy in those heart-stopping eyes. Banged the pan on an element to cook the bacon; added the spaghetti to the water. Concentrated on cooking. Ignored the old grief threatening to engulf him.

'Are these the colours you've chosen for the repaint?' Sasha had moved away from the table and now waved some colour swatches in the air.

'I'm going for neutral: Spanish White and Whipped Cream. Should appeal to more punters than if I let my inner being out.' His lungs squeezed out the air they were holding. Sasha had become more beautiful than ever. Her pregnancy made her face glow even while exhaustion dragged her down. Her body was curvier than before, and he itched to hold her, cup her butt in his hands, feel her breasts pressed against his chest.

A soft chuckle brought him to his senses, made him force aside those fanciful pictures as she said, 'I can't imagine painting this room in your favourite rugby team's colours would appeal to many.'

Sasha was grinning at him. And that brought his libido up to speed. Stuck his tongue to the roof of his mouth. Set his nerve endings to tingling. Would it be rude to demand she leave now before he followed through on the need rushing through his body? Knowing he couldn't touch her didn't stop his body reacting in the only way it had ever known.

'Who is your favourite team at the moment, by the way?' she asked in a voice that sounded calm and un-affected. How could that be when he was burning up with need?

'Still the red and blacks. I've followed them from afar.' Another memory flipped over. The ceiling of this room filled with helium balloons, red and black for his team. His mates and their girlfriends hanging around, beers in hand, as the rugby game unfolded that one winter holiday he had ever had here. Their team had won and Dad had handed out more beers and laughed till he'd cried at the whopping score.

Chop, chop. Toss the bacon into the melted butter. So much had gone down during those shocking weeks after Dad had died. So much that he hadn't been able to deal with. Things he'd cruised through by pretending he was handling them well. Making the biggest blunder of his life.

Hiss. Boiling water spilled over the side of the pot. He snatched the lid up, let the bubbling die down. Get a grip, man. Any moment now Sasha was going to charge out of here and call for the paddy wagon to take him away as he was a danger to himself.

You should never have come back. Should've dealt with selling the house from afar.

'Like how? I couldn't do that to Dad. Or me.' Now he'd spoken aloud. Idiot.

A hand touched his arm, fingers pressed firmly. 'You haven't been back since, have you?'

He turned, and instantly regretted it as Sasha's hand fell away. 'Not once.' And up until you walked in here I was handling it.

Her head dipped in acknowledgement. 'Too hard.' Then she moved away, taking her warmth, her scent, across the room. 'Remember the good things, okay?'

'Sure,' he croaked. But that meant remembering the summer of Sasha Wilson. The summer of promise that had turned to dust. Because he'd done the right thing and stood up for his mother and sisters. Elected to support them and walk away from those heady plans of university with Sash.

'Maybe I should go.' She sounded like she was warring with that idea. Sadness from her eyes ripped him.

What was bothering her so deeply? Not Dad's death, surely? Most likely the consequences. He raised a smile for her because he suddenly did not want to watch her walk out his door. Not yet. 'I'm not eating all this on my own.' He didn't want the quiet of a house empty except for himself and those memories he couldn't face. 'Besides, I haven't told you my plans for tidying up the house over the next month.'

'Guess I'm staying.' Her hand did that maternal thing on her baby belly, rubbing tenderly, her eyes again alight with love and amazement.

His stomach curled in on itself as raw envy crawled up his throat. He wanted that baby to be his. So badly. It was a hunger he hadn't known he had. Until he'd felt that bump when he'd hauled Sasha into his arms for a friendly hug last night. That's when this crazy, mixed-up idea had begun, taking a firmer hold over the day. He wanted to be a dad to Sasha's child. Except the kid already had one. Somewhere.

Her scent warned him moments before her elbow nudged him out of the way. 'The bacon's beyond crisp.' She lifted the pan, set it on a board to take the heat. 'What's next?' Her eyebrows rose and her mouth lifted on one side.

'Add garlic while I grate Parmesan.'

'Now we're cooking.' She gave him a wink.

'Thanks.' She'd brought him out of his funk with a jab from her elbow and a wink. No one did that for him these days.

The savoury smell of crushed garlic cooking tickled his senses as he broke eggs into a bowl. Adding the cream, he whisked the mixture. And relaxed into the simple pleasure of preparing a meal to share with a—friend.

'This is so good,' Sasha murmured around a mouthful a short while later. 'Where did you learn to cook Italian?'

'As compared to charcoaled sausages on the barbie?' Grady scooped up the last mouthful of sauce from his bowl. 'When I was at med school I started watching cooking shows on TV whenever I needed a break from studying. Something that required no thought from me but was entertaining. After a few weeks I found I'd picked up some clues and began incorporating them in the basic meals I prepared for myself and my flatmates.'

'So you've become a foodie?' She grinned as surprise lightened the green in her eyes to emerald.

'A very amateurish one.' He tried not to stare at her. Hard to do when she looked so radiant after a day of appearing drawn and exhausted. Had he made her feel better? If he'd turned her day around with a simple meal then he was happy.

She told him, 'I've been to Italy twice for the skiing. Tina—she's my friend who got married at the weekend—and I worked in Dubai for two years. We're both ski nuts and Italy in winter was a dream come true, especially in the lake district.'

'Also closer to Dubai than New Zealand.'

'Definitely. Those long-haul flights are hideous. I don't know how Dad does it all the time.'

'He's doing the job he loves.' Grady pushed back his chair. 'Want a coffee?'

'Tea? Coffee at this end of the day tends to wind Flipper up and keep me awake.'

'No tea, sorry.' But it was now at the top of tomorrow's shopping list. 'The next best thing I've got is juice.'

She shook her head, swirling her hair around her face. 'Hot water's fine.' And when he winced, she added, 'Truly. I often drink that at night.'

Her wry smile crunched his heart. 'Who'd have thought? You drinking water at night and me cooking pasta. Have we grown up, or what?'

Sasha stretched her legs out under the table and arched her back, rubbing her lower back with her fingers. Baby protruded further than he'd seen so far. 'Did I mention I've quit skiing for now?' She grinned cheekily and sat up straight again. 'Can you imagine me tearing down the slopes, with Flipper leading the way? I'd end up face first in the snow. So not a good look.'

He should've laughed at the image but he couldn't. Sasha wouldn't have fallen on her face, baby or no baby under her ski suit. She'd always been nimble and surefooted, whether she was dancing, water-skiing, or climbing hills.

What had led him back to this place at the same time as Sasha had come home? She must've been home for visits often over the intervening years. But it sounded as though she'd returned for good this time. Had he somehow known he'd find her here? Was there a thread of emotion connecting them? 'How long have you been back in the bay?'

Her smile faded, and she straightened up. 'Nearly three months.'

Grady plugged the kettle in. Got out a mug, spooned in instant coffee and sugar. Filled another mug with boiling water. And once again his tongue got the better of him. 'That when you found out you were pregnant?'

'No. That's when I found out Mum had MS.'

* * *

Sasha winced as that teaspoon Grady had been gripping clanged in the bottom of the sink. He whipped around to look directly at her, impaling her with his unwavering look. For the second time in twenty-four hours shock stunned him; his face still and his eyes wide. 'Muscular sclerosis? Bloody hell.'

Sasha could understand his shock. It gripped her, too. She'd had no intention of telling him anything about Mum's illness. She hadn't got used to the idea yet. 'Mum and Dad need me here now.' Her breathing was shaky. 'Like your mum and sisters needed you.'

They stared at each other for what felt like an eternity. Then he moved, lifted her from the chair as though she weighed nothing, tucked her against his chest and dropped his chin on top of her head.

She wanted this. Had needed it since the day greaseball had told her where to go with their baby. *That* she'd managed to cope with. But the night Dad had phoned to tell her about Mum she'd believed she must've been a very, very bad person for so much to go wrong. Had she been too selfish in her pursuit of adventure? But her parents had always encouraged her and Jackson to follow their dreams. Should she have stayed in Takaka when she finished school and worked on the orchard? Done some of the hard, heavy work? Would that have saved Mum from getting this horrible disease?

Knowing her self-blame was ridiculous didn't mean she could drop it and feel free of everything. This year seemed to be about life catching up, pay-back for all the fun and antics she'd previously got involved in.

Above her head Grady asked, 'Is Virginia's health the reason Ian's giving up flying internationally?'

'He tells me it is.'

Grady leaned back, pushing his hips against Flipper's hideout as he did. 'You're not sure.'

She'd forgotten how in sync they'd been. How they'd read each other's minds as quickly as thoughts had popped in there. She slipped out of those wonderfully safe arms and sat back down. She might be spilling her guts but she'd do it standing—sitting—tall. 'I'm no doubt overreacting. But Dad is tired all the time and he's lost that joie de vivre that was his trademark.' What if Dad's ill, too?

She'd added to his woes. No father liked to have his daughter turning up on the doorstep pregnant by a man she refused to name or even acknowledge.

After placing the mugs on the table, Grady lifted a chair and spun it round to straddle it. With his arms folded across the top he dropped his chin on them and focused his caring eyes on her. 'Stands to reason he's not sleeping too well. He'll be worried sick about Virginia. I'm only surprised he didn't stop work immediately they found out.'

'Mum wouldn't have a bar of it. Said that she was still capable of running the orchard and looking out for herself. Told Dad if he gave up work it would be like giving in to the MS and undermining her determination to remain as independent as possible for as long as possible.'

'And that's why you're here?'

'Flipper is the perfect excuse.' Though hauling those cases of lemons was getting tougher by the week. Mainly because it worried her she might do some internal damage. She'd become incredibly cautious. 'I suspect Mum sees through me, but I'm giving her the opportunity to let go of things in her own time and fashion. Dad's pleased

I'm hanging around. It makes things easier on him to follow Mum's wishes.' Mum and Dad were sorting out a difficult situation by give and take on both sides. Like she and Grady should've done.

'Makes sense.' Grady still watched her with that deep intensity of his.

What did he see? Did her changed persona from wild-cat to tame mother-to-be make him glad he'd left her when he had? He'd always enjoyed the fact that she'd had no restraints when it had come to having fun. No way would she put the Cessna into a spin nowadays just for the sheer thrill of twirling round and round as the plane plummeted towards earth.

Grady broke through her reverie. 'Your parents have always been close, even though it seems Ian's spent half their married life flying round the world.'

'Mum reckons that's what made their relationship so special and strong. They haven't had time to learn to take each other for granted.' She picked at the edge of a fingernail. The lime-coloured polish that had matched her wedding outfit looked distinctly jaded. 'I remember them once sharing a single bed when we stayed at my aunt and uncle's. Mum's sister made some smart comment and Mum told her she'd only had half the marriage time Elsie had had and catch-up was always good.'

Grady grinned. 'How old were you when you heard that?'

She chuckled. 'Twelve. The yuk factor was high, believe me. Of course, I wasn't meant to overhear the conversation going on between the sisters.'

She'd learned more than had been good for her at the time. But now? Now she almost envied her parents.

Would she ever have the caring, loving, understanding relationship with a man that Mum had?

Her eyes seemed to take on a life of their own, lifting and fixing on Grady, studying him thoroughly for the first time since last night. Until now she'd been too busy pretending he wasn't there to really look for who he'd become.

That slightly long hair was as luxuriant as ever, and not a grey strand in sight. But there were lines on his face that hadn't been there at eighteen. Caused by his father's death? Or working to support his mother and sisters? Dumping her? No, not that. He'd known exactly what he'd been doing that day. His words had been clear, leaving no doubt about his intentions. Blink. Shift focus. Those lips still formed heart-melting smiles. Did they still tease with kisses? Kisses on that sensitive spot behind the ear? Between the breasts? Kisses that devoured her mouth?

'Sash?'

She shot upright, the chair toppling backwards to crash on the tiled floor behind her. What had she been thinking? The problem was she hadn't been thinking. No, Grady was the problem. He'd crept out of his box again. Why couldn't he stay put? Why did he want to upset everything? Throw her off beam? She had begun to get her life back on track. She didn't need this.

So why had she agreed to have a meal with him? Why put herself on the line by walking inside this house, where she'd known nothing but fun and love? Why, why, why?

'Time I went home,' she muttered, and searched around for her keys. Found them in her pocket. Snatched up her jacket and turned for the door.

'Sasha.' Grady caught her arm and turned her gently to face him.

Oh, that gentleness could wipe away a lot of grief—if she let it. It crept in under her skin, under her guard, made her feel again. Feel the love she missed, feel the emptiness waiting to be filled by someone special. Yeah, and set herself up to be left high and dry all over again. No way, sunshine.

She jerked her arm free. 'Thanks for dinner.' She ignored the dismay and hurt in those blue eyes watching her too closely. 'And good luck with all your plans for getting the house ready for the market.'

Not that they'd got around to talking about that. Too busy going over the painful stuff. The front door banged shut behind her, cutting off the light as she stomped down the two steps on her way to the car.

Light flooded the yard. Grady strode out to join her, opening and holding her door while she clambered in. She snapped the ignition to 'on' before looking up into that familiar yet changed face she'd been denying for so long. She locked gazes with Grady, and waited. For what, she had no idea.

For a long moment he didn't move then he leaned forward and she figured he was about to kiss her. Her muscles tensed in anticipation, her hormones did the happy-clappy. Her brain tossed a coin—was this good or bad? When his lips brushed hers she knew it was good. More than good. A girl could get lost in that soft kiss, and when he deepened it, she didn't have a clue about anything but the man kissing her. It was like honey on ice cream, sweet and cool. Delicious. Then his tongue sought hers and cool went to scorching in an instant. So Grady. So them.

Until Flipper got in on the act, delivering a heavy kick to her side. Sasha gasped, rubbed her side.

Grady reared back. He muttered something that sounded like an oath, still staring at her, swallowing hard more than once. Finally he seemed to calm down but kept his distance. 'Where is the baby's father?' He asked so calmly and quietly she wasn't sure she'd heard correctly. But when he added, 'Who is he?' she knew she had.

'He doesn't exist.'

'What?' Grady gaped at her.

'He who doesn't deserve to be acknowledged no longer exists as far as I'm concerned.' Except as greaseball in her head. She looked away. 'He wants no part of my baby's life.' Too much information.

Now he stepped closer, reaching for the ignition to turn it off. Then he peeled her fingers away from the steering-wheel and wrapped her hand in both his. 'The bastard.'

How could two words hold so much anger plus hurt for her, as well as concern and affection?

Lifting her head, she met his gaze. 'The bastard,' she repeated softly. 'He dumped me when the going got tough. Said it had been fun and he'd loved being with me but he didn't love me enough to stay around.'

Grady's hands squeezed tight around hers, loosened. His chest rose sharply. 'Just as I did.'

She said nothing. What was there to say?

'Is that what you think, Sash?'

Gulp. She tugged her hand free, leaned further away from the open door. 'Why wouldn't I?' Shut up, girl. Don't say another thing. Don't show your feelings to this man who stomped on them once already. Don't let him know how worthless he'd made you feel. He used to tell you how strong you were. He wasn't about to find out how untrue that had turned out to be.

'What if he's like me, Sasha?'

Her lips pressed tight, holding back words that had been stewing for years: words she needed to get past. Her hand shook as she reached again for the ignition.

'What if he's lying? What if he does want you and comes back one day?'

Her hand banged down on her knee. Her chin shot out and she fixed him with a glare. Anger, pain, despair all combined to roll up her throat and spill out between them. 'He's worse. He's dumped his baby daughter. He doesn't want to be a part of her life.' She reached out to grab the front of his shirt and shake him. 'That makes me the worst mother possible because my girl won't ever know her father. I didn't plan on getting pregnant but I still thought I was with a man who cared for me, who would care for his child.' She wouldn't have had a relationship with him otherwise. 'I made a bad choice.'

She refused to think about the implications of Grady's revelation. That he might want to come back for her. It wasn't possible. And even if he did it wasn't going to happen. She was done with risking her heart.

Grady placed his hands on her shoulders. 'We all make mistakes, Sasha. But please stop thinking your baby's mother is bad. You are so special. She'll never want for love or kindness. You have those in bucketloads. You love her so much already it's amazing to see. When you touch your tummy your eyes go all misty with it.' His Adam's apple bobbed. 'She's a very lucky little girl.'

Talk about knocking her for six. Never would she have imagined Grady saying something so heart-warming, so caring. 'Thank you' was the best she could manage around the tears clogging her throat. She reached up to place her hand on his cheek. 'I needed to hear that.'

His eyes locked with hers. So much emotion streamed out at her. Too many emotions to read. 'If you did then I'm glad I told you.'

Her stomach hurt from clenching. Her head throbbed from holding in the tears. Her heart ached—because in a different world, at a different time, Grady would've been the perfect man for her.

She turned away. 'I'd better go home and get some shut-eye. I seem to need more of that these days.'

As he began closing her door he whispered, 'Good-night, Sasha. Sleep tight.'

CHAPTER SIX

'SLEEP TIGHT. LIKE HOW?' Sasha asked into the dark for the umpteenth time as she slapped her pillow into shape. Dropping her head back down, the air whooshed out of her lungs. 'Any sleep at all would be good.'

Flipper gave her a wee nudge.

'You need to sleep, too, sweetheart. Swimming's over for the day.' Sasha ran her hands over her stomach, revelling in the tightness of her skin and the life under her palms. This pregnancy might've been unplanned but it had turned out to be the most exciting and life-changing thing to happen.

Don't forget the most worrying. Not that being pregnant was troubling, but what came afterwards was. Being a full-time mother, making all the decisions regarding her daughter and praying she got them right. There was no one to fall back on when she needed reassurance. Once she'd have had her parents but really they now had too much to deal with to need their daughter demanding help with a problem she'd caused. No, she was on her own for this ride.

Nothing in her life had undermined her confidence as pregnancy had. The stack of books on the bedside table about caring for a baby underscored that. The contents list on her internet screen highlighted that. She soaked up all the available information, ignored her colleagues' comments that nurses worried too much, and read some more.

'I've totally confused myself. For every expert who says do one thing there are as many saying the opposite.'

'You'll be fine,' Jess kept telling her. 'The moment I place your baby in your arms it will all come together. Believe me. I felt the same before Nicholas was born.'

Which did nothing to bolster her confidence. It wasn't as though she could go bang on the doors of the experts who got it wrong and give them a telling-off. She didn't know who was right or who was wrong.

She sighed. 'Grady's shown up and all these unwanted needs are ramping up inside me.' Another sigh, softer this time. 'He kissed me goodnight.' Her finger traced her lips. Never in all the intervening years had it occurred to her she'd receive another Grady kiss. She should've rammed the car in reverse and shot out of his yard faster than a 747 on take-off. But she hadn't. Because? That kiss had sneaked up on her. It had been wonderful. Exciting, caring, hot. Grady. *Did he regret leaving me?*

He'd said something about wanting to come back. To her. That didn't make sense when he was planning to sell the house. Had he been testing the waters? Or had he been consumed with the need to taste her, to find he'd done the right thing when he'd left her?

Her fists banged down on the mattress. 'Go away, Grady. Take your kiss with you. Climb back in your box and leave me alone. Please.'

'Please,' she whispered again. Deep breaths. In, out.

In, out. Relax. Arms first. Fingers uncurled, hands loose, lower arms. Upper arms. Toes.

The urge to roll on her side and face the empty half of her big bed was relentless. Refusing to give in, she stared at the ceiling, her hands clenched at her sides, and breathed deeply. Uncurled her fingers, shook her hands loose.

Imagined Grady in that space next to her. His long legs reaching to the bottom of the bed. His wide chest covering more than his share of the mattress. His head sunk into the pillow beside her. If she rolled over she could move into the warmth of those strong arms he'd placed around her earlier. His hands could splay across her back, holding her safe. That beautiful mouth on her skin. Tonguing her into a frenzy.

She rolled sideways, her hand reaching across the gap to touch—cold, harsh reality. That side of the bed was empty. Chilly. No warm, male body. No Grady.

Grady was not real to her any more. Really? He was hardly an overactive figment of her imagination. Those hands that had held her shoulders earlier had been warm and strong and real. That mouth that had smiled and grinned and grimaced and kissed her had been real.

Her eyes filled, the tears burst over her eyelids, flooded her face, her pillow, her dreams. 'Real or not, I can't give you my heart again, Grady.'

Grady finally went back into his box.

Every muscle in Sasha's body complained of fatigue, as it had all day long. If she didn't get some decent, deep sleep tonight she'd be toast tomorrow. If this was what a couple of less-than-perfect nights did to her then once

Flipper arrived she'd be hopeless. Until now she'd never had trouble sleeping.

'That's because I always exhausted myself physically throughout the day. Can't do that at the moment. And if I turn up at work overtired too often, Mike and Rory are going start asking questions about my ability to do the job.' Fear bounced down her spine. This job was very important. Without it she'd have to leave the bay and head to Nelson. Away from her mother at a time she needed to be here. That made her feel cold just thinking about it. 'So I have to sleep a full eight hours tonight. No argument.'

Rubbing her aching back, she reached for her medical bag and headed up the mud- and rock-strewn driveway to Campbell McRae's bungalow. Behind the outbuildings the high peaks of the Wakamarama Range sent chilly shadows over the surrounding paddocks, keeping the ground damp and cold. Hopefully, at this time of the year trampers weren't walking the Heaphy Track. Too easy to slip over on the muddy track and suffer serious injuries.

The bungalow's front door swung open as she stepped carefully onto the uneven veranda. Bracing for her next call, she smiled. 'Hi, Sadie.'

'Hello, Sasha. Campbell's in a right old snot today.' The middle-aged, squat woman scowled. 'He thinks we should all be at his beck and call.'

Sasha wiped her shoes on the not-so-clean doormat. 'What's bothering him?'

'Just about everything you care to think of.' Sadie had the fortitude of a saint. Her brother's situation made him very bad-tempered, which was completely understandable, but not nice.

'Have you been changing the dressings like I showed

you?' Campbell's leg had been amputated above the knee four weeks ago due to complications with his diabetes.

'When he lets me near him.' Sadie slammed the door shut. 'He's in the lounge.'

Sasha headed down the narrow, dark hallway, trying hard not to trip over any of the myriad objects lying on the floor. 'Afternoon, Campbell.' She'd learned right from her first visit not to say good afternoon as Campbell would instantly dispute the good component.

'You're late. I've been waiting for ages.' The forty-four-year-old grizzled from where he sat by the grubby window, his crutches lying nearby. 'You parked in the wrong place. I've told you about that before. One day that goat's going to run its horns down the side of that fancy wagon of yours and then you'll come complaining to me.'

She'd forgotten about the goat. Blame her jaded brain on a certain man back in Takaka. He'd been following her around in her head all day. 'How's that leg been? Are you doing those lifting exercises I showed you?'

'A fat lot of good they do. It's not like I'm going to be out running around after the stock, is it?'

In other words, no. Sasha explained what she'd explained often. 'You need to keep those thigh muscles moving. You want them strong for when you're fitted with your prosthetic leg.'

Campbell had the grace to look a tiny bit sorry. 'I know you're right, but I don't see the point. Wearing a tin leg won't make it any easier to get around the farm. I can drive the tractor but how do I get on it in the first place? Huh?'

She recognised the self-pity for what it was, and didn't blame him. Who would be happy in his situation? A lot of self-doubt as well as fear went on in an amputee's mind until they accepted their new way of life. Leaning down to remove the dressing from his stump, she asked, 'Have you thought about buying a four-wheeled farm bike? More manoeuvrable and lower to the ground than a tractor.'

'Do you know how much those things cost? I'm no millionaire.'

'You might be able to find a second-hand one. Go on line and see what's around.' Did he have a computer?

'Go on line? That's the modern answer to everything.'

'Yes, it is, and it's not going to change any time soon.' Sasha smiled at him, refusing to let his mood affect her. Carefully touching the wound with glove-covered fingers, she was pleased to see last week's redness and puffiness had gone. 'This is healing nicely. That infection's improved.'

Grunt. 'Jessica stood over me until I swallowed those bullets she calls pills. She's bossier than you.'

Good for you, Jess. Her friend had covered her rounds while she'd been in Christchurch. Sasha cleaned the stump and placed a new dressing over it. 'Okay, Campbell, show me those exercises. I want to see you do them twice before I go.'

Campbell looked away. 'I'm too sore.'

Sasha crossed to a chair, removed the magazines and knitting to sit down. 'I'm not going anywhere.'

Her patient glared at her. 'Anyone ever tell you you're stubborn?'

'All my patients.' She continued smiling, but she was worried. Campbell appeared more belligerent than usual. 'Is something other than your leg bothering you, Campbell?'

His mouth tightened as he stared out the window.

'I've lived here since I was a nipper. Don't know any other way of life.'

'It's the same for Sadie.'

'Yeah, but she can leave any time she likes. Nothing to keep her here.'

A man's man now reduced to hobbling around on crutches. Eventually he'd be able to walk again but he'd never be chasing up the hills and through the valleys with his working dogs the way he used to.

'I'd say Sadie has the same reasons for staying as you. Family, history, the comfort of knowing this place and the land.' Those things had brought *her* back home when the going had got tough. Was she saying the right things? Should she shut up and go back to the medical centre, get Mike to arrange an appointment for Campbell with a counsellor that he'd never keep?

'You reckon?' His belligerence backed off a little. Then he shifted his butt and, gripping the armrest, lifted his thigh off the chair. Put it down. Lifted it again. His face contorted with the effort. 'Weak as a kitten,' he said, self-disgust clear in his voice.

Sasha stood up and crossed over to him. 'What's that wrapper you've stuffed under your backside?'

Campbell's thigh dropped to the chair and stayed there. 'Chocolate.'

'I'll check your glucose level before I go.' She wanted to shake him, tell him he was putting his life in jeopardy, but he knew that better than her. He was already dealing with the consequences of not watching his diet carefully, of having allowed his diabetes go uncontrolled because he'd refused to accept it existed.

Shock rippled down her spine. Was that what she was doing with Grady? Not accepting that they were different now? That they had matured and learned a lot about living? She certainly hadn't forgiven him. Was she meant to? Might help if she did. Might wipe out some of the hurt and anger that had resurfaced in the last two days. Might stop the need for him that crawled through her body, warmed her blood and started an ache in her sex whenever he was near.

'It's twelve point one.'

'What?'

'My glucose,' Campbell grumbled.

'Let's double-check that.' She wouldn't put it past Campbell to have grabbed any figure out of the air.

Two house calls and one hundred and fifty kilometres later Sasha sped into the parking area behind the medical centre and leapt out of her vehicle.

'Please, Flipper, please, please, kick me. Hard as you like. Bruise my ribs. I don't care. I need to know you're okay.' Please.

She skidded on the mat at the back door, righted herself and raced down the hall towards the nurses' room. 'Jess, where are you?' She spilled into the room and ran slap bang into Grady.

Strong hands gripped her shoulders, held her upright. 'Hey, slow down. What's up?'

'Where's Jess?' She wriggled out of his hold and peered behind him, looking for her midwife. 'Jess, I can't feel Flipper moving. She hasn't kicked for hours. Is she all right? Tell me I'm being silly, that she's fine. Jess?'

'Anything out of the ordinary happen today?' Jessica stood up from the desk and came straight to her, reached for her hand at the same moment Grady caught her shoulders again, this time from behind.

'I—I picked up J-Josh T-Templeton for a cuddle and my back t-tweaked.' Why had she bent down to lift the overweight toddler? *Because he's so cute and he was holding his arms up, begging for a hug.* 'Have I hurt my b-baby?' She'd never lift another child, another thing, until after her baby girl was born. She'd sit in a chair and read a book twenty-four seven. Promise. *Just be okay, baby.*

Jess squeezed her hand. 'Deep breaths, Sasha. How long exactly since you last felt her move?'

'I don't want to breathe. I want to feel my baby moving.'

'Sasha, how long?' Grady echoed Jess's question. Those strong fingers on her shoulders began making soothing circular movements.

She didn't want to be soothed. She wanted Flipper kicking as though her life depended on it. She'd take all the pounding she could get to know her baby was safe, and only taking a longer than usual rest. 'Jess, Grady, do something.'

Her knees buckled under her. Grady caught her, held her tight, backed her against his chest. She tried to soak up his strength but it wasn't enough. It didn't answer the overriding question. Was her baby all right? Was she alive?

'Easy, Sasha. I'll examine you immediately but there's probably nothing to worry about.' His tone was soothing but that didn't help either.

Grady was going to examine her? Not in a million years. That would be too weird.

This isn't about you. Or Grady. Your baby's life is all that matters. Who examines you is irrelevant as long as they know what they're doing.

Jessica glared at Grady. 'You're overriding my position?'

Sasha pulled out of Grady's arms, her hands holding her belly. Waiting for a movement, imagining one and knowing she was wrong. Wanting didn't mean getting. She looked from Jess to Grady.

'We'll examine Sasha.'

Something in his eyes must've made Jess feel okay with that because she backed off immediately and gave Sasha a loving smile. 'Let me help you up on the bed.'

But before she could dredge up any kind of answer Grady had taken her arm to lead her across the room. She wanted to relax in against Grady's body and feel safe. But she couldn't. Not when Flipper needed all her focus. Flipper. 'Oh, no.' A chill sliced through her, lifted bumps on her skin. 'Last night I told Flipper to stop swimming and go to sleep. This is my fault,' she wailed. Where had that primal sound come from? Had she made it? Her bottom lip trembled so badly she had to bite down hard.

'No, Sasha, this is not your fault. Babies do this. Chances are your little girl is absolutely fine.' He spoke evenly, quietly. Professionally. He was being a doctor, no more, no less.

That calmed her somewhat, helped her take that breath Jess wanted, got her brain working so she could answer the question she hadn't got to yet. 'I'm not sure of the last time I felt her move. I think I might've while I was with Campbell McRae.' Her lip trembled again. 'But I can't be a hundred per cent sure.'

'Was that your last call?' Grady's hand under her elbow gave her balance as she climbed onto the bed, feeling more than ever like a heavily pregnant hippopotamus.

'I did two more, and then had to drive back from Paton's Rock,' she answered.

'So a couple of hours all up.' Jess stood on the other side of the bed. 'The usual thing to do now is make you lie down for one or two hours and relax—'

'Relax?' she shrieked. 'When I haven't felt anything from my baby all that time? I don't think so.'

Jess's calm smile didn't help a bit. 'Let me finish. You've been racing around all day, visiting patients, right?'

Sasha pursed her lips and glared at her friend. 'So?'

'So when you're busy you won't always notice baby's movements as much as when you're taking it easy. Lie back, Sasha, place your hands on your tummy and wait quietly.'

'Since when have I ever done quietly?' she grumbled, but lay back on the pillows.

'Since you left that loser and came home,' Jessica told her.

My own fault for asking. Jess had never hidden the truth, at least not about greaseball whom she'd never met but had an opinion about anyway. 'Thanks, pal.'

'You're welcome.' Jess gave her a big smile. 'Now, relax, will you?'

Beside her Grady lifted her wrist, pressed his fingers onto her radial artery. She watched his lips moving as he counted her pulse. His eyes had become inscrutable. Because of that loser comment? This was probably as strange a situation for Grady as it was for her. But if she could handle it then so could he. Only the baby mattered. Not his bruised ego or hers. Despite last night's conversation about the past they were trying to be friends, and this was a good way to start. Don't think about the kiss.

'Pulse is normal.' He laid her wrist down as though it was made of the finest crystal.

'Why did you even take it? I wouldn't have thought it necessary.'

'Gives me something to do.' He gave a deprecating smile. 'Jessica's got everything covered.'

'What about listening in? Flipper might have something to say.'

'Why not? Can't do any harm.' Friendliness had taken over his gaze.

But when Sasha tugged her top up, exposing her rounded belly for all to see, it was Grady's bobbing Adam's apple that caught her attention. So he was having massive trouble with the situation. She shouldn't have suggested he do this bit. Should've asked Jess.

She turned in entreaty to Jess. Her friend nodded once in understanding and shoved the earpieces in her ears before placing the cold bell on her abdomen.

Sasha crossed her fingers and held her breath, and bit down on that quivering lip again. Please, please, please, please…

She watched Jess closely, looking for any change in her eyes or mouth, her expression. She knew Jess well, had learned to read her over the months as their friendship had deepened. But she saw nothing. Panic roared up her throat. She bit down hard to block off a cry. Her hands turned into fists and she thumped the bed at her sides.

'Shh.' Grady's hand covered one of hers. 'You're making it hard for Jessica to hear anything.'

She shifted her stare from Jess to Grady, locked eyes with him. Saw nothing but concern and caring, not fear and worry. *Masking the Truth from Your Patient 101?*

'I hear a heartbeat.' Jess gave her a tense smile. 'Grady?' She handed him the stethoscope and picked up Sasha's other hand. 'That's good, Sasha. The relaxing will help—if you ever get around to following my instructions.'

Grady still held her gaze, having reached blindly for the stethoscope, and now she saw a crack in his demeanour. Relief? Worry? Love? No, couldn't be that. Had to be the anxiety one friend naturally felt for another in this predicament. She had Jess and her parents with her on this journey but she also knew whatever Grady was feeling she had him with her too, at least until Flipper was born. Some of the chill racking her loosened.

He asked, 'Do you mind if I listen, Sasha?'

'Go for it. What does it mean if you can hear the heartbeat but she's not moving?' All her nursing training had gone out the door. She was like any other mother, totally freaked out and needing answers that she knew they probably couldn't give.

Grady placed the bell on her abdomen. She stared at him now, watching, waiting for any reaction. He was as good as Jess. Nothing showed.

Okay, guys, you're my friends. Help me out here. What's happening with my baby girl?

Sweat popped on her brow, her palms, thighs, between her toes. She wouldn't think of those questions that had no answers. She wouldn't. She wouldn't. 'Grady? Talk to me.'

At least his fingers weren't shaking as he handed the stethoscope to Jess. 'I don't want you panicking…' His eyebrows rose and his mouth curved upward ever so slightly. 'Okay, no more than you already are. Yes, there's a heartbeat and I'm sure everything is all right. The suggestion of relaxing and waiting is fine if you're living close to a hospital. But since you're two hours away from the nearest one I think as a precaution a cardiotocograph might be appropriate. It's normal in these situations, Sash. Isn't it, Jessica?'

'Absolutely.' Jess looked at her all funny like. As though she was about to cry. 'I'm going to phone the hospital in Nelson right now.'

Sasha sat up, gripping Jess's hand so hard she probably cracked some bones. 'What aren't you telling me? Why are you trying not to cry? What's wrong with my baby?'

Jess gasped, but didn't pull her hand free. Probably couldn't because of her vice-like grip. 'I think everything's A-okay in there. But I do want you checked out so we can be absolutely sure.' A tear tracked down her cheek. 'Sasha, you're my bestest friend and you're pregnant. More than you can believe, I want this going right for you. You deserve it. You're so brave and strong and big-hearted. The man who gave you this gift already dealt you one bad card. You don't deserve any more.'

Sasha couldn't talk for the tears clogging her throat. Instead, she broke a few more bones in Jess's hand.

On her other side Grady cleared his throat. 'We'll head off very shortly. Jessica can text us about the appointment when she's spoken to the hospital. You also need to tell Ian and Virginia we won't be there for dinner. And why.'

'Mum and Dad.' Glad someone was thinking straight. 'They'll be beside themselves if I tell them what's happening.'

Grady parked his backside on the edge of the bed. 'Let me talk to them. I can reassure them and promise to phone the moment you've been checked over. But you can't avoid telling them. They should know.'

'It will stress them out.' They should hear it from her, not Grady. Especially not from Grady. But she was in a hurry. She had to get to Nelson a.s.a.p. She had to know what was going on in her tummy. Had to know her baby girl really was fine. She nodded, totally at a loss for words.

Jess was already at her desk punching in numbers she seemed to know off by heart. That had to be a good sign, didn't it? This happened so often it was routine. She hadn't heard of an excess of distressed babies being born in Golden Bay.

Then another urgent need caught her. 'I'll be a minute. Then we're out of here.'

When Grady lifted one eyebrow she flushed pink. 'Bathroom.'

His grin was as unexpected as it was fun. 'Babies and bladders, eh? A tricky combination, I'm told.'

A whisper of something rippled through her that had nothing to do with the fear gripping her so tight her muscles felt on the verge of tearing.

I could fall in love with this man all over again.

But right now she didn't have the time or energy. All that was for her baby.

CHAPTER SEVEN

ONCE THEY REACHED the far side of Takaka Hill Grady drove quickly. He still kept an alert eye on the road. The icy conditions of two nights ago had improved to the point that there was little to worry about, but there was no escaping the fact that midwinter reigned and the temperature hovered not much above zero. But he desperately wanted to be at Nelson Hospital and hear someone telling Sasha her baby was fine.

Sasha was too quiet. For her own good. For his heart rate. From what he'd heard through that stethoscope he was satisfied the baby would be all right. It's what he'd have told any patient in the same situation if they'd presented at his clinic, and felt comfortable about it. But this was Sash. So different. So much a part of him. Sash.

He knew she was hurting. The fear lunged out of those green orbs to lance his heart every time she looked at him, which was less and less the further they got from the medical centre. There were dents below her bottom lip from those teeth. She'd broken through the skin in one spot.

Worse, for him anyway, as there was nothing he could do to make her feel any better than what he was already doing. Never had he felt so helpless. In this situation being a doctor hadn't helped one iota. Remaining neutral was impossible.

At least she hadn't argued when he'd said he was driving her across. When he'd spoken to Ian the man had sounded relieved he was going with Sasha. Good to know her father wasn't averse to him being on the scene. There'd been a shade of panic and fear in Ian's voice. He'd hated not being able to totally dispel that. Nothing but the cardiotocograph results would. Favourable results.

Reaching over, he lifted one of Sasha's cold hands in his and rubbed his thumb back and forth over across it. Shivers kept her hand in constant motion. 'Have you thought of real names for your baby yet?'

Slowly she turned to face him. The bewitching green shade of her eyes had dulled and that hit him hard. His stomach sucked in on itself. Pain knotted in the base of his gut. He should be able to allay her fears, take the hurt for her, but he couldn't. Firstly, nothing on earth could make a mother feel unfazed in this situation. And then, well, this baby had nothing to do with him, no matter how much he wanted it to. Like him last night, Jessica had called the father a bastard. No matter what the circumstances, the man had had no right to desert Sasha and their baby so completely.

Just as well I don't know who he is.

'Why?' Sasha whispered.

Why what? What had he asked? Names. 'Just thinking that Flipper could possibly stick even after she's born if you keep calling her that.'

'You weren't thinking Flipper would look wrong on

the headstone if—if…?' Tears diluted her words, her tone, making her sound completely lost. Which she was.

Risking Sash's wrath, he pulled over to the side of the road and turned to pull her into his arms. His hands spread across her back to rub as gently as he could. 'Sash, sweetheart, I promise I was not thinking that at all.' I was trying to divert your thoughts for a very brief moment, only I appear to have made them worse. 'Flipper's going to be fine.' He held off promising. Not only was that going too far without back-up knowledge, it tempted the devil.

'Melanie. That's what I'm calling her.'

'Your grandmother's name?'

'Yes.'

'I like it. Melanie Wilson.' Melanie O'Neil. Worked for him.

She rubbed her face back and forth across the front of his jacket, sniffing and crying. It wrenched his heart. Sash didn't do crying. Okay, she didn't use to. Pending motherhood had changed her. In lots of ways. His arms tightened further around her in the useless hope he could absorb some of her pain and fear. Never had he felt so utterly useless. So unable to do something positive for someone he loved.

'Can we go now?'

At least, that's what he thought her muffled words were. 'Sure.' Afraid of her reaction and yet needing to do it, he dropped a light kiss on the top of her head before straightening up. Then he concentrated on getting his precious cargo to Nelson.

There was so much more he wanted to give her in the future, but that was a slow trip, remember? He couldn't rush her, and certainly not at this moment.

* * *

Sasha gripped Grady's hand as they walked heavily towards the clinic the night-time receptionist directed them to. She'd been doing a lot of handholding since she'd barged back into work as fear overwhelmed her, beat her down. What had happened to her? She used to stand tall, hide all her emotions behind a fixed smile and a smart-assed comment.

Since the advent of Flipper she was an emotional cot case, and totally unable to hide it. 'Will you come in with me?' Talk about asking too much of him, but at this moment, with her heart pounding so hard her ears hurt, she'd have asked the first person she came across if she hadn't got Grady with her.

'Try and keep me away.'

'Good answer.' She tried to smile at him, she really did, but all she managed was a lopsided mouth and an eyeful of tears.

'Hey, hang in there, Sash. Won't be long now before we know what Flipper's up to.'

For the first time she was happy to hear him call her Sash. Now it didn't sound so much sexy as loving. And caring. And right. 'That's what frightens me. There's a huge what-if clanging around my skull that I'm refusing to answer.' Her baby girl had to be all right. Had to be. Was all this squeezing in her gut doing the baby any good? No matter how hard she tried, she couldn't stop the waves of panic gripping and tensing every muscle in her body.

'Here we are.' Grady marched them up to the desk. 'Sasha Wilson for a CTG.'

The guy sitting behind the counter stood up immediately. 'Hi, Sasha, I'm Glen. I've been waiting for you. How was your trip over the hill?'

She didn't have a clue. Apart from that moment when Grady had stopped to hug her she'd been totally unaware of anything apart from her baby. But the guy was trying to be friendly and put her at ease. 'Great.'

'If you go through that door over on the left you'll find a gown to slip into. Leave only your underwear on. There's another door leading out of the cubicle into our room. I'll meet you there.'

She nodded. 'Thank you. Um, can Grady come with me?'

'Of course. Fathers are always welcome.'

'Father?' If only. But it wasn't surprising Glen had made that mistake. Grady was stepping up like an anxious father. She'd have to think about what that meant later. When, if, life ever got back to normal.

Glen turned a deep red and spluttered, 'And friends. It's best you have someone with you.'

In case you find something very wrong. Sasha's bottom lip stung sharply as her teeth dug in again. Running, she reached the door leading into the cubicle and slammed it shut behind her.

'Please, baby girl, please, make your heart go bang, bang, bang for the man.'

Her trousers hit the floor, followed by her jacket, blouse and thermal top. Goose-bumps covered her as the cold air touched her warm skin. The gown she wrapped around herself was thin and inadequate for winter temperatures. *Who cares?*

'Please, Melanie, be all right. We've got so much ahead of us. There're many things I want to show you, teach you, give you.'

Ahh. She stuffed a fist in her mouth to stifle the scream pouring over her tongue. Melanie. Since when had she used the baby's proper name? Since she'd become fearful for her safety. Did this mean—? No. No. No. It must not.

'Sash?' The door opened a crack and Grady asked, 'Are you ready?'

Sniff. *That depends. I'll never be ready if the news is bad.* Dropping her fist to her side, she slipped through the doorway and headed to where Glen waited.

Of course Grady picked up her hand and gave her a squeeze. 'Let's do it, shall we?'

'First we'll check the foetal heart rate.' Glen explained everything.

Sasha's gaze was glued to Glen, watching for every nuance in his expression. Finally she got a thumbs-up. 'Here, look at this. It's all good. Baby's fine.' He tore off a printout from the machine reading the baby's heart rate and handed it to her. Grady's head was touching hers as they stared at the lines in front of them.

Splish, splash. Drops of moisture hit the back of her hands. Her shoulders dropped forward as she curled over her precious baby. 'Oh, Flipper, you're okay, baby. Thank goodness. I don't know what I'd have done if you hadn't been.'

Grady wrapped those strong, safe arms around her and his chin bumped the top of her head. Above her she heard a sniff. 'Grady?' She pulled back just enough to see his face and the tears tracking down his cheeks.

'I'm so glad for you, Sasha.'

Cupping his cheek with one hand, she whispered, 'Thank you. For everything. I needed you here with me.'

Some time later, though probably only a couple of

minutes, Glen cleared his throat and said, 'I'd like to take you for an ultrasound so we can make sure that the placenta is functioning properly and check the transfer of blood and oxygen through the cord to baby.'

'So we're not in the clear yet.' Her smile faded.

'Everything's fine. It's just precautionary. Since you're here we might as well make the most of your trip.' Glen handed her another copy of the printout. 'For your baby album.'

Though her fingers shook as she took it, she felt the awful weight of fear finally lift. *For her baby album.* How normal did that sound?

Grady wound the car slowly and carefully around the hairpin bends on Takaka Hill, determined not to wake Sasha until he reached her cottage. She had exited that hospital quietly, happily and utterly exhausted.

The news had been all good. Sasha had phoned Jessica and then her parents. Everyone would sleep well tonight, though none as well as the woman beside him.

They'd eaten fish and chips parked outside the takeaway shop in Nelson. Make that he'd devoured more than his share while Sasha had pecked at a piece of crispy batter-covered blue cod and a couple of chips. Then she'd fallen sound asleep, curled into the corner made by her seat and the front door.

After clicking her seat belt in place and tossing into the rubbish bin the paper that had wrapped their meal, he'd headed for home. Home. Something tight and warm settled under his ribs. He'd been searching for a place to call that ever since he'd left Sasha.

Returning to Nelson from Golden Bay that day eleven years ago to go and see the transport company's boss and make arrangements for taking over Dad's contract had been hard. With every kilometre he'd driven he'd felt his heart being torn further from his chest, pulled by the girl he'd left behind, yanked by his mother's needs in Nelson.

He'd never regretted changing his plans of going to university in order to support Mum and the girls. It's what any man worthy of being called that would do—step up for his family. The price had been high, though. Sash. He might've grown up in Nelson but it hadn't felt like home since that day.

He'd known only despair. A week earlier his father had gone for ever. That day Sasha had gone, forced out of his life by him. Gone. For ever, if that heart-tearing, gut-slicing look in her eyes as the truth had dropped home in her mind had been anything to go by.

In reality, Golden Bay had never been home for him either, just the place he'd gone with his family for the most amazing, carefree summer holidays—and Sash.

Now, from the moment he'd set eyes on her at the accident scene, that word had been creeping into his vocabulary on a regular basis. Already he'd changed his mind about what colour to paint the inside of his house from those bland, neutral shades. Earlier in the day he'd phoned through an order for paint a shade of terracotta that made him feel happy and warm. He'd also called on the local plumber for bathroom brochures, to see what they had on offer.

You're setting yourself up for the biggest fall. Just because it's starting to feel like home in Golden Bay it doesn't mean Sash will want a bar of you in any other way than as friends.

He also didn't have a job to keep food in the pantry and petrol in the tank.

The shuffle of Sasha's jacket had his eyes flicking sideways. Her hand circled her belly. In the almost-dark of the car's interior he couldn't see if she had woken.

'Sash?' he whispered, as he focused back on the road.

Nothing. So even in sleep she was conscious of her baby. He liked that.

Finally, nearly two hours after they'd set out from Nelson he turned into Sasha's drive and cut the motor. Now what? Sasha was sleeping the sleep of emotional exhaustion. He so did not want to wake her. But he couldn't go scrabbling around in that massive bag of hers for keys to the house. He couldn't take her to his place with only one bed.

Now, there's a thought. Down, boy. Hard not to react to Sash when she dominated his mind all the time, tormented his body. Go find a way into the cottage and put those thoughts of hot sex on the back burner.

The house key sat under the potted lemon tree on the top step. 'Nice one, Sash.'

With the door open and lights on, Grady returned to Sasha. Opening the door carefully so as not to dump her on the drive, he scooped her into his arms and headed inside, pushing the door shut behind them with his butt.

Now that the panic of hours earlier had gone he allowed himself to breathe in the sweet scent of Sash. Honeysuckle. Reminding him of summer days and nights. Anything to do with Sash reminded him of hot summer days and hotter nights. Tightened his gut with longing. Sent waves of heat through his body, all aiming for his sex. Her warm body tucked against his chest did nothing to halt these waves of desire cascading over him. His body had missed hers. Had longed to plunge deep inside her, to feel her heat surround him, to know her passion as she shattered in his arms.

Great one, O'Neil. Just what the doctor ordered. A full-blown hard-on. One that would have no release. Sasha wasn't his. Hadn't been in ages, and wasn't about to become so. She carried another man's baby. It didn't matter that the man had left her high and dry.

Yeah, and you still lust after her. Still love her.

Yeah, and I can't do a thing about that.

What happened to trying to woo her back slowly?

I just ran out of patience. And, I suspect, opportunity— if I ever had that. Sasha had made it very plain she wasn't interested in a rerun of their previous relationship. What about a newer version? A grown-up, take-all-life's-punches relationship? She wasn't interested in that either. She might be saying her baby's father was a bastard but there'd been a ton of hurt in her voice, indicating she might still be in love with the guy.

Ignoring his painfully squeezing heart, Grady turned into her bedroom and nudged the light switch with an elbow. The big bed beckoned. It would be so easy to lie down with Sash and hold her close as she slept. If she woke he'd have to rethink that because he doubted he'd be able to keep his hands off her. Patience had always been his middle name—until he'd returned to Golden Bay and seen this woman currently in his arms and drooping in all directions as though she was boneless.

Yet the moment she woke she'd remember all that fear brought on by her baby's silence and those muscles would tighten up.

And he still had a boner to contend with. Seemed a dose of cold, hard reality hadn't quietened that down.

Best put her to bed. Don't go there, he warned his southern brain. Behave.

Sash stirred as he placed her on the bed. When he tucked the sheet and quilt up to her chin she blinked her eyes open. 'Grady?' she croaked.

'Shh. Go back to sleep, Sash.'

Her eyes opened wider. 'Why are you putting me to bed?'

'Because it's late and you were sound asleep in my car.' He stepped back from that tempting picture of sweetness. Run, man, while you still can. Because whatever you want, Sash will hate you tomorrow if you take advantage of her right now.

But Sash wasn't thinking straight. Her hand slid out from under the covers and grabbed at his shirt. 'Grady.' She tugged him. When he didn't budge she pushed up the bed and leaned closer. 'Thank you for today. For being there. For being you. I needed all of that.'

Another tug, and this time he didn't resist. Couldn't resist. Those lips were smiling, those eyes drawing him in, that honeysuckle tickling his sensory receptors. He bent down, wrapped his arms around her and pulled her up close so that he could feel against him the length of the body he craved in the deep of the night.

Sash twisted her head so that her lips locked on his. Finally, finally he tasted her. When her tongue slipped into his mouth he knew he'd found his Sash. And yet this was not his Sash. A different woman, confident in a less brash way. Gentled by her baby? By circumstances? Then her hands gripped his biceps and her swollen breasts pushed into his chest and he forgot to think. Just savoured the moment, the bone-melting kiss. He was home.

Lifting his hands to her head, his fingers combed into her silky hair. So soft. In response she pressed her hips forward. Rubbed up against his obvious need for her.

And reminded him with her baby bump why he shouldn't be doing this. Dropping his hands to her shoulders, he separated their bodies, put air between them. Let go his hold. Stepped back further. 'Sash.' Swallow. 'Sasha, I'm sorry.'

Her butt abruptly landed on the edge of the bed, as though her legs couldn't hold her up without any assistance from him. The ring-covered fingers of her left hand pressed into her lips. Surprise glittered out of her eyes. 'You're sorry?' she asked around those fingers. 'Then so am I.' Taking her hand away, she stared up at him. 'Grady, I shouldn't have kissed you. It was obvious you were moving away from me and in my sleep-hazed state I had to follow.'

Hit me in the gut, why don't you? 'I understand. It's okay.' Lying was all right sometimes, wasn't it? For sure, he wasn't about to lay his heart in those trembling hands twisting in her lap. She wasn't ready for that. She might never want him again, despite that kiss. He'd still have to try, but not this way. Slowly, slowly. In other words, be patient.

'I need to get into bed now. Properly.'

'Of course. Do you want a hot drink once you're sorted?'

'Is hot chocolate on the menu?' Her smile was shy and sliced right in deep, twisting through his heart.

'Coming right up,' he gasped, and turned abruptly for the door and the chill of the other rooms. Her bedroom had become hotter than an inferno. To the point he half expected to melt into a puddle of need at her feet.

In the pokey kitchen he banged cupboard doors as he looked for a mug, some chocolate and sugar, clanged the pot onto the element, slammed the fridge door shut after finding the milk.

He'd never be able to walk away from her again. At least, not until he'd tried everything possible to win her back. That kiss, short though it had been, had proved how much he still loved her.

As if he hadn't known.

Turning the gas on to low, he stood watching the milk heat ever so slowly, thinking about Sasha and what she'd done in the intervening years when they'd both been carving out careers and turning into grounded adults. Funny how they'd both always wanted medical careers. He'd once tried to talk Sash into studying to become a doctor. She'd told him he was crazy to even think about it.

It wasn't as though she didn't have the smarts. She had as much, if not more, intelligence as any doctor he knew. Her school grades had been embarrassingly high. She'd been school dux, topped science and biology, and yet she'd refused to consider med school.

'Too big a tie,' she'd say with a grin. 'At least six years with no free time for flying, skiing or just doing.'

'Just doing' had been her favourite expression and it encompassed all things physical or fun or non-studious.

He'd argued back, 'Six years isn't all that long. And we'd be studying together.' Talk about selfish, but he hadn't been able to imagine not being all but glued to her side. If only he'd known then what the future held just around the corner he'd have kept his big gob shut.

'Two points you're missing.' She'd wagged her fore-finger at him. 'It takes a lot of money to go to med school and I'm not asking Dad to fork out for me. Then there's the fact I hate being tied down too long. Can you imagine me studying twenty-four seven for years on end? I don't think so. I want to be a nurse, do the hands-on caring stuff, help people when they're feeling at their most vulnerable. I know there's a lot of study involved but not as much as it takes to become a doctor.'

He hadn't been able to argue with that and in the end he'd been the one to walk away from all their plans anyway.

The milk bubbled to the top of the pot and he deftly poured it into the large mug and stirred rapidly, swirling the dissolving chocolate through the liquid. Thinking about Sash, Sash, Sash.

Back in her bedroom the bedside light had replaced the main light, giving off a soft glow. Sash lay tucked up under her quilt, her eyes closed and her golden hair spread over the pillow. His heart felt like that chocolate in the hot milk. All gooey and swirling.

'Sash?' he called softly, in case she'd already fallen asleep.

Her eyes opened slowly. 'Hey, Grady. That smells yummy. You're spoiling me.'

Placing the mug on the bedside table, he headed for the door, where he turned to look at her. 'Get a good night's sleep, Sasha. I'll be out in the lounge if you need anything.' He wasn't leaving her in the house alone. Not after today. She'd had a huge fright and if she woke during the night he wanted to be there to reassure her that everything was fine with her baby.

Shrugging, he continued down the short hall. Who did he think he was fooling? He was staying because he had an excuse to, because he didn't want to leave her.

Not until he absolutely had to—which no doubt would be tomorrow when she was back to being her normal self and kicked him out.

CHAPTER EIGHT

SASHA DRAGGED HER eyes open and peered through the gloom of her bedroom to the sunlight trying to filter in around the edges of her blinds. 'At least it's going to be a nice day, by the look of that.'

Her hands went to her stomach. 'Hey, Flipper, how're you doing in there this morning? All over yesterday's quiet spell?'

She'd fought sleep last night—and lost—afraid that she'd not notice if the baby stopped moving again. Twice she'd woken during the night when she'd tried to roll over onto her stomach and immediately she'd felt a kick from inside. The relief had been enormous, but nothing like that moment when the hospital technician had shown her the printout with her baby's heartbeat looking absolutely normal.

Didn't mean she'd stop worrying for the rest of her pregnancy, though.

Stretching her toes to the end of the bed and her arms above her head, she revelled in the sheer indulgence of lying in bed. If only it was the weekend and she could stay all snug and warm in here for another hour or so.

'Got to get up, lazybones. You've got a full load of patients today. You're not supposed to be late, remember?'

And judging by the light filtering in, she was well on the way to being just that. It was as if something was testing her, making her earn this job by throwing obstacles all over the place to check her determination to turn up at work on time every day.

Reaching for her robe lying at the end of the bed, she shoved into it and headed for the kitchen. Stopped in the doorway. 'Grady? What are you doing here?'

Grady finished filling the kettle and plugged it in. 'I slept over. In case you had any more problems with baby.'

Warmth stole through her, heating her cheeks, her everywhere bits, and especially her heart. He'd looked out for her. He'd been doing that from the moment she'd rushed into the nurses' room beside herself with fear for Flipper. She so wasn't used to this.

'Where did you sleep?' The cottage didn't run to a spare bed. She'd already started preparing the tiny second bedroom for the baby, collecting cute little knick knacks in pink, buying a bassinet and change table. Until Flipper she hadn't even liked pink. Too girly.

'Your couch folds out into a bed of sorts.' He rolled his neck and she heard it click. 'Not the most comfortable, I admit, but I managed to get some sleep.'

Now she felt indebted to him. 'You should've gone home. I was fine.' To think she hadn't known he was here. Her radar had failed. She stared at him, and the man she used to love watched her back. If that kiss was anything to go by, she ran the chance of falling for him all over again. That would be an unfortunate error on her part, because they weren't going anywhere with this fledgling friendship.

Entrusting her heart to Grady again would have to be right up there with leaping out of her plane without a parachute. Not because he was a bad person. Far from it. His heart was in the right place. Hers had difficulty making good decisions. She seemed to have a flaw that made men leave around the time when she started to relax with them.

Admittedly, it had been slightly different with this particular man watching her from under those thick black eyebrows. She'd been relaxed and involved and in love with him from the first time they'd met. It had been a very intense relationship and she'd believed he was equally as happy until he'd walked. But he had walked, leaving her shattered and shocked.

She was beginning to understand what it had cost him to help his family, though. He'd not only forced her away, he'd put his whole life on hold, including the career he'd worked so hard for with the high grades to get him into medical school. If only she'd stopped to think it through at the time, they might've come up with some arrangement to keep their relationship working. The only good thing to come out of Mum's MS was that she'd started seeing what Grady had had to deal with. It might be too late for her and Grady, but at least she'd be more careful in the future.

With a heavy heart, she told him, 'Thanks for staying over even when it wasn't necessary. I'm going to have a shower and head into work. I guess I'll see you around over the next few days.'

His lips whitened and he shoved his hands deep into those muscle-hugging, butt-defining jeans he wore with such nonchalance. 'How about I see you in forty-five minutes' time when I pick you up and drive you to work? Your car's still at the medical centre, remember?' Then he headed away.

She stared at her front door as it closed behind that straight back and tight shoulders. 'Now I've gone and upset him.'

But it was probably for the best. She had to put the barriers back in place to keep him at a distance.

Sasha tried to relax for the fifteen-minute ride into work. Not easy with Grady less than a stretch away. He was completely focused on driving and avoiding school kids on bikes who veered out into the middle of the road. Totally ignoring her.

Finally they pulled up at the centre. She had to say something or she'd spend the rest of the day feeling terrible. 'Grady, I'm sorry. You went out of your way to help me and then I pushed you aside.' She gripped her bag. 'I made a mistake last night when I kissed you.' Though it hadn't felt like a mistake at the time. 'We need to keep our distance. You're here for such a short time and I have a lot on my plate at the moment.'

'It's all right, Sash. I get it. There's to be no rerun of the past.' Did he have to look so disappointed? Nah, couldn't be. Had to be that he was angry with her for kissing him in the first place and then making it sound like he was the problem here.

She headed inside, turning when she realised Grady was following her. 'You don't have to escort me right into my room.'

'I'm working this morning.'

Keeping that distance just got harder. 'Are you coming to the staff meeting?'

'Yep.'

Wonderful. A glance at her watch showed she had time

to top up her medical kit beforehand. 'White and one, thanks.' She cracked Grady a smile. 'I'll be five minutes.'

'Yes, ma'am.'

Jess jumped up from the desk the moment Sasha walked into their room. Engulfing her in a huge hug, she sniffed. 'Told you Flipper would be all right.'

Sniff back. 'Guess that was the first of millions of crises my girl's going to cause. I hope I'm cut out for this.'

Stepping back, Jess grinned. 'Welcome to my world. Nicholas brings me so much happiness and worry all wrapped up together, it can be scary, but I keep reminding myself there are millions of kids out there with parents who feel the same and they grow up fine.'

'That's supposed to make me feel better?' She grinned back. 'I'm going to buy you a cellphone that is only to be used to talk to me, because you're my first line of defence when I can't cope.'

'I signed up for friendship so bring it on.' Jess's grin wavered. 'You do have your parents on standby.'

Unlike Jessica. Another hug was called for. 'You know, if you called her Mum would be on your doorstep before you'd finished saying you needed help. She adores you and Nicholas.'

'Great, now look what you've done.' Jess rummaged around for the tissues. 'Sasha, you're in for the most amazing experience. Having a baby is wonderful beyond description. Yeah, it can be frightening, doing it on your own, but the rewards more than make up for that. Anyway, apparently I'll be on the end of the phone all the time. That's if I'm not glued to your hip.'

'Now, there's an idea.' She sucked in her trepidation. 'Guess we'd better get to that meeting.'

She grinned at the coffee waiting on the table. Everyone asked about her baby before they got down to the business of discussing patients.

Then Sasha told everyone about Campbell McRae and her concerns for his mental state. 'I'm going to visit him again today, more to check that he's not become any further depressed than anything else. But I did wonder if some counselling sessions might help.' Rory was Campbell's doctor.

'It would, but do you honestly see Campbell turning up for them? Especially as he'll have to drive over the hill to see anyone.'

Beside him Grady sat, tapping the tabletop with his finger. 'Want me to go with Sasha to see him? Give him a medical assessment?'

They needed to be fixing the problems she'd already noted. 'Medically Campbell's doing fine, apart from ignoring his exercise routine and letting his glucose levels creep up a little with the occasional intake of chocolate. It's the head stuff that needs dealing with.'

Rory answered before Grady even got his mouth open. 'I like the idea of Grady visiting him. The guy enjoys being made a fuss of. What bigger fuss than a doctor calling in?' He glanced at Grady, and something passed between them.

Something that made Sasha sit up. Those men were too smug. 'Grady can head up that way while I go in the other direction. He'll be saving me time when I've got a long list of patients to see today, starting up the Cobb Valley.'

What was Grady doing here anyway? It's not like he had a job at the centre. Oh, no. She shivered. He didn't, did he? He hadn't told her anything about his current job, where he worked, what he intended doing after he'd got that house ready for the market. Had she missed a vital clue somewhere between the Donovans' accident and last night's kiss?

That kiss. She swallowed a groan. What had she been thinking? And there was no way she could blame it on Flipper's little sleep that had sent her into a mad panic for hours. Her hand brushed her bump. Almost simultaneously felt a kick. *Yah, good girl. Love ya.*

Glancing around the table, she found all eyes on her. 'What?' Had she missed something? Something monumental? Like there was yoghurt on her chin?

Oh, no. It had to do with Grady. She just knew it. Worse, Grady and her. What crazy scheme were the doctors hatching? She flicked Jess a 'what's going on?' look, got a shrug in return. Traitor. Friends stuck together through everything. Break-ups, reunions, uninvited babies, family crises.

Grady cut in. 'There's a patient on your house call list that Roz wants seen by a doctor as well as you. Mary Stanners. Are you aware of her case?'

'She had a car accident last month and spent four weeks in hospital with a fractured femur and hips, a ruptured spleen and both lungs punctured. She's now at home under the care of her elderly mother.'

Roz added her bit. 'The situation worries me, Sasha. Mary should've been kept in hospital for at least another week but they were short of beds. I think it's wise to keep an eye on her. I'd also prefer it if we didn't ask her to make that long and uncomfortable drive in here until her pain level has improved.'

'Makes sense.' And keeps Grady in my vehicle. Why didn't I do midwifery instead of stopping at general nursing?

Mike added, 'We're making use of Grady while he's

here. For either Roz or I to take a couple of hours to do the round trip visiting Mary takes a huge chunk out of the clinic schedule. Since Mary is already on your list of patients, it makes sense for Grady to accompany you.'

'And this has absolutely nothing to do with my worry over lifting Josh up yesterday and hurting my back. Nothing to do with my mad dash over to Nelson last night.'

'Of course not.'

'Not at all.'

Sasha felt her brow wrinkling, and forced it smooth again. They were babysitting her because of yesterday's drama. It was kind of nice, if Grady wasn't going to be her constant companion. Her hormones were in for a long, exhausting day. But arguing with these guys wouldn't get her anywhere. She'd accept the deal for today, get on with her patient list, come up with a solution to get rid of Grady by tomorrow.

'Not a problem. We'll go and see Mary first and then I'll drop Grady back here before heading to the Cobb.' Didn't have to give in gracefully, did she?

Grady wanted to throttle Sasha and laugh out loud all at the same time. She absolutely hated to be bested, and she knew that's exactly what had happened. Mary Stanners lived less than thirty minutes from the farmlet Roz and Mike lived on. It would be no problem for one of them to call in on the way home at the end of the day. Roz had apparently been doing that every day anyway.

'I'll go get my files and kit. See you in ten.' Sasha gave him an 'I'm still in charge' glare as she rinsed her mug under the tap and placed it in the dishwasher. 'The car needs fuelling on the way out.'

'Yes, ma'am.' He resisted throwing a salute. They had to spend the day together.

'Being smug doesn't suit you,' she muttered as she pushed past him on her way out.

'Still always have to get the last word in.' His grin wavered as his nostrils filled with honeysuckle scent. Closing his eyes, he watched a rerun of the image in his mind of Sasha curled up in the front seat of his car, sound asleep. Then, bang, that kiss flashed across his brain, filled his body with heat and need. Snapping his eyes open, he strode resolutely to the office where he would find Mary Stanners's complete medical records. Anything to keep his mind on the job and off Nurse Wilson.

'Sheree, can I please have a printout of all the hospital reports on Mary Stanners?' he asked the receptionist the moment she put the phone down after taking an appointment booking.

'Sure.' Her fingers began clicking away on the keyboard of her computer, and the phone began ringing again.

'Sheree, has the courier dropped off a package from the medical supplies company?' Sasha bounced into the office.

Damn it, woman, give me some space here. It's bad enough I'm going to be sitting in your vehicle, sucking up all that honeysuckle smell, for hours on end, not to have you following me around the medical centre as well.

Grady watched the computer screen over the receptionist's shoulder, refusing his body's command to turn and look at Sash. But he knew the instant she came to stand on the other side of Sheree. Why had he put his hand up to go on the rounds with her? What little devil had been playing havoc inside his skull this morning?

He should be at home, preparing the lounge for painting, doing sensible, sane jobs that would get him out of town quickly. *If he was still leaving.* Focus on the screen, stop thinking about—anything.

Sheree glanced at Sasha and pointed a pen in the direction of a bench on the back wall of her office while talking to someone on the phone and printing off the notes he wanted. Wonder woman. Who said medical centres relied on their doctors and nurses to keep things on an even keel? Without Sheree this place would fall apart before the first tea break.

Without her he'd be negotiating his way around the alien program on the computer in the staffroom, trying to extract the notes he needed, and wouldn't be losing his mind over Sasha.

They hit the road five minutes later than Sasha had intended and headed for the petrol station. The moment she pulled up to the pump Grady hopped out and made to fill up the vehicle's tank.

'You don't have to mollycoddle me. Refuelling my vehicle is very simple. Baby brain can still manage that.'

'Go and sign for the petrol, Sasha. I'd be doing this for you no matter what your situation.' Did he sound as tired as he felt? Probably. Sasha's eyebrows had risen at his tone.

But at least she stomped inside after a curt, 'Thanks.'

Back on the road the silence was deafening. Grady replayed the previous night and wondered where he'd gone wrong. He'd looked out for Sash all the way. Except for that kiss—which Sash had started. *Oh, yeah, of course you hadn't been thinking about kissing her, definitely didn't want to.* One step forward, ten back.

He'd concentrate on the calls they'd be making and

hopefully soon Sash would relax enough to start talking freely with him. 'Who's your first patient?'

'Janice and Julie Daniels, seven-year-old twins. They've had a severe vomiting bug and their mum's keeping them in isolation. No point in spreading the bug to all their schoolmates.'

What about you? Shouldn't you be staying away from them too? Dehydration due to vomiting is not good for your baby. He bit down on the words that would cause a greater rift between them and went for, 'Has anyone else in the bay had this bug?'

The corner of her mouth lifted in a wry smile. So she'd known what he was thinking anyway. Might as well have said it.

'Not so far. Kathy Daniels thinks the girls caught it while over in Nelson with their cousins.'

'Let's hope we keep it contained.' He wasn't thinking only of the twins' schoolmates. The woman beside him was his number-one priority.

'Thanks, mate,' Sasha growled. Mud and muck splashed onto the windscreen, thrown up by the stock truck they were now following up a narrow, metal road. She flicked the wipers on and pressed the cleaning liquid button. Soapy water briefly turned the windscreen opaque and Sasha slowed, dropping back far enough not to collect any more mess. 'There's one call not on the list that we'll make after the twins. I always drop in on Mr Harris whenever I'm out this way. He's in his eighties and lives with his son and daughter-in-law. He's got a history of cardiac failure.'

'Are you talking Old Jack, the man my father used to go fishing with every Christmas Eve?' When she nodded he continued. 'They'd get blue cod for Christmas breakfast. Dad bought the beach house from Jack when he moved up to the farm with his family. They hit it off and that fishing trip became a ritual. I'd wondered if he was still around.' The memories were warm, comfortable.

'He's as spry as a sixty-year-old. Refuses to let his heart condition dominate what he does, though I don't think he gets out fishing any more. No one to go with, and his son's always too busy with the farm.'

'I could take him out if I get a chance to put the boat in working order.'

Sasha glanced his way. 'Mr Harris would love that. So you've still got a boat?'

'The same old aluminium runabout. I tested the motor the other day. Needs a bit of TLC but nothing major.'

'At last.' Sasha slowed to a stop as the stock truck negotiated the turn onto the farm they'd been driving beside. 'Guess that's a load of beef heading for market.' She nodded towards the yards a hundred metres away by a cluster of sheds. 'Sirloin on legs. Yum.'

'Makes that chicken-and-salad-filled bread roll you bought at the service station seem lame.' And the ham sandwiches he'd bought just as unappetising.

Ten minutes later they pulled up at a large old villa sitting in the middle of immaculate lawns and gardens that spoke of many hours of weeding and pruning. 'That's stunning.'

'Isn't it? Whenever I see this I think I'd love a garden to spend time in.' Sasha laughed. 'Then I remember the only time I tried growing radishes, which anyone can supposedly grow, and how they were the biggest flop ever. I was only five but my schoolmates all grew plump, delicious radishes. Got right up my nose, that did, and I never tried again.'

'Bet they can't fly a plane.'

'True.' She slid out of the vehicle and collected her pack of supplies. 'Coming?'

Julie and Janice were very unwell little cuties who still had enough energy to sit up in their beds the moment Sasha entered their bedroom. Grady laughed when they told him knock, knock jokes, and chuckled as they kept finishing each other's sentences, commiserated when they told Sasha how many times they'd puked.

Kids, eh? He'd not given having a family of his own much thought. Hadn't seen the point when he was seriously single. But apparently a few days around Sash made a huge difference in his outlook. Having children would be kind of cool. With the right mother, of course. Funny how his gaze tracked immediately to Sash. Like that was going to happen, no matter how patient he was and how much he tried to fool himself she might give him a second chance. Not after her warning that morning.

Sasha took temperatures and listened to their chests when Kathy said they'd started coughing during the night. 'Their temps are still a little high, but I think the worst of that bug is over.'

Grady also felt their tummies and listened to their chests. 'I'll write out prescriptions for antibiotics. I think they're both presenting with the beginning of a chest infection. Double trouble,' he said, as he handed the prescriptions over.

'Double love,' Kathy said, as she passed the prescriptions on to Sasha.

'We'll drop this in when we get back to town and then Sheree will bring it out on her way home.' Sasha clipped the piece of paper to the outside of Julie's file. 'She's Kathy's sister and lives two farms down the road.'

'Small communities have their advantages.' Grady picked up the stethoscope to place it in its pouch in Sasha's kit.

'Sometimes,' the women answered in unison, then burst into laughter.

'Not when you want to keep something secret, eh, Kathy?'

Kathy's cheeks reddened. 'You can talk, Sasha Wilson.'

'Time we were on the road.' Sasha slung the pack over one shoulder and waved at the twins. 'See you two scallywags tomorrow.'

Back in the four-wheel drive, Grady dared to ask, 'What was your great secret that the town found out about?'

'I didn't ride into town and announce to all and sundry I was pregnant. Apart from telling Mum and Dad, I kept it to myself for a while. Thought I'd give them time to get used to the idea before I started letting it out, but I hadn't counted on Kathy guessing. Not that she went wild with the news, but she made me realise I couldn't keep Flipper hidden for ever.'

'I take it they knew at the medical centre?'

'I was up front with them right from the start. Had to be. I'm there to cover Karen's maternity leave, but Mike and Rory have indicated there might be a permanent job at the end of it.' Worry darkened her words, tightened her brow.

'What will you do if the job doesn't eventuate?'

'That's not an option.' She leaned forward to peer through the windscreen, and instantly eased off on the accelerator and wound down her window. Cold air filled the cab.

'What's up?' Grady asked, as he craned his neck to see past her head.

'I'm not sure but those guys are running towards the shed, carrying someone between them.'

'I see them. That's the farm the stock truck turned into.' Unease made him wary. 'We'd better go and see if we're needed.' Men didn't usually run around with one of their mates swinging from their arms.

'On our way.' Sasha turned sharply, bounced the vehicle over the cattle stop and drove directly to the shed. 'Stock truck's still here, parked over behind that second shed.'

'Drive right up to that door where those men ducked inside.' Grady undid his seat belt, ready to follow the men.

Before Sasha had pulled up, a man appeared in the doorway, carrying a rifle under his arm. 'What the heck?' She stuck her head out the window. 'What's happening, Jason?'

'Sasha? That was quick. Murts is in a bad way. That bull went berko when we tried to load him. Got Murts in the gut I don't know how many times.' The man who was apparently Jason strode over to them. 'I'm going to put a bullet between his eyes.'

'What do you mean, that was quick?' Grady asked as he climbed out. 'We've been up the road, visiting patients, and saw you all running inside the shed.'

Jason looked across at him, then back to Sasha, a question in his eyes. 'I phoned 111 and McKentry used his truck phone to call the medical centre. Mike's getting the ambulance and heading out here as soon as he can.'

Sasha joined Jason. 'This is Grady O'Neil. He's a doctor.'

'Some good news.' Jason pushed Grady towards the shed. 'Go, man. Murts needs you real bad.'

Grady called over his shoulder to Sasha, 'Bring your pack with you.' Not that it contained half the equipment he'd give his right arm for at this moment. He hated to think of the injuries this guy Murts had suffered every time that bull's head had slammed into his gut.

The man lying on the floor of the shed looked worse than even he'd imagined. Covered in blood from head to foot, he was shaking and groaning as his friends knelt beside him, helpless to do anything. 'Hey, guys. Grady O'Neil. I'm a doctor.'

In the shed the relief was almost palpable. As the three men scrambled out of the way they tripped over themselves. 'Thank God,' one of them muttered, then added, 'Hello, and we've got Sasha. Murts, this is your lucky day, dude.'

Unable to see anything lucky in being gored by a raging bull, Grady kept his mouth shut and knelt down on the hard dirt. Sasha joined him on the other side and immediately began taking a pulse. Make that tried to take a pulse. Her finger pressed on the carotid, moved a smidge left, right. Then, 'At last,' she whispered.

Grady spoke to the patient. 'Hello, Murts. I'm Grady, a doctor. And Sasha's here, she's a nurse.'

'Glad to see you,' the guy wheezed around his obvious pain, and opened his eyes for a brief moment.

'Murts, how old are you?'

'Forty-eight.'

A clear verbal response, and Murts had opened his eyes. 'Can you feel my hand?' Grady asked as he touched his patient's hand, and felt a small clenching around his fingers. 'GCS thirteen,' he told Sasha. Not bad in the circumstances.

'Pulse weak and low,' she responded.

Not good. Grady settled further down on his haunches. 'Murts, can you tell me where the pain is coming from?'

'Everywhere.'

Okay. Try again. 'What about your head?'

'Yes, bad.'

'Your chest?' Grady asked. There could be a pneumothorax if that solid head had hit Murts's ribs hard enough. Or often enough.

'Agony,' Murts muttered.

Grady said in an aside to Sasha, 'How do we go about calling for the rescue helicopter?' Without that, this man was unlikely to survive. A two-hour trip over the hill was not an option.

'I imagine Mike would've put them on standby the moment he got the call. They have to come from Wellington or Nelson, about equal flying times.'

'Can you get Mike on the phone for me? Then see if any of these men saw the attack and where the bull got Murts, other than in the gut, as already mentioned.'

'Sure.' She stood, tugged her phone from her pocket and punched buttons. After handing the phone to him, she strode across to where the three men hovered anxiously.

He heard Mike answer his phone and got on with getting what he needed. 'We're with the man attacked by a bull. Can you make that helicopter a go? Needed here a.s.a.p.'

'Onto it. I'll be with you in ten.' The phone went dead.

Continuing with his examination, Grady worked his hands over the chest he'd just exposed by tearing away what remained of Murts's shirt. Beneath his hands the man writhed and groaned. Pain or cerebral irritation? What he wouldn't do for a fully equipped theatre at this moment, and an X-ray machine. Or even that ambulance with at least essential equipment.

Sash squatted down again. 'The bull rammed into Murts continually pretty much everywhere. The guys reckon at least twenty times.'

Grady closed his eyes briefly. Murts was lucky to be alive.

Sash wasn't finished. 'His head whipped all over the place, often connecting with the wooden fence rails. His legs took some hits as well.'

'So we're looking at internal injuries, possibly broken ribs and a punctured lung, and brain injuries.'

'Could be bleeding out internally, too.' Sasha began counting Murts's resp rate again.

'I need to insert an artificial airway before he gets into that helicopter. I'm presuming there are the right drugs in that ambulance so that I can do an RSI?'

'Resp rate fifty-two. Too low,' she murmured, as she looked directly at him, the worry for Murts obvious in her eyes. 'They're in the pack that Mike will bring from the surgery. As there are no ambulance personnel qualified to use most drugs, they're only carried when one of the doctors attends an incident.'

'Good policy, though right now I could do without it.'

'I think both femurs are broken,' Sasha's hands were carefully working down the length of Murts's left leg.

'We're going to have to straighten them and apply splints before loading him in the helicopter.'

'We'll wait for that drug kit and some morphine.' He began checking the right leg, working in sync with Sasha. Amazing how well they worked together. But it shouldn't be a surprise. They'd always done things well together.

A shot rang out, quickly followed by another.

Grady saw Sasha shiver and reached over to run a finger over her hand. 'Had to be done.'

'I know, but doesn't mean I have to like it.'

The men gave a cheer. 'That'll show him,' one of them muttered, as they headed outside.

'What was that you said about sirloin on the way in?' Grady asked Sasha with a smile, trying to lift her spirits.

Her face paled. 'No, thanks. Think I'll stick to my chicken now.'

'You squeamish about where your meat comes from?' He held back a chuckle. Probably get slapped hard for that.

'Not normally, but being pregnant has changed a lot of things. Like craving for prunes. Used to hate them as a kid and they were Mum's favourite fix for everything that ailed us.' Colour started returning to her face and she began counting Murts's resp rate again.

Murts gave a deeper groan than any before.

'Murts? What's going on?' Grady gently palpated the abdomen area where the man's fist was tapping. 'Pain here?'

'Ye-es. Ahh.'

The sound lifted the hairs on the back of Grady's neck. 'The ambulance is nearly here, and the helicopter is on its way. You hang in there, right? We'll get you sorted and into hospital where they can fix you up in no time.' Don't you dare die on us. Don't you damn well dare.

Sasha rubbed the back of one of Murts's hands. 'Who do you want to go to hospital with you? Sally or one of those lugs outside?'

'Sally's in Nelson, doing the shopping,' Murts wheezed.

'So one of those lugs it is. I'll go see who's available.' Sasha stood, leaned closer to Grady. 'Resp rate dropping. Now forty.' Then she headed out to find the men.

The sound of tyres on the gravel outside was very welcome, as was the bag of medical goodies Mike carried in moments later. 'Hey, there, Murts, hear that bull of yours went a little crazy.'

Sasha returned carrying leg splints and a stretcher from the ambulance, accompanied by Rebecca.

Grady shook his head at Sasha. 'What was wrong with getting Rebecca to carry that stretcher?'

Her face squeezed into a scowl. 'It weighs next to nothing.' But she did quickly place it on the ground near their patient, before handing the splints to Grady. 'I'll head off on my round now. With Mike and Rebecca here, you won't need me any more.' There was a hint of mischief in her eyes as she nailed him with a stare.

Sash thought she'd found a way to get rid of him for the rest of the day, did she? That sucked. Hurt, too, if he was honest. She really didn't want him accompanying her for the day. Did she dislike him now? No. Her kiss negated that theory. So his presence was stirring up memories or emotions she'd prefer weren't stirred up. Was that it? Hope flared, nudged the hurt aside. He could still rattle her cage. Cool. 'Guess what?'

When her carefully styled eyebrows lifted in a 'this had better be good' way he answered his own question.

'I'm coming with you to see Campbell McRae. Or had you forgotten that?'

The eyebrows dropped. But her mouth slid upwards into a reluctant smile. 'I'd hoped you had.'

CHAPTER NINE

SASHA SAID GOODBYE to Mrs Callahan and headed outside to the car. Mrs Callahan hadn't wanted Grady there while Sasha examined her hysterectomy wound.

'Call me old-fashioned but my woman's bits aren't for everyone to see.'

Sasha had smiled her understanding and refrained from pointing out that no 'woman's bits' would be on show anyway. Sixty-year-old Mrs Callahan was entitled to her privacy, though that was likely to go out the window when she started radiation for her cervical cancer next week in Christchurch. Sasha carefully picked her way over the rough cobblestones on the pathway. Such a nice, kind lady, known for her good deeds in the community, and she'd been dealt a bad card. Cancer didn't care who it attacked.

Rounding the corner of the house, she stopped. Grady was leaning against her vehicle, talking on his phone, and looking so sexy in his thick jacket and his butt-hugging trousers.

Her mouth dried. No wonder she'd kissed him last night in her half-awake—or was that half-asleep—state. Kissing Grady had always been a favourite pastime. And what those kisses had led to. Thank goodness he'd put the brakes on before they'd gone any further last night. Had he wanted her? In that way? Or had her kiss turned him completely off her? Or her baby bump? That had to be a dose of reality for any man. Kissing a woman who carried another guy's baby had to be the biggest turn-off imaginable.

But look at him. Not just sexy beyond belief. Solid, reliable, caring. Special. Grady. The man she'd once intended marrying, intended sharing her future with.

Her head pounded. The blood beat along her veins. Exhaustion swamped her. Being tired beyond belief made dealing with Grady too much. Too complicated, involved, difficult. One half-assed kiss didn't mean everything had been righted in her world. Far from it.

Flipper nudged her more gently than usual. 'Yeah, I know, baby girl. It's just you and me.' She continued down the path. This had been the last call. What with rampaging bulls and Campbell taking his time to size up Grady, and then not letting him go until he'd talked and talked and talked, they were very late. 'Time to head home and put my feet up.' Now she sounded like an old lady. Thank goodness Dad was home. She didn't have any energy to spare for packing citrus today.

'Murts has just had surgery to put rods in his femurs.' Grady shoved his phone into his jacket pocket as she approached. 'The head injuries are causing concern, as are his punctured lungs.'

'But he's alive.' A sigh rushed over her lips. 'That's got to be good news.' Poor Sally would be beside herself with worry.

'You okay?' Grady's eyes clouded with concern.

'Absolutely fantastic.' I've seen a guy who'd been battered half to death by a bull, a lovely lady dealing with cancer, and I had the biggest scare of my life yesterday. 'I'm just fine.' But she walked up to the passenger side of her vehicle and opened the door, hauled herself inside and hunched back against the seat, her eyes closed.

Grady, to his credit, didn't say a word, just walked round to the other side, adjusted the driver's seat and drove them back to town.

She'd rest on the way and then she'd be up to shopping at the supermarket and deciding what to have for dinner. Flipper was probably getting sick of soup and toast, or yoghurt. Monday night's meal at Grady's had been delicious and made her think she should be trying harder to cook tasty meals. But making them just for herself was a bore. And required energy she didn't have today.

'What would you like for dinner?' Grady's skin-lifting, emotion-grazing voice penetrated her fogged mind.

'Trying to decide between two-minute noodles and canned spaghetti,' she muttered. She wasn't lying. Suddenly having to stand at the stove at all seemed beyond her.

'How about sweet and sour pork with stir-fried rice?'

She blinked. 'What planet are you on? There's no Chinese takeaway around here.'

'Did I say anything about takeaways?' He flicked her a cocky grin.

'You're cooking again?' Her hand rested on the point her baby was currently toeing.

Grady's gaze dropped to her hand then returned to the road ahead. 'Didn't you know you can get sweet and sour pork in a packet? Just add water and stir.'

'I've been missing out on gourmet delights.' She

laughed, her tiredness taking a step back. Grady was making her feel good. 'Any other flavours?'

'Not tonight.' As they neared the medical centre he said, 'Are you up to driving home from here? I need to get some groceries, mainly pork and rice, and then I'll come to your place to cook dinner.'

'I can manage fifteen minutes behind the wheel. I'm going to drop into the parents' on the way. They'll want to feel Flipper do her goal-kicking practice to make them totally happy all's well in there.'

'Okay if I let myself in if you're not home when I arrive?' He pulled up outside the medical centre.

'Go for it. The key's under the lemon-tree container.'

'Where I found it last night.'

Of course he had. She shook her head at him. 'Not the cleverest place to...' she flicked her forefingers in the air '...hide it, I know, but it's there for when I forget to take my key ring with me.'

Last night. When he'd driven her back from Nelson. After he'd sat with her, held her hand figuratively while she'd freaked out big time. A girl could get used to that if she wasn't careful. Last night—when she'd kissed him. Swallow. Maybe having Grady in her house again so soon after that faux pas was a mistake. Because those memories she refused to admit to were getting harder to deny by the minute.

But pork and fried rice sounded so much tastier than those two-minute noodles sitting in her cupboard. How pathetic was that? Unfair on Grady, too. Hey, he was a big boy. In more ways than one. He'd cope. He wouldn't have offered if he didn't want to do this. One thing about Grady—he didn't do anything he didn't want to.

Shuffling over to the driver's side, she reached to pull

the door closed that Grady had left open. 'See you in a while.' She crashed the gearstick into place and jerked her foot off the accelerator, sending the four-wheel drive bunny-hopping out of the car park.

'Excellent, Sasha. Now you're a ballet dancer on wheels.' In the rear-view mirror she saw Grady standing, hands on hips, shaking his head. 'So you don't like dancers. What do you like these days, Grady O'Neil? Who are the women you've dated since I last saw you? Beautiful ones, I'll bet. Exciting and fun, or serious and safe?'

Her good mood evaporated. She hated the thought of those other women with Grady. Even though she'd had other men, and had loved one a lot. Grady had been hers. But not any more.

'Hey, Dad, how was your trip?' Sasha wrapped her arms around her father and hugged tight. One of the good things about returning home was Dad hugs. They'd been a part of her life from as far back as she could remember.

'A darned sight less drama-ridden than things back here.' He squeezed her and stepped back, his eyes dropping to her protruding tummy. 'How is my granddaughter today?'

Sasha grabbed his hand and placed it where Flipper was kicking up a storm. 'She's been making up for lost time all day.' Watching Dad's eyes mist over as he felt the movement, her throat clogged with emotion. 'Melanie's doing fine, Dad. Everything's on target.' She winced as another kick caught at her. 'Right on target. I think I've got a women's soccer rep in there.'

'Melanie?' Dad whispered as he raised his eyes to

meet her gaze. 'You're naming her after your grand-mother? My mother?' he emphasised.

'Yes. Melanie Wilson the second. I'm giving her a lot to live up to, I know, but I'm sure she'll manage.'

Mum handed Dad a box of tissues and shunted him aside. 'My turn.' Her arms wrapped around Sasha's neck and she planted a soppy kiss on her cheek. 'That baby gave us a huge scare yesterday. When Grady phoned I had a wee cry.'

Grady. The name dropped between them. Mum would have a thousand questions. Dad might, too. They'd both liked Grady and had been hurt when he'd dumped her.

Sasha unwound Mum's arms, noting the slight tremors, and tried hard not to show any tears. No way did Mum want any sympathy, went nuts if anyone said anything about her illness. Which left Grady to talk about, and she so did not want to go there. 'Sorry I didn't phone. I was almost incoherent with panic.' She met Dad's gaze. Saw the empathy there for her predicament. 'So much for being the cool, calm nurse.'

'Yesterday you were a mother, not a nurse,' Mum told her. 'Are you staying for dinner?'

'Not tonight, sorry. It's been a long day and I really want to get home.' That wasn't a fib.

'What are you cooking?' Dad asked, his shrewd eyes watching her every movement.

'Sweet and sour pork with fried rice.' That wasn't quite a fib either.

'Where did you find Chinese food? Has a new place opened in the week I've been away?' He turned to Mum, who shook her head, turned back. 'Sasha?'

'Grady's cooking. He insisted and I didn't have the energy to keep saying no.' Neither was that a fib.

'Good for him.' Mum grinned.

'Are you seeing Grady again?' Dad asked, a load of caution lacing his voice.

'No, Dad, I'm not. He's been doing some hours for the medical centre so there's no avoiding him. Then, Grady being Grady, he insisted on driving me over to Nelson last night.'

'Thank goodness he did.' Mum seemed determined to make the whole Grady thing a rosy picture. Did she want a father for Flipper? Did that make her prepared to welcome Grady into the family so easily?

'Look…' Sasha drew a shaky breath. 'Grady's back here to prepare his house for sale and then he's heading off again. We are not getting back together. Not now, not ever. It would never work.'

Dad laid his hand on her shoulder. 'Trying too hard to convince us? Or to convince yourself, love?'

The trouble with her father was that he knew her too well, had always been able to read her like a book, because they were so similar in character. Reaching up on her toes, she placed a kiss on his cheek. 'I'll be over to help with the avocados after work tomorrow. I'm sure they need thinning.'

'No need. We've got it covered.' Dad went to the front door with her, held it open as she stepped out into the cold night.

She noted the clear sky and the condensation in the air in front of her mouth. 'Could be a frost tonight.'

'Tread carefully, Sasha.'

As she slid back into her vehicle she knew Dad wasn't talking about the slippery steps or path.

She waved as she drove out onto the road home. And dinner with Grady. 'I'm trying really hard, Dad, believe me. But nothing seems to be going according to plan right now.'

The delicious aroma of fried rice teased Sasha's nostrils as she let herself into her cottage. She could so easily get used to this. Squeezing into the kitchen, she told Grady, 'That smells divine.'

He turned from the bench where he was stirring soy sauce and crushed garlic together. 'Better than your box of noodles?'

I shouldn't have agreed to this. The tiny kitchen couldn't hold both of them without them rubbing against each other. Crossing to the alcove that served as her dining room, she stopped. The table was set, waiting for her. 'Oh. Right.' Now what? She turned back to the kitchen. 'Do you want a beer or something?'

Grady lifted an open bottle from the bench. 'Sorted, thanks.'

Okay. Um, guess there wasn't anything to do except wait for that food that looked so good in the deep pan he was using as a wok. 'I'll go and change out of my work clothes, then.' She shot past him, ignoring the raised eyebrows and quirky smile on his gorgeous face. Gorgeous face?

Yeah, Dad, as you can see, I'm trying really hard to keep my distance.

'Don't be long. I'm almost ready.' Grady's voice followed her down to her bedroom. So ordinary, normal. Grady in the kitchen, preparing dinner, while she'd been visiting her parents. Now they'd sit down together and eat, talk about their day. Like a couple. A couple with their first baby on the way.

Yeah, Dad, I'm trying really hard.

Grady would be a super father. The kind any kid would want to rush home to at the end of school and tell him about all the things she'd done during the day. Did her baby need a father? Right from the day she popped out?

Flipper had needed one yesterday. As she'd needed Grady. Hard to imagine how she'd have coped without him being there for her.

'I'd have done what I always do—sucked it up and got on with it. Having Grady hanging around made it easier to give in to the fear and panic gripping me.'

She sank onto the edge of her bed, stared around the room she'd made cosy with the quilts she'd inherited from her grandmother. They were works of art, full of vibrant colours and intriguing patterns. Apart from the terracotta and cream-coloured log-cabin quilt on her bed there were three others in greens, blues and more terracotta lying on the chair in the corner and over the wooden clothes rack in the opposite corner. All made by her grandmother.

Closing her eyes, she could picture Grandma hand-piecing together intricate shapes of fabric, slowly, painstakingly, creating another magical quilt. Grandma. Sasha's hands went to her tummy. Melanie.

What are you going to be like, baby girl? Sweet and kind, like your great-grandma? Tough and determined, like your grandma? Daredevil and wild, like your mum and grandfather?

Please, not like Dad and me. I don't think I could bear to have to sit at home, waiting for you to return from some dangerous escapade.

This whole motherhood thing was huge. Terrifying. Exciting. Massive. Was she up to it? Too late. It had been too late since she'd gone to Fiji for a week with grease-ball Freddy. Her hands gripped the quilt on either side of her butt. He might've turned out to be a waste of space but he had given her Flipper, and no matter what the future brought she'd be grateful for that. She might have to work hard at being the best mother but nothing would get in the way of her trying.

'Sasha?' Grady stood in the doorway. 'You okay?'

Forcing her hands to relax, she plastered the facsimile of a smile on her mouth and stood up. 'Perfectly fine.' Now, that was a fib.

'Dinner's ready.' He didn't move away, remained with his thoughtful gaze cruising over her. What was he thinking? Did she measure up to his expectations after all this time? Did he even have any expectations? And what did it matter? They had no future together.

'I'll be there in a minute.' Go away. Take those all-seeing eyes with you. Give me some space. You're crowding me, turning any rational thinking into a mire of questions and memories. Enticing crazy ideas to blossom in my skull. Ideas about you and me and my baby.

Picking up her trackpants, she waved them at Grady. 'One minute.'

The moment he turned away she untied her belt and let her trousers drop to her ankles. Stepping out of them, she tugged her trackies on and changed her blouse for a loose sweatshirt that downplayed her baby bulge. Trackpants weren't exactly a fashion statement, wouldn't flatter her or remind Grady of sex, but they were darned comfortable and comforting.

Did she want to remind Grady of sex? With her? Of

course not. But having him thinking she looked a frump
was hard to swallow, too. Those new trousers with the
loose waistband looked okay if she wore a long top over
them. Reaching into the wardrobe she heard Grady calling again. Too late. Frump look it was.

'That was as delicious as it smelt when I arrived home.'
Sasha pushed her plate away after her second helping of
rice and pork. 'I'm impressed.'

His grin was cocky. 'Wait till you taste my seafood
paella.'

'Guess I'll have to give that a miss. Seafood is out
while I'm pregnant. Listeria is a concern.'

'So if I go out scalloping with Ian next week, you
won't be able to eat any?' His grin just got bigger. 'You
will hate that.'

'True. But the season will still be open when my baby
arrives so I'll make up for any I've missed out on then.'

Grady gathered up their plates. 'Are you going to work
right up until you have her?'

'Definitely. Unless something goes wrong, high blood
pressure, that sort of thing. I don't see why not.' She
needed the money.

'When is the girl you're covering for due back?'

'Karen's returning about a month after I'm due. Jess
is going to cover for both of us during that time. Nicholas, her little boy, will have to go to playgroup every day,
but that's no hardship. He loves it.'

Grady placed the plates in the sink and asked, 'Do
you want ice cream? It's boysenberry.'

Still her favourite flavour. 'Low blow. How can I resist?'

Opening the freezer, he asked another question. 'What

will you do for a job after your maternity leave is up? You said something about a permanent job but with Jess and this other nurse the centre won't need you, will they?'

'There's talk about me job sharing with Karen so we both have time off with our babies.' Half-pay would be better than none. Once she was more confident with Flipper she might have to look at moving over to Nelson and a full-time position, but at the moment she didn't intend worrying about that. She had saved and invested a lot of money during her years working in Dubai, though that was for a deposit on a house some time, not for everyday expenses. But enough of talking about her. 'Have you got a job to return to once your house is on the market?'

He leaned that mouth-watering butt against the bench and folded his arms across his chest. His eyes seemed to be searching her face, looking for who knew what. His answer, when it finally came, rocked her. 'There's a contract waiting for me to sign at the practice I qualified from in Auckland. But I like the idea of being a locum for a while. Being here and working a couple of shifts has got me thinking.'

'About working here?' she squeaked. 'As in Golden Bay?' Please, no. Not that. For a start, there weren't any vacancies at the medical centre. Though the three doctors were often bemoaning the fact they never got much time off.

'Would that be so bad?' He was serious.

For her peace of mind, yes, it would. She was still getting used to being back home herself, starting to really relax and let go the past that involved city living, a big job and lots of people always in her face. People who hurt her, broke her trust.

But at the same time Golden Bay and Grady went

hand in hand—for her anyway. She'd only known him since she was a teen but that year she'd met him on Pohara Beach had been big. She'd given him her heart in this place. She'd planned a future with him here.

Grady was waiting for her reply, still leaning against the bench, only now he looked as though he needed the cabinet's support. His eyes had darkened as they bored right inside her.

Hopefully he didn't see her confusion. Because she sure didn't understand her own feelings right now. She wasn't sure she couldn't trust him again. She also knew he made her feel safe, made her feel as though he'd do anything for her. Made her feel, full stop.

On the table her hands were shaking so she shoved them on her thighs out of his sight. 'No, Grady, it's not a problem for me.' That was the biggest fib she could've come up with.

Her reply didn't make him look relieved. Not at all. 'But you'd prefer it if I didn't.'

Standing up, she crossed to stand directly in front of him. 'Grady, I'm still settling in myself. It's a permanent move for me.' She crossed her fingers. 'Mum's going to need more and more attention as the MS progresses, though hopefully that will be a while away. And I'd like Flipper to start her life in a place that teaches community values, where she has family and friends who'll always be there for her, no matter what.'

'The same things that are making me feel more comfortable than I've felt in years, and I didn't grow up here.' With his forefinger he lifted a strand of hair from her cheek and slipped it behind her ear. 'The things that remind me of you.'

Gulp. Move. Away. From. Grady. Now.

Her feet were lead weights, so heavy she couldn't shift. Lifting her gaze, she locked eyes with him. Saw a need in those cerulean orbs. A need for her. Gulp. This is not meant to be. *So move.*

He said, 'Want to go for a walk along the beach? There's a full moon tonight.'

Hello? Weren't we talking about you maybe moving to Golden Bay? 'Sure, I'd like that.' Huh? What happened to moving away from him, putting distance between them?

'Grab a coat, then. We'll cut through the properties at the end of the road. Hopefully the moonlight will be enough.'

'Almost daylight,' Sasha quipped, as she tripped over a large piece of driftwood at the edge of the sand.

Grady draped an arm over her shoulders and tugged her in beside him. 'You're supposed to watch where you're going.'

'Then I wouldn't see the stars above or the tide rushing up the beach, tossing shells in front of it.' Somehow her arm found its way around his waist. Walking on the beach with Grady brought back so many beautiful memories. 'We brought the CD player down to the beach and danced the night away. You ran the cable for it from your house through the flax bushes to the beach. Anyone coming down to join us tripped over the cord and let us know they were coming.' Giving us time to straighten ourselves up a bit.

'We fell asleep on the sand and woke up when the tide came in, soaking us. Didn't do the CD player any good.'

'We went skinny-dipping after everyone had gone to bed.'

'Except half my mates were already out here, doing the same thing with their girlfriends.' Grady laughed;

a deep, full laugh she hadn't heard once since he'd turned up again in Golden Bay.

Warmth seeped under her jacket, stole through her heart. 'You used to laugh a lot.'

'We didn't have a care in the world, did we? Thought life was wonderful and couldn't understand how quickly and drastically it could change.' Removing his arm from her shoulders, he took her hand in his as they continued along the beach.

Sneaking a glance up at him, a smile curved her lips. His generous mouth that could kiss her blind was also smiling. This she had missed. Face it, she'd missed Grady and hadn't been able to replace him, no matter how hard she'd tried. Swinging their joined hands, she let go of the tension that had been gripping her for days and made the most of walking in the moonlight with the man who'd stolen her heart so long ago.

They turned for home and Grady stopped, placed his hands on her shoulders and gently drew her closer. Her body leant towards him, bending slightly at the waist, or where her waist used to be. Her lips parted as her tongue slid out over the bottom one. Like she wanted to taste him.

She couldn't resist him. It was beyond her. When his head lowered and his mouth covered hers she leaned closer. Inhaled that spicy man scent that was Grady. The scent that had been driving her nuts in her vehicle. The man who'd been waking her up, day by day, bringing her out of hibernation to feel again. To remind her of great sex, of love, of needs that had been shut down far too long. Her mouth opened under his, welcomed his probing tongue.

This is Sash. My love. Grady shifted slightly, wrapped

his arms around Sash's waist and pulled her as close to his body as possible. His muscles remembered her. Especially those south of his belt. As he lost himself in kissing her, tasting her, feeling her plastered against his chest, belly, thighs, he went into sensory overload.

Forgot everything except Sash. The sweet honeysuckle scent on her skin. Her mouth that teased and tormented as it went from sweet and demure to saucy and sexy in a flash. As though he'd woken her up. Those breasts pressed against his chest were bigger than he remembered, ripe from her pregnancy. His hands itched to touch, cup them; his thumbs needed to rub her nipples until they peaked.

Her hands were holding his head so that he couldn't lift his mouth from hers. Her fingers were threaded through his hair, pummelling his scalp with their tips.

He felt something against his lower gut. What the—? Comprehension rushed in, had him peeling his lips off hers. 'Is that the baby? Did I just feel her kick?'

'You felt Flipper?' Astonishment crossed her face, dashed away the slumberous look that had been growing with the deepening of their kiss. 'Truly?'

'There was a small thud.' He stared in wonder at the baby bulge resting against him. 'Unbelievable.' He'd once had the opportunity to feel a baby's movements when he'd been doing his training, but this—this couldn't be more different. This was Sasha and her baby.

That green-eyed monster stirred. Grady pushed it right back where it had come from. He didn't own Sasha. She owed him nothing. He'd sent her packing, freed her from loving him, so he had no right to feel jealous of the man she'd obviously had more than a passing fling with. But where was the man?

Sasha pushed out of his arms, tugged her shirt up and then grabbed his hand to place it on her belly. 'Here.'

His palm on her skin, his fingers pressing against her flesh. Unbelievable. Sensory overload. Then he felt it. A nudge from inside Sash's belly. Wow. And again. 'That's… That's amazing.'

Sash was grinning like crazy. 'Isn't it? Amazing. That's going on in my tummy. My baby girl. She's something else.'

His other hand seemed to have a life of its own, reaching for Sash's face, cupping her cheek. His thumb traced over her jaw, along her chin and up to her sweet, sexy mouth. 'I have never known anything so unbelievable. This is real. Your baby. Nothing like what I learned in med school.'

She chuckled. 'I'd hope not. Though it is exactly the same really. But it is amazing. I never get tired of feeling Flipper go ballistic in there.'

'Especially after last night.'

'Exactly.' Her face contorted briefly.

'Another kick?' He slid his hand across her stomach to where her hand flattened and pressed down. 'Here?'

Her head dipped in acknowledgement. Her eyes glittered with love and excitement. 'I can't wait to meet her. To see what she looks like, what colour her hair and eyes are.' Then the glitter faded, replaced with worry. 'I shouldn't have said that. I'm tempting fate. I don't know what I'd do if it happened again.'

Wrapping his arms around her waist, he tugged her close, enjoying that pushing stomach against his solar plexus. 'You are so lucky.'

'You think so?'

'I know so.' In more ways than one. Hell, he'd been

an idiot when he'd told her to get on with her life without him.

Those lush lips spread into a wide smile. 'So do I.'

That smile hit him in the gut, sending desire spinning out of control, heating the corners of his body, his heart, where he'd been cold for eleven long years. When his mouth covered hers a groan rolled up his throat from that pool of need and spilled into her mouth. Under his lips her mouth opened further, allowing him deeper access. He tasted Sash. Her fire and sweetness, her softness and strength. And he was lost.

He had to have her. Taking her hand, he began pulling her along the beach as fast as it was safe to go in the near dark. 'We might have wonderful memories of what we got up to out here but it's winter, not summer. Let's carry this on back at your place.' As long as she didn't change her mind about kissing him before they got there. Leaning down, he held her close for a quick kiss. Raced a few metres and stopped for another one. They ran and kissed all the way back to the warmth of her cottage.

Immediately they got through the front door he pulled her into him, as though they could melt into one. He knew only the woman in his arms. Then her breasts slid up his chest as she stretched up on her toes to push her fingers into his hair. Breasts that had swollen with pregnancy. Breasts that felt soft and yielding, yet their peaks were as hard as pebbles as they moved against his oversensitised chest. And then they were filling his hands where he'd slipped under her bra.

Then Sash twisted in his arms, feverishly tugging her shirt over her head, reaching behind to unclip the annoying bra. At the same time her baby bump rubbed up against him and he dropped his hands to touch and feel and hold. When she stood naked from the waist up a lump blocked his breathing. 'You are so beautiful,' he finally managed to croak as his hands kept caressing her extended belly. 'Utterly beautiful.'

And then he couldn't think any more as those small hands gripped his shirt and pulled him near. Her fingers plucked at the buttons of his shirt, working their way deftly down from his neck to his waist, exposing his chest bit by bit, her lips touching him with each new exposure.

Swinging Sash up into his arms, he strode to her bedroom and lowered her onto the bed, all the while kissing that swollen mouth, unable to break the contact.

Sash pulled her mouth free. 'Make love to me, Grady.' Her hands trembled as they unzipped his trousers and took his manhood, caressing and teasing.

He needed no invitation, had been waiting for this since the night on Takaka Hill when she'd slipped back into his life. He shucked his trousers, helped Sash remove hers, and then he was touching her intimately. She was wet for him, instantly arching into his hand.

'Sash, baby, take your hand off me.'

Her slumberous eyes blinked at him. 'No way, sunshine. I like what I'm feeling.'

'Sash,' he ground through clenched teeth. 'I won't last if you keep doing that.'

'You're not meant to. Ahh,' she gulped. 'Don't stop, whatever you do. Don't. Stop. That.' And then her body was convulsing against his hand. And still she rubbed him. And then he rose over her, pushed inside, felt her heat envelop him and knew no more except the waves of hot need exploding from him as he drove into Sash again and again.

CHAPTER TEN

SASH TUGGED THE quilt over their naked bodies and snuggled against the hard, muscular length filling her bed that was Grady. His arm encircled her below her baby bump, pulling her as close to him as possible.

Her brain was sluggish, filled with warmth and the aftermath of their lovemaking. 'I've missed that,' she whispered to herself. The instant inferno that always came with Grady touching her. She'd even begun to believe it was all in her imagination, made brighter as each year passed. Now she knew she'd been right. And her body wanted it again.

His hand slid over her breast to cup it. When he stroked her nipple she luxuriated in the erotic sensations flicking out from that point to touch her toes, her thighs, both breasts, lips and fingers. Her tummy.

My pregnant tummy.

The reason she should not be lying naked in bed with Grady. Her baby girl would expect her not to make mistakes, did not deserve to have her mother bring a man into their lives who'd sooner or later leave them. Not even when she might be falling in love with that man again.

Oh, help. What have I done?

Sent Grady all the wrong messages for a start. Sent

those same messages to her heart as well. Now she had to undo it all.

'Sash?' Grady murmured by her ear. 'You okay?'

No. No, she was not okay. She'd just made the biggest mistake of her life. Rolling out of his arms, she pushed to the other, cold side of her bed and sat up, tugging the quilt under her chin and all around her.

'Sash? What's up?' Grady sat up, too, reached to take her hand.

She moved right to the edge of the bed. 'No, Grady. Don't.'

Click. Yellow light flooded the room from her bedside light and Grady focused that steady gaze on her. 'I'm not understanding what's going on here.'

Neither did she. What had possessed her to have sex with him? Like she could've stopped. She'd been seized by such an overwhelming need for him her brain had fried and all reason had evaporated. Now she had to face reality, only it had just got complicated. 'This has got to stop. We can't do this again. It shouldn't have happened at all. We are not getting back together, ever.'

'Why not?'

Snapping her eyes shut, she prayed for control. She so wanted to hurl herself into his arms and beg him to make love to her again. But it was wrong. Completely wrong. Opening her eyes, she stared at him, forced a wave of need aside, and struggled to remain calm and focused. 'You can't possibly think we're going to have an affair while you're here?'

'Unless you're still in a relationship with your baby's father, why can't we get to know each other again? The chemistry's certainly still there.'

He wasn't listening. 'I do not want a relationship.'

How blunt could she be? Did she need to bang him over the head to get him to understand? She leapt out of bed, fumbled around for her robe and shoved into it.

Grady stood, too, those thoughtful eyes watching her closely, hurt mingling with confusion as he asked, 'Are you hanging out for the baby's father to return to you? Because if you are, I would understand.'

A shudder rocked her. 'I never want to see Freddy again. Of course, if he changes his mind about being a part of Flipper's life then I won't deny him access. She deserves a father, even Freddy.' But move back in with him? No way.

His shoulders relaxed a little as he began dressing. 'Sash—'

'Stop calling me that,' she all but yelled. Being called Sash undermined her determination to stop whatever was going on between them before it got out of control. If it hadn't already. Being called Sash reminded her of so many things about Grady she did not need to remember as she fought to keep him at arm's length.

That hurt in his gaze deepened. 'Talk to me, Sasha. Tell me what's really behind this? Do you not feel anything for me? Apart from the sex?'

Pain scudded through her heart. He didn't deserve this. Oh, he'd been doing a good job of stepping up for her lately. But she had a child to consider, to put before him or even herself. And she'd do anything for her baby. Sucking in a deep breath, she let rip. 'Just go, Grady. We are not meant for each other. Otherwise you'd never have dumped me.'

'I did it out of love for you.'

Make it worse, why don't you? 'Sorry, I'm not buying into that.' She brushed past him on the way out of her bedroom. She had to make him leave. Now. Before the threatening flood of tears won out over her precarious control. She headed straight for the front door, hauled it open, and shivered in the icy blast of night air. 'Please, go.' Her voice squeaked around that ball of tears.

He stood in front of her, his hands in his pockets, legs splayed and chest forward. His gaze was unwavering. 'I did it for you, Sasha. Believe me.'

'Really? You hurt me so much I went completely off the rails so that I nearly killed myself by pushing the boundaries too far. You did that for my own good?' She was nearly screaming at him now and the words would not stop. 'I have lived with the knowledge that the man I once loved with all my being did not love me back. Not enough anyway. He didn't want to share his pain, his family, his future with me. I was only good enough for the fun times, not the real nitty-gritty living stuff.'

His hands slapped his hips, his fingers white where they dug in, but he didn't step away from her tirade. 'I believed I was looking out for you by giving you your freedom to get on with the plans you'd made for your career and future. You own the dangerous stuff.'

'My future was with you.' Nothing had been more important than Grady.

'You'd dreamed of being a nurse since you were ten.'

'I could've trained in Nelson while you looked after your family. Did that ever occur to you? Did you ever think to ask me if we could rearrange our plans?' Her mouth snapped shut, her teeth banging hard. Her throat clogged with years of emotions. Those darned tears began falling. She had to get away from Grady. But more words spewed forth. 'Of course you didn't. Because apparently you didn't love me. You do remember telling me that, don't you? And now you have the audacity to say you did it for me.'

'I'm not denying anything. I did tell you I didn't love you because you wouldn't listen to me. I—'

'You're making it my fault now?'

'No, Sasha, I'm not.' His hands gripped tighter. 'It was a weird time. I was struggling to deal with Dad's passing, with having to put my plans on hold and step up for Mum, and then there was you. I didn't feel I could ask you to hang around waiting while I sorted my family out.'

Her heart squeezed. Not for her, but for Grady. 'You could have said what you've just said now. We might've been able to sort something out.'

'Would you have listened?'

'I'd have done anything to be with you.' Had she missed something back then? If she had, then so had Grady. He hadn't understood what her love for him meant. 'Anything.'

'I couldn't ask that of you.'

With one hand on his shoulder she pushed him out the door. 'Go home, Grady. We're done.'

That hurt was back in his beautiful eyes. 'You're sure about that?'

No. Not at all. It would be so easy to curl up against his chest and let him take over, be strong for her, love her. But the little girl kicking her tummy right now needed her to find her own strength. 'Yes, I am.'

'Meet me at the café for lunch,' Jess muttered, as she walked out of the office at the medical centre.

'Not hungry,' Sasha muttered back, as she avoided bumping into Grady.

'Maybe not, but you need some girlfriend time. You're looking like hell this morning. Twelve o'clock. Don't be late. I've got a full afternoon.' Jess disappeared down the hall to the nurses' room.

She could always rely on Jess to be honest. And bossy. 'Too honest for your own good,' she complained at her friend at midday as she slid onto a wooden chair in the café. 'What's this?' She eyed the bowls of pumpkin and bacon soup alongside the plate of freshly baked bread rolls before her.

'It's called food. Something Flipper needs.' Jess leaned back against her chair and studied her in a very disconcerting way.

'What? Have I got bird droppings in my hair?'

'What's with you and Grady this morning? It's like you're both afraid to go near each other.' No mucking about with Jess.

'Sort of.' Afraid of where another touch from Grady might lead, more like.

'Spill.' Jess spread a light dash of butter on her warm bun and bit into it. Her eyes lit up. 'Heaven. Jonesy knows a thing or two about baking bread.'

About to take the diversion and run with it, Sasha hesitated. Stirring her spoon round and round in her soup, she thought about Grady and making love and kicking him out afterwards and how she felt she'd done the wrong thing. She did need to talk. 'Grady stayed late last night.'

Jess looked funny with her jaw stopped in mid-chew. 'As in he and you did it?'

'Something like that.'

'Either you did or you didn't.'

'Yeah, we did.' Sipping the hot soup gave her time to

rerun through her mind her final words to him. 'Then I kicked him out. For ever.'

'Why?'

Placing her spoon down on the plate, she gave up pretending to want to eat. 'We talked about back when we broke up.'

'That's good. Isn't it?'

Her shoulders lifted, dropped. 'Probably. But he won't accept that I'd have stayed with him if only he'd told me what was going on with his mother and sisters. He didn't want me to give up my plans for him.'

'Sounds kind of noble,' said the voice of reason opposite her.

'He didn't give me any choice, made my decisions for me.'

'I wouldn't have left him. But I guess he knew that and that's why he said he'd stopped loving me. Why didn't I think about the whole situation, Jess? Why didn't I ask him how he could say he didn't love me when a week before he'd told me he'd die if anything came between us?'

'Melodramatic, but he was only eighteen.' Jess buttered another bun. 'Same as you. I don't think we have all our brain cells functioning properly at that age, especially when hormones are involved.'

'And now I'm dealing with babymones.' Should she wait until Flipper was born to think this through? As if that would work.

'Yep. Give yourself time, spend some of it with Grady, get to know him all over.'

Did that last night. 'You mean all over *again*.' Picking up the spoon, she tasted the soup and rolled her eyes. 'This is yummy.' Maybe eating wasn't such a bad idea after all.

'Want to go to the pub one night soon? Have some fun? I hear they're doing a great milk and vanilla cocktail for pregnant women.'

A girls' night out sounded perfect right now. 'What about Nicholas? You could leave him with Mum and Dad.'

'I'll call them tonight. So we're on? Cool. Now eat some bread with that soup. It's good for you both.'

Grady hauled the rope in, hand over hand, straining as the weight of the dredge tried to defy him. 'Reckon we've got a full load in this sucker.'

Ian leaned over the side and peered down into the murky water. 'I see it. Look at all those lovely scallops. My mouth's watering already. Sasha's going to hate us for getting these.'

Sasha hates me already. A few scallops won't make the slightest difference. 'The blue cod will make up for not being allowed shellfish.'

'You think?' Ian's eyes twinkled as he took one side of the dredge and helped haul it into the boat. 'These are her favourite shellfish.'

Yeah, he remembered. She used to eat them raw while they were opening the shells, and then be back for a large helping when they'd been cooked on the barbecue.

Together he and Ian tipped their catch onto the deck, along with the seaweed and starfish also caught in the dredge. 'We must have at least a hundred good scallops in that lot.'

Jack slowly lowered to his knees and began tossing the obviously too small scallops back overboard. 'This

is a good haul for so early in the season. Don't tell anyone about it.'

'This is Golden Bay. People will know before we hit
the beach.' Ian hunkered down too.

'Want to do another run?' Grady looked up at the
sky. 'I take that back. The weather's starting to close in.
Better head for home.'

He began coiling the rope attached to the dredge,
making meticulous loops in the bin before placing the
dredge on top. Then he washed down the deck with buck-
ets of salt water, getting rid of the worst of the mud and
mess. A good hose down back home would finish the
job. It'd also help keep him occupied and his mind off
Sasha. As if that was at all possible.

'How's the redecorating coming along?' Ian asked,
as he tossed a handful of large shellfish into the bucket.

'I'm over watching the paint dry, that's for sure. Painting in the cold winter air was asking for delays. I've got
the plumber doing a refit of the bathroom next week.'
He'd never intended doing that but on Saturday he'd
walked in for a shower and found a crack in the old
glass panel. Then he'd taken a really good look at the
room and gone to phone the plumber. 'So much for just
a lick of paint.'

Jack paused his sorting to ask, 'You doing the place
up for yourself, or putting it on the market?'

'Probably selling it, if I can. I haven't used it since
Dad died. It's gone backwards over the years. Needs
someone living there most of the time to breathe life
back into it.' But a big part of him did not want to let the
place go now that he'd had time back here.

Staring out over the sea as he directed the nose of the
boat for the shore, he could hear the laughter of nights

spent on the front lawn of the house with his family and friends. Eating barbecued fish and scallops, drinking beer, having plain old, carefree fun. His heart yearned for that again. Yearned to be able to get up in the morning, every morning, and pull back the curtains to reveal the bay spread as far as the eye could see. To know the sea and sand would be waiting when he got home from work. To have a family to enjoy it with. To share the barbecued food again.

To have the impossible dream.

It all came back to Sasha.

CHAPTER ELEVEN

'ANOTHER WEEK NEARLY OVER.' On Friday Sasha stopped in at home for a late lunch before heading out on the rest of her house calls. Thank goodness the weekend was nearly here. Unfortunately the week had been quiet, keeping her hanging around the medical centre more than usual, stocking shelves with bandages and syringes, cleaning out her kit, doing inventories. Ignoring Grady when he turned up to do a half-day for Rory on Wednesday and again on Thursday.

'At least we had antenatal clinic this morning, eh, Flipper? Kind of fun being with other pregnant mums and doing their check-ups.' Jess had gone with Nicholas and his playgroup to visit Natureland in Nelson. 'Nicholas was so excited about seeing the monkeys he nearly wet himself. His little face was wide with excitement. Think you'll like monkeys, my girl?'

No answer from in there.

'Okay. What do you want for lunch? One of those fruit buns I bought yesterday or reheated tomato soup?' None of it sounded very appealing. 'I promise to go to the supermarket on the way home and get us some proper food.'

Her cell rang as Flipper nudged her. A glance at the screen and, 'Hi, Mike. What have you got for me?'

'Tamara Tucker, eighteen years old, has severe back and abdomen pains. She's out at Totaranui Camping Ground and doesn't have any way of getting into town to see us. I want you to head out there.'

'Totaranui?' About an hour away over a rough, narrow winding road that could be slippery at this time of year. 'She had to have got out there somehow. It's not on a main road to anywhere.'

'Tell me something I don't know. Apparently she and her boyfriend were dropped off on the other side by the charter boat and walked across to the camping ground where friends were supposed to have joined them for a few days.'

'The friends haven't turned up.'

'You've got it. Now, Sasha…' Mike's tone changed, turned quiet and calm.

What was she in for now? Bumps lifted on her skin. 'Ye-es?'

'Can you pick up Grady on your way? He's getting ready as we speak. Just in case this is an emergency.'

She'd seen it coming the moment Mike's tone had altered but that didn't prevent the punch to her gut. Grady. In the car with her. For an hour. And another hour on the way back. *Suck it up, girl. This is your job.* 'On my way. Will keep you posted once we get to Totaranui in case we need outside help. Is the warden there?'

'According to Tamara's boyfriend, he left early this morning for supplies in town. There aren't any other campers either.'

'Who in their right mind would be out there at this time of year?' Sasha asked Flipper, as she stuffed two buns in a plastic bag and filled her water bottle. 'At least I don't have to decide what we're having for lunch.'

Outside Grady's house she tapped the horn but he didn't appear. Climbing out of the Jeep, she stomped up to the wide-open front door. The smell of fresh paint hit her. No wonder all the windows were also open. The house would be freezing inside but getting the paint dry was obviously a problem. 'Grady? You ready?'

Silence.

She'd taken one step inside when Grady appeared, striding out of one room on the way to the kitchen. Rubbing his hair with a towel. Naked as the day he was born.

She stared, unable to even blink. Her mouth dried as she took in the sight of moving muscles, that wide chest with its sprinkling of fine black hair, of a washboard stomach, of his male tackle. Two weeks ago she'd slept with him, had had him inside her, and yet nothing measured up to the sight filling her eyes. He was stunning. He'd filled out into a very beautiful man from the teen he'd been last time she'd known him.

'Grady,' she squeaked, as he reached the kitchen doorway.

Unfortunately he heard her, because she hadn't intended making her presence known.

Grady stopped, leaned back to look directly at her. 'Sash. I didn't realise you'd be here this soon.'

Obviously. 'I'll wait for you outside.' She ran to her vehicle, leapt in and slammed the door. His image followed her, filling her head, sending her hormones into a riot of activity, heating the chill that had lain over her since she'd sent him away. Ten minutes ago she'd thought having to ride with Grady would be difficult. Now she knew it would be impossible.

What was she supposed to do? A young woman needed help from both of them. Somehow she'd have to dig deep and pull on a mantle to hide behind for as long as this job took. She couldn't do it. She had to. It was impossible. Tough. Do it. Now. Before Grady comes out of that house and gets in beside me.

The passenger door opened and Grady's large frame, fully clothed, filled the periphery of her view. 'I'd been sanding the table and was covered in dust when Mike rang. Thought I'd have time for a shower before you turned up.'

As far as an explanation went she couldn't fault it. Didn't make the trip into Totaranui any easier, though. Funny how, even when concentrating hard on the difficult road, she still had that image of Grady firmly in the front of her head.

They hadn't even come to a stop when a young man ran towards them from a nearby hut. 'Am I glad to see you. Tamara's in a lot of pain. Screaming and crying all the time.'

Grady hopped out and extended his hand to the young guy. 'Grady O'Neil, doctor, and this is Nurse Sasha Wilson. You are…?'

The lad's hand shook when he gripped Grady's hand. 'Sorry. Tamara's boyfriend. Kevin Sparkes. She thinks it's her appendix. She's got a rumbling one or something.'

'Right, Kevin, how long has Tamara been having pain? And where is it centred mostly?' Grady took the medical kit off Sasha and ignored the scowl she gave him.

Kevin began filling them in with details as he led them to the cabin he and Tamara had hired. 'Man, she's hurting, curling up with the pain at times. I was real frightened, man. Especially when she started getting worse. Didn't know what to do. There's no one here.' He waved a hand around the camp site. 'No one.'

'You did the right thing phoning the medical centre.' Sasha trotted along on Kevin's other side.

In the cabin Tamara lay across the bunk; a large girl dressed in loose trackpants and sweatshirt. She was moaning and gripping her stomach. Then she stopped, breathing deeply.

Grady figured he knew what the problem was immediately but had to approach Tamara and her situation delicately. After he'd introduced Sasha and himself, he waited while Sasha went through the motions of checking her pulse and BP. The loaded glance Sasha gave him as she said, 'All normal,' told him she was onto it, too.

Sitting on the edge of the bunk Grady asked, 'Tamara, is it all right if I lift your top and feel your abdomen area?'

The girl nodded. 'What do you think is wrong with me?'

Uh-huh. His hand felt the contraction as Tamara suddenly gasped and snatched at Kevin's hand. A scream filled the small room, piercing in its intensity. Grady waited, nodding at Sasha who'd grabbed the girl's other hand.

When the contraction had passed, Sasha asked quietly, 'When did you last have a period?'

'Why?' Tamara blinked. 'I don't remember. I'm never regular. What's that got to do with anything anyway? This is my appendix, right?'

Grady drew a long, slow breath. 'You're having a baby, Tamara.'

The girl stared at him as though he'd lost his marbles. 'No way. That's not possible. I'd have known. You can't just have a baby and not know. I'm not stupid.'

Sasha still held her hand. 'No one's saying you're stupid. If you don't have regular periods then you wouldn't necessarily notice when you missed them. Have you had one in the last few months?'

'Yes, of course I have.' But Tamara's focus was directed on the wall behind them. Tears were oozing down her face. 'I must have.'

Kevin spoke up for the first time in a while. 'A baby? We're having a kid? No way, man. We're too young. I haven't even got a job. No, can't happen.' He pushed Grady out of the way and hauled his girlfriend into his arms. 'I'll get you to another doctor, Tam. This is crazy.'

Another contraction rippled through Tamara and she screamed louder than ever, holding onto Kevin as though her life depended on him.

As soon as the pain faded Grady said, 'I know you don't want to believe me but think about it. You're having contractions. That's what the pain is.'

Sasha added, 'I've been timing them and they're quite close. We need to examine you internally, Tamara. Are you okay about that?'

The girl nodded slowly, gulping as more tears splashed down her pale face. 'I guess. Um, it feels like I have to push my stomach out. Is the baby trying to come out?'

'I imagine so,' Grady told her. 'Let's take a look and then we'll know what's going on.' So much for a lead-in time while everyone got a little bit used to this unexpected situation. How hadn't Tamara detected any changes in her body over the previous several months? She was a large girl but she must've noticed some weight gain. Glancing across at Sasha, he saw her doing that tummy rub thing and looking a little baffled at the situation. Hadn't Tamara felt the baby kicking?

Hell, she won't have had any bloods taken for blood grouping or antibody checks. Too late now. He'd cross his fingers and hope for a normal delivery with no hidden problems. Because, even without looking, he doubted they had time to get back to Takaka before this baby made an appearance.

Sasha helped Tamara remove her pants and gently settled her back on the bunk before placing a glove-covered hand on her knee. 'I know this isn't easy, Tamara, but try to relax. Let your legs drop wide. There, that's it. Dr O'Neil will examine you. Are you all right with that?'

'Yes,' she whispered, and grabbed for Kevin's hand again.

One look and Grady turned to Sasha, asking, 'Have you got a sterile blanket in your medical kit?'

'We always carry one in a sealed pack, in case of exactly this. Not that I ever thought I'd have to use it.' She shook her head. 'I can't imagine…'

The look of disbelief in her eyes made him want to haul her in tight and reassure her. She'd done everything right so far. Sash didn't turn a blind eye to the tricky things life threw at her. No, she pulled those shoulders back and straightened her spine to face the world head on. 'Sasha, get the blanket, will you?' Grady nudged her towards the door. 'Quickly,' he added quietly, so as not to panic Tamara. 'I don't think we've got long to wait.'

Tamara went rigid as another contraction hit. This time she held back her scream, instead burying her face in Kevin's shirt. Almost as though now she knew what she faced the fear generated by the pain had gone. But she'd have more fears later when her situation really sank in.

Kevin seemed to be in total shock, barely managing to hold Tamara as she clung to him. 'We need to get to a hospital. She can't have her baby here.'

These two were barely more than kids themselves, and they'd just learned they were about to become parents, that life as they knew it was over for ever. Or had they even got that far yet? Probably not.

'The baby's head's crowning,' Grady told the young couple. 'That means it's coming out. We don't have time to take you back to town.'

'What? You mean Tam's having the baby here? But she can't. That's wrong. What if something goes wrong?'

'It won't,' Grady told Kevin. 'Now, this is how you can help Tamara.'

And they got down to the business of delivering a baby in a cabin in the back of beyond. It happened so fast no one had time to raise any more doubts.

Soon Grady was handing a tiny baby into Sasha's safe hands and the wrap she'd found in her bag of tricks so she could clear the airway and wipe out his mouth. 'Tamara, Kevin, congratulations, you've got a little boy.'

Kevin whistled. 'A boy. How cool's that, man?'

'A boy? Truly?' Tamara's eyes followed every movement Sasha made with her baby. 'It's Jordan. He's come back.'

'Who's Jordan?' Grady asked.

'My little brother.' Tamara stared at the baby, hunger filling her eyes. 'Let me see him. Can I hold him?' Tamara tried to push herself upright.

Grady leaned to give her a hand. 'Not too far. The afterbirth's coming.'

Kevin filled them in. 'Jordan was killed when Tamara's aunt backed over him in the driveway. No one in her family's been the same since.'

Sasha froze for a moment. 'That's utterly terrible.' Then she resumed checking the baby's vitals. He gave a little cry. 'There you go. His first cry. He's so cute. Here, Tamara, meet your son.' Tears streamed down Sasha's face as she, oh, so gently placed the baby in his mother's arms. 'He's just beautiful. Look, ten toes, ten fingers. And look at all that dark hair.' The tears became a flood before she turned and ran outside, banging the door behind her.

Tamara and Kevin didn't even notice, they were so absorbed in their baby. Grady cleaned up as best he could and then said, 'I'll give you a minute to yourselves,' and headed out to find Sasha leaning against the car, sobbing her heart out.

Grady placed an arm around her shoulders, tugged her close, handed her a fistful of tissues he'd snatched from her medical kit on the way out. 'Hey, look at you. If you're like this for Tamara's baby, what'll you be like when Flipper arrives?' He grinned down at her. Swallowed at the awe glittering in her eyes. 'Guess seeing this is different for you now.'

'When I was training as a nurse and saw babies being born I never knew this tugging of the heart. I fell in love with each one but…' She waved a hand in the direction of the cabin, 'Oh, wow. He's so cute and tiny and vulnerable and helpless and all covered in mucky stuff.'

'Yep, all of those. And some.' Her body shook against him and he wrapped her closer, rubbed her back in circular motions to ease the tightness he felt in her muscles. 'And very special. Just like Flipper is.'

'How are those two going to manage?' she sniffed. 'They didn't even know.'

'Yes, well. It's kind of sad. But who knows? They could step up to be the best parents ever.' Grady continued to rub her back. 'I wonder where they come from? They've obviously been through a huge trauma with her brother.'

'We need to get them to Takaka and in touch with their family. This baby's arrival might be what they all need.' There was a waver in her voice, and under his hands he felt Sasha straightening, stiffening her shoulders, putting on her brave face again. The moment of tears was over.

Dropping a kiss on the top of her head, he stepped away, and instantly felt cold. Sash was such a part of him he didn't know how to stop missing her whenever he wasn't touching her. Which was almost all the time, especially since they'd made love and she'd kicked him out. Hell, he missed her all the time, full stop.

'You sure you're okay?'

'It's babymones.' He must've looked blank because she explained. 'Pregnancy hormones. A Jessica word. They knock me sideways at the most unexpected times. Have me crying and doing things I shouldn't be doing.'

Like making love with me. It hung between them. He could see the truth in her eyes before she turned for the cabin. She was blaming her hormones for giving in to the need that had rolled through her the other night. Newsflash, Sash. Sex was all about hormones, too. And love, and being with someone special. He must have babymones, too. Because he sure hadn't been in control that night either.

* * *

Sasha yawned and stretched. Where was she? Peeling her eyes open, she stared at the interior of her car, then looked outside at the house she was parked in front of. 'That's Colleen Simmonds's house, Flipper. How did I get here? Did you drive?'

Right then the answer appeared at the house's front door. Everything clicked into place. 'Grady.' He'd offered to drive her on her rounds after they'd dropped Tamara, Kevin and the baby at the maternity unit in town.

'Sleeping Beauty awakes.' The vehicle rocked as Grady slid behind the steering-wheel. 'Well timed. We're finished for the day.'

'I'm sorry. Don't know what came over me.' Sasha yawned. Had she really slept through the whole round? Couldn't have. But she'd been exhausted. This was going to look bad when Mike and Rory found out. Not the way to impress them. It would be another black mark against her when her performance assessment came up. That permanent job seemed to be slipping ever further away. 'Why didn't you wake me?'

'You needed the sleep and I can handle a few dressings and BP readings.' He gave her that gut-crunching grin. 'Just.'

'Thanks. But there's a problem. The doctors at the centre are hardly going to give me a permanent job if I don't do the one I've already got properly.'

'They don't need to know any different.'

'Right, Grady. This is Golden Bay, not Auckland.'

'True.' He seemed damned pleased with himself as he drove.

'Okay, I admit I'm grateful. Thank you.' She'd deal with Mike and Rory on Monday.

Then Grady pulled into his drive, and turned to look at her. 'Would you like some blue cod for your dinner? Freshly caught this morning.'

She should say no. It wasn't fair to banish Grady from her life and then take the fish out of his hands. But who turned down fresh blue cod? She licked her lips. 'Yes, please.'

Grady's eyes seemed stuck on her mouth. When was she going to learn not to do things like that around the man? His eyes were lightening with desire that in turn sent shivers of desire over her skin. Take control, Sasha. Get the heck out of here.

No way was she sliding across from one side to the other while he sat gawping at her. Shoving her door open, she stepped out to go round the front of the car. But her action had distracted that gaze. Grady was out of the car and striding up to his front door. 'Come inside while I put the fish in a bag.'

She shouldn't go in there. The house wasn't big enough for the two of them. Seemed her feet had other ideas because she quickly found herself standing in the lounge, looking around at the new paintwork. A soft terracotta shade covered the walls, making the room feel warm despite all the windows being open. It was lovely, inviting. 'What happened to the Spanish White colour?' she called through the door.

'It was too neutral for my taste.' Grady stood in the doorway, watching her. 'Don't you like it?'

'I love it.' But what colour he painted his house had nothing to do with her. She picked up a glossy brochure.

Kitchens. Flicking through the pictures and plans, it seemed awfully exciting to be revamping a house.

'I like the first and third designs. What about you?' Grady stood in front of her.

Flicking back and forth, she decided, 'Definitely the second one. More workable bench space and all the cupboards seem to flow into one another better.'

His lips pressed together as he nodded. 'I'll take that on board. Now, come and look what I've done with the dining table.'

She followed him outside to the shed where the large table that held so many memories stood. 'You've sanded it back to the wood.' She ran her hand over the smooth surface. 'That's going to come up beautifully.'

'Isn't it? I'm pleased with the result so far.' There was a ton of pride in his voice.

Why would he go to all that trouble if he was going to sell it with the house? Why had he changed his mind about paint colours when he'd said he wanted to attract as many potential buyers as possible? Why look at new kitchens? Her stomach sucked in on itself as the truth hit her hard. 'You're staying.' She shook her head from side to side. 'You're going to live almost next door to me.' *Just when I'm settling down and coming to grips with my new lifestyle.*

She'd never be able to get him out of her system this time if she had to see him every day. 'Have you taken a job at the medical centre? Is that what this is all about?'

'Thanks a lot, Sasha,' Grady drawled. 'You really know how to make a guy feel good.'

'Why now, Grady? Why can't you let me have this one little piece of New Zealand? I'm trying so hard to make this work for my baby and me. All I want is to be safe, secure and able to bring my baby girl up in a good community. But you're not going to play fair, are you?' Gulp. 'Do you think I'll let you back into my life? Just go away, Grady. Leave me be.'

Uh, hadn't she been the one to kiss him? Heat swamped her cheeks. She probably had been out of line but this was too much. 'I'm going home.'

Before she'd made it to the car Grady called after her. 'Sash, I'm not staying permanently. I'll be heading back to Auckland on Sunday. For now this is going to be my holiday retreat.'

Don't call me Sash.

Grady sank down on his haunches and watched Sash leave, speeding away to put as much distance between them as possible. His heart banged painfully in his ribcage. His head pounded behind his eyes.

'I love you, Sash. More than ever.'

She'd socked it to him about not wanting him in her life. He hadn't been expecting miracles but those words had stabbed him, sliced his heart open, exposed his needs, showed how pointless this all was.

So much for coming here and getting his life sorted so he could move on. Finally he understood totally that he didn't want to sell his house and all the memories that went with it. For the first time in eleven years he was comfortable with his father's death, could enjoy recalling all the fun times. So he'd keep the house and visit once or twice a year. If that gave Sash peace of mind then that's what he had to do.

There'd been so much hurt and confusion in those brilliant emerald eyes as she'd yelled at him, her hands on her hips, her breasts pushed forward.

He'd seen that hurt once before. The day he'd told her he didn't love her. She'd loved him then. Did that hurt mean she loved him now? How was he to know? There hadn't been any real indication.

Oh, yeah?

She'd instigated more than one of those scorching kisses.

She'd been more than happy to take him into her bed.

She'd let him feel Flipper kicking.

She'd been more than grateful he'd gone with her to Nelson when Flipper had stopped moving, even gone so far as to acknowledge she'd wanted him there.

Yet when it occurred to her he might be staying, she'd flipped her lid and told him in no uncertain terms to go someplace else.

Yeah, and what am I doing about it? Walking away, heading to Auckland in two days' time. For her sake. Doing the same as I did last time. What happened to standing tall and trying to make things work? Sash might love me, she might not. But I'm never going to know if I leave.

He'd never stopped loving her, had spent years trying to find her match and failing miserably every time. 'I love Sash Wilson. End of. And I'm going to fight for her. Patiently. One day at a time. One hour at a time. But first I have things back in Auckland to sort out.'

CHAPTER TWELVE

SIX WEEKS LATER Grady walked out of the Nelson Airport terminal and across to the aero club, where Ian waited with his plane. 'Thanks for this, Ian. I could've got a rental car.'

'Nonsense. I enjoy taking the old girl up for a spin. Don't do it often enough these days. Climb in. I've done the checks.'

Grady latched the door shut, buckled the seat belt and slipped the headset over his head. The last time he'd flown in something so small had been with Sasha the day of her sixteenth birthday when she had officially been allowed to take passengers. The calls Ian made to the control tower to report his start up were so familiar.

As the older man taxied the plane across the grass towards the runway, Grady asked, 'How's everything in Takaka?' *How's Sash keeping? Is she taking it quietly now that she only has a few days to go before giving birth? Has she missed me?*

'Sasha's fine. And behaving—for her.' Ian changed the subject. 'Those builders you employed have been working their butts off. You're going to be amazed at the changes.'

I hope I'm doing the right thing. 'I hear there was a

hold-up with the new kitchen and that they're working overtime this weekend to finish it.'

'It's all hands to the fore tomorrow to lift two of those units inside. That's a big kitchen you've got there, son.'

Son. If only. 'It's the kitchen Sasha liked when she was flipping through the catalogue.'

'Yeah, I figured.' Ian stopped talking to him to call up the control tower again and Grady sat back to enjoy the flight over the hill. In the weeks he'd been in Auckland he'd missed Golden Bay and the relaxed lifestyle. He'd missed Sash even more. He'd been gutted eleven years ago when he'd sent her packing, but this time had been so, so much worse. He loved her in so many ways, for so many things. He did not want to go back to life without her. He was being patient, but patience sucked big time.

'Virginia's cooking you dinner tonight. We're looking after Nicholas while Sasha and Jess have their fortnightly girls' night. It had been arranged before we got your call to say you were coming down.'

Grady sucked in on the wave of disappointment rolling through him. He could wait another day to see Sash. Just. 'I look forward to dinner.' How lame did that sound? But what else could he say? Virginia and Ian had gone out of their way to make him feel at home with them, which on a positive day he took for a good sign.

He stared down at the sun-kissed waters of Tasman Bay as they flew along the coastline. So different from the icy night he'd first bumped into Sash again. Ian had opted for the long way round instead of going over the hill. Ahead he saw Totaranui and the camping ground, which prompted him to ask, 'How's Kevin settling in with helping Virginia on the orchard?'

Ian grimaced. 'He's got a lot to learn but I think he'll

come right. His heart's in the right place. He wants to provide for his unexpected family.'

It had been a surprise for everyone when Kevin and Tamara had decided they wanted to live in Takaka with little Jordan, and not return to Christchurch to her family. 'At least he's stepping up for them.'

Which was a hell of a lot more than Sash's Freddy had done. But if he was honest he was kind of glad about that. He'd hate it if Sash decided she had to marry the guy because he was her baby's father.

Ian was still talking. 'I like that Kevin's there for Virginia. I hate that she might do something strenuous when I'm not around. Thank goodness I've only got a few months before I quit the job.'

'The Wilson women can be so stubborn.' Grady grinned across at this man who'd accepted he was trying to win over his daughter.

'Forget that at your peril.' Ian grinned back, before preparing to land at Takaka's minuscule airstrip.

Sasha walked out of Grady's house with Jess right behind her. The workmen were about to lift the huge main unit into place and had asked the women to get out of the way for their safety.

Grady apologised, looking very disappointed when Sasha told him she'd be off home. 'You just got here.'

'I'll call in again later. Jess has to pick up Nicholas from his friend's house.' Shock still held her in thrall. Had to be why she'd made that promise, but the relief in his eyes had been worth it. But 'Why did he choose that particular kitchen style?' she asked Jess when they were in the car.

'Why wouldn't he?'

'It's the one in the brochure I liked.' Sasha shook her head, trying to clear it. Grady had rung that morning to invite her over to see how his house was progressing. Like an idiot, she'd given in to temptation. She'd missed him more than she'd have believed possible. To the point she had even looked at airfares to go up to Auckland for a weekend. But Flipper was too close to arriving and she'd had to be sensible. Another first.

Jess chuckled. 'The guy will try every trick in the book to get you back.'

Sasha rubbed her lower back before getting into the car. 'You reckon?'

'Yep. He's up front about wanting you. Now all you have to do is admit that you love him, too.'

'If only it was that easy.'

Jess slapped the steering-wheel. 'Sasha, when are you going to learn? It is that easy.'

'You've been in this situation?' Sasha rubbed her back again. It ached like crazy.

Jess ignored her question. 'Grady's nothing like he was when his dad died and he had to cope with his responsibilities. His mother and sisters needed him then. I know you did too but give the guy a break. He was only eighteen and trying to do the best for all of you. Now he could cope with all of that and some.'

'I get all of that.' Really got it. To the point she didn't understand why she was stalling.

'You're made for each other.' Jess went on and on.

Sasha tuned out. Until an icky sensation of moisture made her mutter, 'Jess, shut up. My waters have broken.'

'What? They have? In my car?' Jess shook her head and pulled to the side of the road. 'No, you're wrong. I'm the midwife. I'll tell you when your waters have broken.'

Sasha gaped at her friend gone mad and started to smile. The smile stretched into a grin, and then she was laughing hard enough to bust her sides. 'Jess, you idiot.' Laughter poured out. 'Don't stop here. Get me somewhere.'

Jess had turned in her seat to stare at her, her eyes shining as she began laughing, too. 'What's funny?'

'I don't know. I'm having a baby? Like now. In your car.'

'You can't. I— We— Okay, what should we do?'

More laughter burst out of Sasha. 'Aren't you the midwife around here?' Then pain struck and the laughter disappeared. 'Oh. My. God. That really hurts.'

Jess immediately started driving again. 'We'll go to the birthing unit and I'll time your contractions. Though it is much too soon for the baby to come. You've only just started. There's a way to go yet.'

'Watch out for those bumps. They hurt.'

Jess waved a hand at her. 'If I go any slower the car will stall.'

'Seems too soon to go to the unit.' She hadn't really started full labour, had she?

'What else are we going to do, then? We can't just creep around aimlessly. One of Toby's men will lock us up in the police cells for loitering.'

Another pain gripped Sasha. Her hands clasped her belly. 'Call Grady. Now.'

Through every contraction Grady held Sasha with his strong arms as she stood, leaning into him. It was the most comfortable position she could find. Which was excruciatingly painful. His hands rubbing her back soothed, irritated, comforted and annoyed her. He took it calmly and reasonably when she had a momentary loss of sanity and swore at him. Then when she blamed men in general for her predicament he hugged her.

He never left her side for the fourteen hours Flipper took to make her entrance into the world.

Tears were streaming down Jess's face when she finally handed over the precious bundle. 'Say hello to your beautiful baby girl, Sasha.'

Tears poured out of Sasha's eyes as she hungrily peered into the folds of the soft pink wrap to see her daughter. 'She's so beautiful.' She repeated Jess's description. 'So, so beautiful,' she whispered as a humongous lump clogged her throat.

Tears slid down Grady's cheeks too as he leaned over to get his first glimpse of her little girl. 'Hey, gorgeous, you look just like your mum. Beautiful.' He choked out that last word and smeared the tears across his face with the back of his hand.

Sasha smiled at him and went back to studying her baby. Her baby felt so light and tiny and yet real and precious. 'Hello, Melanie. I'm Mummy.' Then she couldn't utter another word for all the love clogging her throat.

Grady's hand curved over her shoulder, squeezed gently. 'Your mummy is going to be the best in the world, Melanie. You are a very lucky girl to have her.'

She couldn't remove a hand from her baby to touch him. Not when she'd waited so long for this moment, to hold Melanie, but she managed to look up into his eyes and smile. 'You reckon?'

'I know.' His return smile cracked her heart wide open. So wide that she could no longer hold onto her doubts about him. Not when she didn't believe them any more, hadn't for months, if she was honest. No, now she wanted to show him how much she loved him. Words alone wouldn't cut it. There was only one thing she could give him at this moment that showed her true feelings. 'Grady, would you hold Melanie?'

His face lit up as though she'd given him the best gift possible. 'Can I?' His mouth split into a big grin as he ever so carefully took her baby from her arms and held her to his chest, his hands enormous against the small baby. His eyes were filled with wonder as they fixed on Melanie, drinking in the sight of her. And those tears started again, fatter, faster this time. 'Hello, sweetheart. Anyone told you how cute you are?' he whispered.

Sasha felt her own eyes watering up again. What a perfect picture. Grady holding Melanie as though he'd give his life for her. Which he would. Without a doubt. Her body was exhausted and yet exhilaration sped along her veins. Now she really was a mum. For ever. There'd be no going back. 'I'm a forever mum.'

Grady raised his head, locking those love-filled eyes on her. 'Goes with those forever legs.'

More tears slid down her cheeks. She'd turned into such a crybaby lately. Running her hands down her cheeks to wipe them away, she said, 'Guess these aren't babymones making me topsy-turvy any more.'

'You reckon?' Jess grinned. 'I'm going to head out for a while, give your parents a call while you three have some family time.'

'Family?' Her lungs stalled. Family. Yeah. Her gaze tracked back to Grady, found the same stunned look in his eyes as must be in hers. 'Family,' she whispered to him as the door closed quietly behind Jess.

Wariness filtered into his gaze. 'Sash? What are you saying?'

'I love you.' Okay, that was little bit blunt. 'It's taken me a while to admit it. I've been holding out for some crazy, inexplicable reason, denying it to myself.'

'Babymones,' he croaked.

Laying her hand over the one of his that rested on Melanie's blanket, she shook her head. 'That's an excuse. I've hung onto the fact that you dumped me for too long. If I'd been more mature, less self-centred that day, I might've seen what you were doing. I should've seen your pain and dilemma.'

His hand turned over to wrap around hers. 'Neither of us knew how to cope with everything going down at that time.'

Squeezing her fingers around his, she told him, 'Maybe, maybe not. But I know we can manage anything thrown at us now if we're together. I love you so much.'

'Patience. I knew it.' A hint of smugness?

'Pardon?' She smiled at this wonderful man.

'I had to keep putting the brakes on my need for you. I'd have had you in my bed that same night we met on the hill if I'd had half a chance. I had missed you so much it hurt. But it was like putting my hand in the fire every time I tried to get close. So I kept telling myself to be patient, take my time, and hopefully I'd win your trust, your heart.'

'You do love me.' Relief and happiness and excitement poured through her, made her hands shake.

'Never stopped. I admit to trying bloody hard to forget

you, but some things are impossible. You're a part of me, Sash.'

'I love it when you call me Sash.'

'I know.'

'Looking smug doesn't suit you.' She grinned and leaned in for a kiss, careful not to squash her baby girl between them. 'You're looking quite the dad, too.'

Grady looked as though he never wanted to let Melanie out of his arms. 'She's lovely. Hello, Melanie Wilson.'

Sasha said quietly, 'Melanie O'Neil.'

Grady's eyes bored into her. Did he think she'd finally gone totally bananas? She drew air into her lungs, reached for Grady's hand, locked gazes with him and said loudly, clearly, 'Why not? I love you. So…' Her voice faltered. Huffing out the breath she'd been holding, she drew another and quickly asked, 'So will you please marry us?'

Melanie was placed, oh, so carefully in the baby crib and then Sasha gasped as Grady scooped her off the bed and into those strong, safe and trustworthy arms.

'Typical Sash. Got to get the first word in.' He grinned. 'That had been my next question for you.' His lips brushed hers. Teasing, tantalising. 'My answer is…' He stopped to kiss her, more thoroughly this time. 'Yes. I love you so much, Sash. So, yes, try stopping me now that you've asked.'

Sasha kissed him this time. 'I won't be stopping you. I think I've done too much of that already.'

Their kiss deepened, holding so much love and promise Sasha knew winter had gone for good. Finally tugging her lips away from that wonderful mouth, she asked, 'Let's have a summer wedding. Just a small one.'

Grady groaned. 'You've never done anything small in your life, Sash. Why start now?'

There was a tiny cry from the pink bundle in the crib beside her. Sasha reached in and lifted her daughter out, feeling her breasts tighten in response. Oh, my. This motherhood thing was amazing. Her baby might've left her body but they were still so connected. 'They don't come much smaller than this.' She grinned at him through another deluge of tears.

'You done good.' He grinned back. 'Summer wedding it is.'

* * * * *

THE MIDWIFE'S SON

BY
SUE MacKAY

Published in Great Britain 2014
by Mills & Boon, an imprint of Harlequin (UK) Limited,
Eton House, 18-24 Paradise Road, Richmond, Surrey, TW9 1SR

© 2014 Sue MacKay

ISBN: 978 0 263 90770 4

Harlequin (UK) Limited's policy is to use papers that are natural,
renewable and recyclable products and made from wood grown in
sustainable forests. The logging and manufacturing processes conform
to the legal environmental regulations of the country of origin.

Printed and bound in Spain
by Blackprint CPI, Barcelona

Dedication

Thanks very much to Kate Vida for her medical help.
Any mistakes are mine.
And to Deidre and Angela, because I can.

CHAPTER ONE

JESSICA BAXTER STARED at the champagne glass twirling between her thumb and forefinger. It was empty. Again. How had that happened? Best fill it up. She reached for the bottle nestled in ice in the silver bucket beside her.

'You planning on drinking that whole bottle all by yourself?' The groomsman sat down beside her, his steady green gaze fixed on her. Eyes so similar to his sister Sasha's, yet far more dramatic. The way they were sizing her up at this moment sent shivers of anticipation through her. But it was more likely she had whipped cream and strawberry compote on her nose rather than anything earth-shatteringly sensual going on.

Her finger shook as she wiped the top of her nose. Nope. All clear of dessert. So what was fascinating Jackson Wilson so much that his head seemed to have locked into position and his eyes forgotten how to move? Maybe if she answered him he'd get moving again.

So she told him, 'Yes.' Every last drop.

'Then I'll have to get my own bottle. Shame to have to move, though.' Jackson smiled at her, long and slow, making her feel as though she was the only person in the marquee. The only woman at least.

Which was blatantly untrue. Apart from Sasha, who

was looking absolutely fabulous in a cream silk wedding gown, there had to be half the female population of Golden Bay in this marquee. Hadn't Sasha said she wanted a small wedding? Define small. Jess looked at the bottle in her hand. Had she drunk too much? Not yet. 'This has to be the best champagne I've ever tasted. Your father went all out.'

'Can't argue with that.'

She wasn't looking for an argument. Her mouth curved upwards. Just some more champagne. The bubbles sped to the surface as she refilled her glass. The sight was enough to turn a girl on. If you were the kind that got turned on easily. Which she definitely wasn't. Her eyes cruised sideways, spied Jackson's legs stretched far under the table, and stilled. Well-toned thighs shaped his black evening trousers to perfection. Her tongue stuck to the top of her mouth, her skin warmed, and somewhere below her waist she felt long-forgotten sensations of desire. Maybe she was that kind of girl after all.

She lifted the bottle in Jackson's direction. 'Got a glass?'

'Of course.' He presented one with a flourish. 'I never go unprepared.' That gaze had returned, stuck on her, apparently taking in every detail of her face.

She paused halfway through filling his glass, raising a well-styled eyebrow. 'Has my mascara run or something?'

Jackson shook his head. 'Nope.'

Spinach in my teeth? Except spinach hadn't featured on the wedding dinner menu. So what was he looking at? Looking for? Jackson Wilson had never taken much notice of her before. They hadn't even liked each other much during the two years she had gone to school here; both had been too busy trying to steal the limelight.

The last time she'd seen him had been at their school graduation party. Thirteen years ago. He'd been the guy every girl had wanted to date. She'd been the girl everybody had invited to their parties because she could supply anything money could buy. They'd never hooked up.

'Hey, stop.' He said it quietly, in that bone-melting voice of his. 'My glass runneth over.'

'What?' Eek. Bad move. She'd been so distracted she'd started pouring again without realising. So unlike her. Worse, he knew exactly what she was distracted by—him. Suck it up, and get over him. He's a minor diversion.

Jackson raised his fingers to his mouth and lapped up the champagne. Had he heard her telling herself to suck it up? She shivered deliciously. The gesture was done so naturally that she had to presume Jackson hadn't meant it as a sexual come-on. But, then, why would it be? She'd be the last female on earth he'd come on to. They probably still wouldn't get on very well; she was a solo mum, he was used to glamorous, sexy ladies who didn't sport stretch marks on their tummies.

Wait up. He'd only been back in Golden Bay for five days and before today she'd only seen him at the wedding rehearsal. She might have that completely wrong. She was open to having her opinion changed. He didn't look so full of himself any more. No, rather world-weary and sad, if anything.

Then Jackson seemed to shake himself and sit up straighter. Lifting his glass carefully, he sipped until the level dropped to a safe place, before clinking the rim of the glass with hers. 'To the happy couple.'

'To Sasha and Grady.' She should be looking for her friends as they danced on the temporary floor in the centre of the marquee, but for the life of her she couldn't drag her attention away from Jackson. When had he got so handsome? Like so handsome she wanted to strip him naked. Back at school, she'd never been as enthralled as all the other girls, but maybe she'd missed something. His body was tall and lean. His face had a chiselled look, a strong jawline and the most disconcerting eyes that seemed to see everything while giving nothing away.

'Has my mascara run?' he quipped.

Her face blazed. Caught. Why was that any different from him scrutinising her? It wasn't, but she never normally took the time to look a guy over so thoroughly. She usually wasn't interested. 'Yes.'

'Wonderful. My macho image is shattered.' His deep chuckle caught her off balance.

That made her study him even closer. There were deep lines on either side of that delectable mouth. More of them at the corners of those eyes that remained fixed on her. What had caused those lines? To avoid getting caught in his gaze she glanced at his hair, dark brown with a few light strands showing in the overhead lights. Grey, yet not grey. She glanced back to those eyes. 'You look exhausted.'

Jackson blinked, tipped his head back to stare at the top of the marquee. His mouth had tightened, instantly making Jessica regret her words. There was no way she wanted to upset him; she didn't want him to think she was probing, being nosey. 'Sorry. I take that back.' She sipped her champagne, the glass unexpectedly trembling in her hand.

'I am totally beat.'

Phew. Still talking. 'Jet-lag?' She supposed it was a longish haul from Hong Kong.

'Nah. Life.' His hand groped on the tabletop for his drink.

'Here.' She pushed it into his fingers.

'Thanks.' Sitting straighter, he took a deep taste of the nectar. 'You're right. This is superb.'

Again she wondered what hiccups there had been in his life to make him look so shattered. From what she knew, he worked as an emergency specialist in a huge hospital in Hong Kong. That would keep him busy, but many specialists put in the long hours and didn't end up looking as jaded as Jackson did right now. He'd be earning big money and no doubt had a fancy apartment and housekeeper, along with the to-die-for car and a string of women to ride alongside him. Maybe one of those women had caused a ripple in his otherwise perfect life? 'Why Hong Kong?'

'To live? I did part of my internship there and was offered a position in the emergency department for when I qualified.' Now he stared into his glass, seeming to see more than just the bubbles rising to the top. 'Hong Kong was exciting, buzzing with people, and completely different from Golden Bay. It was like starting a whole new life, unhindered by the past.'

'You sound like you hated it here.' What had happened to make him want to head offshore?

'I did at times.' Draining the glass, he reached for the bottle, peered at it. 'We need another one. Be right back.'

Jess watched Jackson stride around the edge of the dance floor, ignoring the women who tried to entice him to dance with them. So he was determined to sit with her for a while and share a drink. Why? Why her of all the people here? There had to be plenty of family and friends he knew from growing up in Takaka, people he'd want to catch up with. Come to think of it, she hadn't noticed him being very sociable with anyone in particular all day. Not that he'd been rude, just remote. Interesting. There must be more to this man than she knew.

Was she a safe bet, unlikely to molest him because she sat alone, not leaping up to shake and gyrate to the music? Well, he'd got that right. She didn't come on to men any more. Not since the last one had made her pregnant and then tossed 'Don't send photos' over his shoulder on the way out, heading about as far north as earth went.

The sound of a cork popping as Jackson returned was like music to her ears. 'What is it about champagne that's so special?' she asked, as he deftly topped up her glass. 'Is it the buzz on the tongue?'

'That, the flavour and the fact that champagne goes with celebrations. Good things, not bad.' Somehow, when he sat back down, his chair had shifted closer to hers.

'I guess you're right.' Goose-bumps prickled her skin and she had to force herself not to lean close enough to rub against his arm. Bubbles tickled her nose when she sipped her drink and she giggled. Oops. Better go easy on this stuff. Then again, why not let her hair down and have a good time? It had been for ever since she'd done that.

'Of course I'm right.' He smiled, slowly widening his mouth and curving those delectable lips upwards, waking up the butterflies in her stomach and sending them on a merry dance. Then he said, 'That shade of orange really suits your brown eyes and fair hair.'

'Orange? Are you colour blind, or what? Your sister

would have a heart attack if she heard you say that. It's apricot.' She fingered the satin of her dress. Being bridesmaid for Sasha had been an honour. It spoke of their growing friendship and being there for each other. One of the best things about returning home to Golden Bay had been getting to know Sasha, whom previously she'd only thought of as the girl about the bay who was younger and wilder than her. But that had been then. Nowadays they both were so tame it was embarrassing.

Jackson shrugged. 'Orange, apricot, whatever. You should wear it all the time.'

'I'll remember that.'

'Do you want to dance?'

What? Where had that come from? Dancing had nothing to do with dress colours. 'No, thanks.'

'Good. I'm hopeless at dancing. Always feel like a puppy on drugs.' His smile was self-deprecating.

'Then why did you ask?' She seemed to remember him gyrating around the floor at school dances.

'Thought you might want to.' He chuckled again. Deep and sexy.

'Luckily for you I'm not into dancing either.' She could get addicted to that chuckle. It sent heat zipping through her, warming her toes, her tummy, her sex. Once more her cheeks blazed, when they'd only just cooled down after the last time. What was going on here? She never blushed. It must be the drink. She stared at her glass belligerently and tried to push it aside, but couldn't. Not when she was letting her hair down for the first time in years and enjoying a drink or three. Nicholas was staying with his little friend, Bobby, just down the road at Pohara Beach. Tonight was hers to make the most of, mummyhood on hold for a few hours. Tomorrow reality would kick back in and she'd pick up the reins again. Not that she ever really let them go. But for one day and night it was great to be able to stop worrying.

'How old is your little boy?'

So mindreading was one of Jackson's talents. 'He's four and a handful. A gorgeous, adorable handful who keeps me on my toes nonstop.' He'd looked so cute at the marriage ceremony in his long trousers and white shirt.

'What happened to his dad?'

This man was blunt. 'Which rumour did you hear?' she asked, as she contemplated how much to tell.

'That he was a soldier on secondment who didn't take you with him when he left. That he was the married CEO of a big company who liked beautiful young women on his arm.' Jackson drank some more champagne. Was that what had made him suddenly so talkative? 'That he was an alien visiting from Mars for a week.'

Her growing anger evaporated instantly and she dredged up a smile. 'Guess you know you're home when everyone starts making up stories about you.'

'Which is why I hightailed it out of here the day after I finished school.'

'Really?' Jess could feel her eyebrows lifting and brought them under control. How much would he tell her?

The steady green gaze locking onto her lightened. 'Really. I hated it that I couldn't sneeze without someone telling me I'd done something wrong.'

Not much at all. Memories niggled of a rumour about Jackson and a pregnant girl, something to do with a set-up. 'It's like that, isn't it? Claustrophobic.' She shuffled around on her chair, all the better to study him again. 'But there's also security in that.'

'You haven't told me which story is true. I'm guessing none of them.'

Persistent man. Or was he just shifting the focus off himself? She didn't talk about Nicholas's father. Not a lot of point. 'I prefer the alien one.'

He nodded. 'Fair enough.'

That's it? He wasn't going to push harder for information? Most people wouldn't care that the subject had nothing to do with them. She could get to like Jackson Wilson. Really like him. 'How long are you home for?'

'Almost three months.'

Her eyebrows were on the move upwards again. Three months? That seemed a long time when Sasha had mentioned this was his first visit in thirteen years. Of course, his mother had MS now. And there was Sasha's baby girl, Melanie, to get to know. 'Amazing how weddings bring people together from all corners of the world.'

'You're fishing.' He grinned at her.

'Am I catching anything?' She grinned straight back.

His grin faded. His focus fixed on her. Again. She was getting used to his intense moods. 'I need a break. A long one.' He stretched those fascinating legs further under the table and crossed them at the ankles. 'And now you're going to ask why.'

Putting all the innocence she could muster into her gaze, she tapped her sternum. 'Me? No way.' Then, unable to hold that look, she grinned again. 'If you don't tell me I'll have to torture you.'

His mouth curved upwards as his tongue slicked over his bottom lip. 'Interesting.'

Idiot. She'd walked into that one. Now he'd make some smutty comment and ruin the easy camaraderie between them. 'Um, forget I said that.'

'Forgotten.' Did he add, 'Unfortunately,' under his breath?

She so wasn't into leather and handcuffs, or whips and ice. At least she hadn't been. Her mouth twitched. Maybe she should head home now, before the champagne made her say more things she shouldn't.

Where were Sasha and Grady? Right in the centre of the floor, still dancing, wrapped around each other as though they were the only people there. A sudden, deep envy gripped her, chilled her despite the summer heat.

She wanted what they had. Wanted a man who loved her more than anything, anyone else. Who'd put her first. A man to curl up against at night, to laugh and cry with. A man like— Her eyes swivelled in her head, away from the dance floor right to the man beside her. A man like Jackson? No. For starters, he was her best friend's brother. Then there was the fact he was only home for a few months. Add his sophistication and Jackson was so not right for her.

Hold that thought. Focus on it. Believe it. Remember how she'd thought Nicholas's father would give her all those things, only to be shown just how wrong she'd been. Instead, she'd found a man incapable of commitment, even to his wife back in the States. A wife she hadn't had a clue about.

Unfortunately for her, right now, all the reasons for not getting involved with Jackson seemed to have no substance at all.

CHAPTER TWO

JACKSON WATCHED JESSICA. Her brown eyes lightened to fudge and darkened to burnt coffee depending on her emotion, flicking back and forth so fast sometimes she must give herself a headache. Talk about an enigma. One moment all shy and unsure of herself, the next flipping a sassy comment at him like she wanted him. Which was the real Jess Baxter?

Suddenly the months looming ahead didn't seem so long and depressing. Instead, they were beginning to look interesting. Could he spend some time with Jessica and get to know her? Have some light-hearted fun for a while and find the real woman behind that sharp mind and sad face? He enjoyed puzzles, but right now he didn't even know where to begin solving this one. They were hitting it off fine. There might be some fun to be had here.

But— Yeah, there was always a but. He didn't want involvement. Especially not with a woman who'd require him to stay on at the end of those months, to become a permanent resident in the one place that he'd decided before he'd turned fifteen wasn't right for him. Too small, too parochial. Too close and personal. Nasty, even. He'd never forget the gut-squeezing, debilitating hurt and anger when Miriam Blackburn had accused him of getting her pregnant. He'd only ever kissed her once. No wonder big cities held more attraction. Easy to lose himself, to avoid the piranhas.

From the little Sasha had told him, he understood that Jessica had come home permanently. That she'd begun mending bridges with the people she wrongly believed she'd hurt years ago. Apparently she wanted her son to grow up here, where he'd be safe and looked out for. There was no arguing with that sentiment.

He definitely wasn't looking for commitment in any way, shape or form. Commitment might drag him back to the place he'd spent so long avoiding. He wasn't outright avoiding women. But Jessica wasn't like his usual type of woman. Those were sophisticated and well aware of how to have a good time without hanging around the next day. Women who didn't get under his skin or tug at his heartstrings.

Jessica would want more of him than an exciting time. She'd want the whole package. Settle down, have more babies, find a house and car suitable for those children. *And what was so awful about that?* No idea, except it was the complete opposite from what he wanted.

Back up. He mustn't forget why he'd decided to stay on after his sister's wedding. He needed to spend time with his family, to help Mum and Dad as they came to terms with the multiple sclerosis that had hit Mum like a sledgehammer. He'd also like to get to know his niece. Melanie was so cute and, at three months old, had wound him round her little finger. Already, memories of her smile, her cry, her sweet face were piling up in his head to take back with him to Hong Kong.

Then there was the small issue of needing to rest

and recoup his energy, to find the drive to continue his work in Hong Kong and keep his promise to his dead colleague. That motivation had been slipping away over the last year, like fine grain through a sieve. The catastrophic events of last month had really put the lid on his enthusiasm for his work. But a promise was a promise. No going back on it.

Clink. 'Drink up.' Jessica was tapping her glass against his again.

Yeah, drink up and forget everything that had happened in the past month. Let it go for a few hours and have some uncomplicated fun. 'Cheers,' he replied, and drained his glass. Picking up the bottle, he asked, 'More?'

He saw her hesitating between yes and no, her eyes doing that light then dark thing. He made up her mind for her. 'Here, can't let this go to waste.' When he'd filled both glasses, he lifted them and handed over hers, taking care not to touch her fingers as they wound around the glass stem. That would be fire on ice. 'To weddings and families and friends.'

She nodded, sipped, and ramped up his libido as she savoured the sparkling wine, her tongue licking slowly over her lips, searching for every last taste. So much for avoiding contact. She could heat him up without a touch. That mouth… He shook his head. He would not think about her champagne-flavoured lips on his skin. Or her long, slim body under his as he plunged into her. While he lost himself for a few bliss-filled moments. Hours, even.

She was talking, her words sounding as though she was underwater.

Focus, man. Listen to Jess. Ignore your lust-dazed brain. 'What did you just say?'

'Looks like the happy couple are on the move.' Her eyes followed his sister and new brother-in-law as they did the rounds of their guests, hugging and kissing and chatting.

'You and Sasha never used to be mates.'

Jess had been the girl with the rich parents who had bought her anything and everything she could ever have wanted. Yet she'd never seemed genuinely, completely happy, always looking for more. Definitely a party girl, always in the thick of anything going down in Takaka, but at the same time she'd seemed removed from everyone. Like a child looking out the lolly-shop window at the kids gazing in at the sweet treats.

Yet she'd had more than the rest of them put together, having spent most of her childhood apparently travelling to weird and wonderful places. Hadn't she had love? Had that been her problem? It would go a long way to explaining why she'd always bought her pals anything they'd hankered after. Perhaps she had been buying affection and friendship. Talk about sad.

Right now a big smile lit up her face, lightened her eyes. 'The day Sasha walked into the medical centre to start her job we just clicked. Guess that amongst our past friends we're the odd ones out, having left and come back. We've tasted the world, know what life's like on the other side of Takaka Hill, and returned. Though Sasha's done a lot more than I have when it comes to our careers.'

'You didn't work overseas?'

'Nope. I'd travelled a lot with my parents when I was a child. The idea of working in another country didn't appeal. Auckland was enough for me.'

'Are your parents still living here?'

Coffee-colour eyes. And her teeth nibbled at her bottom lip. 'Not often.'

He recognised a stop sign when he saw one. 'Here comes the happy couple.' Jackson stood, placed a hand on Jessica's elbow and pulled her up to tuck her in beside him. Her warm length felt good against his body. The side of her thigh rubbed against his, her elbow nudged his ribs. A perfume that reminded him of Mum's citrus grove teased his nostrils. Her hair, all fancy curls with orange ribbons woven through, tickled his chin when he lowered his head.

I want her. Like, really want her. Not just a five-minute quickie behind the shed either.

Surprise ricocheted through him and he felt his muscles tighten. All his muscles. Especially below his belt. Why was he surprised? Hadn't this need been growing all evening? Against him Jess jerked, looked up with a big question in those pull-you-in eyes.

Don't move. Hold your breath and wish away your out-of-left-field reaction to her before she catches on. Because otherwise she's going to empty what's left in that champagne bottle over your head.

His stomach dropped in time with her chin as she glanced down, over his chest to his waist, and on down. His breath caught somewhere between his lungs and his mouth. She'd have to be blind not to see his boner.

Her head lifted. Her gaze locked onto his. She clearly wasn't blind. Those brown pools were filled with comprehension. Raising herself up on tiptoe, she leaned close and whispered, 'Your place or mine?'

'Yours.' Definitely not his. He was currently staying at his parents' house.

Her hand slipped into his and she tugged him off balance. 'What are we waiting for?'

'I have no idea.' So now he was in the flirty corner of the Jessica puzzle. Fine by him. He'd look into the shy corner another day.

Sasha and Grady stepped in front of them. 'Hey, you two. In a hurry to leave?' Sasha asked, with an annoying twinkle in her eyes. 'Without saying goodbye?'

Jackson removed his hand from Jessica's and carefully hugged his sister. 'You look beautiful, sis. No wonder Grady hasn't moved more than two centimetres away from you all day.'

Then he slapped Grady on the back and stepped away to watch the two women hugging tightly. They'd got so close. Like they shared everything. A small knot of longing tightened in his gut. He wanted that, too. No, he wanted what his sister and Grady had. Wanted to be able to talk about what had happened last month, share his fear and apprehensions, even the promise that hung over him. He would like to know there was someone special to look forward to going home to every night, someone who wasn't the housekeeper.

Jessica? Maybe, maybe not. Though so far tonight she'd been totally in tune with him, not pushing for answers to questions he refused to give, understanding when he wanted to talk and when he didn't. Knowing how his body reacted to hers.

Which reminded him. Weren't they going somewhere? In a damned hurry, too?

'See you two tomorrow,' he told Grady, and grabbed for Jess's hand. He whispered, 'We're out of here.'

And received a big, knowing smile in return. 'Sure are, Doctor.'

As they passed the bar he swiped a bottle of champagne and tucked it under his free arm. 'Neither of us is driving tonight. Let's hope one of those vans Dad organised for transporting inebriated guests home is available.' Like right this minute. Hanging around waiting for a ride and being forced to listen while other guests talked and laughed in their ears would be a passionkiller for sure. Though the beach was a short walk through the flaxes if need be.

They were in luck. The beach could wait for another night. Two vans were lined up so they snaffled one and ten long, tension-filled minutes later Jess was unlocking her front door.

She didn't bother with lights. 'There's enough light from the full moon to see what we need to see. The rest we can do by touch.' Her laughter was soft and warm, touching him in a way none of the sophisticated women he'd bedded had. Was this shy Jessica? Or fun Jessica?

'Where are the glasses?' he asked as he popped the cork on the champagne.

'Come with me.' She reached for his hand. Being tugged through the small house by this gorgeous woman with only moonlight to see by was a breathtaking experience, heightening his senses—and his growing need for her.

Jess's slim outline with those just-right curves outlined by her gown hardened him further. Her backside shaped the fabric to perfection, her hips flared the almost skin-tight skirt subtly. 'How are you going to get out of that dress?'

They'd reached the kitchen, where she removed two champagne glasses from a cupboard and handed them to

him. Her mouth curved into a delicious, cat-like smile.
'That's your job.'

Give me strength. He wouldn't last the distance.
'Right.'

Just then she turned, pressed up against him, her
thighs pushing against his, her lush breasts squashed
against the hard wall of his chest. Her hands slid around
his neck and pulled his head down so her mouth covered his. His pulse went from normal to a thousand in a
flash. Wrapping his free arm around her, he hauled her
close, so close her lower belly covered his reaction to
her, smothered it, warmed it.

'Gawd, Jess. Keep this up and we'll be over before
we've started.'

Her mouth pulled back barely enough for her to reply,
'And your problem is?'

'Why did we stop to get glasses?' His lips claimed
hers again. She tasted sweet, exciting, sexy. She tasted
of what he so badly needed right now. Of freedom and
oblivion. Of recovery.

Somehow she began stepping backwards, taking
him with her, not breaking their kiss at all, not removing those breasts from his chest. Back, back, until they
made it into another room. Thank goodness there was
a bed. A big bed. His knees were turning to something
akin to badly set jelly as desire soared through him. He
was about to explode and that was only under the min-
istrations of her mouth on his. He lifted his head. 'Turn
around so I can free you.'

She spun so quickly she almost lost her balance.
'Oops. I need to slow down.'

'Really?' Jackson reached for her zip. Idiot. He still
held the champagne bottle and glasses in one hand. Oh,

so carefully he placed them on the bedside table. He had completely lost where he was. All he knew was that Jess stood before him and that he wanted her like he'd never wanted a woman before. He was desperate for her. But first he needed her naked. He concentrated on pulling the zip down with fingers that refused to stop trembling. Desire vibrated through him, everywhere, not just his fingers, like this was totally new to him.

It was hard to understand. He hadn't been living in a monastery. Far from it. There'd been a steady stream of women through his bedroom most of his adult life. Yet now he was losing control like the teenager he'd been last time he'd lived in this place, wanting desperately to bury himself inside Jessica Baxter.

'Jackson. What's going on back there?'

'The zip's caught.' Idiot. Couldn't even undo a simple zip. 'Hang on.'

She giggled. 'Hang on? Whatever you want.' Her hand slid behind her and found him. Her fingers slid up and down his covered erection, while the other hand worked his fly, which she obviously had no difficulty with. His trousers were suddenly around his ankles. 'I'm trying to get a hold.'

'Jess, I'll never get you out of this dress if you keep doing that.' And I'll come before I get my boxers down as far as my knees.

Instantly she stilled, her body tense, but he could feel her heat, knew her pulse was working overtime by the way her breasts rose and fell rapidly. She sucked her stomach in so tight it must've hurt. 'Well?'

'Thank you,' he muttered, as he tugged downwards. 'At last.' He slid his hands inside the soft fabric, his fingers sliding over her hot skin, across her back to her waist, round to her stomach and up to cup those luscious breasts. Free breasts. 'You haven't got a bra on.'

'Would've ruined the look.' She wriggled her butt against him. Sucked in her breath. 'Jackson, your thumbs are sending me over the edge to some place I've never been.'

Music to his ears. 'That's nothing to the storm your hand's stirring up.' His erection felt large, hard, throbbing and ready to explode.

She leant forward, teasing him with her rear end as she shrugged her upper body out of the dress and let it fall to her feet. Then she stepped out of the puddle of orange fabric and turned to face him. Insecurity and sass warred on her face, vied for supremacy. 'We haven't kissed. Not once.'

Jackson wasn't sure he'd make it through a kiss. But that uncertainty blinked out at him from her dark eyes and he hauled on the brakes, pulled his hands from where they'd fallen to her waist, and encircled her with his arms. He so wanted to get this right for her. For him. Hell, he knew it would be great for him, but if Jessica wanted a kiss then she'd get one she'd never forget. When his mouth covered hers he couldn't believe he hadn't done this earlier. She tasted of champagne and the promise of hot sex. She also tasted of honest-to-goodness, trustworthy woman with a lot to offer and something to take.

When she pushed her tongue into his mouth to tangle with his he thought he'd died and gone to heaven. His jelly knees melted and they tipped onto the bed, neither breaking their hold on the other. As they rolled and sprawled he continued to devour her mouth. Until now he'd thought kissing highly overrated, but this moment had rewritten his ideas. Kissing Jess went so far off the scale he might never come back to earth.

Then her hand found him again. Forget kissing. His lungs seemed to fold in on themselves as all the air hissed over his teeth. Forget everything. Absolutely everything.

Pulling her mouth away, Jess said, 'You mentioned always being prepared for anything. I guess that means you've got a condom or two in your pocket.'

He froze. Swore under his breath. No. He'd been going to his sister's wedding, had not expected to be bedding a hot bridesmaid.

Hot, shaky laughter filled the room. 'You owe me, buster. Top drawer by the bed. They're probably out of date but better than nothing.'

Within moments she had him covered and her hand was back on him, heat rolling through every cell of his body.

He had to touch her. But suddenly he was on his back and Jess was straddling him. Before he'd caught up with her she was sliding over him, beginning to ride him. His hands gripped her thighs, his thumbs slipped over her wet heat to find her core. She instantly bucked and for a moment she lost the rhythm.

But not for long. Her recovery was swift. This woman had to be something else. He kept the pressure on as he rubbed across her wetness.

Above him Jessica let out a long groan and squeezed tight around him and his brain went blank as he lost the last thread of control over his body.

Careful not to wake Jess, Jackson withdrew his arm from around her waist and rolled onto his back. A comfortable exhaustion lapped at him. It would be so easy to curl back into Jess and sleep for hours. Too easy, which was a scary thought. They'd made love again. Slowly and sensually, and just as gratifying. She'd been generous in her lovemaking, and hungry for her own release. He hadn't experienced anything so straightforward and honest in a long time. And he'd enjoyed every moment.

But now he had to be thinking of getting home. Squinting at his watch, he tried to make out the time. Four twenty-four? The sun would soon be clawing its way up over the horizon. He slid out from under the sheet and groped around the floor for his clothes, which he took out to the bathroom to pull on.

He had to get away from here before there was a chance that anyone might see him leaving. He would not give anyone reason to gossip about Jess. It might be harmless but he knew how it could still hurt, ricocheting around the bay and getting more outrageous by the hour. According to Sasha, Jess wanted nothing more than to blend in around here, and to become a member of the community who everyone could rely on for help and empathy. She most definitely would not want to be the centre of idle chitchat at the corner store or in the pub. Jess wasn't as lucky as he and Sasha were, she didn't have her family to believe in her and stand by her.

Biting down on a sudden flare of anger, he dressed and headed to the kitchen to find pen and paper. He wouldn't leave without saying thank you. Or something. Anything but nothing. He did not want her waking up and thinking he'd done a dash while she'd slept because he hadn't had a good time or couldn't face her in the light of day.

Back in the bedroom he quietly crossed to place the note on her bedside table. Then he stood looking down at her in the glimmer of light from the bathroom opposite. Sleeping Jess appeared completely relaxed. No sass, no uncertainty. His heart lurched. And before he could think about it he bent down to kiss her warm cheek. His hand seemed to rise of its own volition and he had to snatch it back before he made the monumental error of cupping her face and leaning in for one of those brain-melting, hormone-firing kisses.

Another lurch in his chest. She was like a drug; slowing his thought processes, making him forget things he should never forget. So, he was already half under her influence. If he didn't leave immediately he might never go away. Which would cause all sorts of difficulties. He and Jessica were light years apart in what they wanted for their futures. Futures that could never blend comfortably. He didn't need the hassle of trying to make it work and failing, and neither did Jessica.

Walking away was hard, and for every step his heart made a loud thud against his ribs. But he had to—for Jess. Making sure the front door was locked behind him to keep her safe—which also meant he couldn't go back to her—he began the ten-kilometre walk back to his parents' house.

Hopefully, if anyone he or Jess knew happened by at this early hour they wouldn't put two and two together and come up with…four. Because there might be gossip about them spending the night together, but this was one story that would be based on truth.

Three hundred metres on and headlights swept over him. A car sped past, the horn tooting loud in the early morning. Again anger flared, sped along his veins. So much for being discreet. It just wasn't possible around here. Increasing his pace, he tried to outrun the temper threatening to overwhelm him. When would these surges of anger stop? It had been more than a month since the attack. He should have got past that terrifying night by now.

The nearly healed wound in his side pulled as Jackson swung his arms to loosen the knots in his neck and back. There was another reason for leaving before the sun came up. That bloody scar. If Jess saw it she'd have a stream of unwanted questions to fire his way. Somehow she hadn't noticed the rough ridge of puckered skin during the night. Amazing, considering he doubted there was a square millimetre of his body she hadn't touched at one time or another.

'So, Jackson,' he muttered, as he focused on the road and not tripping over some unseen obstacle in the semi light of dawn, 'where to from here, eh?'

His lips tightened as he grimaced.

'That's a tricky one. I don't want commitment, gossip or questions about why I've got an ugly red scar on my body.' That about covered everything.

If only he'd worn running shoes he could be jogging now. Like they'd have been a good match for the wedding clobber he still wore. But who was around to notice? It was weird how quiet it was around here. No hordes of people bumping into him, no thousands of locals talking nonstop as they began their day. Very, very quiet. Peaceful. A complete contrast to Hong Kong.

'Don't get too comfortable. You're heading out of here before the end of April.' He spat the words. 'But I wouldn't mind a repeat of last night with Jess.' Just the mention of her name calmed him, slowed his angry thoughts. A smile began deep in his belly, sending tentacles of warmth to every corner of his body, curving his mouth upwards. 'Oh, yeah. I could do that all over again.'

But would he?

Even if it meant talking about things he preferred buried deep inside his psyche?

Right at this moment he had no damned idea.

CHAPTER THREE

KEEPING HER EYES closed, Jess reached across the bed for Jackson and came up cold. What? She scrambled up and looked around. She was alone.

'Jackson?' she called.

Nothing. No cheeky reply. No deep chuckle. Silence except for the house creaking as the sun warmed up the day.

'Great. Bloody wonderful, even. I hate it when the guy of the night before leaves without at least saying good bye.' Her stomach tightened. Jackson had enjoyed their lovemaking as much as she had. She'd swear to it. 'Maybe he didn't want the whole bay knowing we've been doing the deed.'

Was that good or bad? Did she want the whole of Golden Bay discussing her sex life? Nope. Definitely not. The muscles in her stomach released their death grip.

Did she want to do it again? With Jackson? Oh, yes. Her stomach tightened again. Absolutely wanted that. Which was a very good reason not to. Already she felt the need to see him pulling at her, wanted his arms around her, to hear his sexy chuckle. And that was after one night. Blimey. Was she falling for her best friend's brother? Even when she knew she shouldn't? That was a sure-fire way to fall out with Sasha, especially once Jackson packed his bags and headed back to his job. But there was no helping those feelings of want and desire that seemed to sneak out of her skull when she wasn't looking.

Throwing the sheet aside, she leapt out of bed. He might've left but, darn, she felt good this morning. Despite the uncertainty of today and, in fact, every other day of the coming months with Jackson in the bay, she felt great. Just went to show what a healthy dose of sex could do for her.

'What's that?' A piece of paper lay on the floor by the bed. Picking it up, she read:

Hey, sleepyhead, thought I'd get away before the bay woke up. Thanks for a great night. See you at brunch. Hugs, Jackson.

Hugs, eh? That was good, wasn't it? Seemed he wasn't hiding from her if he'd mentioned the post-wedding brunch. What was the time? Eight-thirty. Yikes. She was supposed to be at the Wilsons' by nine-thirty and she had to pick up Nicholas. Her boy, the light of her life. She might've had a fantastic night but she missed him.

The piping-hot shower softened those aching muscles that had had a rare workout during the night. Singing loudly—and badly—she lathered shampoo through her hair while memories of last night with Jackson ran like a nonstop film through her mind. Hugging herself, she screeched out the words to a favourite song.

The phone was ringing as she towelled herself. Knowing she had no babies due at the moment, she wondered who'd be calling. Sasha would be too busy with Grady, it being the first day of married bliss and all that.

'Hello,' she sang.

'Is that Jessica Baxter? The midwife?' a strained male voice asked hesitantly.

Her stomach dropped. 'Yes, it is. Who's this?'

'You don't know me, but my wife's having a baby and I think something's wrong. It's too early. Can we come and see you? Like now?'

No. I'm busy. I'm going to have brunch with the most amazingly attractive, sexy-as-hell guy I've ever had the good luck to sleep with. Except, as of now, she wasn't. She swallowed the disappointment roiling in her stomach. 'Let's start at the beginning. Yes, I am Jessica. You are?'

'Sorry, I'm panicking a bit here. I'm Matthew Carter and my wife's Lily. We're up here for the weekend from Christchurch. Staying at Paton's Rock.' The more he talked the calmer he sounded. 'She seems a bit uncomfortable this morning.'

'How far along is your wife?' Why had they come away from home and their midwife when this Lily was due to give birth?

He hesitated, then, 'Nearly eight months. Everything's been good until this morning, otherwise we wouldn't have come away. But my cousin got married yesterday and we had to be here.'

'You were at Sasha and Grady's wedding?' She didn't remember seeing any obviously pregnant women, and as a midwife she usually noticed things like that.

'No, Greg and Deb Smith's.'

No one she knew. There were often multiple weddings

in the bay in January. The golden beaches were a huge attraction for nuptials. 'Right. Tell me what's going on.'

'Lily's having pains in her stomach. Personally I think she ate too much rich food yesterday but she wants someone to check her out.'

'That sounds wise. They could be false labour pains. Can you drive into Takaka and meet me at the maternity unit? It's behind the medical centre. I'll head there now.' She went on to give exact directions before hanging up.

Immediately picking the phone up again, she called the mother of Nicholas's friend and asked if it was all right for him to stay there a while longer. Then she phoned Sasha's mother.

'Virginia, I'm very sorry but I have to bail on brunch, or at least be very late. A pregnant woman from Christchurch is having problems.'

'That's fine, Jess. You can't predict when those babies will make their appearance.'

Yeah, but this wasn't one of hers. Then there was the fact it was coming early—if it was even coming at all. 'Can you tell Sasha and Grady I'm sorry? I really wanted to be there.' And can you let your son know too?

'Sure can. What about Jackson?'

Ahh. She swallowed. 'What about him?'

Virginia's laughter filled her ear. So that's where Jackson had got that deep chuckle. She'd never noticed Virginia's laugh before. 'Seems he had a bit of a walk home at daybreak. We shared a pot of tea when he got in. He doesn't realise how little I sleep these days. It gave him a bit of a shock when he crept in the back door just like he used to as a teenager.'

So much for Jackson trying to stop the town knowing about their night of fun. But his mother wouldn't be one for spreading that particular titbit of gossip. Or any other. She didn't do gossip. And...Jessica drew a breath...*she* didn't need to know what he'd got up to as a teen.

'Tell him thanks.' Oops. Wrong thing to blurt out to the man's mother.

'For what, Jess?' That laughter was back in Virginia's voice.

Too much information for Jackson's mother. 'For...' she cast around for something innocuous to say, came up blank.

Virginia's laughter grew louder. 'I'll tell him thanks. He can fill in the blanks. Good luck with the baby. Come round when you're done. We'd love to see you.'

I'm never going to the Wilson house again. My face will light up like a Christmas-tree candle the moment I step through their door. Apparently Virginia had a way of getting things out of a person without appearing to be trying.

Hauling on some knee-length shorts and a sleeveless shirt, she gave her hair a quick brush and tied it in a ponytail. There wasn't time to blow-dry it now and as she wasn't about to see Jackson it didn't really matter any more.

Pulling out of her driveway, she saw her neighbour, Mrs Harrop, waving at her from the front porch. They both lived on the outskirts of town in identical little houses built back in the 1950s. Mrs Harrop took care of the gardens for both of them while Jess made sure the other woman had proper meals every day by always cooking twice as much as she and Nicholas needed.

'Morning, Mrs Harrop. Everything all right with you today?'

'The sun came up, didn't it? How was the wedding?

Who was that man I saw leaving your place in the early hours?' There was a twinkle in the seventy-year-old woman's eyes.

Damn. Usually her neighbour was half-blind in full daylight. 'Mrs Harrop…' Jess couldn't help herself. 'You won't mention anything to your friends, will you?'

'Get away with you, girl. My lips are zipped.'

Now, why did she have to mention zips? Jess's brain replayed the memory of Jackson undoing the zip of her dress last night. Oh, and then of her hand on his fly, pulling that zip down. Turning the radio onto full blast, she sang some more cringeworthy words and banged the steering-wheel in an approximation of the song's beat, and drove to town.

Jess made it to the maternity unit fifteen minutes before the distressed couple arrived. She filled in the time making coffee and nipped next door to the store to buy a muffin for breakfast. Nothing like the big cook-up she could've been enjoying at the Wilson establishment. But way better for her waistline.

The man she supposed to be Matthew helped his wife into the clinic and stood hopping from foot to foot, looking lost and uncomfortable.

After the introductions, Jess helped Lily up onto the examination bed. 'This is where they used to tell the husbands to go and boil water.'

Matthew gave a reluctant smile. 'Thank goodness the world is far more modern these days. But I admit having something concrete to do would help me right now.'

'You could hold your wife's hand while I examine her.' Try being a comfort to her, rubbing her back. She's the one doing the hard work here.

'Speaking of water, Lily did pass a lot of fluid just before I rang you.'

'You're telling me her waters broke?' What was wrong with letting me know sooner?

Matthew looked sheepish. 'Lily wouldn't let me look and I wasn't sure.'

Jess wanted to bang her head against the wall and scream. These two really weren't dealing with this pregnancy very well. After an examination she told them, 'Baby's head's down, and its bottom is pointing up. You're definitely in labour.'

Lily said nothing, but her face turned white. 'Now? Here? We shouldn't have come.' The eyes she turned on her husband were filled with distress and something else Jess couldn't quite make out. Blame? Fear?

'Matthew told me you're nearly eight months along.' When Lily nodded slowly, Jessica groaned internally. She'd have preferred to be dealing with a full-term baby when she didn't know the patient. 'I need to talk to your midwife. Lily, have you timed how far apart your contractions are?'

'She wasn't sure they were contractions,' Matthew replied.

'So this is your first baby?' Jess asked.

'No, our second.' Matthew again.

So far Lily had hardly got a word in. Maybe that boiling water was a good idea after all. Jess pasted on a smile before saying, 'I really need to talk to Lily for a moment. Have you timed the pains?'

Lily nodded, her face colouring up. 'They're four minutes apart.'

'Okey-dokey, we've got a little lead-in time, then.' Possibly very little, if this baby was in a hurry, but there was no point in raising Lily's anxiety level any further. 'You can fill me in on details. Like who your midwife is and how I can get hold of her for a start.'

I so do not like flying blind. A perfectly normal pregnancy so far, according to Matthew, but that baby was coming early. Too early really. Jess punched the cellphone number Matthew read out from his phone.

'They're where?' the other midwife yelped when Jess explained the situation. 'I warned them not to leave town. Lily has a history of early delivery. She's only thirty weeks. The last baby didn't survive.'

'Thirty weeks? You're sure? Sorry, of course you are. Damn it. Why would Matthew have said nearly eight months?' Jess would've sworn long and loud if it weren't the most unprofessional thing to do.

'To cover the fact he shouldn't have taken Lily away at all.' The other midwife didn't sound surprised.

'He's brought his wife to a place where there's no well-equipped hospital or any highly qualified obstetricians and paediatricians.' All because he'd wanted to go to a family wedding. The closest hospital by road was Nelson, a good two hours away. Now what? She had to call one of the local doctors. At least she knew where they all were. At the post-wedding brunch. She needed help fast. And probably a rescue helicopter. Those guys would have Lily in Nelson with every chance of saving her baby's life in a lot less time than any other form of transport.

Lily groaned her way through a contraction. It would only get worse very soon, Jess thought after another examination of Lily. 'Your baby has definitely decided on Golden Bay for its showdown.' But she'd do her damnedest to change that. 'Do you know if you're having a boy or a girl?'

'A girl,' Matthew answered.

A discreet knock at the door had her spinning around to see what her next crisis was. Another patient was not on her agenda.

Heat slammed into her tummy. 'Jackson?' Yes, please, thank you. 'Come in.' Perfect timing. 'What brought you here?'

'Mum's truck.' He grinned. 'When she told me why you'd phoned I thought I'd drop by and say hi.'

'I'm really glad you did.' Then Matthew glared at her and Jackson so she quickly made the introductions.

'Good. A doctor is exactly what we need,' the guy had the temerity to say straight to her face.

Lily would've had any number of those if only they'd stayed in Christchurch. 'Lily, Matthew, I need to talk to Dr Wilson. We'll be right back.'

She dragged Jackson out of the room before anyone had time to utter a word. Her hand held a bunch of his very expensive shirt, the likes of which wasn't usually seen around Takaka. In other circumstances, she'd have been pulling that gorgeous mouth down closer so she could kiss him hard and long. But today wasn't her lucky day. 'I know you don't start covering for Grady for a few more days so I can phone Mike or Roz, but I'd like some assistance here.' She quickly ran through all the details the midwife had given her. 'I think it would be best if the rescue helicopter is called. I do not want to risk that baby's life.'

'I'm with you.' Jackson caught her hand to his chest as she let go of his shirt. 'The baby will need all the support it can get right from the moment it appears.'

'She. It's a girl.' Jess spread her fingers across the chest that only hours ago she'd been kissing. 'You need to make the call. I'm not authorised to except in exceptional circumstances.' Which this could arguably be.

'No problem. I'll examine Lily first and then I'll know what I'm talking about when I phone the rescue service. Can you get me the number? And the midwife's? I'd like to talk to her, too.' His green gaze was steady. 'I'm not undermining you, Jess. I prefer first-hand information, that's all. Especially since it's been a while since I delivered a baby.'

The relief that he was sharing the burden swamped her, although she knew it shouldn't. She had experience in difficult deliveries, though always in places where back-up was on hand. 'Not a problem, I assure you.' She turned to head for her patient. 'Come on, we'll talk to those two again. Together.'

Jackson still held her hand, tugged her back against him. 'I had a great time.' His lips brushed hers. 'Thank you.'

You and me both. But she couldn't tell him because of the sudden blockage in her throat and the pounding in her ears. So she blinked and smiled and then made her way into see Lily.

Jackson made the phone calls and returned to check on baby Carter's progress. He was angry.

Breathe deep, in one two, out one two.

This mother and baby should not be here, jeopardising their chances of a good outcome. His hands fisted.

In one two. Out one two.

Sure, everything could work out perfectly, but at thirty weeks the baby would still need an incubator and special care. The father was a moron. Especially considering the fact their last baby had died. How did Jess remain so calm? Maybe she'd had time to settle down and get on with what mattered most, appearing confident in the current situation and ignoring the if-only's. 'Lily, you're going to Nelson Hospital to have this baby. It's too early for us to be bringing her into the world here.' His tone was too harsh.

In one two. Out one two.

'I'm not driving Lily over that awful hill in her condition. It was uncomfortable enough for her on Friday and she wasn't in labour then.' Matthew stared at Jackson as though it was his fault they were dealing with this here and now.

Jackson ground his teeth and fought for control. Losing his temper would do absolutely nothing to help. Finally, on a very deep, indrawn breath, he managed to explain without showing his anger. 'The rescue helicopter will be here in approximately one hour. Jessica, where do they land?'

'In the paddock out the back of the medical centre. I'll go and see if there are any sheep that need shifting. Matthew, you can give me a hand.' Jess winked at Jackson before she led the startled man out the door.

'Go, Jess.' Jackson grinned to himself, his anger easing off quicker than usual. Starting an examination of Lily, he talked to her all the while, explaining what was happening. And calmed down further. These sudden anger spurts were disturbing. He was usually known for his cool, calm manner in any crisis and he'd hoped taking time away from his job would fix the problem. It seemed he was wrong or maybe just impatient.

'Will my baby be all right?' Lily asked through an onset of tears.

He would not promise anything. 'We'll do everything we can towards that outcome.'

The tears flowed harder. 'I didn't want to come to the wedding but Matthew insisted. He can be very determined.'

Try selfish and stubborn. 'We can't change the fact that you're in Golden Bay at the moment so let's concentrate on keeping baby safe.'

'Grr. Ahhh.' Lily's face screwed up with pain as another contraction tore through her.

Jackson reached for a flailing hand, held it tightly. The contractions were coming faster. All he could do was prepare for the birth and hope like hell the emergency crew would get here first. How fast could they spin those rotors? Where was Jess? She'd be more at ease with the situation than him. It's what she did, bringing babies into the world. Admittedly not usually this early or with this much danger of things going horribly wrong, but she was still more used to the birthing process.

'Hey, how are we doing?' A sweet voice answered his silent pleas. Jess had returned, dissolving the last of the tension gripping him.

Stepping away from the bed and closer to this delightful woman who seemed to have a way about her that quickly relaxed him, he murmured, 'Remind me to buy you another bottle of champagne when this is over.'

The fudge-coloured eyes that turned to him were twinkling. Her citrus tang wafted in the air when she leaned close to whisper, 'I might need some of that brunch first. My energy levels need rebuilding.'

Jess would drive him crazy with need if he wasn't

careful. And did that matter? Of course it did. Didn't it? He'd hate to hurt her in any way. 'You'll have to wait. How was that paddock? Any sheep?'

'Nope, all clear. The windsock is hardly moving so the landing should be straightforward. How's Lily doing?'

'Starting to panic. And who can blame her?'

Jess crossed to the woman. 'We're all set for that helicopter, Lily. Ever been in one before?'

'N-no. I—I don't like flying.'

Jackson groaned quietly. This day was going from bad to worse for the woman. 'They're quite different to being in a plane. Perfectly safe. The pilot will probably go around the coastline instead of over the hill so you won't be too far above ground level.'

Jess added, 'This is definitely the best way to keep your baby safe. Now, with the next contraction I want you to stand. You might find it easier to deal with the pain.'

Lily's smile was strained as she clambered off the bed. 'Thank you. I know you're trying your best. I'll be okay.' Then all talk stopped as she went through another contraction.

This time Matthew held her as she draped herself over him and hung on. 'You're doing great, Lily.'

Finally, just when Jackson thought they'd be delivering Baby Carter in the medical centre the steady thwup-thwup of the helicopter approaching reached them inside the hot and stuffy room. 'Here we go. Your ride has arrived, Lily,' he said needlessly.

Everyone had heard the aircraft and Matthew had gone to watch the landing. Jackson followed him out and once the rotors had stopped spinning he strode across to meet the paramedic and paediatrician as they disembarked and began unloading equipment.

'Glad to see that incubator.' He nodded towards the interior of the craft. 'You might be needing it.'

'Baby's that close?' the man who'd introduced himself as Patrick asked. His arm badge read 'Advanced Paramedic'.

'The mother has the urge to push. But I'm hoping she can hold off for a bit longer.'

'Let's take a look before we decide how to run with it. I don't fancy a birth in mid-air.'

In the end, Baby Carter made their minds up for them. She arrived in a hurry, sliding out into the bright light of the world, a tiny baby that barely filled Jackson's hand. Handing her carefully to Jess, he concentrated on repairing a tear that Lily had received during the birth.

Matthew stood to one side, stunned at the unfolding events. 'Is Lily okay? What about my daughter? Is she going to make it? At least she cried. That's got to be good, doesn't it?'

The last baby didn't cry? Jackson looked up and locked gazes with Matthew. 'The baby's breathing normally, and Lily's going to be fine. Have you decided on a name for your daughter?'

'Yes, but we were afraid to mention it until we knew if she'd be all right.' Matthew's eyes shifted to the right, where his daughter was being attached to monitors inside the incubator. 'Alice Rose,' he whispered, and brushed the back of his hand over his face.

'Alice Rose Carter.' Jess spared the man a sympathetic glance. 'I like it. Pretty. And so is she. Come over here and see for yourself.'

The paediatrician continued adjusting equipment as he

explained, 'Alice Rose is very small, as to be expected. At thirty weeks her lungs aren't fully developed so this machine will help her breathe until she grows some. But…' the man looked directly at Matthew '…everything so far shows she's looking to be in good shape despite her early arrival. I'm not saying you're out of trouble yet. There are a lot of things to watch out for, but one step at a time, eh?'

Matthew blinked, swiped at his face again and stepped closer to his daughter. 'Hello, Alice. I'm your daddy.' Then he sniffed hard.

Jess handed the guy a box of tissues. 'Hey, Daddy, blow your nose away from your baby.' She said it in such a soft tone that Jackson knew she'd forgiven the guy for being rather highhanded earlier. 'You're going to have to learn to be very careful around Alice Rose for a long time to come.'

Jackson helped Lily into a sitting position. 'I'm so sorry you can't hold your daughter yet.' That had to be devastating for any new mother. During many long phone calls last year Sasha had often told him that she could barely wait for Melanie to be placed in her arms and to be able to give her that very first kiss. Lily and Matthew weren't going to have that for a while.

'I'm grateful she's doing all right so far. Not like last time. We knew straight away little Molly wouldn't make it.' Lily's bottom lip trembled. 'No. I'm lying. I want to hold her so much it hurts. By the time I do she won't be a newborn.' The tears flowed, pouring down her cheeks to soak into the hospital gown that she still wore.

'You're going to need to head across to Nelson as soon as possible,' Jackson told her, shifting the subject to more practical matters. 'There's a shower next door, if you want to clean up first.'

'Thank you. It all seems surreal. I've just been through childbirth and there's no baby in my arms to show for it.' Tears sparkled out of her tired eyes as she gathered up her clothes and headed towards the bathroom.

His heart squeezed. For this couple who'd blown into their lives that morning with a monumental problem? Or could there be more to his emotional reaction? Since the attack he'd never quite known where his emotions were taking him, they were so out of whack. Coming home had added to his unrest. Having spent so many years being thankful that he'd escaped Golden Bay, it was difficult to understand why regrets were now filtering through his long-held beliefs.

He'd never really given much thought to having a family of his own. It wasn't that he didn't want one. It was just a thought that had been on the back burner while he established his career and got over his distrust of women enough to get to really know them. Then his career had grown into a two-headed monster, leaving him little time to develop anything remotely like a relationship. The women who'd passed through his life hadn't changed that opinion. Probably because he'd chosen women who wouldn't want to wreck their careers or their figures by having children. He'd chosen women who wouldn't lie to him or about him.

But honestly? He wasn't against a relationship where he settled down with someone special. The problem was, he couldn't see it working in the centre of Hong Kong surrounded by high-rises and very little green space. As that city was where his life came together, where he was the man he'd strived so hard to become, he could see that there'd be no children in his life for a long while.

He looked around and found Jess regarding him from

under lowered eyelids. Could she read him? Did she know that if he ever changed his mind she might be the one woman he'd be interested in? Get a grip, Jackson. Until last night he wouldn't even have had these thoughts. One very exciting and enjoyable night in the arms of Jessica Baxter and he was getting some very weird ideas.

Because, love or hate Golden Bay, there was a lot to be said for the outdoors lifestyle and bringing up kids in this district. The district where his career would fizzle out with the lack of hospitals and emergency centres.

CHAPTER FOUR

THE HELICOPTER LIFTED off the paddock, the wind it created whipping at Jess's clothes, moulding her shirt against her breasts. 'Right, I'd better go and pick up Nicholas. I promised he would get to see Sasha and Grady before they left on their honeymoon.' Jess glanced at her watch. 'Brunch is probably well and truly wrapped up by now.'

Jackson's gaze was on her breasts. 'What did you say?' he almost shouted.

She grinned. Deafened by the aircraft or distracted by her boobs? 'I need to collect Nicholas. And hopefully catch Sasha and Grady before they leave.'

Jackson finally lifted his head enough to meet her gaze. 'Okay.' He tossed his keys up and down in his left hand. 'I don't think they were heading off until about one. Their flight leaves Nelson at four and they're staying overnight in Auckland.'

'Two weeks in Fiji sounds sublime.' Jess sighed wistfully and headed inside.

'Not just Fiji, but Tokariki Island. Tiny place, catering for only a few couples at a time. Heaven.' Jackson grinned at her as he strode alongside, sending those butterflies in her stomach on another of their merry dances.

'You are so mean. I'd love to go to the Islands.' With

a hot man. Not that it was ever going to happen. She was a mother with a four-year-old who needed her more than anyone. 'Let's get out of here before the bell rings and we're stuck fixing cuts and scrapes for the rest of the day.' Leading by example, she turned off the lights and headed for the outside door.

'Can I come with you to pick up your son?'

Jess stopped her mad dash for freedom and spun round to come chest to chest with Jackson. He'd startled her with his simple request, and judging by the look of surprise in his eyes he'd startled himself as well. 'Did I hear right? You want to share a tiny car with a loud, boisterous little boy who talks nonstop, never letting anyone else get a word in?'

She waited for him to back off fast. But instead he nodded. 'Guess I do. Is Nicholas really that noisy?'

Laughter rolled up her throat. 'Oh, boy. You have no idea.' This would test their burgeoning friendship. Her son was no angel. In fact, she had to admit he was getting very much out of control and she didn't know what to do about it. Loving him to bits meant saying no which didn't come easily for her.

But one day soon she was going to have to grow a backbone when it came to Nicholas or they were in for a very rocky ride as he grew up. It was just that she needed to lavish him with love, show him how much he mattered to her. She would not become her parents, throwing money at every situation when more often than not a hug would have sufficed. No. Nicholas would always know how much she cared about him. Always.

A big, warm and strong hand cupped her chin, tilted her head back so that she stared into Jackson's green gaze. 'Jess? Where have you gone? Something up?'

With an abrupt shake of her head she stepped away from that hand and those all-seeing eyes. It would be too easy to lean into him, burden him with her problems. That would certainly put the kibosh on getting to know him better. He'd suddenly have so much to do she'd not even see his delectable butt departing for all the dust he'd raise on the way out. She mightn't be sophisticated but she knew the rules. She'd invented some of them.

Keep it simple.

Do not get too close.

Don't ask him for more than fun. And great sex.

Her skin sizzled. What they'd shared last night had gone beyond fun, beyond description. She grimaced. What rule had she broken there?

'Jessica, you're going weird on me.' Jackson was right beside her as she punched in the security code for the alarm system.

Pulling the door shut and checking it was locked, she dug deep for a nonchalant answer and came up with, 'Not weird, just pulling on my mother-in-charge persona.'

'You're two different people?' His eyes widened, making him look surprised and funny at the same time.

She couldn't keep serious around him. Bending forward at the waist, one hand on her butt like a tail and the other creating a beak over her mouth, she headed towards her car. 'Quack, quack, quack.'

'Hang on, who are you? Where's Jess gone? Bring her back. I'm not getting in a vehicle with a duck.'

'Quack, quack.'

Jackson chuckled. 'Is this how you bring up your son? The poor little blighter. He'll be scarred for life. I need to save him.'

Jess felt his arms circle her and swing her off the

ground to be held against that chest she'd so enjoyed running her fingers up and down during the night. She slid her hands behind his neck and grinned into his face. 'You're not going to kiss a duck?'

He groaned. 'I must be as crazy as you.' Then his mouth covered hers and she forgot everything except his kiss.

Heat spiralled out of control inside her. Her skin lifted in excited goose-bumps. Between her legs a steady throb of need tapped away at her sanity. Sparks flew. Whoever had invented electricity obviously hadn't had great sex.

Without taking that gorgeous, sexy mouth away from hers, Jackson set her on her feet and tugged her hard against him. She could feel his reaction to her against her abdomen. She clung to him. To stop holding him would mean ending up in an ungainly heap on the ground.

His lips lifted enough for him to demand, 'What's that code you just punched in?'

'Why?'

'We need a bed. Or privacy at least.'

He was right. They couldn't stay in the very public car park, demonstrating their awakening friendship. Not when he'd made sure no one had seen him leaving her place early that morning. She glanced down at Jackson's well-awake evidence of their needs and grinned. 'Three-two-four-eight-one.'

'I'm expected to remember that in the midst of a wave of desire swamping my brain?'

Thank goodness he returned his mouth to hers the moment he'd got that question out. She couldn't stand it when he withdrew from kissing her. Could this man kiss or what?

Cheep-cheep. Cheep-cheep.

'What the—?' Jackson's eyes were dazed as he looked around.

Reality kicked into Jess. 'My phone.' She tugged the offending item from her pocket and glared at the screen. Then softened. 'It's probably Nicholas, using Andrea's phone.' As she pressed the talk button she gave Jackson an apologetic shrug. 'This is another side of being a mother. Always on call.' Then, 'Hello, is that my boy?'

'Mummy, where are you? I want to see Grady now.' He'd taken to Grady very quickly. Perhaps it was a sign he needed a male figure in his life?

'I'm on my way to get you.' She turned from the disappointment in Jackson's eyes. He might as well get used to the reality of her life right from the start. Presuming he wanted to see more of her, and that bulge in his jeans suggested he did.

'How long will you be, Mummy? I want to show you the fish the seagulls stole.'

'Nicholas, you know I can't talk to you while I'm driving so you'll have to wait until I get there to tell me about the seagulls. Okay?'

'Why won't the policemen let you drive and talk to me? It's not fair.'

Jess grinned. 'It's the law, sweetheart.' Knowing Nicholas could talk for ever, she cut him off. 'See you soon.'

Jackson's hands were stuffed into the pockets of his designer jeans as he leaned against the vehicle he'd borrowed from his mother. 'Want me to drive?'

'You still want to come with me?' Now, that surprised her. As far as she knew, Jackson wasn't used to little kids and this particular one had interrupted something fairly intense. 'Are you going to growl at him for his timing?'

'No.' He flicked a cheeky smile her way. 'The day will come when someone interrupts him in his hour of need.'

She groaned and slapped her forehead. 'I do not want to think about that. He's four, not thirty-four.'

'Thirty-four?'

'That's when I'll think about letting him out on his own to see girls.'

'Good luck with that one.' He crossed to the driver's side of her car and held his hand up for the keys. 'Let's go.'

'Um, my car. I drive.'

He just grinned at her. Really grinned, so that her tummy flip flopped and her head spun. So much that driving could be dangerous.

'Go on, then.' She tossed the keys over the top of her car. 'Men.'

'Glad you noticed.'

How could she not? His masculinity was apparent in those muscles that filled his jeans perfectly, in his long-legged stride, in the jut of his chin, in that deep, sexy chuckle that got her hormones in a twitter every time. She climbed into the passenger seat and closed the door with a firm click. Then something occurred to her. 'We're going to Pohara Beach. Shouldn't we take both vehicles, save a trip back into town later?'

'Nah. I'll go for a run when it cools down, pick up the truck then. Mum won't be needing it today.'

'Running? As in pounding the pavement and build-ing up a sweat?' She shuddered. 'You obviously need a life.' But it did explain those superb thigh muscles. And his stamina.

Jackson just laughed. 'You're not into jogging, then? Knitting and crochet more your style?'

Thinking about the cute little jerseys she'd made for Nicholas last winter, she smiled and kept quiet. *If only you knew, Jackson.*

Then he threw another curve ball as they headed towards the beach. 'Who held you while you had Nicholas? Who smoothed your back and said you were doing fine?'

The man wasn't afraid of the big questions. 'No one ever asked me that before.' Not even Mum and Dad. Especially not Mum and Dad.

'Tell me to shut up if you want.'

That was the funny thing. She didn't want to. Jackson touched something in her that negated all her usual reticence when it came to talking about personal things. 'Two nurses I was friendly with took it in turns to hold my hand and talk me through the pain.' She'd trained with Phillip and Rochelle, and when they'd got married she'd been there to celebrate with them. They'd been quick to put their hands up when she'd announced she was having a baby, offering to help in any way they could. It had been more than three years since they'd left to work in Australia, and she still missed them.

'That must've been hard.'

Because Nicholas's dad wasn't there? No, by then she'd known she'd had a lucky escape. 'Not so bad. It was worse afterwards when I wanted to share Nicholas's progress, to talk about him and know I was on the right track with how I brought him up. That's when single mothers have it tough. That's what I've been told, and going by my own experience I have to agree.' It was also probably why Nicholas got away with far more than he should. There was no one to share the discipline, to play good cop, bad cop with.

'So how do you cope with the day-to-day stuff of being a solo mum?'

'Heard of the headless chook? That's me.'

'When you're not being a duck, you mean?'

She giggled. 'That too. I don't think about how I manage, I just do. I wouldn't want to go back to before I had Nicholas. Being a mother is wonderful. Though there are days when I go to visit Sasha or your mum for a bit of adult conversation and to help calm the worry that I'm getting it all wrong.'

'Even two parents bringing up a child together have those worries.'

'Guess it will never stop.'

Jackson turned onto the road running beside Pohara Beach. 'I was watching Lily and Matthew earlier. They were desperate to hold their baby and it hurt them not to be able to.'

Again she thought she could read him. 'Believe me, if you want to be a part of your child's life then you're not going to miss that first cuddle for anything. Sad to say, but my boy's father truly didn't care. He came to town for three months, had a lot of fun, and left waving a hand over his shoulder when I told him I was pregnant. He didn't even say goodbye.'

It was silent in the car for a minute then she pointed to a sprawling modern home on the waterfront. 'There.'

Jackson pulled up on the drive, switched the engine off and turned to her. 'He wasn't interested in his child?'

'There was a wife in Alaska.' It had hurt so much at the time. She'd been an idiot to fall for him.

'The jerk.' Jackson lifted her hand and rubbed his

thumb across the back of it, sending shivers of need racing through her blood. Again.

'It's Nicholas who misses out. He'd love a dad to do all those male things with. Apparently I'm no good at football.' She pushed out of the car. All the better to breathe. Despite the conversation they were having, sitting beside Jackson in her minuscule car did nothing to quieten her rampaging hormones.

'Mummy, here I am.' Nicholas's sweet voice interrupted her internal monologue and reminded her who was important in her life. Here was the only person she should be thinking about.

'Hey, sweetheart, have you had a good time?' She reached out to haul him in for a hug but he'd stumbled to a stop and banged his hands on his hips.

His head flipped back at Jackson. 'What's your name?' he demanded.

Jackson stood on the other side of the car, studying her boy in that searching way of his. 'I'm Jackson Wilson. You saw me at the wedding.' He came round and put his hand out to be shaken.

But Nicholas hadn't finished. 'Why did you drive my mummy's car?'

The corner of Jackson's mouth lifted but he kept his amusement under control. 'I like driving and haven't been doing very much lately.'

'Mummy likes driving, too.' Nicholas stared at the proffered hand. 'Are you a friend of ours?'

'Yes, I am. That's why I'm waiting to shake your hand. Want to put yours in mine, sport?'

Jess could barely contain her laughter as she watched her son strut across and bang his tiny hand into Jackson's much larger one. They both shook.

'See, Mummy. That's how it's done.'

'So it is.' What she did see was that Nicholas really did need some male influence in his life. He picked up on anything Grady said, and now, if she wasn't mistaken, he was factoring Jackson into his thinking.

A chill ran through her veins. Not good. Jackson would soon be going away again, and if Nicholas got too fond of him, they were in for tears. Some of those might be hers, too. Already she felt comfortable around him in a way she rarely felt with men. There were a lot of hidden depths to Jackson, but she liked the way he took the proper time with her son. Amongst other things. Then her face heated as she recalled how there'd been no time spared last night when they'd first fallen into bed.

'Do I get my hug now, Nicholas?'

Dropping the strut, her boy ran at her, barrelling into her legs. 'I missed you, Mummy. Did you miss me?'

Swinging him up in her arms, she grinned and kissed his cheek. 'Big time.'

'Hi, Jess,' Andrea called from the porch of the house. 'How was the wedding?'

Andrea's question might have been directed to Jessica but her gaze was fixed on Jackson. He seemed to have that effect on most women. Including her. Even now, when there was no alcohol fizzing around her system, she definitely had the hots for him. She knew that if they were alone with time to spare she'd be requesting a repeat performance of last night's lovemaking.

But she wasn't alone with him. Her son was waiting to go and see Grady, and Andrea was waiting for a reply to her question. 'Sasha looked stunning, and Grady scrubbed up all right, too. They're leaving on their honeymoon shortly so I'd better get Nicholas around there to say goodbye. Thank you so much for having him to stay. I hope he wasn't any trouble.' He could be. She knew that. He hated being told what to do and could throw a paddy that matched the severity of a tornado. It was something she needed to work on.

He wriggled to be set down as Andrea waved a hand in his direction. 'You were very well behaved, weren't you, Nicholas? I wish Bobby could be half as good.'

Huh? Did Nicholas only play up for her? 'Thank goodness for that.' Jess checked he'd put his seat belt on properly before walking around to get back in the car.

Jackson started backing out the driveway. 'What did you get up to with your friend, Nicholas?'

'We played soccer, and Bobby's dad took us in his truck to get a boat. I wanted to go fishing but we weren't allowed because no adults wanted to go with us.' On and on he went, detailing every single thing he'd done since she'd dropped him off after the wedding service and before the reception.

Warmth stole through her, lifting her lips into a smile. 'That's my boy,' she whispered. Though thankfully they were pulling up outside Virginia and Ian's within minutes. Jess didn't want Jackson bored to sleep while driving. But he was the one to unclip Nicholas's belt and help him down. 'There you go, sport. Let's see if there's any of that brunch left for us to enjoy.'

'What's brunch?'

'Breakfast and lunch all mixed together,' Jess told him as she straightened his shirt.

'Why do you mix them?'

'So you only have one meal.' She rubbed his curls and got a glare for her trouble.

'That's a dumb idea.' Nicholas, as usual, got in the last word.

There were still a lot of people milling around, obviously in no hurry to leave. Jess hoped Virginia was coping. Yesterday had been tiring enough for someone with her disease. 'I'm going to see if I can do anything to help,' she told Jackson.

'I'll go and find Dad,' he told her.

'Hey, there you two are.' Grady strode across the lawn towards them.

The way he said it suggested she and Jackson were a couple. That would surely send Jackson off to hide amongst the guests.

'Howdy, Grady. How's married life treating you so far?' she asked.

'No complaints,' he answered, before swinging Nicholas up above his head and holding the giggling, writhing body of her son aloft. 'Hey, Nicholas, how are you doing, boyo? Did you have fun at Bobby's house?'

'Yes, yes,' Nicholas shrieked. 'Make me fly, Grady.'

'Please,' Jess said automatically.

Too late. Grady swooped his armful earthward and up again. How his back took the strain she had no idea. 'Where's Sasha?'

'Inside with Virginia, getting some more food. Man, these people can eat.' Swoop, and Nicholas was flying towards the ground again.

'You okay with Nicholas while I go see what I can do to help?' she asked Grady.

'She thinks I can't look after you, Nicholas. Women, eh?'

'What do you mean, women?' Nicholas's little face screwed up in question.

Jackson laughed. 'Get yourself out of that in one piece, Grady.'

'Better that he knows all he can as soon as possible.' Grady grinned. 'Leave the lad with us, Jess. We'll teach him all our bad habits.'

'That's what I'm afraid of.' She tipped her head to one side. 'You are grinning a lot this morning, Mr O'Neil. I'd better go see what Mrs O'Neil has been up to.' Jess headed to the house, ignoring the ribald comments coming from the two men she'd just left.

Inside she found Sasha and Virginia busy plating up leftover dessert from the wedding dinner. One look at Sasha told her everything. 'Oh, yuk. You look as happy as Grady. Must be something in the water out here.'

Sasha grinned and rushed to hug her. 'Morning. You're not looking too unhappy yourself.'

Uh-oh. Jess looked over at Virginia who suddenly seemed very busy placing slices of fruit on a pavlova. 'Of course I do. I've just delivered a baby. Although she was ten weeks early.'

'Is that why the helicopter went over earlier?' Virginia finally lifted her head. Dark shadows stained her cheeks, and her smile was a little loose.

'Yep. Now, Virginia, I'd love nothing better than a good old chinwag with Sasha before she leaves on her honeymoon. Want to let me finish that while I talk? Jackson's outside somewhere.'

Jess held her breath. She knew better than to out and out insist that Sasha's mum should take a rest.

'Good idea. I've been waiting to have a chat with that boy of mine.' She had the audacity to wink at Jess.

'I think he's with Grady, though he said he wanted to find Ian.'

Virginia hadn't even got to the door when Sasha rounded on Jess, grabbing her arms. 'What's this about my brother staying the night at your place?'

Didn't Sasha approve? She should have known it wasn't wise to get too close to her friend's brother. Hell, none of last night had been wise, but it had been a lot of fun. Though if it would come between her and Sasha then she'd learn to get over Jackson fast. Which wasn't a bad idea. She didn't want a serious relationship. 'Your mother's been talking?'

'Her words were, "Maybe there's enough of an attraction here to keep Jackson from returning to Hong Kong."' Sasha locked her eyes on Jess's, looking right inside her. 'It's okay, you know. In fact, I wholeheartedly approve.'

The air in Jess's lungs whooshed across her lips. 'I'm glad it isn't going to be an issue between us. But you and your mother are getting ahead of the game. One night doesn't automatically lead to a wedding.'

'Got to start somewhere.' Sasha grinned again.

These lovesick grins were getting tiresome. But, then, hadn't she been smiling and laughing more than normal this morning? 'Great sex does the trick every time.'

'Excuse me?' Sasha's eyebrows rose and her brow wrinkled.

'You and Grady, going around like those clowns at the show with big grins that won't close.'

'Oh. Like the one on your face right now? Bet there's one on my brother's mug, too.'

Jess couldn't help it. She burst out laughing, and grabbed Sasha into another hug. 'Guess we should get these pavlovas done.'

'You always change the subject when it gets too hot

for you.' Sasha resumed hulling the bowl of strawberries on the bench beside her. 'By the way, thank you for that painting you gave us. It's fabulous. How does the artist do such intricate work? Looking at that gull on the post with the sea in the background makes me feel the sun on my face and the salt air in my nostrils.'

'He's very good, no doubt about it.'

'Yeah, well, we love it and thank you so much. Of course, I could say you shouldn't have spent that kind of money but then I'd have to give the painting back and I'm not parting with it.'

'Damn. My cunning plan failed.'

They talked about the wedding as they worked, reminding each other of everything that had happened from the moment they'd started getting ready early yesterday morning.

Loud masculine laughter reached them through the open kitchen windows and Jess stopped to stare out at Jackson as he stood talking with Grady and Ian. Those butt-hugging jeans and a T-shirt that outlined his well-defined muscles made her mouth water. Her heart bumped harder and louder than normal, and those pesky butterflies in her tummy started their dance again. 'Sasha, what does love feel like?' she whispered.

Sasha came to stand beside her and looked in the same direction. Slipping her arm through Jess's, she answered softly, 'It feels like every day is summer, like the air is clearer, and at night the stars are brighter. Love feels as though nothing can go wrong. As though everything is bigger. It makes you laugh and smile more.'

Jess bit down hard on her lip. *I've fallen in love. Overnight. Or did it happen the moment I saw Jackson standing beside Grady as they waited for us to arrive and the wedding ceremony to start? Does it even matter? It's happened. And it's not going anywhere.*

Sasha nudged her gently. 'The sky's very blue today, isn't it? Sparkling with sunlight.'

'Yes,' she whispered. *What the heck do I do now?*

'The colour of love, I reckon.'

CHAPTER FIVE

'WHO'S LOOKING AFTER Nicholas while you're working all these extra hours?' Jackson asked Jessica, as she folded the towels just back from the laundry and stacked them in the storeroom. It was Wednesday and he'd missed her every minute since the weekend. At least working here at the medical centre he got to see her occasionally but most of the time they were both too busy for more than quick snatches of conversation.

'He's at day care until Andrea picks him up after she collects her little boy from school. Bobby started school on Monday and Nicholas is so jealous. June can't come quickly enough for him.'

'I bet. It must be hard to leave him while you work.' She doted on her boy.

'It is. His little face turns all sad, which hurts to see. But it only happens a couple of days a week unless I'm covering for someone here.' Her face was turning sad now.

'You wouldn't think of not working at all?' What was her financial situation?

'Thanks to my parents...' she winced '...I could afford to stay at home, but not having a partner I need some adult contact. The brain needs some exercise, too.'

'I can understand that. It won't hurt Nicholas to be mixing with other kids his age either.' Do not wrap her up in a hug. Not here at work. 'Do you like doing Sasha's job as well as your own?' From what he'd seen so far, she coped remarkably well. Nothing seemed too much for her. It made him wonder if people took advantage of that.

Jessica shrugged. 'Two weeks is nothing. And I get to keep my other nursing skills up to date.'

'Do you often do the nursing job?'

'First and foremost I'm the midwife, but if either nurse wants time off I cover for her. I like the variety and there are times when I've got no babies due and need to be busy.' The face she lifted to him was beautiful. Those big brown eyes were shining and her mouth had been curved in a perpetual smile all day.

'That chicken dish you dropped at home yesterday was tasty. When did you find the time to make it?' He and Dad had come in from the orchard late to find that Jess had dropped by with the meal. 'Mum was grateful, though, be warned, she's not likely to tell you.'

'I know. Not a problem. The wedding took its toll on her.'

'Which is why I haven't had time to call round to see you since Sunday.' Not for lack of trying. 'Dad's had a lot to do, clearing away everything and getting on with the orchard needs.' He'd ached to visit Jess but knew his priorities lay with his parents for a few days at least. His guilt at not having been here for so long could only be kept at bay by working his butt off, doing chores for them. Leaving in April was not going to be easy. 'My tractor skills have been in demand.'

'I understand.' The hand she laid on his arm was warm, but the sensations zipping through his blood were red hot. 'Virginia's worked nonstop on wedding plans since the day Sasha proposed to Grady. She had to crash some time.'

Jackson grinned. 'Sasha proposed to Grady? Are you sure?'

Nodding, Jess told him, 'Absolutely. She did it minutes after Melanie was born.'

'That's so Sasha. I'd have thought Grady would've been chomping at the bit to ask her to marry him. He's besotted.'

'Isn't he? Sasha had been keeping him at a distance. Afraid he might leave her again, I guess.'

Jackson stepped back, away from the citrus scent, away from that body that he so craved. Otherwise he was going to haul Jess into his arms and kiss her senseless. Something he wanted to do every time he saw her. Something he very definitely couldn't do while at work in the medical centre. But they could catch up out of the work zone. 'I've been checking the tides and it's looking good for a spot of surfcasting. How about we take Nicholas down to the beach when we're done here and he can try some fishing?'

Her eyes were definitely fudge-coloured right now. 'You'd do that? I'd love it, and you'll be Nicholas's hero for ever.' Then the light gleaming out at him dimmed. 'Maybe that's not so wise.'

Jackson stepped back close, laid his hands on her shoulders. 'I promise to be careful with him. And Grady will be back to replace me in my male role model position.' He suddenly didn't like that idea. Not one little bit. For a brief moment he wished he could be the man who showed Nicholas the ways of the world. But he wasn't being realistic at all. It was not possible to be there for

Nicholas for more than a few weeks. So having Grady in the background was good. He had to believe that, or go crazy, worrying about the little guy.

Under his hands her shoulders lifted, dropped. 'You're right. But just so as you know, I don't want Nicholas getting high expectations of your involvement with him. Not when you're not staying around.'

At least she hadn't said anything about his involvement with her. While he hadn't worked out where their relationship was headed, he didn't want the gate closing before they'd spent more time together. 'I understand, Jess.'

'Do you?' She locked her gaze on him, like she was searching for something. 'I worry because I know what it's like to have expectations of adults and never have them met.'

'Your parents?' He held his breath, waiting for her to tell him to go to hell. To say it was none of his business.

But after a moment she nodded. 'Yeah. I'm sure they loved me. But they never needed me. I was a nuisance when all they needed was each other and their busy life outdoors, studying native flora and fauna, and how to protect it for generations to come. They tried. I'll give them that. I always had more money than even I could spend. Occasionally they took me on trips to places in the world most people aren't even aware of. All far away from civilisation, from the fun things a kid likes to do. I guess growing up I never wanted for anything. Except hugs, and sharing girl talk with my mother, and being able to brings friends home for sleepovers.'

When she started spilling her heart she didn't stop easily. The pain in her words cut him deep. No one should ever feel that they came second best with their parents.

No one. To hell with being at the medical centre. He wrapped his arms around her, held her tight, and dropped kisses on the top of her head. 'You already give Nicholas far more than that.'

'I hope so,' she murmured against him, her warm breath heating his skin. 'It's a work in progress.'

'You think you don't know how to love? From what I've seen, you're spot on.' She exuded love—to Nicholas, to Sasha, his parents, her patients. Did she have any left over for him? Because he really wanted some. Correction, he wanted lots. And what would he give her in return? Love? Full, hands-on love? Or the chilly, remote kind, like her parents'? From afar, in a city that was not conducive to raising a small boy with an apparent penchant for the outdoors.

His hands dropped away and he took that backwards step again. It was too soon to know. Did he want to know? He knew he didn't want to hurt Jess. *Don't forget you're heading out of here come mid-April. No way will Jessica and Nicholas be going with you.*

Jess rocked sideways, regained her balance. Gave him a crooked smile. 'Thanks. I think. Fishing after work would be lovely.' Then she spun round and became very intent on those damned towels again, refolding already neatly folded ones. Shifting them from stack to stack.

'Jackson.' Sheree from Reception popped her head around the corner. 'Mrs Harrop's here to see you.' Her voice dropped several octaves. 'She's not the most patient lady either.'

'On my way.' He stared at Jess's ramrod-straight back, waited for the other woman to return to her desk out front. 'We'll have fish and chips for dinner on the beach. That okay with you? And Nicholas?'

'Sounds great.' Jess turned and he relaxed. Her grin was back. Her eyes were like fudge. 'I'm looking forward to it.'

So was he. A lot. Too much for someone who wasn't getting involved. Face it, taking a woman and her son to do regular stuff like fishing was a first.

'And, Jackson?'

He turned back. 'Yes?'

'Mrs Harrop is a sweetie underneath that grumpy exterior.'

'I'll remember that.' How come Jessica stuck up for the underdog so much? Maybe it was because she'd been the odd one out in those two years she'd been to school here. He'd had the loving, sharing family *and* all the friends at school, and yet he stayed away.

'Mrs Harrop, it's been years since I saw you. Do you even remember me?' Jackson showed the rather large, elderly lady to a chair in the consulting room he was using while Grady was away.

'Could hardly forget the boy who kicked his football through my front window.'

Jackson winced. That had been at least fifteen years ago. He gave Mrs Harrop a rueful smile. 'Sorry about that.'

'You've been away too long, my boy,' she muttered, as she carefully lowered herself onto the seat. 'But you're here now.'

As this was about the fifth time he'd heard almost the exact words since arriving in Golden Bay Jackson didn't react at all. He might even have been disappointed if people hadn't commented on his return, even though it wasn't permanent. After all, since one of his reasons for leaving was that everyone here knew everything about people's business, he'd feel cheated if his actions were no longer justified.

'I wasn't going to miss the wedding. Sasha would never forgive me.' He wouldn't have forgiven himself. He loved his sister. 'She's so happy, it's wonderful.'

'That Grady was always meant for her.' Mrs Harrop was pulling up her sleeve. 'You going to take my blood pressure, or what?'

'I sure am. But first, how've you been feeling?' He'd read the patient notes before asking Mrs Harrop to come through and knew that she'd had two arterial stents put in six months ago.

'Old, tired, and a lot better than I used to.'

'How's your diet been? Are you sticking to fat-free?' Jackson saw that her last cholesterol test had been a little high but nothing dangerous.

'Your lady makes sure of that.'

'My lady? Mum? Or Sasha?' He wound the cuff of the sphygmomanometer around her upper arm.

'Pssh. I'm talking about Jessica. She's very good to me. Always delivering healthy meals and telling me how she's cooked too much. You'd think she'd have learned a new excuse by now. She's the best neighbour I ever had. Very kind. She genuinely cares about people.'

Alarm bells began clattering in his head. Mrs Harrop was calling Jessica his woman and they'd only spent one night together. Wasn't this why he left Golden Bay in the first place? 'You live in the house next to Jess?' Guess that explained her comment about his woman. At seventy Mrs Harrop might have old fashioned ideas about him spending a night with a lovely young woman.

Without waiting for Mrs Harrop's answer, he stuck the

earpieces in and squeezed the bulb to tighten the cuff. Then he listened to the blood pumping through her veins and noted the systolic and diastolic pressures. 'Moderately high. Have you been taking your tablets daily?'

'Yes, young man, I have. But I need a new prescription.' His patient pulled her sleeve down to her wrist and buttoned it. 'She bought both houses.'

'I think you need a different dosage.' Jackson began tapping the computer keyboard. 'She what? Who bought both houses? Jessica?'

Mrs Harrop's chin bobbed up and down, and her eyes lit up with satisfaction. 'Of course, Jessica. She saved my bacon when she bought mine. And now she lets me rent it back for next to nothing. I know I should be paying more but I can't.'

Jackson slumped in his chair. Jess owned both those homes? She hadn't said. *But why should she? She might've talked about her parents earlier but that didn't mean she would be telling you everything. Like you, she can play things close to the chest.* Another vision of that chest flickered through his brain before he had time to stamp on it. Beautiful, full breasts that filled his hands perfectly.

Apparently Mrs Harrop hadn't finished. 'You see, that boy of mine cleaned out my savings and left me with only the house. I wouldn't even have had that if my lawyer hadn't made me get a trustee to oversee any sale I might want to make.'

'I'm sorry to hear that.' But Jess had saved this woman from heartbreak.

'The day Jessica decided to return to Golden Bay was my lucky day.'

'So it would seem.' *Good for you, Jess. You're an absolute star.* Money had never been in short supply in her family, yet she drove a joke of a car and gave her neighbour cheap accommodation. 'Now, Mrs Harrop, here's your prescription. I've upped the dosage a little and I want to see you again next week.'

'Thank you, Doctor. I'll make an appointment on the way out.'

Jess was taking bloods from Gary Hill when he walked back from showing Mrs Harrop out. He asked, 'Hi, Gary. You still into motocross?'

'Gidday, Jackson. Sure am. Though the body's a bit stiff these days and I don't land so easily when I come off. Break a few more bones than I used to.' The guy appeared flushed and lethargic, but had plenty to say. Some things didn't change.

'Maybe it's time to give it up.'

Jess turned to him and rolled her eyes. 'Even when he broke his clavicle and humerus, there was no stopping Gary. You honestly think he'll give up because his body's getting rumpty on him?'

'Guess not.' Jackson was puzzled as to why Jess was taking bloods. 'So what brings you here today? I'm seeing you next, aren't I?'

'I've got a fever. I got malaria last year when I was riding in Malaysia and this feels exactly the same as the previous two bouts.' Gary shrugged. 'Just hope I'm not on my back too long. I'm supposed to be heading away to the Philippines in eight days.'

'Sorry, Jackson, but the courier's due to pick up medical specimens and Roz suggested I take Gary's bloods while he waited to see you.' Jess labelled the tubes of blood for haematology and biochemistry, then made some thick blood smears. Next she stuck a tiny plaster on the needle entry site on Gary's arm. 'There you go. We should hear back tonight about the malaria.'

Back in his room Jackson began to read Gary's file on the computer screen as he asked, 'Any symptoms other than the fever?'

'Hot and cold, hell of a headache, and I keep wanting to toss my food.' Gary eased himself onto a chair, rubbing his left side.

'You're hurting?' Was that his spleen giving him grief, engorged through trying to remove malarial parasites from his blood system?

'That's my old injury from when I came off the bike and broke my pelvis. Still hurts on and off. Guess the arthritis is starting to set in. I was warned.' He yawned deep. 'Yeah, this is familiar. The bone-numbing tiredness.'

Jackson found a thermometer and slipped it under Gary's tongue. 'Seriously, you ever think about slowing down?' The guy was only thirty-four but at this rate he might not make forty in reasonable working order.

Gary kept his lips sealed around the thermometer and shook his head.

'Fair enough. Your call.' Reading more of the file, he commented, 'I see your malaria was diagnosed as falciparum. Common in Asia. Had you taken anti-malarials at the time?'

A nod.

Reading the thermometer, he told Gary, 'That's way too high. I hope you've been taking lots of fluids. Let's get you up on the bed so I can check your spleen.'

Jackson gently felt Gary's abdomen. 'Your spleen's definitely enlarged, which fits the diagnosis.'

'Guess I already knew. Can't blame me for hoping I was wrong.'

'When did you start getting symptoms?'

'Started feeling crook night before last, but I was working up the Cobb Valley and wanted to get the job done.'

'You've got to take care of yourself, mate. This malaria can be very serious if you stall on getting treatment.'

'I live hard,' Gary growled. 'With my family history of bowel cancer taking my dad and two brothers, I'm packing in as much as I can in case I'm next.'

It made sense in a way. Jackson asked, 'You married, got kids?'

'Kate Saunders and I got hitched ten years back. Got two youngsters. What about you?'

'No, no kids or wife.'

'What are you waiting for? None of us are getting any younger. You don't want to be in your dotage, with anklebiters hanging on to you.'

'I'll remember you said that.' And try not to think about Jess in the same moment. 'I suggest we get you over the hill to hospital today. I don't want you waiting here until we find out those results. You need intravenous fluids ASAP.'

'Figured you'd say that. Kate's packed my overnight bag.'

He remembered Kate from school, a quiet girl who'd followed the crowd around. After signing a referral to hospital, Jackson went with Gary out to the waiting room and explained everything to Kate. 'It's great to see you both again.'

'You stopping here permanently?' Gary asked.

'No.'

'Why not? I travel a lot but this is the greatest little place on earth.'

Exactly. Little. Too little for him.

Thankfully Jessica joined them and diverted Gary's focus as she handed him a package. 'You might as well take your bloods with you. Save time at the other end, and prevent the need to be jabbed again.'

'Jess, line one for you,' Sheree called. 'It's a Lily Carter.'

'Cool. I hope that means good news on baby Alice Rose.'

'Let me know,' he called after her. That had been their first time working together and he'd enjoyed it.

So far, buster, there hasn't been anything you haven't enjoyed doing with Jess.

Five minutes later the woman swamping his brain popped her head around the door. 'Lily says hi and thank you for everything we did on Sunday. Alice Rose is doing very well and we're getting the credit.' That smile she gave him would get her anything she wanted.

'That's good news. I hated seeing her pain, and I'm not just talking about the labour. She's had more than her share of misfortune.'

'If they have another baby, I don't think Matthew will be taking her far from home. She hated her helicopter flight.'

'What a waste.' He grinned.

A light offshore breeze lifted Jess's hair as she sat on the sand, watching Nicholas trying to fling the fishing line into the water. Unfortunately it kept getting stuck in the sand and seaweed behind him as he threw the rod tip over his shoulder. She chuckled. 'Go slowly with that rod, Nicholas. You don't want to break it.'

'I'm doing what Jackson showed me.'

Right, shut up, Mum, and let the men get on with the job of fishing. 'I guess he knows best.'

'I'm a man, remember. We know these things from birth.' Jackson flicked a cheeky grin her way before carefully lifting the tip of Nicholas's rod out of the sand.

Of course she remembered he was a man. A perfect specimen of a man. Why else had she gone to bed with him? *Because you were so attracted to him you couldn't think straight.* Yeah, well, there was that, too. Which only underlined the fact he was male. She lay back on her towel to soak up some of the end-of-day summer warmth, and glanced at Jackson again.

He was still watching her but now his gaze had dropped to cruise over her scantily clad body. She saw his chest rise and his stomach suck in.

Guess her new bikini was a hit, then. Sasha had told her she would be nuts not to buy it when they'd spent a day in Nelson shopping two weeks ago. While they'd gone for last-minute wedding accessories they'd got side-tracked with lingerie and swimwear for Sasha's honeymoon. Bikinis all round.

Jackson croaked, 'What did I tell you? Orange really suits you.'

'You're close. Burnt orange this time.' Pulling her eyes away from that tantalising view of rock-hard muscles and sexy mouth, she tipped her head back to look up at the sky. Bright blue. The colour of love. Gulp. Her gaze dropped back to the man who'd snatched her heart. Thankfully he was now focused on fishing with Nicholas so she could study him without being caught. Tall, lean and as virile as it was possible to get. Yep, this was definitely love. How fast that had happened. So fast she couldn't trust it. Yet.

Four days after that heady night with him she still didn't know what to do. She'd been surprised when Jackson hadn't taken off at the first hint of her talking about something as personal as her misguided parents. He'd even hugged her, reassured her. Yeah, he wasn't hard to love. Too darned easy, in fact.

'Mummy, something's pulling my line. Look. Mummy, come here, quick. It's jiggling.'

Jackson was holding the rod upright. 'Wind the line in as fast as you can, Nicholas. That's it. Keep it coming. You don't want the fish jumping off the hook.'

'Mummy, look. Is it a fish? Jackson?'

'Yes, sport, you've caught your first fish.' Jackson reached for the hand net on the sand and raced to scoop up the flapping trophy. 'Look at that. Well done, Nicholas. You're a proper fisherman now.'

'Can I see? I want to hold it.' Nicholas dropped the rod and ran at Jackson, who scooped him up and carried boy and net up onto the sand.

'If we tip the fish out here, away from the sea, we won't lose it back in the water.' His long fingers deftly unhooked the ten-centimetre-long herring and handed it to Nicholas. 'Put your fingers where mine are, by the gills. That's it.' In an undertone he added, solely for her benefit, 'I hope you brought the camera, Mum.'

She did an exaggerated eye-roll. 'Would I forget the most important thing?'

After at least ten photos, capturing the biggest smile she'd ever seen on her boy's face, she made Jackson kneel down beside Nicholas and snapped a few more of the pair of happy fishermen. Those would look great in her album. Along with the wedding shots of her and Jackson standing with Sasha and Grady.

'I want to do it again, Jackson.'

'Like a true fisherman.' Jackson retrieved the rod, baited the hook and handed it to Nicholas, then took the herring aside to deal with it.

'Can we have my fish for dinner, Mummy?'

Yuk. Herring. But this was her boy's first fish. 'I guess, but it's very small for three people to share.'

As Nicholas's little face puckered up, ready for an outburst, Jackson saved the moment. 'You know, herrings are usually used for bait to catch bigger fish. Why don't we put it in your mother's freezer for when we go out in the boat after big fish?'

'Okay. What's for dinner? Fishing makes me hungry.'

'Now, there's a surprise.' She blew him a kiss before glancing across to Jackson, who was smiling at Nicholas.

'We're having fish and chips as soon as we've finished fishing, sport. What do you reckon? Had enough with that rod yet?'

'No. I'm going to get another he-herring.'

He did. Two more. Then they packed up and headed to the motor camp and the fast-food shop.

'Fish and chips on the beach in the fading sunlight, with sand for extra texture, and lukewarm cans of soda. I can't think of a better meal,' Jess said an hour later, as she unlocked her front door. Behind her Jackson carried Nicholas from the car.

'Talk about picky. What's wrong with a bit of sand crunching between your teeth?' He grinned. 'Bedroom?'

What a silly question. Of course she wanted to go to her bedroom with him. Her body was leaning towards him like metal to a magnet. That dancing feeling had begun in her stomach.

'Which is Nicholas's room?' Jackson's deep voice interrupted her hot thoughts. A wicked twinkle lightened his eyes.

Oh, yes, Nicholas. She gave herself a mental slap and led the way into the second, smaller bedroom. 'Definitely bedtime for my boy.' He was out for the count, had been all the way home, after talking excitedly non-stop about his fish.

'Whatever else were you thinking?' The bone-melting chuckle played havoc with all her thought processes so that she stood waiting for Jackson to lay Nicholas on the bed.

'Jess? The bedcover?'

Blink. Another mental slap. Concentrate. Heat raced up her cheeks as she hurriedly snatched the quilt out of the way. Then her heart rolled over as Jackson placed Nicholas ever so gently onto his bed and reached for the quilt to tuck it up under his chin. It wouldn't take much for her to get used to this. This was what she wanted for her boy, for herself. Sharing parenthood. Sharing everything.

'Thanks,' she whispered around a thickening in her throat. She found Teddy and slipped him in beside Nicholas, before dropping a kiss on her boy's forehead. She sniffed back her threatening tears, and grinned. 'Yuk. He smells fishy.'

'Only a little.' Jackson draped an arm over her shoulders. 'All part of the fun.'

Sniff, sniff. 'How come you don't reek? You handled those herrings more than Nicholas did.'

'I used the bathroom at the takeaway place. I thought Nicholas had, too.'

'Little boys have to be supervised at cleaning time.' She nudged his ribs with her elbow. 'Want a coffee before you head home?'

His finger touched her chin, tilted her head back so their eyes met. 'Any chance I can stay longer than a coffee?'

She melted against him. 'Every chance.'

'What's this?' Jess's fingers were running over Jackson's flat belly, seeking pleasure, hopefully giving pleasure, as they lay luxuriating in the aftermath of great sex.

Under her hand he stilled. 'An old wound.'

Didn't feel that old to her. The scar was still soft with a rough ridge running through the puckered skin. 'Define old.' If he refused to answer she'd back off. Everyone was entitled to privacy.

'Five weeks.'

'That is a long time.' She smiled into the dark.

'Seems like yesterday.' He rolled onto his side and ran a finger from her shoulder down to her breast, flicked across the nipple, sending shards of hot need slicing through her.

Okay, so this was the sidetrack trick. She'd run with it. She might be missing out on something important but amazing sex wasn't a bad second.

Then Jackson said, 'I was knifed.'

'What?' She bolted upright and stared down at him in the half-light from the hall. A low-wattage light always ran in case Nicholas woke up needing the bathroom. 'You must've really annoyed someone.'

'Come back down here.' He reached and tugged at her until she complied, sliding down the bed and finishing up tucked in against him. 'You don't want to know.'

'Wrong, Jackson. I do.'

She felt his chest lift as he drew a breath. Then he told her. 'In Hong Kong there's a group of doctors and nurses I belong to outside the hospital. We look after the poor and underprivileged during the hours of darkness. We mostly visit night shelters but occasionally the police call us to look at someone who refuses to get help.'

'You do this as well as work in the emergency department of a large hospital?' No wonder the guy looked exhausted most of the time. 'This is what you were referring to the other night when I asked why you were so tired.'

'Not quite.' He leaned in and dropped the softest of kisses on the corner of her mouth. Then he lay on his back, hands behind his head, and stared up at the ceiling. 'It was Christmas Eve. Fireworks displays out on the harbour. Plenty of tourists and locals enjoying themselves.'

Jess wound an arm over his waist and laid her cheek on his chest. 'Lots of booze.'

'Lots and lots of booze.' Jackson was quiet for a long time. Under her cheek she could feel his heart thudding. Tension had crept into his body. Her hand softly massaged his thigh. Finally, he said, 'The unit I worked with was doing the rounds of the usual haunts when we had a call from the police to meet them three streets over where they'd found a woman claiming she'd been raped.'

Running her fingers back and forth over his skin, Jess waited. He'd tell his tale in his own time, and she had all night.

'It was a set-up. We were attacked the moment we turned the corner. The nurse with me…' His Adam's apple bobbed. 'It should've been me, not Juliet who got the fatal blow. But she was always a fast sprinter.'

'Your friend ran into the attackers?'

'Slap bang onto the knives they wielded.'

'So you feel guilty because you didn't take the hit.' Her hand smoothed over those tense muscles. 'How were you to know that would happen?' About now he'd go all silent on her. 'Is this why you get angry at times?'

'Yeah.'

She waited quietly, only her hand moving as it swept his skin.

Exhaling, he continued. 'Frustration, guilt, vulnerability all add up to an ugly picture. It's debilitating.'

It took a brave man to tell her that. She wrapped herself around him, held him tight. Just listened.

'She didn't make it. I tried. Believe me, I did everything in my power to save her. But she'd been struck in the heart. There was absolutely nothing I could do but wait for the ambulance, hold her hand and keep talking. Noting the things she wanted me to tell her family, dreading that I might forget even one little detail.'

'She knew she was dying.'

'Yeah.' His sigh was so sad it tugged at her heart. 'I couldn't hide that from her. She was too experienced in emergency medicine.'

'You were wounded, too.'

'Yeah. But I survived.'

With one hand she traced the outline of the scar that ran down his thigh. 'Why did they attack you?'

'No one knows. So far the men who did this haven't been found. The police put every resource they had into finding them but no one's talking. The cops don't think it was personal, in that it wasn't me or Juliet they were targeting but more likely the organisation we worked for.'

'Will you continue with that when you return to Hong Kong?'

'Juliet made me promise not to give up our work on the streets because of this.'

That was a big ask. Jess chilled. No wonder Jackson wasn't staying in Golden Bay. He believed he had to go back even if he didn't want to. That promise would be strong, hanging over him, adding to his guilt if he even considered not returning. 'She didn't say not to quit if you had other compelling reasons.' *Like your mum. Like me.*

'I think I need to go back, if only to get past what happened. I don't mind admitting I'll be scared witless the first time I hit the streets, probably see knife-wielding attackers at every dark corner. At the same time I find myself wondering what it would be like to create a life outside medicine.'

Jess caught her breath. What sort of life? Where? Breathing out, she admitted her disappointment. He hadn't said he intended changing hospitals or countries. 'Guess you've got time to make that decision.'

'True. Doesn't get any easier, though. I don't know if I'm reacting to the attack or if I'm genuinely ready for a change.'

Her hands began moving up his sides, lightly touching his skin, gentling the tension gripping him. Her lips kissed his chest, found a nipple and she began to lick slowly, teasing him to forget the pain of that night. Gradually his reaction changed from tension caused by his story to a tension of another kind, pushing into her thigh. Shifting slightly so that she held him between her thighs, she slid a hand between them and began to rub that hard evidence of his need.

'Jessica,' he groaned through clenched teeth. 'Please don't stop. I need this. I need *you*.'

She had no intention of stopping. Not when her libido was screaming for release. She had to have him—deep inside her.

Suddenly she was flipped onto her back. Jackson separated her thighs to kneel between them. His hands lifted her backside and then he drove into her. Withdrew. Forged forward. Withdrew. And her mind went blank as her body was swamped with heat and desire and need.

CHAPTER SIX

A VOICE CUT through Jess's dreams, dragging her cotton-wool-filled mind into the daylight. 'Who—?'

'Now for the seven o'clock news. Last night—'

The radio alarm. She shut the annoying drone out, concentrated on why she felt so languid this morning. 'Jackson.' Why else? Who else?

Rolling her head sideways, she saw what she already knew. He'd gone. Sneaked out some time in the early hours while she'd been snoozing, gathering her energy around her. For another round of exquisite sex? Turning to glance the other way, she smiled. A note lay on the bedside table.

'Didn't want to be around when Nicholas woke in case it caused trouble. See you at the medical centre. Hugs, J.'

Thoughtful as well as sexy. Great combination, Jackson. And I still love you. But you are going away again and I can understand why. Unfortunately.

Leaping out of bed, she tugged the curtains open. Yep, the sky was as blue as the lightest sapphire. The colour of love. Love meant letting go and waiting for him to come back.

'Now for the weather forecast.' Behind her the voice

droned on. 'Expect showers this morning and if you're thinking of going out on the briny, maybe you should find something else to do. Forty-knot northerlies are predicted from around lunchtime.'

Showers? The day was light and sunny. 'Get a new forecast, buddy.' She clicked the pessimist off and headed for the shower.

Twenty minutes later Nicholas bounced into the kitchen and pulled out a chair at the table. 'I want cocoa pops.'

'Please,' Jess said. Placing the bowl and box of cereal on the table, she did a double take. 'What are you wearing?'

'My fishing shirt. This is the lucky shirt. Jackson told me I should wear it every time I go fishing with him.'

So there were to be more fishing expeditions? 'That's fine, but you're going to play centre this morning, not fishing. Take it off and put it in the washing basket.'

'No. I'm wearing it so my friends can see it.' The cocoa pops overflowed from the bowl onto the table. 'I'm going to tell them all about the three fishes I got.'

Removing the carton from Nicholas's hand, she put it back in the cupboard, out of reach. 'That's more than enough cereal. Let's put half those pops in another bowl before you add the milk or there'll be a big mess.'

Too late. The puffed rice spilled over the rim on a tide of milk. 'Whoa, stop pouring now.' She snatched the milk container away.

'I want more milk.' Nicholas banged his spoon on the tabletop. 'More milk, more milk.'

'Sorry, buddy, but you've got more than enough.' She spooned coffee granules into a mug, added half a teaspoon extra, then two sugars. As she dropped two slices of wholegrain in the toaster the front doorbell rang.

Behind her a chair slammed back against the wall. 'I'll get it.' Nicholas raced out of the kitchen.

'Hello, Mr Fisherman.' A deep, sexy voice echoed down the hallway before Jess had made it to the kitchen doorway. Her stomach turned to mush as she peeped around the doorframe and drank in the sight of this man who seemed to hold her heart in his hand.

'Mummy, it's Jackson,' Nicholas yelled, as though she was already at the medical centre.

'Morning.' Jackson had somehow moved along the hall to stand in front of her. 'You're looking good enough to eat this morning.'

Corny. But nice. 'Want a coffee?'

'Please, ta.'

Nicholas jumped up and down in front of Jackson. 'I'm wearing my fishing shirt. See?'

Jackson flicked a question her way. 'Not your idea?'

She shook her head.

'See, here's the thing, Nicholas. Fishing shirts are special and we men have got to look after them. They need washing after you've caught fish, and then put away in the drawer until next time you go to the beach.'

Nicholas was nodding solemnly. 'Okay. I'll go and change.'

Jess stared after Nicholas as he sped out of the room. 'How did you do that? I could spend ten minutes arguing myself blue in the face about that shirt and he'd still wear it to play centre.'

'Hey. Solo parenting can't be so easy. You've got to make all the calls.' A friendly arm encircled her shoulders, tugged her in against a warm, strong body. 'From what I saw last night, you have a good relationship with Nicholas. Don't be so hard on yourself. It's not like you have family here to support you or give you a break.'

The more she got to know Jackson the more talkative he got. 'Thanks.' Reluctantly she pulled out of his hold. 'Have you had breakfast?'

'Toast on the run. Sam's sheep got into Mum's orchard overnight. I helped Kevin round them up and get them back in their rightful paddock.'

'Kevin's turning out to be very helpful.'

'Where'd he come from?'

Jess handed him a coffee as she answered. 'He and Tamara had an unexpected baby, which Sasha and Grady delivered. There are some terrible family issues involving Tamara's family. Seems the young couple got so much help when the locals heard about the baby and everything else that they decided to stay here. Your dad offered Kevin work on the orchard, helping Virginia, and since Sam's accident he hasn't been able to go back to driving full time so Kevin fills in for him as needed.'

'That's why they're living in the orchard cottage.'

'Yep. Sasha moved in with Grady after Melanie was born. Kevin and Tamara needed somewhere to stay. Simple.'

'Is this shirt okay, Jackson?' Nicholas bounded back and climbed onto his chair.

After silently checking with her, Jackson gave his approval. 'You'd better get on with your breakfast, sport. It's nearly time to go to play group.'

Jess held her breath. But the kitchen became quiet except for the steady munching of cocoa pops. She shook her head and turned to Jackson. 'That's a turnaround. You sure you're not staying for good?'

His smile faltered then returned. 'Can I take a rain-check?'

Her eyes must have been out on stalks. They'd certainly widened so that they were stretching. Her mouth dried. As she stared at Jackson he shoved a hand through his hair, mussing it nicely.

'You are making it so tempting, believe me.' His chest rose. 'But I have to be very honest here. I can't see me staying. For a start, there isn't an emergency department for me to find work at.'

'There's one two hours away over the hill.'

His lips pressed together and she knew she'd gone too far. But this wasn't a one-sided conversation. Was it?

'Like I've already explained, I don't see myself settling back into such a small community. I didn't much like it the first time round.' His chest rose and fell. 'Not to mention my promise to Juliet.'

She couldn't complain that he hadn't given her the facts. He was more honest than she was. But she had no intention of telling him she'd fallen in love with him. Not when she knew deep down she couldn't start a serious relationship. Her son was more important than her love for any man. So that meant keeping her mouth shut and enjoying whatever happened between her and Jackson. 'Thank you for being honest.'

'Jess,' he called softly. 'Am I asking too much if I say I'd like to carry on with what we've got? Is that selfish?'

'It would only be selfish if you were the only one getting something out of it.' Even to her, the smile she made felt lacklustre. Trying again, she came up with something stronger, warmer. 'I...' I'm stuck for words.

'It's okay. You don't have to say anything.'

But I do. I want to. 'Until Saturday night I never expected to meet a man I'd feel so relaxed and comfortable with. You touch something within me, and—' Oh hell, why wasn't this easy? Maybe she should come out with it, tell him she loved him. Except she had to remember that she carried her parents' genes—she would never be able to trust herself to be a good parent when she was in love with someone else. Mum and Dad were devoted to each other, to the point she'd always felt like a spare part in their lives. She'd never do that to Nicholas. 'Jackson, you're special and you make me feel the same way. So, yes, let's carry on with whatever it is we've got.'

Did that sound like a business arrangement? Nah, who had hot sex with their business partner? She started to giggle. This really was an oddball situation, and she had no intention of dropping it. Her giggles turned to laughter.

'What's funny, Mummy?' Nicholas tapped Jackson on the arm. 'Mummy doesn't like laughing.'

Jackson's eyes widened. 'Must be my fault. She laughs a lot around me.'

'That's because you're funny,' Nicholas told him as he got down from the table.

'Funny ha-ha or funny strange? No, don't answer that, either of you.' Jackson grinned at her boy.

'Funny cool.' Getting herself under control, Jess noticed Nicholas heading for his bedroom. 'Nicholas, come back and put your bowl and spoon in the sink, please.'

'You do it. I'm getting my school bag.'

'Nicholas. Do as I say. Please.'

'No. Too busy.'

Jackson glanced at her then down the hall. 'Hey, sport,

that's not the way for a boy to talk to his mother. Better come and do as she says.'

She held her breath, and waited through the sudden silence that descended on her home.

'Okay, coming,' her son called, moments before he bounced back into the kitchen. There was the clatter of his plate dropping in the sink, followed by the spoon. Then he snatched up the cloth and wiped the spilled milk further across the table. 'There, Mummy, all clean.'

Jess rescued the cloth from sliding off the edge of the bench and rinsed it under the tap. 'Thanks, Nicholas. You can finish getting ready for play group now.' As she re-wiped the table she didn't know whether to be pleased or unhappy at Jackson's help. He'd certainly got a good response from Nicholas. Far more than she'd managed. 'Thank you,' she whispered.

'Like I said, you're a good mum, Jessica Baxter. You're too hard on yourself.' Those arms she was coming to rely on for comfort were winding around her again.

Sighing she pulled back and looked up into those green eyes that reminded her of spring and new growth. New love? Don't think like that. Some time soon Jackson will twig what you're thinking and then where will you be? Out in the cold. 'Guess we'd better get cracking. The centre opens in fifteen and I've got antenatal clinic this morning.'

At the medical centre Jackson sat at the staff kitchen table, a strong, long black coffee in hand, and listened to Roz and Rory discussing their patients. 'Seems there's no end of people needing lots of care.'

Jess hadn't had a moment to spare during the day. Mike was at home, catching up on sleep after a night up on Takaka Hill helping Search and Rescue haul a caver out of Harwood's Hole. The man had slipped and fallen fifty metres, breaking both legs on landing at the bottom.

Rory told him, 'Summer is always busier. The influx of holidaymakers adds to our workload something terrible. Not to mention numerous cavers and trampers getting out into the wilderness.'

Roz added, 'It's as if people leave the cautious side of their brains at home when they pack to go on holiday.'

'You must remember what it was like when you were growing up here, Jackson,' Rory said.

'Sure, but I wasn't a doctor. I got to see a few incidents that occurred amongst my mates. I don't remember anything too serious happening.'

'What about when those guys took a dinghy out with too big a motor for the size of the boat? They flipped the boat and nearly drowned themselves. Saved by another boat going past. And by you swimming out to rescue one of them. He would've drowned if it hadn't been for you and the doctor on board the second boat.'

When had Jess come into the room? When had his antennae failed him? He always knew when she was within metres of him. Or so he'd thought. 'Ben and Haydon. Damned idiots they were.'

'Lucky idiots, by the sound of it.' Rory picked up a printout of a lab result. 'I see it's confirmed Gary's got another bout of falciparum. We need to look into what else can be down to prevent further attacks. Jackson, do you see much malaria in Hong Kong?'

'We get quite a few patients presenting but then they're passed on to the medical team and that's it as far as the emergency department is concerned. But I can give you a contact at the hospital if you like.'

From under lowered eyelids he watched Jess as she filled her water bottle. The movement of leaning slightly forward over the sink accentuated her sweet curves, especially that butt he'd cupped in his hands last night. His mouth dried while below his belt muscles stirred. Was there such a thing as having too much of Jess? Not in this lifetime.

'Have you got many house calls, Jess?' Rory asked.

'Five for this afternoon, which isn't too bad. I'll stop by and see Claire Johnston and baby Max on my way home.'

Jackson sat up straighter. 'I'll give you another prescription for antibiotics for Max. Talking to Claire earlier, she said the baby still has a wheezy cough.'

Jess gave him one of those heart-melting smiles of hers. 'Sure. Send it through to the pharmacy and I'll pick it up on my way.' She pulled a pen from her pocket and scribbled a note on the back of her hand. 'There, shouldn't forget now.'

'Right.' Roz pushed her chair back and stood up. 'Might as well get this show on the road.'

Rory stayed seated, twirling his mug back and forth in his hands, like he was waiting for the others to disappear.

'Baby Carrington's due any day now so I'll be hovering.' Jess shoved her water bottle in the fridge and followed Roz.

Jackson drained his coffee and stood up. 'You want to say something?' he asked Rory.

The mug kept moving back and forth in those big hands resting on the table. 'Are you fixed on returning to Hong Kong at the end of your leave?'

'Definitely. Nothing to keep me here.' Why did an

image of a pair of all-seeing, fudge-coloured eyes suddenly dance across his brain?

'Pity.' Rory lifted his gaze from the table to Jackson. 'Will you go back to working on the streets at night?'

How did he know about that? 'Of course. There's no end of work out there.'

'Your near-miss with a knife hasn't changed your attitude?'

Disappointment was a hard ball in the pit of his gut. 'Jess has been talking too much.' So the very thing that had made him wary about being here had come back to haunt him—in less than three weeks.

Rory's eyebrows lifted. 'Jess?' Then understanding dawned. 'Not Jess. Dr Ng Ping.'

What was going on here? Ping was his department head, and probably the closest he had to a friend in Hong Kong. Why had he and Rory been in touch? 'You care to explain?' Jackson's blood started to simmer. If anyone had anything to say about him, they should say it to his face.

'Dr Ng rang to ask after your health. Said whenever he talked to you, you only ever told him you were fine.'

'Wait until I see Ping. He had no right to do that.' The simmer was becoming a boil. How could Ping do that behind his back? He, more than most, understood how important it was to him to be above board in everything.

'He told me he was a concerned friend who wanted to know you were doing as well as you said. That you are getting over the incident.'

Had Ping told Rory about his meltdown in the middle of the department one particularly busy night? Yes, Jackson would bet everything he owned on it. Pulling out a chair, he straddled it and eyeballed Rory. 'I still have small temper surges at the most unexpected moments, but they disappear quickly, and they happen less and less often. Nothing has happened here at the centre, and no patients have any reason to be concerned. Neither do you and your partners.' Bile soured his mouth. And he'd been stupid enough to think loose-tongued people only lived in Golden Bay.

'Relax, Jackson. I have absolutely no qualms about you working with us. No one else knows about that call either. I figured it wasn't necessary.'

'So where's this headed? I'm sure the waiting room is bursting with people wanting our services.' The threatening temper outburst backed off a little.

Rory got up and shut the door, came back to the table but didn't sit. 'I'm getting antsy, want to head home to Auckland. But my conscience won't let me leave these guys in the lurch. Not before I've tried all avenues I can think of to find a replacement.'

Jackson stared at him. 'You're asking if I want to stay on permanently?' Of course, the man knew next to nothing about him and how he'd left the moment the school bell had rung for the last time on his school life. Hell. How had his parents coped with that? He'd never stopped to ask. Maybe he should. *Only if you can handle the answer.*

'Yeah, something like that.' Rory grimaced. 'Your face tells me all I need to know. But if Jess manages to change your mind, let me know, will you?'

Jackson felt his mouth drop open. Was it really that obvious? Guess so if Rory had noticed. *Grady, the sooner you're home the better for me. And as for Ping— I'm ringing you tonight. Pal.*

His stomach tightened and his hands balled into fists

as his head spun. Damn you, Ping. Thankfully Rory had disappeared out the door without seeing this tantrum.

'Hey, what's up? You look ready to shoot someone.' Jess was back. Her hand gripped his shoulder, shook him softly.

'My so-called friend in Hong Kong has been checking up on me. Rory took a call from Ping and now knows about the attack.'

Jess smiled. Smiled? This was serious.

'Jackson, friends do that. This Ping obviously cares about you, wants to make sure you're doing okay.' Her mouth came close, caressed his cheek with the lightest of kisses. 'He's doing the right thing.'

And just like that, the tension disappeared. The anger evaporated. His arms encircled this wonderful woman. 'You are so good for me.' And he kissed her, thoroughly. Until there was a knock on the door.

'Mind if I get a coffee?' Sheree asked.

Jess leapt back and winked at him. 'Just leaving.'

In his consulting room Jackson studied the notes of his first patient for the day. Dawn Sullivan, thirty-nine years old, no major health issues during the five years she'd been coming to the Golden Bay Medical and Wellbeing Centre.

He turned to study the woman sitting opposite. Her cheeks appeared unnaturally pale. 'So, Dawn, what brings you to see me today?'

'I'm so tired all the time I can hardly get out of bed some days. I've got the attention span of a fly, which is great considering school started this week and I'm a teacher.' Even as she spoke Dawn was yawning.

'You don't have any history of anaemia. How are

your periods? Heavier than usual? Or do they last longer these days?'

Shaking her head, his patient told him, 'All much the same as ever. But I do get lots of stomachaches. Actually, I ache everywhere at times. It's like I've got the flu full time. I'd planned on finally painting my house over the summer break but hardly got one wall done I've been that short of energy. Not like me at all. Ask anyone around here. I always used to be on the go.'

'How long has this been going on?' he asked.

Dawn looked sheepish. 'Months. At first I went to the naturopath, who gave me vitamins and minerals. Fat lot of good they turned out to be and nearly bankrupted me in the process. Whatever I've got is getting worse. I've lost a bit of weight, which normally would make me happy but right now worries me sick.'

Jackson felt as though he should be sitting in the back of a classroom as Dawn's voice carried loudly across the small gap between them. He read Dawn's blood pressure—normal; checked her eyes—they showed signs of anaemia. 'Can you get up on the bed and I'll examine your abdomen.' After a few moments of gently pressing over the area he stepped back. 'I can't feel anything out of the ordinary.'

'So what do you think is going on?' Dawn sat up and pulled her top back into place.

'I'd say you're anaemic but the cause needs to be checked out. We'll do some blood tests. Any changes in diet? Or are you a vegan?'

Dawn shuddered. 'No, love my meat too much for that.'

'We'll start with these blood tests.' He glanced at the patient notes on his computer screen. Something was bothering him. 'Your house is going to have to wait a little longer for its new coat.'

'Right now I'd be happy to have enough energy to teach all day.'

Jackson tapped his forefinger on the desktop. Checking Dawn's address, he tried to remember the style of houses in that road. 'Your house—how old is it?'

'About seventy years. It's a bungalow. The wide boards and wooden window frames type. Mighty cold in winter.'

'Did you do a lot of preparation for the paint job? Sanding off old paint, for example?'

'Yes, I spent weeks with an electric sander, getting down to bare boards. From what I could see, it hadn't been done properly in for ever.'

Bingo. 'I might be wrong but I have a hunch that what you're suffering from is lead poisoning. The old paints are notorious for having a lead component. Did you wear a mask while you were using the sander?'

'No. I can get lead from inhaling dust granules?' Dawn sank down onto the chair, looking shocked. 'It's bad, isn't it? Lead poisoning? Really?'

The more he thought about it the more certain he was. On the screen he ticked boxes on the laboratory form. 'We won't know for sure until the haematology results come back but I think we're onto something. So let's forget those vitamins and wait for a couple of days. If you do have lead in your system, it has to be removed by chelation therapy.'

'Meaning?' Dawn's voice had grown smaller, no longer the booming teacher's tone.

'You'd be given chelation agents that absorb the lead from your body tissues, which is then passed out through your urine. It's an effective way for cleaning up the lead and then we can treat the residual effects, like that lack of energy, which will be due to an anaemia caused by the poisoning.' Signing the form, he added, 'Take this through to Jess. I don't think she's left for her rounds yet.'

'Thank you, Doctor.'

'It's Jackson, and I'll phone you as soon as the results come through.'

'Again, thank you. Guess this means the house and my job are on hold.'

'Talk to the school board and see if you can take on reduced hours for this term.' He held the door open and ushered Dawn through, before going in search of his next patient.

Kelly Brown walked carefully and slowly into his room and eased her bottom onto the edge of the chair. Her face, arms and every other bit of exposed skin was the colour of well-ripened tomatoes. She wore a loose dress that barely reached her thighs and probably had nothing on underneath.

Jackson sat down and said, 'You're here for that sunburn?'

Kelly nodded. 'It's awful. Can you do anything to stop the heat? Or the pain? I can't wear clothes or lie under the sheet. It hurts all the time.'

'I'll give you a mild painkiller. I hope you're drinking lots of water.'

'Mum nags at me all the time.' Kelly moved, grimaced.

'Where did you get so much sun? It was overcast here yesterday.' Or so he'd thought.

'A group of us went over the hill to Kaiteriteri Beach. Everyone got a bit of sunburn but nothing like this.'

Jackson typed up details on her notes. 'Do you have naturally fair skin?' When she nodded he added, 'You should know better, then. Lots of sunscreen all the time. Any blisters?'

'On my back and all down the front. I've always been sort of careful but yesterday I forgot to take the sunblock with me and thought I'd be safe if I got out of the sun after an hour. But I fell asleep sunbathing.'

'Cool showers, lots of fluids and a mild analgesic is all I can recommend, Kelly. And stay out of the sun in future.'

Taking the prescription he handed her, she said, 'Think I'll move to Alaska. Should be safe there.'

He laughed. 'Might be eaten by a bear.'

'At least that'd be different.' Kelly hobbled to the door. 'Thanks, Doctor. I hear you're only here while Grady's away. Can you tell Jess I won't be able to babysit this week?'

'Your cellphone not working?' Why the hell did this teen think he should be passing Jess her messages?

'Nothing wrong with it. Thought you might like an excuse to talk to her.' With a cheeky wink the minx left his room.

Jackson stared after her. Small towns. There was no getting away from the fact everyone knew everyone's business. How many weeks before he caught the big tin bird back to Asia? Too many.

Then he thought of the woman he was supposed to pass Kelly's message on to and took back that thought. Not nearly enough days left.

CHAPTER SEVEN

JESS HELD BABY Carrington while his mother wriggled herself into a comfortable position on the bed.

'Is this going to be hard? Painful?' Anna asked, anxiety in her voice, as she reached for her baby.

'No and no.' Jess carefully placed the baby in Anna's arms. 'But remember I told you your milk mightn't come in for the first few days. You'll most likely be feeding him colostrum, which is full of goodies he needs.'

'How do I hold him? Oh, hello, gorgeous. Aren't you the most beautiful baby ever?' Anna beamed as she studied her son.

'He's a little cracker, absolutely beautiful.' As they all were. When Nicholas had been placed in her arms for the very first time she couldn't believe her overwhelming sense of love for her son. She'd seen exactly the same reaction in every mother she'd delivered before and since Nicholas's birth, only nowadays she understood how deep the bond ran. How it was the start of something that stayed with mothers for the rest of their lives. Life-changing, empowering. Frightening.

Anna finally raised her gaze. 'Show me how to hold him so I can feed him.'

Tucking the baby in against Anna so she supported

his shoulders, Jess then placed Anna's hand on his head. 'Holding him like that means he can access your nipple easily. That's it. Now rub his mouth against your nipple to encourage him to suck. That's it. Perfect.'

'Wow, that's awesome. Oh, my goodness, I'm feeding my baby.' Anna's eyes grew misty. 'Danny, look at this.'

The baby's father was transfixed, watching his son. A bemused expression covered his face. 'That's amazing.'

Jess felt a similar sense of wonder. This was always a wonderful sight, mum bonding with baby. Memories of Nicholas tugged at her heart again. *I'd love to do it all over again. Have a brother or sister for Nicholas.* And where on earth had that idea come from?

Jackson. Of course. Loving him had sparked all sorts of weird ideas. Ideas she wouldn't follow through on. Nicholas needed all her attention. It wouldn't be fair to expect him to share her with Jackson. *What about that baby you suddenly want? Can you spread your love between two children without depriving one or the other?* Surely that would be different? A mother's love was very different from the love she felt for Jackson.

Besides, it was one thing to find herself a solo mother of one, but of two? That would be plain irresponsible. Jackson wouldn't be staying, baby or no baby. That was unfair. He was a very responsible man. But she wouldn't be wanting a loveless—make that one-sided—relationship.

Anna's question cut through her turmoil. 'How will I know when he's hungry?'

Jess dragged up a smile. 'Believe me, he'll let you know. His lungs are in good working order.'

Danny grinned. 'Just like his dad.'

'I feel so much happier now that I've tried feeding

him. It isn't the nightmare I'd thought it might be.' Anna gazed adoringly at the baby. 'He's looking sleepy.'

'Carefully take him off your breast. You need to wind him now. Place him on your shoulder and rub his back gently. That's it. You're a natural at this.'

'Who'd have believed it, huh? It's not like my day job as a gardener gave me any clues.'

'I'm going to leave you two to get to know your son. What are you naming him, by the way?'

'Antony.'

'Michael.'

Jess grinned. 'Right, you definitely need to sort that out. Call the nurse if you have any problems with anything, otherwise I'll be in to see you later.'

She went to find Sheryl and hand over her patient. 'I'm off. I doubt you'll be needing me, though I'll drop by later. That baby might've been two weeks late but the birth was straightforward and Anna's already managing feeding.'

Sheryl waved her out the door. 'Go and enjoy the weekend. It's a stunner of a day.'

It certainly was. Summer had turned on its absolute best for the weekend, which had brought people in droves from Nelson and other towns to their beach houses. At home Jess stood on her deck with a glass of icy water and looked around. Bright blue skies—the colour of love—sparkled above and not a whisper of wind stirred the leaves on the trees in the neighbour's yard. The sparrows and finches were singing while the tuis were squabbling over the last few yellow flowers of a kowhai tree.

'Mummy, can I go swimming at the beach?'

'After lunch has settled in your tummy I'll take you down to Pohara.' She'd picked him up from Bobby's on the way home. Studying him now, that feeling of awe that had struck her as she'd watched Anna and her baby bonding returned in full force.

Was Nicholas missing out because he didn't have a sibling? When she'd been young she'd pestered her mother about why she didn't have a sister like her friends did. Her mother had always told her that she got more love being the only one but somehow that had never washed with Jess. There hadn't been much love. She'd grown up fast, only having adults around to talk to most of the time. She hadn't spent a lot of time in places where there were other kids for her to play with.

'Why can't Jackson come with me?' Nicholas rode his bike round and round the lemon tree, making her feel dizzy watching him.

'He's busy picking the avocados for Virginia.' Nicholas definitely missed out by not having a father. Balancing that against what he'd miss out on if the man she loved lived with them, she suddenly didn't know what was best for them all.

'Actually, I've finished that chore,' a familiar deep voice said from the corner of the house. 'Got up with the birds to do the picking. I've even graded and packed the avocados, ready to go to the markets.'

'Jackson, look at me,' Nicholas shouted, and pedalled faster than ever until he forgot to watch where he was going and rode into the lemon tree.

Jess winced and rushed to lift him back onto his bike. 'Nicholas, be careful, sweetheart.'

'Okay, Mummy.'

Jackson moved up beside her. 'Hey, you're looking great.' Sex oozed from that voice, lifting bumps on her skin.

'Go easy around you know who,' she warned, at the same time noticing how his gaze cruised over her legs. She'd pulled on very short shorts and a singlet top the moment she'd got home, feeling the need to make the most of the sun after hours shut inside that small delivery room. 'Anna Carrington had her baby this morning.'

Jackson's eyes softened. 'So you've been up most of the night?'

'All of it.'

'You don't look like you're wilting.' He ran a finger down her arm. 'What did she have?'

'A boy.' She couldn't help the sigh that slid across her lips.

'That cute, eh?'

'Yes. I never get tired of seeing new babies.'

'You sound as though you're yearning for another of your own.' Jackson's finger hovered over her wrist.

Her feelings were too obvious if Jackson was picking up on them. 'It's easy to wish for another baby when they're brand-new and behaving and I'm not at home alone trying to balance everything like a one-winged bird.'

Jackson turned to stare across her lawn, his eyes following Nicholas as he again rode faster and faster, happily showing off. 'You'd have to choose a father.'

She sucked in a breath. Odd way of putting it. 'Not doing that. I do not want to have another child on my own, no matter how cool it would be for Nicholas to have a sibling. It's not fair on the children.'

'Or you. It's hard work, for sure.' He still watched Nicholas, but what was going on in his head?

'It's not about the hard work. It's about having two role models, a male perspective as well as mine. Anyway, I don't know why we're having this conversation. It's not going to happen.'

Jackson turned then, his hands reaching for her arms. 'You sound so certain.'

Because I am. Because you're going away. Because I couldn't trust myself not to be able to share my love between you and Nicholas and any other child even if you did stay. 'I'm being practical. No point wishing for the impossible. Takes too much energy.' She stepped back, pulling her arms free. 'Want to go to the beach with us?'

Disappointment blinked out at her. 'You're changing the subject.'

'Are you staying on in Golden Bay come April?'

He hesitated, and she held her breath. Until, 'No.'

Now it was her turn to feel disappointed, despite knowing the answer before he'd enunciated it. Swallowing hard, she said, 'Then of course I'm changing the subject. We're going to the beach. Want to join us?'

'Yes, Jackson, you've got to come.' Nicholas let rip with another shout as he spun around on his bike too fast and tipped over. 'I want you to,' he yelled, through the too-long grass covering his face.

'How can I refuse that demand?' Jackson shrugged in her direction, puzzlement in his eyes. So he'd picked up on what she hadn't said. That she'd be interested if he was hanging around.

'I guess Nicholas has a way with words.' If only it was that easy for her to get Jackson to do what she needed. Because it was slowly dawning on her that she wasn't going to be able to let him go as easily as she'd first thought. For a moment there she'd almost wished he'd said he was staying and that they might make their relationship more permanent. For a moment she thought she could see past her fears and take a chance. For a moment.

Jackson went to right the bike and held it while Nicholas climbed back on. 'You're going to need a bigger bike soon.'

'I told Mummy but she said I had to wait.'

A bigger bike meant further to fall. 'There's no hurry.'

'Have you got sun block on, sport?'

'Yes.' Nicholas nodded gravely. 'Kelly got burnt at the beach. She said it hurt a lot.'

'That's right, she was bright red. You don't want to look like a fried tomato.'

Jess watched the two of them: Jackson so patient and Nicholas so keen to show off his skills. They looked good together. If only this relationship could last as it was, but the weeks were cranking along, disappearing unbelievably fast. The first of March was only a couple of days away, and that heralded the end of summer. Then it would be April and some time during that month it would be the end of her affair with Jackson. Swallowing down on the sudden sadness engulfing her, she vowed to make the most of whatever time she had with him. For someone who did not want a permanent relationship with any man she was making a right hash of keeping Jackson at arm's length.

'You're daydreaming again.' Jackson stood in front of her.

'Must be the heat.' She poured the last of her water down her throat.

'Shucks. Here I was thinking I might be the reason you had that far-away look in your eye.'

'Nope. That was pollen from the lemon flowers.'

His finger ran along her bottom lip, sending zips of

heat right down to her toes. 'Is that why you always smell of citrus? You spend a lot of time hauling Nicholas out of the lemon tree?'

Rising onto her toes, she nudged his hand out of the way and kissed those full, sexy lips that knew how to tease and tantalise her for hours on end. 'Try reading the label of my shampoo bottle. Less exotic but more practical.'

He took over the kiss, deepening it until she had to hang on to keep her balance. Pressing her body up against his, she felt the hardening of his reaction to her. Not now. Not here. Hands on his chest, she pushed back. 'Nicholas.'

His sultry eyes widened. 'God, I'm like a crazed teen around you, forgetting everything except what you make me feel, want.' Jackson stepped back, tugged at his shirt to cover the obvious reaction to their kiss. 'Better do something else before the trouble really starts.'

'I'll get towels and things for the beach.' How mundane was that? It should dampen their ardour.

Jackson followed her inside. 'I came around to ask you what you think about camping.'

'As in a tent? Sleeping bags and air mattresses? That sort of camping?' It had been years since she'd done that and then it had been in the Australian outback with her parents. She'd spent her whole time sitting up with the thin sleeping bag zipped right to her throat, terrified a snake would come into her tent and bite her.

'Is there any other sort?' Jackson grinned. 'A friend from way back has a bit of land by the beach out at Wainui Inlet. There's a shed with bathroom and cooking facilities. I figured we could go out there and pitch a tent, go swimming and fishing. Nicholas can take his bike and ride around the paddock when we're tired of the beach.'

Jess grunted. 'Like that's going to happen. It's usually a battle to get him out of the water. A prune is wrinkle-free compared to what he ends up looking like.'

'I've got steak, potatoes wrapped in foil to bake, lots of salad stuff, and fruit for afterwards. How can you refuse?' Jackson implored, looking at her like a little boy intent on winning his case.

'Steak? You don't have any faith in your fishing skills?'

'Fishing? Are we going fishing?' Nicholas leapt between them, looking excited already.

Jackson locked eyes with her. 'Are we? Fishing and camping?'

There wouldn't be any snakes or other creepy-crawlies for her to worry about. 'What are we waiting for?'

Of course, it took nearly an hour to pack clothes, towels, more food, toys and the bike into the truck. Nicholas hindered progress but as he was trying so hard to be helpful Jess didn't growl at him once. His excitement level escalated until it was almost unbearable, and then Jackson stepped in.

'Hey, sport. Take it easy, eh? You need lots of energy to go fishing and swimming, and the way you're going now you'll run out before we leave.'

'Sorry, Jackson. I'll be good, promise.'

Jess shook her head. 'How do you do that?'

'I'm very good at getting my way. With little boys and their wicked mothers. Okay, make that singular. One boy and his mother.' Jackson's hand cupped her butt, squeezed gently. 'Nicholas will go to sleep tonight, won't he?'

Finally she let go of the hurt that had sprung up when Jackson had told her he wouldn't be staying. 'Come on,' she teased him. 'The kid's never been in a tent before. He's going to be wide-eyed all night long.' Chuckling when disappointment darkened Jackson's eyes, she added, 'You can leave behind any condoms you've packed.'

'Which reminds me. Be right back.' He headed outside to the truck. Returning, he handed her a parcel the size of a book.

'What's this?'

'Open it before your young man comes back inside.'

She tore the paper off, became even more baffled at seeing the plain cardboard box. With her fingernail she slit the tape holding down the lid and flicked it open. 'Bleeding heck.' She stared at the condoms. 'You planning on staying around for a while, or just being very busy?'

'That first time? You told me I owed you and I always pay my debts.' Leaning in, he kissed the corner of her mouth. 'Now put them out of sight. I hear small footsteps coming this way. I won't complain if you put a handful in your pocket for later, though.'

'A handful? Yeah, right.' Laughing all the way to her bedroom, she slid the box into the drawer of her bedside table and, yes, shoved some condoms into her overnight bag.

Jess slipped the air-filled bands up Nicholas's arms. 'These'll help keep you afloat in those waves.' Tiny waves that suddenly seemed big compared to her wee boy. 'Hold my hand.'

Small fingers wrapped around hers. 'Will there be fish in the water, Jackson?'

'Not around you. They'll see your legs and swim away fast.' Jackson took his other hand. 'You like swimming, sport?'

'I only like the pool.'

Uh-oh. How did I not know that? Jess bit her lip. 'We'll stay on the edge where it's shallow.' She sank to her knees in the water, the waves reaching the top of her thighs, and reached for Nicholas.

He leaned against her, studying the waves, worry darkening his eyes. 'Why does the sea go up and down like that?'

'Sometimes the wind makes it happen.'

'But there isn't any wind.' Nicholas stared around the small bay.

Jackson squatted down beside them, those well-honed thighs very distracting. 'There might be further away. Or a big boat might've gone past. Engines on boats stir the water like when Mummy makes a cake, and that sends waves inshore.'

'My cakes resemble the sea?'

Jackson grinned and lifted a strand of hair off her face. 'Don't know. You've never made me one.'

'Be grateful.'

Nicholas sank down lower, sucking in his stomach as the water reached his waist. 'It's not cold, Mummy.'

Right. So why the shivers? 'Let's play ball.' Hopefully a game would distract him enough to relax and have fun. She made to take the beach ball from Jackson and came up against hard chest muscles, the hand holding the ball well out of reach. Her gaze shot to his face, caught the cheeky grin. Right, buster. Carefully removing her other hand from Nicholas she turned and shoved at Jackson, toppling him into and under the water.

'Nicholas, help me. Your mother needs controlling.' Jackson coughed out salt water, that grin wider than ever. 'Let's show her she can't play dirty tricks and get away with it.'

Her son didn't need any more encouragement, leaping onto her, wrapping his arms tightly around her knees. Jackson showed no sympathy, helping Nicholas dunk her.

She leapt up, shaking her sodden hair, water streaming down her body. 'Right, who's next?'

'You can't catch me, Mummy.' Nicholas forged through the water, parallel to the shore, shrieking at every splash he made.

Jackson took her hand and they pretended to chase him hard, keeping close enough to reach him quickly if needed but letting him think he was winning. Inevitably he tripped himself up and went under. Jess felt the air stall in her lungs. He'd panic and choke.

Jackson lunged forward, caught Nicholas and stood him on his feet. 'You okay, sport?'

Wide-eyed and grinning, Nicholas shouted, 'Yes. Look at me, Mummy.' He jumped up, tucking his knees under his chin and dropped into the water again.

'Guess he likes the sea as much as the pool, then.' She was relieved. Living in Golden Bay meant he'd spend a lot of time on or near the water and if he feared it then he wouldn't learn to master it.

'What happened to that ball?' Jackson looked around. 'Oops, it's heading out. I'd better retrieve it before it gets too far away.' He dived in and swam for it, his strokes strong and powerful, pulling his body quickly through the water.

'Mummy, I want to swim like Jackson.'

Thank you, Jackson. Until now, learning to swim had been the last thing Nicholas had wanted to do. The pool had been about splashing and jumping. She ruffled his wet hair. 'I'll sign you up for lessons this week.' And thank Jackson in an appropriate fashion once her boy was asleep.

'Help me collect driftwood for a bonfire, Nicholas.' Jackson threw an armful of wood down on the damp sand. The tide was receding fast and they'd be able to light a small fire before darkness set in.

'Why are we having a fire?' the boy asked.

'So we can toast marshmallows on sticks and eat them after dinner.'

'Won't they melt?'

Sometimes Nicholas was smarter than he should be for his age. 'Not if you're quick.'

'Are we all sleeping in the tent?' Nicholas picked up the end of a huge piece of wood and staggered along the beach, dragging it behind him.

'Yes.' Damn it. He hadn't thought that far ahead when he'd had this camping brainwave. Hadn't considered the frustration of lying with Jess and not being able to make love to her because Nicholas would be with them. It had seemed like a brilliant idea to come out here and give the boy a new experience. Guess he'd have to rein in his hormones for the night. Unless they found a secluded spot away from the tent but close enough to hear if Nicholas woke and got frightened.

'Hey, you two,' Jess called from down by the water's edge. 'Come and help me collect some cockles to cook for dinner.'

'What are cockles?'

'Shellfish,' Jackson told him. 'They're yummy.' If you got rid of all the sand in the shells.

'Why don't we catch them with our rods?'

'Because they live in the sand and mud. You've got to dig for them. See, like Mummy's doing.' Jess looked stunning in that orange bikini she wore. All legs and breasts. His mouth dried. When she'd asked if he intended staying on at Golden Bay he'd struggled to say no. Which meant he should be hightailing it out of the country now, not planning a way to get into her sleeping bag tonight.

There was no denying Jess had sneaked in under his skin when he'd been busy looking the other way. Leaving her was going to be incredibly difficult. But he couldn't take her and Nicholas with him. His eighteenth-floor apartment was definitely not conducive to raising a young child. No, Nicholas was in the perfect place for a boy—swimming and fishing on his doorstep, farms with real animals just as close in the other direction.

'I want to do the digging, Mummy.' Once Nicholas got started there was no stopping him. Finally they had to drag him into the water and clean off the mud that covered him from head to toes. 'Why are you throwing them away?' he asked when Jackson tipped half their haul back into the mud.

'Because we're not allowed too many.'

'Will the policeman tell us off if you don't put them back?'

'Yes. It's so that we don't use them all up and can get more another day.'

'Okay.'

Okay. Life seemed so simple for Nicholas. Give him

an explanation and he was happy, not looking for hidden agendas. 'How about you and I cook the cockles so that Mummy can have a rest?' Jess's all-night haul at the birthing unit appeared to be catching up with her. He'd seen her hiding a yawn more than once. 'Jess, why don't you curl up in the tent and have a snooze?'

'Because I'd probably not wake up till morning. I don't want to miss out on anything.' Her smile was soft and wistful.

'I promise to call you for dinner.' He knew what all-nighters with patients were like. They drained you so that putting one foot in front of the other became hard work. 'Go on. Nicholas and I will put our rods in the water and see what we can catch. On your way to the tent can you put those cockles in fresh water so they spit out the sand?' He wasn't giving her a chance to argue.

'You promise to call me?'

'Promise. I'll have a glass of wine waiting. The potatoes will be cooking and the steak ready to sizzle.'

Another yawn stretched her mouth and she shrugged. 'Guess I can't argue with that.' Picking up the bucket of shellfish, she trudged up the beach and across the road to their camp site.

Jackson only tore his eyes away from her when she reached the tent. His heart ached with need. With love. Love? No way, man. He hadn't gone and fallen in love with Jessica. No way. So why the pain in his chest? Why the need to wrap her up and look after her? Why spend time with her little boy, teaching him things any father would do if he wasn't in love with Jess?

No, he couldn't be. It wasn't meant to happen like that. Lots of hot sex, and plenty of fun; that was how it went. Harmless, enjoyable, no ties, no future.

He dropped to his haunches and picked up a pebble to hurl it across the water. Where had he gone wrong? How had he made such a monumental error? Right from that first night he'd had no intention of getting too close to Jess. Because no matter what happened, what she hoped for, he was going home to Hong Kong. To his frantic life, his orderly life. His now frightening life—and that damned promise.

Another pebble skimmed across the wavelets. Dropped out of sight under the water. And another, and another. A lonely life it may be, but at least he wasn't letting anyone down by being too busy for them.

What about Ping's words of wisdom last week when he'd finally caught up with him on the phone? *You are ready to return home. Hong Kong isn't home for you.* Ping had sounded so certain that he'd found he couldn't argue with his friend. Not that he'd done anything stupid like hand in his notice. No way. But he hadn't been able to shut Ping out of his brain, especially in the early hours while he lay in bed, waiting for the sun to lift above the horizon so he could go for a run. Ping often came out with Chinese proverbs or other wise bits of advice, but this time Jackson would ignore him.

He might be falling for Jess but he wouldn't be doing anything about it. He wasn't prepared to live in the back of beyond where his medical skills would be wasted. And he couldn't ask Jess to move when she'd only recently settled here and begun making a secure environment for Nicholas to grow up in.

'Look at me. I can throw stones in the water like you.' Nicholas stood beside him, his little face earnest as he tried to toss his pebbles as far as the water's edge.

Might be time to head away, get out of here earlier

than planned, save any further heartache that being with Jess would cause. Then there was this little guy who took everything at face value and had accepted him as a part of his life.

'You're doing great, Nicholas.' Jackson stood up and moved behind him, took his elbow and gently pulled it back. 'Swing your arm back like this. Now fling it forward as hard as you can.'

They continued throwing pebbles until Nicholas tired of that game. 'Can we go fishing now?'

'Sure. I'll go and get the rods and bait.'

'I'll do it.' Without waiting for Jackson, Nicholas raced up the beach. 'I know where the rods are.' He was nearing the road too fast.

'Nicholas, come back here now.' Panic had Jackson charging after him. 'Don't you go on that road, Nicholas,' he roared. He thought he could hear a vehicle approaching at speed. 'Nicholas. Stop.'

'I'm looking both ways.'

'Wait for me.' Jackson skidded to a stop beside him at the road's edge. His hand gripped the boy's shoulder. 'Never run towards a road, sport,' he gasped around his receding fear. 'Cars go a lot faster than you do and the driver might not see you.'

'Mummy told me that.' Nicholas wriggled his shoulder free and looked right, left, then right again. 'See. Nothing's coming. Can I cross now?'

That vehicle had to have been in his imagination because now he'd stopped his mad dash up the beach Jackson couldn't hear it. Quickly checking both ways, he said in an uneven voice, 'Yes, you can. Let's go quietly so we don't wake your mum.'

* * *

Over an hour later Jackson and Nicholas returned from their fishing expedition with all the bait gone and no fish to show for it.

'I wanted to catch a fish.' Nicholas pouted. 'It's not fair.'

'That's the way of it, sport. If fish were too easy to catch, there'd be no fun in it.' Jackson stopped at the tent entrance and peered in. Jess lay sprawled face down across the bigger of the two air beds, her hair spread over the pillow. How easy it would be to curl up beside her and push his fingers through that blonde silk. Fishy fingers, he reminded himself.

He turned to Nicholas. 'Let's go clean ourselves up. Then we'll get dinner cooking and wake your mother.'

'I'm hungry now.'

'Wash your hands first. You smell of fish bait.'

'I want something to eat first.'

Jackson sighed. No wonder Jess gave in to Nicholas so often. Otherwise she'd be sounding like the big, bad wolf all the time. 'You can have a banana as soon as you're clean.' He swung Nicholas up under his arm and carried him to the ablutions block, tickling him and getting ear-piercing shrieks for his efforts. So much for keeping quiet, but at least the temper tantrum had been avoided.

With the potatoes baking on the barbecue hot plate and the cockles in a pot ready to steam, Jackson poured a glass of wine and headed for the tent. 'Wake up, sleepy-head.' His heart blocked his throat at the sight inside. Jess had rolled onto her back and spread her arms wide, like an invitation. In sleep she had lost that worrying look that had him wondering if she'd got too involved with him, making it easier for him to believe they were merely having an affair that he would shortly walk away from unharmed. Except he already knew it would hurt, that he was too late to save his heart. But he would still have to go.

'Jess.' He nudged her foot with his toe. 'Time to wake up, lazybones.'

'Go away,' she mumbled, and made to roll over.

'Mummy, you've got to get up now.' Nicholas bounced onto the bed and dropped to his knees so close to Jess that Jackson feared she'd be bruised.

Her eyes popped open. 'Hello, you two.' Her voice was thick with sleep. Rubbing her hands down her cheeks, she yawned and then stretched her feet to the end of the bed and her hands high above her, lifting her breasts as she did.

His breath caught as he ogled those sweet mounds pushing against her singlet top. The glass shook in his hand, spilling wine over his fingers. 'I'll see you outside. Do you want this wine in here?'

'No, I'll join you in a minute.' Already she was scrambling onto her knees and delving into her bag to haul out a jersey.

Nicholas had arranged the outdoor chairs so that they could see down the grass to the beach. Jackson sank down on one and picked up his beer. His hand still shook. He knew how it felt to hold Jess in his arms and make love to her, the little sounds she made in pleasure, the way she liked to wind her legs around his afterwards. He wanted to know all those things again and again.

Making love to Jess was nothing like the sex he'd had with those women he usually dated. But he hadn't really dated Jess. They'd just got together. At work, at his parents' place, and mostly at her home, where they enjoyed each other whenever Nicholas wasn't around or was tucked up in bed, sound asleep.

'Where's the TV?' Nicholas asked as he crossed over to Jackson.

Laughter rang out, sweet and clear, from the tent. 'There's no TV out here, sweetheart. When you go camping you don't have power for things like that.'

As the boy's face began to pucker up Jackson reined in his smile and said, 'Think about telling your friends how you spent the night in a tent and that you ate food cooked outside, and how you dug for shellfish. Isn't that more exciting?'

'Can I catch a fish tomorrow?'

'We'll give it a darned good try, sport.'

Jess slid onto the chair beside him, her light jersey covering those tantalising breasts. 'You have a knack with him.' She sipped from her glass. 'Perfect.'

'Should've got champagne, knowing how much you enjoy it.'

'You'd better stop spoiling me. I might get used to it.' She stared out across the water, seeing who knew what. The glass shook in her fingers, as it had moments ago in his.

Laying a hand on her thigh, he squeezed gently. 'Jess, I can't—'

She turned, placed a finger on his lips. 'Don't say anything, Jackson. I know this has to come to an end, have known it all along, but I don't want to spoil our time together talking about things we can't change.'

He could not argue with that, so he didn't.

CHAPTER EIGHT

'So Melanie's getting a little sister or brother. That's cool.' *And I'm fighting something very like jealousy here.* Jess watched Sasha's face light up with excitement, felt her own heart thump harder. *A baby—with Jackson— would be perfect.* She breathed in deep, exhaled slowly. *Get real.*

'Yeah, isn't it? I can't wait. So unlike last time, when I was dealing with the defection of Melanie's father and coming to terms with returning here, this time I've got Grady right beside me.' Sasha grinned and wrapped her arms around Jess in a big hug. 'Know a good midwife?'

'I might.' She squeezed back. 'A summer baby.'

'Not like Melanie. She kept me warm through last winter.' Sasha stepped away and opened the fridge, where she found the salmon Jackson had placed there earlier. 'Did Jackson go out to Anatoki for this?'

Anatoki was a salmon farm where customers could fish for their dinner in large holding ponds. 'He took Nicholas and let him catch the salmon. In fact, Jackson let him catch and release two before bringing this one home. I don't think my boy will ever stop talking about that. I'm surprised he hasn't told you every minute detail. I couldn't get his fishing shirt off him so he does reek a little.'

Sasha shook her head. 'I haven't spoken to him yet. He's following Jackson everywhere, glued to his hip.'

'There's a certain amount of hero worship going on, for sure.' Which would soon turn into a big problem. The weeks were speeding by and when Jackson headed away she'd be left to pick up the pieces. As well as deal with her own broken heart.

Sasha looked up from stuffing the salmon with herbs. 'You're worried?'

'Big time. Maybe I should've stopped seeing Jackson right after your wedding and kept him out of Nicholas's life.' Like she'd have been able to manage that easily. She'd fallen for him so fast she'd been spinning.

'Maybe you should tell Jackson how you feel about him.' Sasha cocked her head to one side. 'Hmm?'

'No way. We've been up front right from the start. No commitment, no demands on each other. Have a good time and sign off come April.' Why did that sound so flippant? Because it was. Casual maybe, but not normal. 'But I haven't, and won't, tell him I've fallen for him. It would ruin everything.'

Her friend's lips pressed tight for a moment and Jess knew she was about to get a lecture. 'Leave it, Sasha. I'm not asking Jackson to stay on when he obviously doesn't want to. Don't forget I'm not interested in tying myself to anyone either. It wouldn't be fair on Nicholas.'

'That's getting a little monotonous, Jess. You've got a big heart, big enough for more than your son. You've spread it around the community and he hasn't suffered.' Hadn't she already heard that from Jackson? Unfortunately, Sasha wasn't finished. 'There are still a few weeks for you to talk to him, lay your feelings on the line.'

Jess shivered. She couldn't do that. Too scary. 'Do we want to make the salads now?'

Sasha wasn't about to be sidetracked. 'Think about it. What have you got to lose? A broken heart? That's coming anyway, regardless. But you might find my brother has changed his mind about his mighty Hong Kong hospital and lifestyle. He was moody when he first arrived home, got angry at the smallest things, but that's not happening so much now. Mum says he sometimes sings in the shower. That's unheard of. You've got a role in all this. He's keen on you, really keen.'

Jackson hadn't told his family about the stabbing. He didn't want them worrying about him when he returned to Hong Kong. Opening the fridge again, Jess removed the vegetable bin containing everything needed to put together a crisp, healthy salad. Jackson might be keen on her, as Sasha put it, but he didn't want her trailing after him all the way to Asia. That also would mean putting her needs before Nicholas's. How could she explain to her boy that living in an enormous city was as good as being in Golden Bay with beaches and fishing?

Loud laughter rolled through the open windows. Jackson and Grady were playing soccer with Nicholas on the front lawn. Her son wore a huge grin as he charged after the ball and stole it from under Jackson's foot. He dribbled it towards the makeshift goal until he fell over the ball and landed on his face. Jess held her breath, waiting for an explosion of tears, but Nicholas bounced back up and took off after the ball that Grady had stolen while he was down. Her boy was lapping up the male attention. 'Grady will still have some time for Nicholas, won't he?'

'You know he will, though it won't be the same as having Jackson's undivided attention.' Sasha handed her a glass of champagne. 'You'll have to drink my share now that I'm pregnant. Let's join Mum and Dad on the deck. The salmon will take a while.'

Jess continued to keep one eye on Jackson, filing away memories of how athletic he looked, how his long legs ate up the ground as he chased the ball, how his laughter sneaked under her ribs and tickled her heart. She collected even more mental images during dinnertime.

But. Nothing was going to be the same ever again. Grady might be there for Nicholas when he had time, but he had his own children to put first. She'd do anything to make her son's life perfect—except tell Jackson she loved him.

But as Sasha had pointed out, what did she have to lose? Honesty was good, wasn't it? What if Jackson had already guessed her feelings for him? Was he waiting for her to say something? Or crossing his fingers she'd keep silent?

'You're very quiet tonight.' Jackson leaned close.

Unnerved that he might read her mind, she shivered. 'Sorry.'

'You're cold. I'll get your jersey.'

She let him go and find it. Cold had nothing to do with that shiver. But—but all to do with cowardice. She was afraid if she told Jackson she loved him he'd laugh at her or, worse, commiserate and beat a hasty retreat. So she'd remain silent. Coward. If her heart was big enough for more than Nicholas, as people kept telling her, then what was holding her back? Nothing ventured, nothing gained, as they said. Or nothing lost.

But. She was hanging onto her belief that she'd turn

out to be like her parents. Did Sasha have a point? Was this belief just an excuse to hide behind because she was afraid of putting her heart on the line? It had hurt when Nicholas's father had done a bunk, and now, compared with her feelings for Jackson, she saw she hadn't been as invested in that relationship as she'd thought.

'Here.' Jackson held out her jersey. 'Have you taken to buying everything you wear in orange since the wedding?' Those delicious lips curved upwards, sending her stomach into a riot of fluttering.

'No, but I have bought things in apricot shades.' Underwear, two shirts and the sexiest pair of fitted jeans. 'Online shopping is an absolute boon when living here.'

Jackson did an eye-roll. 'Women will always find a way to shop, even if they're living on Mars.'

'Sexist.' Jess and Sasha spoke in unison.

Virginia added her bit. 'So says the man with the biggest, most expensive wardrobe I've ever seen.'

'Nicholas. Want another game of soccer, sport?' Jackson grinned.

'After dinner. I want to eat more salmon. It's yummy, Mummy. Can you take me to catch more?'

Giving Jackson a mock glare, she answered, 'You've been spoiled today. This is a treat.'

'We'll go next time I come home, sport.'

She'd have sworn she was trying not to look at him, but she was—staring. 'You might come home for another visit?' she croaked in a squeaky voice that had everyone staring at them both. *Don't. It won't be fair on Nicholas. Or me.*

'We'd love it if you do.' Ian filled the sudden silence. 'But we understand how busy you are over there.'

Jackson looked embarrassed, like he'd made a mistake. 'I've got more leave owing but it's hard to get away. There's always a shortage of temporary replacement staff.' Backpedalling so fast he'd fall on his butt if he wasn't careful.

Jess forced her disappointment aside. What had she expected? Glancing around the now quiet table, she saw that Jackson's statement had taken a toll on everyone. Of course Ian and Virginia wanted their son staying home. Now that Virginia was ill it would be more important for them. Sasha would want her brother on hand to help out on the orchard and to be a part of her children's lives. Everyone was affected by Jackson's decision and yet he should be able to continue with the career path he'd chosen.

Her gaze stopped on Jackson, noted the way his jaw clenched, his lips whitened. This was the first time he'd got angry in a couple of weeks. Was he angry at himself for hurting his family? Reaching under the table, she laid a hand on his thigh and softly dug her fingers into those tense muscles. 'Do they make apricot-coloured fishing rods?'

Green eyes locked with hers. Recognition of how she was trying to help him flickered back at her. His Adam's apple bobbed. Then his mouth softened. 'No, but I'm sure I can find you an orange one.'

The chuckles around the table were a little forced but soon the conversation was flowing again, this time on safer topics.

Not all the questions buzzing around inside Jess's head retreated. Instead, they drove her loopy with apprehension, making her feel like she was on a runaway truck, with no hope of stopping, and only disaster at the end. When Jackson offered to drive her home, she shook her head. 'Not tonight. My boy's exhausted and so am I. An early night is what we need.' She needed space to cope with the growing fear of how she'd manage when he left.

'You're mad at me for saying earlier I'd go fishing with Nicholas again some time.' He stood directly in front of her, hands on hips, eyes locked on hers.

'Not mad, Jackson, disappointed. Nicholas is young. He only sees things in black and white, and everything happens now.' That was only the beginning of her turmoil.

'Yeah, I get it. I'm very sorry. I'm not used to youngsters and how their thought processes work.'

'Says the man who has been absolutely brilliant with Nicholas these past two months.' She dug her keys out of her bag. 'Just so you know, I'm not going home alone because of what you told him. I'm bigger than that. I really do need some sleep.' Some space in my bed so I can think, and not be distracted by your sexy body and persuasive voice.

His lips brushed her cheek. 'I get that, too. I think. Let me put Nicholas in his car seat.'

She watched with hunger as he strode into the lounge where Nicholas was watching TV with Ian. She watched when he came back with her boy tucked against his chest, Nicholas's thumb in his mouth as he desperately tried to stay awake. Her hunger increased as he carefully clicked the seat belt around her son and brushed curls off his face. She shouldn't have turned him down. Climbing inside her car, she watched as he bent down and kissed her, long and tenderly. So tenderly he brought tears to her eyes. And a lump to her throat. She needed to be with him. She needed to be alone.

* * *

Jackson watched Jess drive out onto the road for the short trip back to her place. It took all his willpower not to run after her, to follow her home and slip into bed to hold her tight.

How the hell was he going to leave Jess? His heart ached now and he still had four weeks left to be with her. Impossible to imagine how he'd feel once he stepped onto that plane heading northeast.

Don't go. Stay here. Everyone wants you to. That much had been painfully obvious at dinnertime. Surprising how easy it might be to do exactly that. Stay. Become a part of the community he'd been in such a hurry to leave when he'd been a teen. If he stayed, what would he do for work? On average he'd have one emergency a week to deal with. Unless he worked in Nelson. Only two hours' drive away. He could commute or get a small apartment, return home on his days off. Not the perfect way to have a relationship but it had worked for Mum and Dad. Nah, he did not want that for him and Jess.

As the taillights of Jess's car disappeared he headed for the deck and some quiet time. Inside, Sasha and Mum were arguing light-heartedly about who had the best chocolate-cake recipe. Dad was still watching TV. Or was he catnapping, as he often did when he thought no one was looking?

Family. He loved them. Leaving Golden Bay back then hadn't been about them. Being young and brash, he'd always believed they would be around for ever. That whenever he chose to return, family life would be as it had always been. And it was. Yet it was different. There were additions: Grady, Melanie and the unborn baby. Dad no longer disappeared to the other side of the world every second week. Then there was Mum. His rock when he'd been growing up, always there with a ready ear and a loving word. Now he should be here for her. That promise shouldn't keep him from those he loved, yet he was afraid to ignore it. His word was important.

He was avoiding the real issue. Jessica Baxter.

Jess hadn't had what he and Sasha got from Mum and Dad, yet she'd slotted into his family: best mates with Sasha; a surrogate daughter to his parents. Often she could be found helping out in the orchard or doing the ironing or scrubbing the floor. If anyone was the outsider in his family it was him. Only because he lived so damned far away, but it was reason enough.

'Want a beer?' Grady's question cut through the crap in his head.

'Thanks.' He took the proffered bottle, dropped onto a chair and swung his feet up onto the deck railing. The cold liquid was like nectar. 'That's bloody good.'

'Nothing's ever easy, is it?'

He presumed Grady was talking about the things going on in his head. 'Nope.'

They sat in a comfortable silence, drinking their beer, replenishing the bottles when they dried up, not bothering with unnecessary talk. They both knew the situation. Why keep talking about it? As far as brothers-in-law went, Sasha had got him a good one.

The temperature had cooled, and the air felt heavy with dew. Summer was giving way to autumn and the temperatures were beginning to reflect that, day and night. Soon the holiday homeowners would clean down their boats and put them away for winter. They'd lock up their houses and go home. What would Jess do over winter? Would she hunker down for the cold months or get out there, continuing to visit people: checking they had enough firewood to see them through; taking food and books to the older folk living outside the township boundaries; keeping an eye on their health?

No guesses there. He knew the answer. Jess was generous beyond generous. No matter that she thought it was about repaying folk for the bad things she'd done as a wild teenager. It wasn't that at all. Jess was kind and generous to a fault. Couldn't help being so good to others.

'Time we went home, Grady.' Sasha stepped into the light spilling from the windows. 'Melanie has finished feeding and needs to be tucked up in her cot.'

'Not a problem, sweetheart.' Grady unwound his long body and stood up. 'You want to do a spot of fishing tomorrow, Jackson? We could put the tinny in before breakfast and go find ourselves something for brunch.'

'I'm on. See you about six?' Fishing always relaxed him. Unless he was with Nicholas and had to spend the whole time baiting hooks and untying knots in the line. Which was kind of fun, in its own way.

'Six? Just because you're sleeping solo tonight, you want to drag me out early.'

'Five past?' Jackson laughed, but inside he felt lonely. Grady was a good bloke, but he wasn't what he needed right now, at night, in bed. No, she had elected to go home alone.

Jess might've desperately wanted to sleep, but that didn't mean she got any. At two o'clock she gave up and went out to the kitchen to make some chamomile tea. Sitting in the lounge, she switched on the TV and watched the second half of some out-of-date rerun of something she'd first seen when she'd been about fourteen. And still the thoughts about what she should tell Jackson before he left went round and round her skull.

'Hey, Jackson, I love you. So if you ever change your mind about coming home or wanting a life partner, you know my number.'

Yep, that would work. She could see him rushing up and kissing her and telling her that was the best news he'd had in a long time. Not.

Okay, what about, 'Jackson, I love you and would love it if Nicholas and I could move to Hong Kong to be with you.'

He probably wouldn't bother packing his bags, just run for the airport.

What about just shutting up, keeping her feelings to herself, and getting on with enjoying the remaining weeks?

Yep, that might work.

Except she'd heard Sasha loud and clear. It was time to risk her heart, lay it out there for Jackson to do with as he pleased. At least she'd know exactly where she stood with him.

Thought I knew that already.

They were having an affair; no more, no less. She'd fallen in love with him the night it had started but she'd known from the beginning that the fling had no chance of becoming anything else. It'd be breaking the rules to tell Jackson her true feelings.

Rules were made to be broken, weren't they?

Apparently, but...she drew a deep breath...this could backfire so fast, so badly, she daren't do it.

She had to do it. It was eating her up, not being honest with him.

Why had she fallen for him? Why Jackson, of all

men? Because he was out of reach and so she'd be safe? Wouldn't have to relinquish her long-held beliefs that she couldn't love more than one person thoroughly?

Newsflash. You already do love Nicholas and Jackson, and you haven't once let your boy down in the weeks you've been seeing Jackson. You are so not like your parents it's a joke.

The annoying voice in her head hadn't finished with her yet. 'You love Jackson because he's Jackson, because of all the little things that make him the man he is. The good things and the not-so-good things.' Huh? 'The immaculate clothes that are so out of place here, the need to be in charge.' Oh. 'Remember the colour of love is sky blue. Happy blue with bright yellow sunshine.'

CHAPTER NINE

THE COLOUR OF love was absent the next morning as Jess drove to the Wilson household. The sky was grey with heavy, rain-filled clouds and they were going nowhere. The moist atmosphere felt chilly after such a hot summer.

Her heart was out of whack, like it didn't know what rhythm it should be beating. It sure clogged her throat any time she thought about her mission.

'So don't think about it.' Yeah, sure.

'What can't I think about, Mummy?'

'Sorry, sweetheart. I was talking to myself.' Turning into the long driveway leading up to Ian and Virginia's house, her foot lifted off the accelerator and the car slowly came to a halt. *What am I doing? Is it the right thing?* The resolve she'd found at about six that morning had deserted her. *Turn around and go home. No. That's cowardly.*

Before she could overthink what she'd come to do, she pressed her foot hard on the accelerator and the car shot up the drive like she was being chased.

'Hi, Jess, Nicholas. You're out early.' Ian sauntered over to them from his packing shed. 'Just like the boys. Grady was around here before the sparrows woke to take Jackson out fishing.'

Her heart stopped its erratic tattoo as relief whooshed through her. *Coward. This is a delay, not the finish of your mission.* 'Isn't it a bit rough out on the water today?'

Ian shook his head. 'No. Flat calm at the moment. Perfect conditions. Though it is forecast to kick up early afternoon, but they'll be back long before then. Hopefully with a bin of fish for lunch.'

'Fishing? I want to go, too.'

'No, Nicholas, you can't.' Thump-thump went the dull pain behind her eyes. The last thing she needed was Nicholas throwing a paddy because he hadn't gone with Jackson. Picking him up, she hugged him tight. 'Sorry, sweetheart.'

Ian ruffled Nicholas's hair. 'Sorry, boyo, but Grady and Jackson were having some man time. None of us were invited.'

'What's man time?' came the inevitable question.

Jess held her breath as Ian answered, keen to know what this fishing trip was all about if not catching fish.

'It's when close friends want to spend time talking or not talking and doing something together that they enjoy.'

What did Jackson and Grady have to talk about that they hadn't already discussed last night around the dinner table?

'Guess we'll go back home, then.' She sighed. Home, where she could pace up and down the small lounge. Or make herself useful and bake cookies for her neighbours. Or, 'Think I'll go see Sasha.'

Ian frowned. 'Don't go before you've seen Virginia, will you? She's a bit shaky this morning and I don't mind admitting she worries me. I never know how she's really feeling, she's so intent on hiding the truth from me.'

Guilt assailed her. She'd become very selfish recently, putting her own concerns before those of her friends. See, loving Jackson did divert her from the other people in her life. 'Of course I'm going to see Virginia. Is there something you want me to check out?'

'No. There are two doctors in the family taking good care of her. Driving her insane with all their questions if you want to know the truth. But while I can sympathise with Virginia, I need those boys doing the doctor thing.' Ian looked glum as he ran a hand through his hair. Like father, like son. 'Just give her some cheek and pretend everything's normal, will you?'

'Come on, Nicholas. Let's go say hello to Virginia.'

'He can help me in the shed, if you like.' Ian looked at Nicholas. 'We've got boxes to make up for the avocados.'

'Yes, please. I want to help.'

'Guess that's decided, then.' Jess headed for the house, torn between being relieved Jackson wasn't around to talk to and being disappointed she hadn't got it over and done with.

Jackson wound hard and fast, bringing the line in before the barracuda bit into the blue cod he'd hooked. 'Get lost, you waste of sea space.'

'You've got two cod on those hooks.' Grady grinned. 'Talk about greedy.'

'Saves time.' Jackson swung the straining line over the side of the boat so that his catch landed in the big bin they'd put on board. 'Nothing wrong with either of them either. Definitely not undersized.' He grinned. Not like Grady's last two.

'Next you'll be saying you've caught the biggest of the day.'

'Too right.' One of the cod had swallowed the hook, making it tricky to remove. He found the special pliers and wrenched it free. The other fish was foul-hooked around the mouth and didn't take much to undo. 'Got my brunch. How're you doing?'

'I'm onto getting enough for the rest of the family.' Grady wound in a fish and Jackson nearly split his sides laughing.

'Not even Nicholas would get enough to eat from that.'

'Says the expert,' Grady grumped, and carefully slid the undersized cod back under the water. 'You and that boy get on okay.'

'He likes fishing.' Hopefully Grady would take him out occasionally. 'I'll miss him.'

'What about his mother? Going to miss her, too?'

'Definitely.' More than he'd have believed possible. Hell, he missed her now, missed her whenever they were apart. It had hurt last night when she'd wanted to go home alone. But she was entitled to her space. He didn't want to encroach on everything she did. Not much, anyway.

'There's a job going at the Nelson Hospital ED.'

That he did not want to know. It added to his dilemma about heading away, leaving everyone behind. 'I've got one, thanks.'

Grady dropped his line back in the water. 'Just thought you should know.'

A tug at the end of his line gave Jackson the distraction he needed. Winding fast, he soon had another cod in the bin. 'One to go and we've got our limit.'

And we can head home to the family. My family. And Jess and Nicholas.

* * *

Jess placed the tray of shortbread in the oven and set the timer. It was quiet in her house. Nicholas had stayed on with Ian, doing man stuff apparently. Thank goodness there were men like Ian to give her boy a male perspective. Jackson was Nicholas's firm favourite. Unfortunately. His little heart would be broken soon. Had she done wrong, encouraging Nicholas to get on with Jackson? Probably. But, then, life was like that and the sooner Nicholas learned he had to look out for himself the better.

Her cellphone vibrated on the bench. 'Hello?'

'I think I'm in labour.'

'Constance? Is that you?' The thirty-six-year-old woman wasn't due for ten days.

'Yes.' Grunt. 'Can you hurry? You know how fast my babies like to be.'

'On my way.' Turning the oven off, she ran for her car, whilst phoning Virginia. 'I've got an eminent birth. Can Nicholas stay there until I'm finished?' She hated asking when Virginia had enough to deal with, but right now she didn't have the time to collect her boy and deposit him with Andrea and Bobby. 'I can phone Andrea and see if she'll pick him up later.'

'Nonsense. We love having him here. Don't worry about him at all. Just go and deliver that baby safely.'

Nicholas waved furiously as they turned up the drive. Jackson looked around, felt a tug of disappointment when he didn't see Jess's car. 'Hey, sport. What have you been up to all morning?'

'Making boxes. Did you get any fish?' Nicholas jumped up and down by the boat, trying to get high enough to see what they'd caught.

Jackson swung him up and into the boat. 'Take a look in that bin.'

Nicholas's eyes popped out wide. 'That's lots. They're very big.' He delved into the bin, ran his hands all over the cold, wet fish. Jess would be thrilled when she caught up with her stinky boy.

'Where's Mummy?' The question was out before he'd thought about it.

Grady rolled his eyes and hefted the bin out of the boat.

'She's getting a new baby.' Nicholas picked up a rod and handed it to him.

Grady's eyes widened and his mouth twitched. 'Interesting.'

'Careful of those hooks, sport.' Jackson took the rod and stood it against the side of the boat and waited for the second rod to come his way. Jess was at a birth. He remembered when Baby Carter had been born and the misty look of longing that had filtered into her eyes. Did she really want more children? Or did she get like that with every birth she attended?

'You're looking dewy-eyed.' Grady nudged him.

Jackson snapped his head around. 'What? I don't think so. I am definitely not interested in babies. Not when I've got to go back to Hong Kong anyway. No, sir.'

'The man protests too much. Come on, Nicholas. Help me clean up these fish.' Grady strolled off to the outside sink and table to fillet the fish, Nicholas stepping along beside him.

Do I want children? Now? With Jess? Turning the hose on, he began hosing down the boat and trailer to remove any traces of salt water.

Yes. Someday. Yes. Cold water sprayed down his trousers, filled his shoes. Damn. Concentrate on the job in hand. Stop asking himself stupid questions. Whatever he wanted, it wasn't going to happen.

So whose baby was Jess delivering?

'Abigail is absolutely beautiful.' As Jess handed Constance her daughter she heard a vehicle pulling up outside the house. 'You've got a visitor, Tim.'

Tim groaned. 'Bad timing.' He didn't move from where he sat on the edge of the bed his wife had just given birth in.

'Want me to go give whoever it is a nudge?' Jess figured these two needed time alone with Abigail and it was an excuse to take herself out of the room.

'Would you mind?' Tim looked hopeful. 'Though I guess if it's one of our parents there's no stopping them.'

'Leave it to me.' She was already halfway out of the room. The doorbell chimed before she reached the front of the house. Pulling the door wide, the breath stuck in her lungs.

Jackson stood there, beaming at her. 'Thought I'd drop by and see if you needed any support.'

Leaning against the doorjamb for strength, she waited for her breathing to restart. 'You're too late. Abigail arrived ten minutes ago.'

His brow creased. 'That was fast. From what Mum said, you've only been gone a little over an hour.'

'Constance has a history of short labours, hence the home birth. She didn't fancy giving birth in Tim's truck on the way to town.'

Nodding, Jackson said, 'So you're all done here? Heading back to town now?'

'I've got some cleaning up to do, and I like to hang

around for a while in case there's anything not right. Though Constance is a seasoned mum, this being her fourth baby.' But she wasn't about to leave because of that. 'I'm about to make coffee. Want one?' Hopefully the caffeine wouldn't set her heart racing any faster than it already was. One sight of Jackson and it lost all control over its rhythm.

'Sounds good.'

Pushing away from the jamb, she straightened. 'How was the fishing?'

'Brilliant. You've got blue cod for dinner.' He caught her elbow, held her from moving away. 'Did you get any of that sleep you wanted? You're looking more peaky than ever.'

'Flattery will get you anything.' She tugged free, only to be caught again.

'What's bothering you, Jess?' Those green eyes bored into her, seeing who knew what? Probably everything she was trying to hide from him.

So stop hiding it. Get it over and done. Stepping past him, she tugged the door shut and went down the steps to the path. Rotating on her heels, she faced him, locked eyes with him again. 'You. Me. Us. That's what's keeping me awake at the moment.'

He froze, stared at her like he was a deer caught in headlights. His Adam's apple bobbed. The tip of his tongue slid across his bottom lip. Fear tripped through that green gaze. 'Us.'

Nodding slowly, she added, 'I know we agreed to an affair for the duration of your time here.' Damn, that sounded too formal, but how else did she say what needed to be said? *Try coming straight out with it.* 'But I fell in love with you.'

His face paled. Not a good sign. At all. Might as well give him the rest. Might help put him at ease. 'You're safe. I said at the time I had no intention of ever getting into a permanent relationship with anyone. That hasn't changed.' *You are so wrong, Jess. You'd settle down with Jackson in a flash, given the opportunity.* Yes, now she understood she would. No argument.

The next thing she knew his arms were around her, holding her tight against his chest. Under her ear his heart was speeding faster than a rabbit being chased by hounds. 'I'm so sorry, Jess.'

'I think that should be my line,' she muttered. But why? What had she done wrong? It wasn't as though she'd been able to avoid falling for him. It had happened in an instant. Yet she repeated in a lower voice, 'I'm sorry.'

'Ahh, Jess, this is all my fault. I've been so selfish. But I couldn't stay away from you.' Still holding her around the waist, he leaned back to lock eyes with her. 'You are beautiful, inside and out, Jessica Baxter. I've never known anyone like you.'

'Yet you're still going away.' Wanting to pull away before she melded herself to him so he had to take her with him, but needing to stay in his arms for as long as she could, she stood irresolute, fighting threatening tears.

'I'm sorry.' His voice was low, and sad, and trembling. 'Very sorry for everything.'

Jess spun out of his arms and tore down the path out onto the roadside, gulping lungful after lungful of air as she went. Get a grip. She'd known this would hurt big time. Yeah, but knowing and experiencing were poles apart. This hurt so bad she felt like she might never be able to stand straight again. She loved Jackson. End of story. There'd be no happy ever after. Funny how now that she knew that for real, she realised how much she actually wanted it. Desperately.

'Jess.' Jackson had followed her, stood watching her through wary eyes. 'Are you all right?'

'Oh, I'm just peachy.' She gasped, tried to hold onto the words bursting from her throat, and failed. 'Of course I'm not all right. I've spent days agonising over whether to tell you or not, but honesty got the better of me, and now I've spoiled what we might've had left before you head away.' The floodgates opened and a deluge poured down her cheeks, and there was nothing she could do to stop them.

Strong arms wrapped around her, held her close to his hard body. The rough beating of his heart against her ear echoed her own. Jackson's sharp breaths lifted strands of her hair and wafted them over her face. 'I'd like to promise I'll be back, but that'd be selfish. I honestly don't know what's ahead.'

Lifting her head just enough to see his face, she told him, 'I understand. Truly. It's not as if you lied to me. Golden Bay has never been big enough for you.'

'It will be a lot harder leaving this time than it was at eighteen. There's so much that's important to me here.' His hand rubbed circles over her shoulder blades.

She raised a pathetic chuckle. 'At eighteen you left in such a hurry you scorched the road.'

'True. If only I hadn't made that promise to Juliet.'

She pulled out of that comforting hold and slashed a hand over her wet cheeks. 'I'd better go check on Constance and Abigail.'

He looked hesitant.

She put him out of his misery. 'Go home, Jackson.

I won't be long and then I'll be doing the same thing.' Which meant collecting Nicholas from his parents' house. This just got harder and harder.

'Jess…' He hesitated. 'It might be in both our interests if I leave for Asia sooner than I'd planned.'

She gasped. She hadn't seen that coming. 'What about Virginia? She'll be upset.'

Wincing, he replied, 'I'll talk to her, explain, hopefully make her understand. After all, it was Mum who taught me to be honest and to live by my beliefs. But I will come home often, no more staying away for years on end.'

She had no answer to that. Her heart ached so badly it felt as though it was disintegrating inside her chest. 'Will I see you before you go?'

Shock widened his eyes, tightened his mouth. He reached for her, took her shoulders and tugged her close. 'Most definitely. I won't walk away without saying goodbye.'

For the second time since he'd turned up here she spun away and put space between them. Goodbye? A cruel word. A harsh reality for her future. A bleak future without Jackson in it. Behind her the truck door slammed shut and the engine turned over. She didn't look as he drove away. If she did she'd have started running, chasing the truck, begging him to stop and talk to her some more.

She didn't even know his feelings for her. Somewhere along the way she'd started to think he might care for her a lot, even love her a little. Not that knowing would have changed what happened, but it might've been a slight salve for her battered heart.

At seven o'clock on Tuesday morning Jess woke with a thumping headache. The alarm was loud in her quiet bedroom. She'd lain awake until about four then drifted into a fitful sleep. Now all she wanted to do was stick her head under the covers and go back to sleep, where she wouldn't notice Jackson leaving.

'Mummy, I got myself up.' Nicholas bounced onto her bed, creating havoc inside her skull.

'Good for you, sweetheart. What are you going to have for breakfast today?' She wouldn't be able to swallow a thing. When would her appetite return?

'Toast with honey. Can I cook it by myself?'

That had her sitting up too fast, her head spinning like a cricket ball in flight. 'Wait until I'm out there with you.' Slipping into her heavy robe, she tied the belt at her waist and followed him out to the kitchen.

While Nicholas made toast, along with the usual mess, she drank a cup of tea that threatened to come back up any moment.

A knock on the back door sent Nicholas rushing to open it. 'Mummy, it's Jackson.'

She tried to stand up, she really did, but her legs failed her. Her hands gripped her mug of tea as her eyes tracked Jackson as he entered the room and came towards her. Dressed in superbly cut trousers and jacket, he looked like something out of a glossy magazine, not the man in shorts and T-shirt she'd been knocking around with for the last couple of months.

'Jess.'

'Jackson.'

He'd dropped in last night to tell her he was flying out today, bound for Auckland, and on to Hong Kong on Saturday. Said it was for the best. That's what she'd spent most of the night trying to figure out—how could it be good for him or for her?

'Jackson, I made my own breakfast.' Nicholas seemed impervious to the mood in the room.

'That's great.' He looked down at her boy, and swallowed. 'Nicholas, I'm leaving today, going back to where I live.'

Her eyes blurred, her hands were like claws around the mug. *Give me strength.*

Nicholas stared up at the man he'd come to accept as part of his life. 'You can't. I don't want you to. Mummy, tell him to stay.'

There were tears in Jackson's eyes as he hunkered down to be on Nicholas's level and reached for him. 'I'm sorry, sport, but I have to go.'

'No, you don't.' Nicholas began crying, big hiccupping sobs that broke her heart as much as Jackson's leaving would.

'Can I send you emails? You can answer, telling me how your swimming lessons are going, how many fish you catch with Grady?' Sniff, sniff. Jackson studied her boy like he was storing memories to take with him.

Nicholas nodded slowly then his eyes widened in panic. 'I don't know how to email. Mummy?'

'I'll show you.' Was it a good idea to let these two stay in touch? Would Nicholas feel let down, or would he slowly get over Jackson's disappearance?

Jackson stood, Nicholas in his arms. 'I want you to look after Mummy, for me. She's very special, you know.'

Stay and look out for me yourself. 'That doesn't give you licence to do what you like around here, Nicholas.' Her smile was warped, but at least it was a smile.

'What's licence?'

'I think your mother means you can't do whatever you like without permission.' Jackson squeezed him close then dropped a kiss on his head before handing him to her. 'See you later, alligator.' His voice broke and he turned away.

She cuddled her little boy, comforting him, comforting herself. 'Ssh, sweetheart. It's going to be all right.' Like hell it would be, and now she'd lied to Nicholas. She kissed the top of his head. 'Jackson, you'd better go.' *Before I nail you to the floor so you can't. Before I fall apart, the way my boy is.* 'Please,' she begged.

He turned back to face her. 'Sure.' But he didn't move. Just stood there, watching her, sadness oozing out of those beautiful green eyes.

'Go. Now. Please.'

He stepped up beside her, his hand took her chin and gently tilted her head back. His kiss was so gentle it hurt. Her lips moulded to his, fitted perfectly, for the last time. She breathed in to get her last taste of him, a scent to hold onto and remember in the dark of the night.

And then he was gone. Her back door closed quietly behind him. Nicholas howled louder. Jess sat there, unable to move, and let the tears flow.

Jackson had gone.

CHAPTER TEN

JESS PULLED THE bedcovers up to her chin and listened to the rain beating down on the roof. It hadn't let up all night. She'd never heard rain like it. And according to the radio it wasn't about to stop.

'Heavy rain warnings for the Cobb Valley and lower Takaka' had been the dire message, again and again.

'Not a lot I can do about it. Might as well stay snug in bed. At least until Nicholas decides he wants up and about.' The rain suited her mood. The mood that had hung over her, keeping her gripped in misery, for the two days since Jackson had walked out of her life.

It was time to get over that. Yeah, okay, time to paste a smile on her face and pretend everything was fine in her world. Going around looking like someone had stolen her house when she hadn't been looking didn't help. Starting from now, she'd enjoy these quiet moments before Nicholas demanded her attention. She flicked the bedside light on and reached for her book. 'Bliss,' she pretended.

The light flickered. Dimmed, came back to full strength. Went off.

'So much for that idea.'

'Mummy, it's gone dark,' Nicholas yelled from his bedroom. 'I'm getting up.'

'Me, too, Sweetheart.' Jess leapt out of bed and quickly dressed in old jeans and T-shirt. It didn't matter that she looked like a tramp; Jackson wasn't around to notice. The familiar tug of need twisted at her heart, tightened her tummy. She missed him. So much. Let's face it, she'd already been missing him before he'd left.

The moment he'd said goodbye and walked away she'd shut down, squashing hard on the pain threatening to break her apart. She'd gone through the last two days at work like a robot. One day she'd have to face up to the end of her affair with Jackson, and deal with it. But right now it was a case of getting through the minutes one at a time.

With a smile on her face. No matter how false that was.

'Hey, Mummy. Can I go outside and jump in the puddles?' Nicholas appeared in her doorway, dressed in his favourite shirt—his fishing one, of course.

Another tug at her heart. At least she could be thankful that after his first outburst of disappointment Nicholas hadn't been as sad as she'd expected. But that could be because her son didn't get what goodbye really meant. Up until now anyone who said that to him always came back—from Nelson, from school, from just about anywhere. But not from Hong Kong.

'Let me see what it's like outside first. There's been a lot of rain and those puddles might be very deep.'

Jackson would still be in Auckland. He'd left Golden Bay with days to spare before the first flight he could get to Asia, running out as though dogs had been snapping at his gorgeous butt. He was staying with an old med-school pal he'd kept in touch with over the years since graduation. Or so Sasha had told her as she'd handed Jess the tissue box. There'd been a lot of tissues used in the past two days. Who'd have believed one person could produce so many tears? She could probably singlehandedly meet Golden Bay's salt requirements.

Pulling the curtains back, Jess stared at the sight of her front yard with puddles the size of small swimming pools. A trickle of concern had her heading out the front door to check what was happening with her neighbours and the road. Wet, wet, wet. Water was everywhere, and rising. She'd never seen anything like this. It looked like her house had been transplanted into the sea.

Back inside, she reached for her cellphone. At least that was working. 'Hey, Grady, just checking everything's all right over your way. We're inundated with water here. The power's out as well.'

Grady sounded calm as he told her, 'Sasha and I are with Ian and Virginia. Might be a good idea for you and Nicholas to join us. The area is copping huge runoff from the hills. That's probably what you're getting. About an hour ago it started coming across the farms, over the road and through the properties on this side.'

'I'm sure we're safe but, yeah, I might come over before it gets worse. I don't want to be stuck here with Nicholas. At the moment he thinks this is all for his benefit but if we have to wade out it won't be pretty.' Besides, there was safety in numbers and all that.

'Take your phone and call if you think you're going to get stuck. Actually, no. Stay there. I'll come and get you in the four-wheel drive. That little hybrid thing of yours won't stand a chance if there's more than a few inches of water on the road.' Click, and Grady had gone.

'Nicholas, put a jersey and your shoes in a bag. Get

your rain jacket and gumboots ready too. Grady's coming to pick us up.'

'Ye-es, Grady's coming.' He leapt up and down all the way down the hall to the laundry, where his bag hung on the back of the door.

Quickly stuffing some warm clothes in another bag for herself, she slipped into her heavy-duty jacket and went around making sure all light switches were off and everything was locked up tight. Then she grabbed another handful of Nicholas's clothes. There was no way her boy would stay dry today. Too much temptation outside.

'Nicholas…' She waited until she had his full attention. 'When we get to Mrs Wilson's you are not to go outside. It's dangerous out there. Do you understand?'

'Yes, Mummy.' He looked so innocent that she crossed her fingers. But thanks to Jackson he was more amenable these days.

Jackson. What she wouldn't do to have him walking in the front door right now.

'Grady's here.' Nicholas raced for the door to drag the poor guy inside.

Once aboard the four-wheel drive, she told Grady, 'Thanks for taking us to your in-laws'. I didn't fancy hanging around watching that water getting higher by the minute.' Mentally she crossed fingers that her house would be safe.

'No problem. The situation's going to get worse before it's over.'

Less than an hour later Jess heard from the police that her house had a torrent of water pouring through it, as did the other few houses in her immediate neighbourhood, including Mrs Harrop's place. Thankfully the old lady had gone to Nelson for a few days. The cop told her, 'Half a kilometre back the road has been undermined with a deep and wide cut made by the force of the ever-increasing volume of water. That caused it to build up and surge forward through your area.'

Her heart sank. 'At least we're safe. Thank goodness Grady came and got us.' But what about her home? All her things? Nicholas's favourite toys and books? Tears spurted down her cheeks. 'They are only possessions,' she muttered, slashing at her cheeks with the back of her hand. 'But this has turned into the week from hell.'

Sasha hugged her. 'Those things are *your* things. I get it. It isn't fair. Maybe it won't be as bad as you think.'

Jess looked at her friend and shook her head. 'You reckon?'

Then Ian burst in through his back door yelling, 'The water levels are rising fast. I need to shift the sheep out of the orchard into the yard around the house. All hands on deck.'

Virginia said, 'I'll look after Melanie and Nicholas while you're all outside.'

Sasha yelled down the phone. 'Jackson, get your butt back home. You're needed. The whole area is flooded. It's serious.'

His heart stalled. 'Is Jess all right? Nicholas?' He looked around the crowded bar, found the TV screen. A rerun of last night's rugby game between the Auckland Blues and the Hawkes Bay Magpies was in full swing. He needed the news channel. 'What about Mum and Dad? I know you said the house was high and dry, but how are they dealing with this?' The orchard had gone under water before but they'd always pulled through. Of course, they hadn't been dealing with other things like MS before. But Jess? How would she fare? Her house was closer to the hills. *Oh, God, Jess, I've let you down.*

Sasha ramped up her yelling. 'Mum and Dad are great. It's Jessica who needs you. Her house's been flooded. She's probably lost just about everything. Including you, you big moron.'

The expletives spitting out of his mouth copped him a few unwanted glares from people sitting at the next table. For a moment he'd forgotten he was in the pub. Up until five minutes ago he'd been having a quiet beer and early brunch with his friend Simon from med-school days and pretending everything was okay. Now he couldn't deny it any longer. He shouldn't be here. Neither should he be going to Hong Kong. 'Tell me about Jess. Is she safe?' His heart finally started working properly and he could hardly hear for the thumping in his ears.

'She's out helping rescue people, patching others up, making sure they've got somewhere to go for the duration of the flood.'

Typical, big-hearted Jess. The woman he hadn't had the courage to tell he loved her. Jackson stood up abruptly, his chair crashing back. He needed to see the flood for himself, to get a grip on reality. 'Has this been on the news?'

'Where have you been, Jackson?' Sasha sounded completely fed up with him. As she had every right to be. He'd been an idiot, thinking he could walk away from them all. Especially from Jess, the love of his life.

'What's up, Jackson?' Simon stood up too, righted the chair and apologised to the people sitting behind them.

'I need to get the bar owner to change to the news channel. It's flooding at home. Badly.' With the phone still glued to his ear, he began picking his way through the crowd.

Simon grabbed his elbow. 'You want to get us lynched? Every single person in this bar has their eyes fixed to that game.'

'Tough. This is important.'

'That's all relative. Come with me. I have a better idea. Besides, I want to live a while longer yet.' Simon was nothing if not persistent. Jackson's elbow was grabbed in something resembling a rugby hold and he was quick-marched outside.

'Where are we going?' he demanded, as fury began roaring up inside him. 'I need to see the news channel.'

'What did you say?' Sasha demanded in his ear.

He'd forgotten all about his sister. 'Sorry, Sasha. Got to go. Simon's dragging me halfway around the city and I need to stop him.'

'Whatever. I got it wrong, didn't I?' Sasha sounded disappointed—in him.

'Got what wrong?' He tugged free of Simon's grip, then stopped as understanding hit. They were outside an appliance store. A store where hopefully someone would listen to his request. 'Thanks, Simon.'

'I thought you cared.' Sasha spoke so softly he nearly missed her words. 'I've got to go. We're dealing with an emergency down here.'

'Wait. Sasha, please. Is the road over the hill a go?'

'Nope. Landslides closed it around lunchtime.'

Jackson opened his mouth to swear again, glanced around the store and saw the row of televisions—all playing the news. Showing Golden Bay like he'd never seen it before. Showing his home town besieged by water. 'Crap.'

Water ran amok, taking trees and kennels and dead cattle with it. Brown, swirling water decimating everything in its path. Suddenly the only place on earth he wanted to be was in Golden Bay, in the thick of it, with Jess, helping her while she helped everyone else. And it had taken a damned disaster to wake him up to that fact.

Simon said, 'I'll run you to the airport.'

'I'll have to hire a private plane when I get to Nelson.' Hell, he hoped he could get on a commercial flight from Auckland to Nelson at such short notice. He didn't fancy the extra hour and a half by road if he had to land in Blenheim. He wouldn't consider the time delay if Christchurch was his only option.

Five hours later Jackson dumped his bags in the corner of the Pohara Motor Camp office and headed for the communal kitchen/dining room being used as an emergency centre. The moment he walked through the door his eyes scanned for Jess, came up blank.

'Where's Jess?' he demanded the instant he saw Grady.

'Hello to you, too. She's seeing to Sam. He's injured himself while trying to dig a ditch to divert water from the house.' Grady reached for a ringing phone. 'She's fine, Jackson.'

Jackson picked his way around people and bags and boxes of food, heading for the white board on the wall. Lists scrolled down the board. Properties damaged by the flood, people being evacuated, injured folk needing house calls. He'd seen some sad sights on his way in from Takaka airstrip, travelling first by four-wheel drive then by boat and lastly on foot.

Jess's house was listed in the flooded properties, as

was her other place, where Mrs Harrop lived. Yet Jess was out there doing what she did best—looking out for others. She was magnificent. And he'd been going to walk away. Idiot. He wanted to run to her, stick by her while she went about her calls. But she'd hate that. Anyway, he could be put to better use, attending patients himself.

Impatience gripped him as he waited for Grady to finish his call. Sounded like someone out past Pohara needed urgent attention from a medic. 'I'll go,' he announced the moment Grady hung up.

'Take my truck. There's a medical kit and hopefully anything else you'll need inside. Tom Gregory, Tarakohe, had his arm squashed while trying to tie his fishing boat down.'

Jackson snatched the keys flying towards him. 'I'll be in touch.'

'Good, because I've already got another call for you out at Wainui Inlet after you're done with Tom.'

Jess shivered. Under her thick jacket her clothes were soaked through. On her way to the truck that she'd hijacked from Ian she'd slipped in the mud and gone into a ditch to be submerged in sludge. It would be weeks before the foul taste of mud left her mouth.

It was well after seven and as dark as coal. This had been the longest day of her life, and it wasn't anywhere near over. Too many people needed help for her to put her feet up in front of Virginia's fire. But what she wouldn't give for a hot chocolate right about now.

Not going to happen. If she was lucky she'd get a lukewarm coffee and a droopy sandwich at Pohara before heading out somewhere else. She wouldn't be the only one feeling exhausted. All the emergency crews had been working their butts off throughout the day. The damage out there was horrendous, taking its toll on people, animals and buildings.

Buildings. As in houses. Her home.

No. She wasn't going to think about that. Wasn't going to consider the damage she'd seen briefly when the police had taken her home to collect some things. At least she'd managed to grab some clothes, a few photos and a couple of Nicholas's favourite toys. The rest didn't bear thinking about.

Hunched over the steering-wheel to peer through the murk and hoping like crazy the vehicle stayed on the road, she drove cautiously towards the temporary emergency centre. Shivering with cold, yawning with fatigue, it was hard to concentrate.

Focus. The last thing the emergency guys needed was her driving into a ditch and having to be rescued.

Finally she pulled up outside the well-lit building, got out and immediately pushed open the door. If she sat still she'd fall asleep. She'd fall asleep walking if she wasn't careful.

The heat exploded as she stepped through the door into the chaos of emergency rescue. Hesitating while her eyes adjusted to the bright lights, she could feel her hands losing their grip on the medical bag she'd brought inside to replenish. She heard it hit the floor with a sickening thud and couldn't find the energy to bend down and pick it up again.

Someone caught her, led her to a chair and gently pushed her down. A cup of tea appeared on the table in front of her. 'Get that inside you, Jess. I bet you didn't stop for lunch.'

Her stomach rumbled in answer. Lunch. What was that? 'The store was shut.' She'd never get that cup to her lips without spilling most of the contents.

'I'll get you a sandwich.'

The rumble was louder this time. She blinked. Looked up at this kind apparition hovering over her. That's when she knew she'd lost her mind. Exhaustion had caught up, obviously tipping her over the edge of sanity. She dropped her eyes, focused on the cup until it was very clear in her mind, no blurring at the edges of her sight. Looking up again, her breath snagged in the back of her throat. Jackson? If this was what not eating did then she'd schedule meals every hour from now on. Seeing Jackson at every turn would put her in the loony bin.

'Hey, sweetheart, you need to eat while Sheree finds you some warm, dry clothes.' A lopsided smile kept her from looking away.

Funny how her lungs seemed to have gone on strike. 'Is it really you?' How could it be? He should be somewhere over Australia by now. The tremors that had been racking her turned into quakes that would knock the socks off the Richter scale.

'Yes, it's me. I'm home, Jess. For good.' Steady hands held the cup to her lips. 'Now get some of this inside you.'

Her lips were numb with cold and the liquid dribbled down her chin, but some ran over her tongue and down her throat. It was good, sending some warmth into the chill. She took another mouthful, this time most of it going in the right direction. 'Define "for good",' she croaked.

'As in for the next fifty years at least.'

She couldn't do the sums. Her brain was struggling

with drinking tea, let alone anything else. But she figured he meant he'd be here for a long while. 'Great.'

Now she really looked at him, concentrating as hard as she had while driving from Sam's. Really, really saw the man hunkered down in front of her, those beautiful deep green eyes fixed on her. Need laced that gaze. So did apology. And concern. Could that be love lingering around the edges, too? Or was she hallucinating?

'I heard your home has taken a hit.'

Oh. Not love. Just everyday concern for someone he knew well. That gave her the strength to murmur, 'Got a bulldozer out in your dad's shed? I'm going to need it.' Her lips pressed together, holding back her returning bewilderment. This was too much. First her home had been all but destroyed. And now the man who had walked away from her two days ago, taking her heart with him, was in front of her, his hand on her knee, looking like he… Like he… That was the problem. She didn't understand any of this. Why had he suddenly reappeared?

Whatever the reason, she really didn't need this right now. She was busy helping folk in the bay. It was what she needed to do, it was how she atoned for being a brat teenager. Had she been even more badly behaved as a young woman than she'd imagined? Was that why all this was happening to her? Would she never pay for her mistakes?

On a long, steadying breath, she told Jackson, 'Glad you're here. They need all the medics they can get.'

'I've been helping for the last four hours. Seems we're all caught up for a while.' He took the plate of sandwiches Sheree arrived with and handed her one. 'Eat.'

'Your jersey's wet.' So was his hair. She hadn't noticed. 'Last time I looked, it was still raining.'

'I need to top up my bag.' Chew, chew. Concentrating on more than one thing at a time was too hard right now.

'I'll see to it in a minute.' He didn't move.

'Jackson,' she growled around another mouthful of bread and ham. 'Why are you here?'

'Because I couldn't leave.' He pulled another chair around and sat in front of her, still holding the plate of sandwiches. 'I was wrong to think I could go, Jess. No, let me rephrase that. I knew I wanted to stay but that bloody promise kept getting in the way, doing my head in.'

Chew, chew. 'Okay.' Was it? Jackson was back, whatever that meant.

'Jackson,' Grady called. 'Got a minute? We've got a young boy needing stitches in his hand waiting in the other room.'

'Sure.' Leaning close, he kissed her cheek so softly she probably imagined it. 'Don't go anywhere.'

Jess watched him stride to the back door and remove his sodden jacket before heading down the hall to the bathroom. 'Did I just see Jackson in here?' she whispered.

Sheree placed a pile of clothes on the chair beside her. 'Definitely Jackson. No one else around here looks so cute in his city clobber, even when it looks like he's been swimming in it.'

'That's because no one else around here wears city clothes.' But Sheree was right. He looked downright gorgeous. Sexy and hot and warm and caring. Even when he was so bedraggled. Jackson. Had he brought her heart back to put her all together?

'Why has he come back?' she asked no one in particular.

'Go and change into those dry clothes, Jess. They'll

be too big for you but at least you'll feel warmer.' Sheree could be bossy when she put her mind to it. 'Jackson isn't going anywhere tonight. You'll get your answer, I'm sure.'

Who'd have believed tears would feel so hot when your cheeks were frozen?

CHAPTER ELEVEN

JACKSON TRIED TO watch Jess as she carefully drove the short distance to his parents' place, avoiding racing water as best she could, driving around fallen trees and bobbing logs. Why had she insisted on driving when she was shattered? Trying to regain some control? Over herself? Or him?

He could barely see her outline in the dark but as they'd pulled away from the emergency centre he'd noted how tight her mouth was, how white her lips were. Her eyes had stood out in her pale face. Worry had turned their warm brown shade to burnt coffee. Now her fingers were wrapped around the steering-wheel so hard he thought he'd be peeling them off for her when they stopped.

'You're staring.'

Yes, he was. Drinking in the dark shape of her in the gloom. She was all mussed, her damp hair fizzing in all directions. Adorable. He'd only been gone a couple of days but he'd missed her every single second of the time. He'd had to fight himself not to return. How bloody stupid was that? Thought he knew what he was doing? Yeah, right. Think again, buddy.

Her voice squeaked as she asked, 'How did you get through? I heard the hill's closed.'

'Hired a plane out of Nelson. I'm glad the airstrip is on higher ground.'

'It's worse around here.'

'Shocking. I haven't seen anything like it before. The orchard's a disaster area, avocado and citrus trees standing deep in the swirling water. Fortunately the house is safe on the higher ground, unscathed by the flood, and full of people Mum and Dad are taking in and feeding.' People that included Jess and Nicholas.

'It's what people do for each other.' He thought Jess glanced at him. 'This isn't the first time this has happened in the bay.' Her tone was sharp, fed up. The turn into Dad's drive was equally sharp.

'Yeah, but I've always been somewhere else.' There lay his problem. He'd done a damned fine job of avoiding being a part of this place when the bad times were going down. Only ever here for some good times. But not any more. 'Jess, there's something I—' He jerked forward as she braked too hard for the conditions.

'Here we are. I can't wait to put on dry, clean clothes, my clothes. And to hug Nicholas.' Slam. Her door banged shut.

'No hugs for me, then.' What had he honestly expected? The band playing 'Welcome home, lover'? Jackson sat shivering from the bone chilling effect of his wet clothes and Jess's avoidance. He watched her stomping across the yard to Mum's back door. Every step sent up a spray of water. Every foot forward, away from him, accentuated the fact she couldn't deal with his return. Didn't want to, more like.

Finally he shoved the door open and dropped to the ground. Tonight wasn't the time for deep and meaningful conversations. Not when Mum and Dad's house was full of neighbours. Not when Jess had her own house situation to deal with. Not when Nicholas would want her attention.

He drew a breath and dug deep for one attribute he didn't have. Patience. Somehow he had to hold back and not rush in waving a flag, demanding that Jess listen to him. Somehow he had to take the time to show he would stand by her no matter what. Help her fix the home she'd been so proud of and that now stood full of muddy water. Wrecked. Not that anyone really knew how vast the damage would be. It'd take a few days before assessors and builders could even begin evaluating the situation.

One thing he knew with absolute certainty—whatever it took, he'd do it to win Jess's heart. For ever.

'Hey, you coming in?' Dad yelled from the back door. 'I've still got some of that bourbon left.'

'That's my dad.' His heart lifted a fraction as he went to join him. But as he approached the porch he noticed how grey Dad had turned, almost overnight. He wasn't coping with Mum's illness, and this situation would have exacerbated everything. His leaving wouldn't have helped matters either.

And I thought I could leave. His gut clenched. 'Dad, I'm sorry.' He wrapped his arms around the man who'd been there for him when he'd stubbed his toe, when he'd caught his first fish, when he'd wanted to know about sex, when he'd shouted he was leaving Golden Bay for ever. 'I'm not leaving again.'

'Tell that to Jess, not me. I'd already worked that out. Even before you had. But that young lady inside is going to take a lot more persuasion.' Dad locked gazes with him. 'She needs you, son. Badly. From what Jonty says, it's really bad news about her property. Both houses are wrecked.'

'Yeah, I saw that on the board at Pohara.' No wonder Jess didn't have time for him.

Dad nodded. 'You're onto it.'

The bottom dropped out of Jackson's stomach. He should be shot. He'd been so sure of himself, acting strong and supposedly doing the right thing. It had taken an act of nature to bring him to his senses. It was going to take a lifetime to prove to Jess he could change, and get it right the second time round. If she even gave him a chance.

Jess forced her feet forward, one slippery step at a time, through her kitchen into the lounge. The mud and sludge was above her ankles, but overnight the water had at last dropped to ground level. Everything dripped moisture. Brown goo stained the walls higher than her waist. Furniture sat like sodden hulks, ruined for ever. The smell turned her nose, curled her stomach.

On the wall photos were buckled from moisture. Seeing one of Nicholas, grinning out at her as he rode around the front lawn, snagged her heart, threatened to break her determination to be strong. She'd sneaked out of the Wilsons' home the moment it was light enough to see her hand held out in front of her. The night had been long and stressful and sleep evasive as she'd tossed and turned on the couch. She'd desperately wanted to see her house, the place she'd made into a home for her and Nicholas. A safe haven where she knew she finally belonged.

Of course she'd known it would be bad, but she had to see it, to know by touch, smell and sight just how bad it really was. She needed this short time alone to absorb it all. That way she'd be able to hold herself together and be strong in front of everyone else, no matter how generous they were with offers of help and new furniture.

Tracking through the mess, she made her way to Nicholas's room and swiped at her cheeks. So much for not crying. The quilt she'd bought at the local fair when Nicholas was two now had a distinct brown tinge but the appliquéd zoo animals were still clear, just dark brown.

'Will I ever be able to wash that clean?'

Pulling open a drawer, she gasped, still able to be surprised at the mess inside.

'Guess we're going shopping for clothes in the next few days, my boy. Thank goodness you wore your lucky fishing shirt yesterday.' The tears became a steady stream.

Another ruined photo caught her eye. How had she missed this one yesterday? There hadn't been time to collect them all, but this one? Reaching out slowly, she lifted it by the frame and stared at the excited face of Nicholas with his first fish. Jackson squatting beside him, an equally big grin on his gorgeous face.

The stream became a torrent. Jackson. Nicholas. The two most important people in her life. The life that had turned into one big mess.

'Hey.' Strong arms wrapped around her, turned her to hold her tight against that familiar, strong body she'd missed so much for the last three days. No, make that since the day she'd told Jackson she loved him.

The torrent turned into a flood, pouring onto Jackson's jersey, like the floodwaters that had soaked his clothes yesterday.

All the time she sobbed he held her against him, his hands soothing her by rubbing her back, his chin settled on the top of her head. Letting his strength soak into her. Calming her with his quiet presence. Not trying to deny that she had a problem but showing he'd be there as she sorted her way through the debris that had become her life.

Finally the tears slowed, stopped. Her heart felt lighter and yet nothing had changed. The house was still a wreck. Jackson would still return to Hong Kong. He might've said he was staying but she couldn't take a chance on that. Time to toughen up. She pulled away, moved to stand in the middle of the room, the photo still in her hand. Wiping her other hand over her cheeks, she told him, 'Thank you. As if there isn't already enough water around the place.'

Jackson winced, but he didn't turn round and hightail it out of her house. 'Let's see what we can save. Throw anything not ruined into the truck and take it back to Mum's to clean before storing. Then we'll check out Mrs Harrop's place.'

It was a plan and she desperately needed something to focus on. Nodding, she walked through to her bedroom and stared around. Looked at the bed where she'd had so much fun with Jackson. Her wardrobe door stood ajar, her shoes everywhere. Bending down, she picked up one of the apricot silk pair she'd worn at the wedding. 'Ruined. But I guess they're only shoes.'

She didn't realise Jackson had followed her until he said, 'No such thing as *only* shoes for women.' When she looked up, he gave her a coaxing smile. 'I'll take you shopping when we've had time to work out what's going to happen with all this.'

That's what she'd said about Nicholas's things. Throw

'em out and get new ones. That didn't seem so easy now. 'I'll get some bags to put things in.'

'Have you called your insurance company yet?' Jackson seemed determined to stick with her.

'Hardly. Too busy yesterday and it's still too early today.' Where were those large black bin liners? They'd be perfect for the damp clothes she needed to take away for washing.

'Jess.' Jackson stood beside her as she poked through a drawer of sodden plastic bags and cling wrap.

'Here we are.' She snatched up the roll and kneed the drawer closed.

'Jess.' A little louder. And when she turned to head to Nicholas's bedroom he put both hands on her shoulders. 'Jess, I don't know if this is the right time to tell you but I love you.'

'Right.' *He loves me. That's got to be good. But it doesn't fix a thing. I need to sort clothes and stuff before the day gets started and I have to go to work.*

Those big hands gripping her gave her a gentle shake. 'I am not going back to Hong Kong. I'm here to stay.'

'That's good. We need another doctor in the bay. Rory's busting to go live with his girlfriend in Auckland.' See, some things did work out if everyone was patient.

Her foot nudged something in the mud covering the floor. Bending down, she retrieved Nicholas's stuffed giraffe, Long Neck. The original yellow and black colours looked decidedly worse for their night in the mud. 'This is one of Nicholas's favourites.' She dropped it into one of the black bags.

Jackson took the roll of bags and tore off a couple. 'I'll deal with Nicholas's room if you like, while you go through your drawers and wardrobe.' He sounded very upbeat. Why? It wasn't like she'd acknowledged his statement.

Some time later she wound a plastic tie around the neck of the last full bag from her room and dumped it on the bed, on top of the beautiful quilt that apparently Sasha's grandmother had made years ago. Jess considered it antique and now it was destined for the trash. What a shame. Hands on hips, she stood at the end of the bed and looked around at what had been her pride and joy. She'd painted the whole place, but here in her bedroom she'd let loose with her creative side, buying beautiful little knick knacks for the top of her dressing table, bedside lamps that matched colours in the quilt and the curtains she'd made. She'd been so damned proud of those curtains and now look at them—sodden, muddy and hanging all askew.

Water dripped onto her breasts. Tears? Surely she'd run out by now. Apparently not. They didn't stop. Her hands began shaking and she had to grip her hips tight to keep them under some sort of control.

'Hey, you're crying.' Jackson suddenly appeared before her with a box of tissues that was miraculously dry. 'Here, let me.' Oh, so gently he sponged up the tears, only to have to repeat the exercise again and again.

Her bottom lip trembled. 'I know it's only little, and very ordinary, but this is my home. I made it how I wanted it to be, a place for Nicholas to grow up in feeling secure and loved. I've been happy here, settled for the very first time in my life.'

Those long, strong fingers touched her cheeks, lifted her face so she had to look into his eyes. 'You think that you've lost all that because your house is a write-off?'

Her head dipped in acknowledgement. That's what she'd been trying to say, yes.

'Sweetheart, the love that permeates this home doesn't come from the paint and curtains and flower vases and books on the shelves. It comes from in here.' He tapped her chest gently, right against her heart. 'From within you. That love goes where you go. It's who you are, and always will be. Nicholas is going to be secure and loved by you all his life, even though he mightn't grow up in this particular home. Even when he eventually heads out into the world on his own, he'll know you love him. Whether you get this place put back together or buy another one with the insurance money, it will be filled with your personality, your love, fun and laughter.'

For Jackson that had to be a record speech. She blinked as the tight knots in her tummy began letting go some tension. The trembling in her hands eased, stopped. 'You really, really think so?' she whispered.

'I know so.' His head lowered so that his mouth was close to hers. 'I really, really know.' Then he kissed her. A quiet kiss filled with understanding, with that love he'd not long ago declared, with his generosity. He was giving her something back after all that had been taken from her since the moment he'd walked out of her life three days ago. 'I love you,' he murmured against her mouth.

Jess leaned forward so that her breasts were crushed against his chest, her mouth kissed his in return, her hands finally lifted from her hips to his neck and held onto him. 'I don't know what to do. I love you so much and yet I can't ask you to stay. You hate it here.'

'I'm staying. End of story. I don't hate it here any more. You taught me what this community is all about.'

'Me? How?' Surprise rocked through her. 'All I do

is try and make up for the mistakes I made when I was young and in need of friends who'd love me.'

'Jess, Jess, you don't get it. Yesterday, when you were dealt a blow here, what did you do? Stand around bemoaning your bad luck? Not likely. You went out caring for other people. That's community spirit in spades.'

'I'm a nurse. That's what nurses do.'

And right on cue her work phone beeped. 'Jessica, I think my waters just broke.'

'Lynley? Is that you?'

'Yes. Ouch. That wasn't nice. I'm having some light pains every ten minutes or so. Guess this is it. Do I go to the centre now?'

A grim smile twisted her mouth. 'You can wait until those contractions are closer, about six minutes between them. Unless it's going to be difficult getting there after yesterday's flood, then I'd suggest making your way there now.' It was going to take some effort for her to get there given the road this side of town had been underwater last night.

'It's a clear run from here. What about you?' Lynley asked.

'I'll be there as soon as possible. You concentrate on that baby's arrival.' She closed the phone and glanced at Jackson, to find him watching her closely.

'Guess we're headed for town, then. Have you got time to pick up some breakfast from Mum's first?'

'The baby's not rushing but I have no idea if the road is manageable.' And why are you coming with me?

'Let's go and find out.' He took the bags of clothes she'd dumped on the bed and headed out to the truck he'd borrowed.

Nothing else for her to do but follow.

* * *

When Jackson had seen Jess's shocked reaction to the state of her home he had wanted to pick her up, hold her close and transport her away from it all. He'd wanted to run her a hot bubble bath and let her soak away her desolation. Not that she'd have let him if he'd even tried. Had she heard him say he loved her? Really heard? Or had his declaration been like words on the wind? Not connecting with her?

He'd been disappointed at her lack of reaction but he figured it had been the wrong time. At least, if she knew how he felt she'd know she wasn't on her own with this. Not that she was. Mum and Dad had had to be restrained from rushing over the moment they'd known where she'd gone this morning. Only by explaining that he'd be helping Jess and that he wanted to tell her why he was home had he managed to make them stay put.

He pressed some numbers on his phone, got hold of Jonty at the fire station. 'Hey, man, how's our road this morning? Is it passable? Jess has a patient in labour in town.'

'It's open but slippery as hell. There's a temporary fix where the road was washed away. Don't let her drive that thing she calls a car. It won't hold on the tarmac.'

'That thing, as you put it, has been submerged most of the night. It's not going anywhere.' He didn't know if Jess had looked in her garage yet, and he'd try to keep her out of there for now.

Jonty groaned. 'Jess has had more than her share of knocks in this flood.'

'She sure has. I'm heading in with her so if anyone needs a doctor over the next few hours I'll be at the medical centre.' He snapped the phone shut, went to find Jess.

'Road's open so let's grab some breakfast and take it with us. We can leave those bags of your belongings at the house.' Mum would probably have everything washed by the time Jess got back.

'You're coming with me? It's a normal birth, Jackson.'

'Sure, but I might be of use at the centre. Besides, there're enough people milling around at home to drive me to drink. It's too soon to start clearing the orchards, so I'm superfluous.' I want to be with you, supporting you, because I don't believe you're totally back on your feet as far as the shock is concerned.

She flicked him a brief smile. 'You're starting to think like a local. You know that?'

'If you'd said that two months ago I'd have run for the hills.'

'Didn't you do just that three days ago? Figuratively speaking.' Those eyes that always got to him were totally focused on him right now.

'Guilty as charged.' His stomach clenched, relaxed. Of course she'd want to take a crack at him. He'd hurt her by leaving like he had. Somehow he was going to make that up to her. But he wasn't barrelling in on this one. They had their whole lives ahead of them. He'd take it slower than he was used to doing with anything.

Parking outside Mum and Dad's house, he pulled on the handbrake. 'I'll tell you something. What you just said about me thinking like a local made me feel warm and fuzzy, not cold and panicked. Guess I'm improving.'

Jess actually chuckled. There was even a hint of mischief in her eyes. 'Watch this space. You'll be standing for mayor before we know it.'

'Get outta here.' Not that Golden Bay had a mayor. There were plenty of people who liked to think they were running the district, but official business was down over the hill.

'Don't let me forget my kit.' She dropped to the ground and reached into the back for two bags. 'Wonder if any of the beach houses are vacant.'

'You thinking of renting one for a while?'

She nodded. 'Got to find somewhere to live fairly quickly.'

Now he had something practical he could do for the woman he loved. 'Leave it with me. I'll ring round, or go online, while you're bringing that baby into this wet world.'

Her gaze lit up as she looked skyward. 'The sun's peeking out, most of the sky's blue, and the rain has stopped everywhere.'

And Jess had started looking a tiny bit more relaxed. Relief nearly made him swing her up in his arms to kiss her soft lips. But as his foot came off the ground to move towards her, caution held him back. Patience, man, patience. Do not rush her. Not today, anyway. He smiled and lifted out two more heavy bags of damp belongings before following that gorgeous butt inside.

Virginia handed her a steaming mug of tea even before she'd got her boots off. 'Here you go, Jess. Get that in you. I tried to get you to have one before you left at sun-up but you weren't hearing anything.'

Jess apologised. 'I had my mind on my home, nothing else.'

'That's what I thought.' Virginia's arm draped around her shoulders. 'You and Nicholas stay here for as long as it takes to sort everything out. No arguments.'

'I'm not arguing. I'm just too exhausted to do anything much about finding somewhere to live today. So, thanks very much.' She laid her cheek against the other woman's arm for a moment, absorbing the warmth and care. 'Thank you,' she whispered again.

Jackson strolled through the farmhouse-sized kitchen and smiled at her and his mother. 'We're heading into town shortly. Anyone here who needs to go that way?' He was definitely sounding more and more like most of the other caring people in the district.

Virginia dropped her arm and handed Jackson a mug. 'Not that I know of. Want to take some food with you? Can't imagine any shops being open today.'

Ten minutes later Jess sat in the passenger seat watching Jackson skilfully negotiate a small washout just past her house. 'It could take months to get everything back to normal.'

Her work phone buzzed in her pocket. 'Hey, Lynley, that you?'

'My contractions are down to five minutes apart and we're waiting at the birthing unit.'

'Nearly there.' She closed the phone. 'That girl is so calm for a first baby.'

'What were you like when you had Nicholas?'

'Terrible. My baby was the first baby ever to be born. No one could've possibly understood what I was going through. I'm surprised I had any friends left by the time I'd finished.' She grinned. 'Labour hurts, big time. And mine went on for thirty-one hours. I swear it's the only time Nicholas has been late for anything.'

'Would you do it again?'

Talk about a loaded question. 'You going somewhere with this?'

'Yep.' He slowed behind a tractor towing a trailer

laden with broken trees. Driving patiently, he kept back from the mud sent into the air by the trailer wheels. 'I'd love to have kids.'

And that had something to do with her? Though he had said he loved her—three times. 'Yeah, I'd do it again. The pain's quickly forgotten when you hold your baby in your arms for the first time.'

Jackson didn't say any more, just concentrated on getting them through the mud and debris littering what used to be a perfectly good road.

The medical centre was surprisingly quiet. 'I think everyone's too busy cleaning up to be bothered with visiting us,' Mike theorised, when they tramped inside with their plastic box of breakfast.

'Where are Lynley and Trevor?' she asked.

'Over in the maternity wing.'

Jackson continued walking through the centre. 'I'm over there if you find you're suddenly rushed off your feet, Mike.'

'You don't have to come with me.' Jess hurried after Jackson.

'I'll make breakfast.'

'You have an answer for everything,' she muttered under her breath.

He leaned close, placed a soft kiss on her cheek. 'Better get used to that.'

Lynley had already changed into a loose-fitting hospital gown. 'Can't stand anything constricting me at the moment,' she told Jess the moment she turned into the birthing room. 'Ahh, Trevor, hold me.' Her pretty face contorted as vice-like pain caught her.

Trevor stood rock solid as his wife clung to him, his hands around her waist. 'Glad you got through, Jess. I heard about your place being flooded. Hope it's going to be all right. If there's anything I can do, give me a call, okay?'

'Thanks. It's too soon to know what'll happen with it. This is Jackson Wilson. He's an emergency doctor and, no, Lynley you're not having an emergency.'

Jackson waved a hand at the couple. 'If you don't want me hanging around just say so, otherwise I'm here to watch and learn.'

When the contraction had passed Jess indicated for Lynley to sit back on the bed and then wrapped the blood-pressure cuff around the mother-to-be's arm. 'Baseline obs first and then I'll listen to baby's heartbeat.'

'Any idea how long this is going to take?' Lynley asked.

'It's like the piece of string. Every baby is different. Your BP's good.' She listened through the stethoscope to the baby's heartbeats, counting silently. 'All good there, too.'

'Now we wait, right?' Trevor said.

'We certainly do. And be grateful that wee boy didn't decide yesterday was the day to arrive.' Jess sat on a low stool and filled in patient observations.

Jackson said, 'I'll make our breakfast. Can I get you anything Lynley? Trevor?'

Another contraction, and again Trevor held Lynley. And again. Jackson returned from the kitchen with a tray laden with toast and jam, and four cups of coffee. More contractions, more observations noted on the page. The morning groaned past and Lynley began to get tired.

'I'm fed up with this pain,' she yelled once.

'Why did you get me pregnant?' she demanded of

Trevor another time. 'Do you know what you're putting me through?'

Jess sympathised, while thinking that at least Lynley hadn't resorted to swearing at the poor guy, like some women did.

Jackson stood behind her and rubbed her back when she rose from the stool. How did he know she ached just there? And did he understand he was knocking down her resistance towards him?

Finally, some time after three o'clock, Lynley suddenly announced, 'I want to push. Now.' She sank onto the bed and leaned back against the stack of pillows Jackson had placed there earlier in case she got tired of standing.

'Let me take a look at you.' Jess pulled on another pair of gloves and squatted on her stool again. 'Push when you're ready. There you go. The head has appeared. Keep pushing, Lynley. That's it. You're doing brilliantly.'

Lynley's attention was focused entirely on pushing her baby out into the world.

Then the baby slipped out into Jess's waiting hands. 'Welcome to the world, baby Coomes.' Jess wiped the little boy's mouth clear of fluid and draped him over his mother's breasts.

'Oh, my goodness. Look at him, Trevor. He's perfect.' Tears streamed down the new mother's cheeks. 'Didn't we do great?'

Trevor was grinning and crying, staring at his son like he was the most amazing sight ever.

Which he was. Jess blinked rapidly. It didn't matter how many babies she'd delivered, today baby Coomes was the most special. Next week there'd be another for her to get all soppy over.

'Isn't that the most beautiful sight?' Jackson spoke quietly beside her, emotion making his voice raw.

Maybe he really did mean to settle down here. 'It is. Once I've dealt with the cord and afterbirth let's take a break and give these two time alone with their son before the families descend. There'll be no peace when they all arrive.' Which was why Lynley had said right from the outset she didn't want anyone knowing she was in labour.

Mike had locked up the medical centre and gone home, no doubt crossing his fingers he'd get a few hours to himself and his wife, Roz. Today everyone's focus would be on clean-up and less on health issues. Tomorrow might be different as reality settled in.

Jess switched on the lights in the kitchen and filled the kettle for a cup of tea. She automatically got out two cups. Then she found the tin of chocolate biscuits Sasha kept hidden in her locker and sprang the lid, quickly stuffing a biscuit in her mouth. 'I need sugar.'

Pulling out a chair, Jackson sat and sprawled his long legs half across the room. 'You must be exhausted. Did you sleep much last night?'

'Next to nothing. My mind would not shut down.'

'I've found three houses for rent that you can look at. Two at Pohara and one at Para Para. You can see see them any time you want. You've got first dibs on all three.'

Leaning back against the bench top, she folded her arms under her breasts. 'Para Para would be lovely. That long, wide, sweeping beach is stunning, though a bit dangerous for Nicholas when it's windy. Which is often.'

'Not too far out of town?'

'Unfortunately, yes. So I'm already down to two.' She gave him a tired smile. 'Thank you for doing this. I do appreciate it.'

'Just want to help.'

Her forefingers scratched at her sleeves. He'd told her he loved her and she hadn't said a word. Yet he hadn't stalked off in a sulk. Far from it, he'd stayed by her side all day. Helping with the birth, making endless rounds of sandwiches and coffee, looking up rental properties, rubbing her back when it got sore.

Raising her head from where she'd been staring at the tips of her running shoes that were never used for running, she looked directly at him and said, 'Jackson, I love you, too.' When he made to stand up she held up a hand. 'But that doesn't mean I'm going to do anything about it.'

It hurt just to say the words. A deep hurt that twisted in her stomach. She wanted him so much, would do almost anything to give in and accept his love and make a life with him.

'Want to elaborate, Jess?' he asked, bewilderment lacing his tone.

'My parents.' This was hard. So hard. 'They love each other very much.' Too much. 'To the point they are selfish with it.' They don't even realise it. 'They excluded me from a lot. Anything that money couldn't buy, really.' Her eyesight blurred. 'Yes, I love you, Jackson. But what if I love you so much I cut Nicholas out of the picture, forget to give him hugs and kisses, miss school plays, send him on expensive holidays to get him out of the way?' Her voice had got quieter and quieter until she could barely hear herself. 'You want kids, but what if I neglect them, too?'

'You won't.' Two little words and yet there was the power of conviction in them. 'I know you, Jessica Baxter. I've seen you with Nicholas. You totally love him.

You'd never be able to avoid hugging him. You'll never want to miss seeing his first proper fish.'

'You're missing the point.' That had been when it had only been her and Nicholas, before she went so far as to admit Jackson into her life properly.

'No.' He stood up and reached for her. With his arms around her waist he leaned back and looked down into her eyes. '*You're* missing the point. You're a natural mother. You'll never be otherwise. But you've got a big heart, Jess, big enough for me as well. And for our children, if we have them. You can love us all. You do love Nicholas and me already. What has Nicholas missed out on since that very first night when we went to bed together? Go on. Tell me.' His mouth was smiling, like this wasn't the issue she'd believed it was. His eyes were brimming with love for her.

'I can't think of anything.' Nicholas certainly seemed as happy as ever when Jackson was around. In fact, he loved Jackson and the things they had done together.

'Do you trust me to give you a nudge if I think you're not getting the mix right? Because I certainly would. But, Jess, I don't believe it will ever come to that.'

He truly believed she wasn't like her parents. Wow. 'I do love you both and I hoped I was getting it right. But it's hard to know. Mum and Dad don't have a clue what they've excluded me from. They honestly believe they've been great parents.'

'I know you're an awesome parent. I wouldn't want anyone else to be my children's mother.' Jackson lowered his head, his lips finding hers. His kiss, when it came, was tender and loving and understanding, and it fired up her passion. 'I love you, Jess. Will you take a chance and marry me? We could have so many babies you'd always be inundated with their demands, and I'll be making arrangements for date nights so I can have you all to myself.'

The eyes that locked with hers held so much sincerity and love her doubts evaporated. For how long she didn't yet know, but she now knew that she could always discuss them with this wonderful man. He'd help her through. 'Go on, then.' At his astonished look, she laughed. 'That's a yes. I will marry you, Jackson. And love you for ever, as well as all those children. Jessica Wilson, here I come.'

This time his kiss wasn't so gentle. More like demanding as he sealed their promise. 'Thank goodness,' he sighed between their lips. 'Thought I'd be spending the next year trying to sweet-talk you into a wedding.'

When Jackson drove up to his parents' house Nicholas was waiting on the veranda. He immediately began waving and leaping up and down.

'Mummy, I've been watching for you for ages.'

Her heart squeezed painfully. Her boy. She loved him beyond reason. Reaching to lift him into her arms, panic struck and she spun around to stare at Jackson.

'No, Jess, you haven't neglected him for other people. You were doing your job and now you're home to hug and hold and love your son. That's normal for most parents.' Jackson stood beside her, lifting strands of hair off her face.

'Thank you.' She sucked in the sweet smell of Nicholas as he wriggled around in her arms. She felt his warmth warming her. Knew he'd always come first with her.

'Mummy, there was a very big eel in the packing

shed. Ian said the flood brought it here. I touched it and it was cold and yucky.'

Jackson took her elbow and led them inside. 'Let's get changed into something clean and warm and I'll break out the champagne. We've got something to celebrate.'

Her mouth stretched so wide it hurt. 'Yeah. We do. But first I need some time with Nicholas. I've got something to discuss with him.'

Jackson nodded his understanding. 'Why don't you go through to Mum's office? I'll make sure no one disturbs you.'

In the office she sat in the one comfortable chair and settled Nicholas on her lap. 'We're going to live in a different house for a while, Nicholas. Our one was flooded.'

His little eyes widened with something like excitement. 'Really? Can I see it with the water in it?'

How easy things were for a child. 'We'll go there tomorrow, but the water's gone now.'

Disappointment replaced the excitement. 'I wanted to see it.'

Drawing a deep breath, she continued with the other important piece of news. 'Nicholas, how would you like Jackson to live with us? All the time?'

The excitement rushed back. 'Yes. When? Now?' His face fell. 'But he can't. We haven't got a house to live in.'

'We'll find another house. Mummy and Jackson are going to get married. You'll have a daddy.'

'Like Robby's daddy?' Hope radiated out of his big eyes.

Shame hit her. She'd held out on Jackson because she'd feared she'd be hurting her son, yet all along the best thing she could've done for him was accept Jackson's love and go with it. 'Just like Robby's father.'

She kissed her boy. 'I love you, Nicholas.'

'I love you, Mummy. I love Jackson.' He slid off her knees. 'Is he really, really going to be my daddy?'

'Yes, darling, he is.'

A whirlwind of arms and legs raced for the door, hauled it open and Nicholas took off to charge through the house. 'Where's my daddy? Jackson, where are you? Mummy and Jackson are getting married. Jackson? There you are.'

Jess made it to the door in time to see Jackson swinging Nicholas up in his arms, both of them grinning like loons.

'Guess everyone in the bay's going to know in no time at all.' She shook her head at Nicholas, her heart brimming with love. 'Quiet has never been one of your attributes, my boy.'

Jackson rolled his eyes. 'It's funny, but I'm happy if the whole world knows I'm marrying you.'

CHAPTER TWELVE

SIX MONTHS LATER, on a perfect spring day, with a sky
the colour of love, Jess walked down the path leading
through Virginia's garden to the marquee once again set
up on the Wilsons' front lawn. Jess clung to Ian's arm,
her fingers digging in hard as her high heels negotiated
the newly laid pebbles. 'Thank you for standing in for
my father,' she told Jackson's dad.

True to form, Mum and Dad hadn't been able to make
it home for the wedding. Something about the gorillas
in Borneo needing their attention. Jess swallowed her
disappointment. She was about to get a whole new family: one that would always be there for her, as she would
be for them.

'I'm thrilled you asked me.' Ian looked down at her
with tears in his eyes. 'I'm getting to be a dab hand at it.
Two weddings in less than a year. Who'd have believed
it? And before we reach that son of mine, who's looking
mighty pleased with himself, can I just say thank you
for bringing him home for us.'

'Thank goodness he didn't have long to go to finish
his contract.' She'd have gone crazy if he'd been away
much longer than the four months he'd had to do. Now

he worked three days a week in Nelson and the rest of the time at the Golden Bay Medical and Wellbeing Centre.

Sasha spoke behind them. 'Come on, you two. We've got a wedding to get under way, and Nicholas and I can't stand around all afternoon listening to you both yabbering.'

Jess turned and grinned at her soon-to-be sister-in-law. 'Yes, ma'am. By the way, you looked lovely in blue.'

'Why do my friends get married when I'm looking like a house in a dress?' For the second time Sasha was standing up for a close friend while pregnant.

Jess grinned and glanced down at Nicholas. He looked gorgeous in his dove-grey suit and sky-blue shirt that matched Jackson and Grady's. 'Let's get the show under way. What do you reckon, Nicholas?'

'Hurry up, Mummy. It's boring standing here.'

Jess grinned. 'Love you too, buddy.' Then she faced the end of the path, where Jackson stood watching her take every step along that path. When she placed her hand on his arm he blinked back tears. 'You are beautiful,' he murmured. His eyes glittered with emotion.

She couldn't say a word for the lump clogging her throat, so she reached up and kissed him lightly.

'Seems we need to get you two married in a hurry.' Diane, the marriage celebrant, chuckled. She looked around at the family and friends gathered on the lawn. 'Jessica and Jackson stand here today in front of you all to pledge themselves to each other.'

Jess heard the words and yet they ran over her like warm oil, soft and soothing. Not once on that day in January, when she'd stood up with Jackson, watching her best friend marry Grady, had it occurred to her that she'd be getting married in this same place, with the same people surrounding them. She hadn't known love like it—the depth, the generosity, the bone-melting sweetness. She hadn't known the colour of love—summer blue with sunshine lightening it. Okay, today it was spring blue, but that was close enough.

In fact, it was brilliant, as Jackson said the vows he'd written himself, declaring his love for her, promising her so much. Her heart squeezed tight with love. This wonderful man was becoming her husband. Handing Sasha her bouquet, she held her hands out to him. The diamond-encrusted wedding ring he slipped onto her finger gleamed in the sunlight.

'Jess, would you say your vows now.' Diane caught her attention.

Taking Jackson's strong, warm hands back in hers, she managed a strong voice. 'Jackson Wilson, today I promise before our family and friends to always love you with all my heart, to share my life with you, to raise our children alongside you. I acknowledge you as my son's father in the truest sense of the word. I love you. We love you.' And then she couldn't say any more for the tears in Jackson's eyes and the lump in her throat.

Sasha placed the gold band she and Jackson had chosen into her shaking hand. Her fingers trembled so much Jackson had to help her slide the ring up his finger. And then he kissed her. Thoroughly. No chaste wedding kiss.

'Okay, that's enough, you two,' Ian interrupted. 'There are children present,' he added, with a twinkle in his eye.

Diane smiled. 'I declare you man and wife.'

'Good, then I can kiss the bride,' Jackson said.

There was a general groan and many quips from the people seated around them, but none of it stopped Jackson placing his lips on hers again.

Once more Ian interrupted by pulling her out of his son's arms into his. 'Welcome to the family, Jessica.'

Then Virginia and Sasha were hugging her, quickly followed by Nicholas, Grady, Mike and Roz, Rory and Mrs Harrop. Time sped by until Ian tapped a glass with a spoon and got everyone's attention.

'Champagne is being brought around. Let's all raise a glass and drink to Jessica and Jackson.'

Champagne. That's where this had all started. Her smile was met by one from her husband. 'Yep, it's the same champagne.'

As they were handed glasses of her favourite nectar, Jess grinned. 'I won't be drinking as much of this as I did the last time. I want all my faculties working on my wedding night.'

Jackson ran his hand through his hair, instantly mussing it up. 'I seem to remember they worked fine that other time.'

He slipped his free hand through her arm and tugged her away from the crowd and through the rose garden that was Ian's latest hobby. 'I want a few moments alone with my wife.'

'You sound very smug, Mr Wilson.'

'Why wouldn't I? I've just achieved a dream. You look absolutely beautiful. That dress with the orange flowers suits you to perfection.'

'Apricot, not orange.' She leaned against him and pressed a kiss to his mouth. 'I love you.'

For a moment they were completely alone. No voices touched their seclusion and nothing interrupted the sense that they were in their own little world. Then Jackson pulled his mouth free. 'I hope you've packed that orange bikini for our honeymoon.'

She'd done what she'd been told to do. Jackson had kept their destination a surprise, only saying that she'd need bikinis, lots of them. 'Of course.' And two other new ones he hadn't seen yet. Not apricot in colour, either of them.

'Our flight to Auckland leaves tomorrow afternoon.'

'Right.' Like she'd be wearing a bikini in Auckland in spring.

'Then on Monday we fly to Fiji.' That smug look just got smugger.

Secretly she'd hoped that's where he'd chosen. 'Fiji?' She grinned. 'You remembered.' Her kiss smothered his chuckle.

'We're away for two weeks, sweetheart.'

'Our house will be finished by then.' There was only the paintwork to be completed and the carpet to be put down in their new home before they were handed the keys.

'That will make you happy. Being back on your piece of dirt where you planned on bringing up Nicholas.'

That was one of the things she loved about this man. He understood her need to put down roots for herself, and how she had done that when she'd bought her little home. Which was why, when the insurance company had elected to bowl over both her houses and pay out the money, they'd had the two sections made into one and started building a house big enough to cope with the children they intended on having very soon.

'Mummy, Jackson, come on. Everyone's hungry and we're not allowed to eat until you sit at your table.' Nicholas burst through the bushes they'd hidden behind. 'Come on.'

'That means you're the hungry one.' Jackson swung

his son up into his arms, and nudged Jess softly. 'Guess we'd better return to our wedding.'

She followed her men back to the front lawn and into the marquee, decorated in apricot and sky blue: the colour of love.

As they sat down at the top table Jackson pinched himself. It had happened. He'd married his love. His beautiful Jessica. She'd changed him, saved him really. Shown him that the important things in life were family, community, generosity. She'd brought him to his senses. But most of all she'd shown him love.

'Didn't I tell you it was time for you to return home?' Ping stood in front of them, nodding sagely.

Standing, Jackson reached over to shake the hand of his best buddy. 'Yes, Ping, you did. Took me a while to hear what you were saying.'

'Jessica's a good woman, that's for sure.' Ping draped an arm over the shoulders of the petite woman standing beside him. 'Like my Chen.'

Chen smiled and elbowed her husband. 'You're talking too much again, husband.'

Ping laughed. 'I can see why this Golden Bay brought you back. It's beautiful. All that land with only cattle on it. And the sea that's so clean.'

'You'll be moving here next,' Jackson told him.

Ping and Chen shook their heads at the same time. 'We've got family that we'd never leave back in Hong Kong. More important than green paddocks and sparkling waters.'

Exactly. Family. There was nothing more important. So important that he would soon quit his days in Nelson and become a full-time partner in the medical centre in town. There was no way he'd be leaving Jess and Nicholas for three days at a time every week. Absolutely no way.

Beside him Jess was talking and laughing with Sasha, as happy as he'd ever seen her. Her eyes were fudge-coloured today, matching that orange ribbon wound through her fair hair. A lump blocked the air to his lungs. He'd do anything for this woman who'd stolen his heart. Blinking rapidly, he looked around the marquee at all their friends and family, here to celebrate with them.

Lifting his eyes, he noted the decorations. Blue and orange ribbons festooned the walls. Orange. He grinned as he heard Jess growling, *It's apricot*. Apricot, orange. Whatever. For him, this was the colour of love.

* * * * *

A sneaky peek at next month…

MEDICAL
ROMANCE™

THE ULTIMATE IN ROMANTIC MEDICAL DRAMA

My wish list for next month's titles…

In stores from 4th July 2014:

❑ 200 Harley Street: The Shameless Maverick
  – Louisa George

& 200 Harley Street: The Tortured Hero – Amy Andrews

❑ A Home for the Hot-Shot Doc

& A Doctor's Confession – Dianne Drake

❑ The Accidental Daddy – Meredith Webber

& Pregnant with the Soldier's Son – Amy Ruttan

Available at WHSmith, Tesco, Asda, Eason, Amazon and Apple

Just can't wait?

Visit us Online

You can buy our books online a month before they hit the shops! **www.millsandboon.co.uk**

0614/03

M?

Join the Mills & Boon Book Club

> Want to read more **Medical** books?
> We're offering you **2 more** absolutely **FREE!**

We'll also treat you to these fabulous extras:

-  Exclusive offers and much more!

- FREE home delivery

- FREE books and gifts with our special rewards scheme

Get your free books now!

visit www.millsandboon.co.uk/bookclub
or call Customer Relations on 020 8288 2888

SUBS/ONLINE/M1